LIGHT *in the* EMPIRE

BLIND AMBITION

CAROL ASHBY

CERRILLO PRESS

Whoever loves father or mother more than me is not worthy of me, and whoever loves son or daughter more than me is not worthy of me. And whoever does not take his cross and follow me is not worthy of me. Whoever finds his life will lose it, and whoever loses his life for my sake will find it.

Matthew 10:37-39 (ESV)

And everyone who has left houses or brothers or sisters or father or mother or children or lands, for my name's sake, will receive a hundredfold and will inherit eternal life.

Matthew 19:29 (ESV)

To my children, Paul and Lydia,
for their love, support, and encouragement,
and especially to my husband, Jim,
who makes life better in every way.

And most of all, to Jesus.

Soli Deo gloria

Note from the Author

Love your enemy. A hard command. Without God's help, an impossible one.

But that's exactly what Valeria does in *Blind Ambition*. She lives in a Roman province where the governor had decreed that any Christian who wouldn't deny Jesus and make an offering to Caesar would be killed. Rome had declared her the enemy, and it was the duty of any military man to enforce that decree. But when she finds a Roman officer dying by the side of the road, she does everything she can to save his life, even though that might cost her own. That selfless love turns the tribune's world upside down as he's forced to rethink everything he ever believed.

I've never really had an enemy, at least not a mortal one. The worst opposition I've ever known was from acquaintances who certainly didn't wish me well, but they didn't wish me dead. But many of my sisters and brothers in Christ do live in a hostile world where the possibility of death for their faith is real. Their world is too much like the Roman Empire, where staying true to your faith might get you killed. And yet they remain faithful and even live out that love for their enemies that Jesus commanded. I think especially of the believers in the Middle East who are risking their lives to help anyone in need, enemy or not. I stand in awe and wonder if I would have the courage to be as faithful to our Lord's command.

But even in my "safe" part of the world, I have opportunities to show God's love to people who don't know him and don't even want to know him. The way I respond to slights, insults, mockery, and sabotage speaks much louder than anything I might say. Do I respond as Jesus said I should? Do I do good to those who hate me? Do I bless those who curse me? Do I pray for those who abuse or persecute me? Do I forgive when I've been hurt, even when the person who hurt me has no regrets? I want to, and with the Spirit's help, I can.

And who knows? Maybe my responding in love when most would get angry and strike back will crack a shell hardened against God, and the Holy Spirit will take that small crack and shatter the shell that keeps someone from seeing how much God loves them.

Blind Ambition is a story about the power of human love to open a man's eyes to whether his life's goal has true value and to open his heart to respond to God's redeeming love.

I hope you enjoy this story of God's reward for loving obedience as much as I've enjoyed living in Decimus's and Valeria's world as I've written it. May God give us all the wisdom to look at the dreams we've been chasing through His eyes and the desire to share His love with everyone, even our enemies.

Carol Ashby

Characters

CORNELIUS LENTULUS FAMILY

Tiberius: (47) governor of Germania Superior, Decimus's father

Decimus: (25) Tiberius's only surviving son; senatorial tribune of XXII Primigenia Legion

Graecus: chief steward of Tiberius in Rome

VALERIA AND LICINIUS CRASSUS FAMILY

Valeria: (19) German, saved and trained as physician by Gaius, devout Christian

Galen: (13) Gaius Licinius Crassus, Valeria's adoptive brother

Rhoda: (9) Galen's sister and Valeria's adoptive sister

Gaius: (deceased) Galen's and Rhoda's father. Fled persecution in Rome, became physician

Priscilla: (deceased) Galen's and Rhoda's mother

BALDRIC'S FAMILY

Baldric: (46) chieftain of Vangiones tribe, friend and protector of Valeria and her family

Adolf: (20) third son of Baldric

Otto: (13) fourth son of Baldric

CLAUDIUS DRUSUS FAMILY

Publius: (49) Tiberius's best friend in Rome; Decimus's mentor and friend

Lucius: (33) Publius's oldest surviving son

Titus: (24) Publius's youngest son and Decimus's best friend

Malleolus: steward of the Claudius Drusus family

OTHER IMPORTANT CHARACTERS

Flavius Sabinus: powerful Senator and friend of the Emperor; political power broker

Cities and Towns

ARGENTORATE: headquarters for VIII Augusta Legion; located on Rhine; present-day Strasbourg

AUGUSTA RAURICA: town on the route from Mogontiacum to Rome; 20 km east of present-day Basel

AVENTICUM: large town on the route from Mogontiacum to Rome: present-day Avenches

BORBETOMAGUS: garrison town on the Rhine between Mogontiacum and Argentorate; present-day Worms

MOGONTIACUM: capital of Roman province of Germania Superior, headquarters of XXII Primigenia Legion; located on the Rhine; present-day Mainz

OCTODURUS: full name Civitas Vallensium Octodurus, provincial capital of Alpes Poeninae; present-day Martigny

Excerpt of map by User:Andrein, with the assistance of EraNavigator - Own work, CC BY-SA 3.0, https://commons.wikimedia.org/w/index.php?curid=26047281

Chapter 1

A Different Choice

Roman province of Germania Superior, Spring of AD 114

The black stallion danced as Decimus guided him through the gray stone arches of the fortress gate. The big horse tossed his head and shook his mane before stretching his nose out to pull on the reins. Decimus leaned forward to pat his neck.

"Patience, Astro. You'll get your gallop after we get out of town."

Tribune Decimus Cornelius Lentulus was leading his troop of six to Argentorate from Mogontiacum, the provincial capital of Germania Superior...again. He'd already traveled the road along the Rhenus six times that year.

The mere thought of another three and a half days riding that same road through the river valley pulled an eye roll and a sigh from him. But as his fidgeting black neared the fork where the road through the western hill country split off from the heavily traveled river road, the corner of his mouth twitched up.

He twisted to face the two young officers riding behind him. "Change of plan. I'm tired of the river road. We'll take the alternate route through the hills. The distance is almost the same."

As top staff officer of the XXII Primigenia Legion, Decimus often received special assignments that took him between the fortress headquarters of the two legions stationed in that province. This time the provincial governor himself had ordered the surprise inspection of the VIII Augusta, the second legion under the governor's command. No one expected them at the Augusta's fortress in Argentorate, so it wouldn't matter if the trip took a few hours longer than normal. Time to satisfy his curiosity about part of the province he'd never seen before.

Decimus's glance fell on the box of his scrolls and codices strapped on the packhorse. He always traveled with something to read, so no one suspected what he carried this time. Its secret compartment concealed the confidential documents and gold he was to deliver to the legate commanding the Augusta.

He allowed only his eyes to reveal his satisfaction that Tiberius Cornelius Lentulus, the provincial governor who was also his father, had called it a stroke of genius when he proposed the concealed transport. No thief would find a box of literature interesting, and they would certainly not expect it to hold secrets or treasure.

He turned Astro down the road to the hill country. There was very little traffic, so he nudged his horse into the gallop the spirited animal had been so eager for. A good gallop down a new road—there was no better way to start a four-day ride.

Two days later

"Death stalks you today. Twice he will miss. The third time..." The Suebian seller of furs shrugged as his mouth turned down. "I saw the flight of crows this morning. In their cries, Nerthus told me the woman who scoffs at her power would be sorry."

Valeria shook her head. "Not so, Brukhard. Nerthus has no power over me. God is my protector. If you knew Him as I do, you wouldn't be afraid of a few crows."

Her warm gray eyes held his gaze, and his frown relaxed into a half-smile.

The full smile that drew in response brightened her voice. "Whenever you want to know more about Him, I'll be very glad to tell you. Perhaps you'd like to follow Him, too."

The Suebian shook his head. "Do you take me for a fool? I trade throughout the province. I see what goes on. Your god doesn't protect his followers from the wrath of the Eagles. Governor Lentulus hunts them in Mogontiacum and Argentorate. He gives one chance to deny your Jesus and sacrifice to Caesar. Some of the fools refuse. If they're lucky, he just cuts off their heads. If he's staging games, they're his favorite food for his wolves."

He patted an ample stomach. "You're a skinny little thing that wouldn't satisfy a wolf cub, but I'd be a rich meal for a pack. I have no desire to risk that."

He turned away, and she led her small bay mare into the village green. After hobbling Placida where she could graze, Valeria returned to her cart.

Today she had something special to sell. Yesterday she'd picked the first ripe strawberries. She lifted the basket to her nose and inhaled. The luscious scent drew a smile. The first fruit of the season always brought a good price, and she needed money for new boots for her brother. Galen's thirteen-year-old feet grew longer every week.

She pulled her vegetable basket from the cart, balanced it on her shoulder, and carried it to her usual place among the roadside vendors. Nine-year-old Rhoda skipped along beside her with the berry basket, her dark-brown braids swinging in time with her steps. Valeria spread out her striped blanket, knelt, and arranged the vegetables in a pretty display while Rhoda placed the berries at the front to tempt hungry shoppers.

The old woman who always sold baskets next to her leaned over and touched Valeria's hand. "Have you heard what happened? It's so horrible."

Valeria took her elderly friend's hand in her own. The basket weaver's worried eyes calmed at her touch. "I haven't heard any news since last market day. What happened?"

"The silver merchant was robbed two days ago on the southern road. They killed him and his whole party. I hope it's not the raiders again." The basket weaver pressed an age-spotted hand against her wrinkled cheek. "You drive that road all the time. I worry about you."

Rhoda inhaled sharply and turned wide eyes on Valeria. "The raiders?"

Valeria stood and wrapped her arm around Rhoda. Her long hair, a light chestnut more gold than brown, brushed Rhoda's cheek as she planted a kiss on her forehead. It had been three years, but any mention of the raiders who'd killed Rhoda's parents still filled her little sister's eyes with dread. Valeria had been only sixteen then, but with God's help she'd managed to keep the farm going while raising the family alone. Still, it was hard sometimes.

"I doubt it. It's too long since they attacked our village. It's probably only some men whose greed has made them murderers, not the raiders at all. Besides, we have nothing worth stealing. Go play with Bertha, and don't worry about it."

Valeria's relaxed eyes and calm smile reassured her adopted sister, and Rhoda skipped off in search of her friend.

Chapter 2

Truly in Control

As Astro trotted under the canopy of branches spanning the road, Decimus congratulated himself on his choice of the alternate route. Patchworks of pines and leafy trees, wildflower meadows, undulating hills—the scenery of the first day and a half had been much prettier than the river valley. He expected the remaining two days to be equally enjoyable.

It was time for lunch as the troop approached a village. He was more than ready to dismount and stretch his legs after the long morning ride. Lunch at an inn in a market town would provide a good break for the horses and a chance to relax with his men.

As he rode by the small group of vendors clustered beside the road, he glanced down and saw the basket on the faded red-striped blanket. Ripe strawberries? This early in the season? The thought made his mouth water. There were plenty to share with his men if he bought the whole basket. Sometimes the food at a village inn was barely worth eating. If those berries were as ripe as they looked, their sweetness would ensure he enjoyed at least part of his meal.

He reined in his stallion, and the Roman troop halted in front of the woman selling the berries.

"Fabius, bring me some of those." He pointed at the basket.

Fabius swung his right leg over his horse's neck and slid to the ground. Without looking at the woman, he scooped up a handful and carried them to Decimus.

Decimus popped some into his mouth. As his teeth broke their skin, a burst of sweet juice squirted across his tongue. A broad smile accompanied his nod.

He took a denarius from the small bag hanging from his belt and tossed it to Fabius. "Buy them all."

◆

Valeria's lips tightened when the young officer took so many berries without a word. Roman troops had a reputation for taking whatever they wanted without paying. Those berries needed to pay for part of Galen's boots. When the officer in charge tossed him a silver coin, her lips relaxed into a smile.

The Roman picked up the basket and handed it to one of the mounted soldiers. He turned toward Valeria to pay and held out the coin for her to take. She kept her eyes on the coin and not his face. Looking into a soldier's eyes could draw dangerous attention.

He held the coin over her outstretched hand. The long pause without him dropping it kicked her heartrate higher. *God, please let him just drop it and go.*

Like a striking snake, his free hand shot out and grabbed her wrist.

"I want something sweeter than berries from you."

He pulled her toward him. The lecherous gleam in his eyes and the cruel twist at the corner of his mouth left no doubt of his intent.

She placed her free hand against his chest and pushed as she leaned away from him. His muscles above the leather forearm guard bulged as he jerked her closer. He gripped both her arms, leaving no hope of pulling free or twisting away from him. With both hands against his chest, she pushed as she dug her heels in, but the blanket prevented secure footing. She slipped, and he pulled her against him. An animal laugh rumbled in his chest as she struggled to free herself.

She forced her voice to sound calm. Pleading would only inflame him. "You're hurting me. Please let me go."

Her gaze was drawn to his cold, merciless eyes. *God, no! Make him stop!*

One arm crushed her to his chest as he reached for the neck of her tunic. She shut her eyes and kept praying for deliverance from what now appeared inevitable.

"Fabius. Enough."

Valeria's eyes sprang open as the arm imprisoning her relaxed. The officer's eyebrow shot up. Frowning, his head snapped sideways to look at the senior tribune, then back at her. The tribune's quiet command had stopped him, but as he released her, he shoved her away hard. As she fell backward onto the blanket, he tossed the coin so it hit her in the face.

Valeria looked up at the tribune to thank him, but he was already riding away toward the inn. The lecherous officer remounted and followed his commander.

Valeria's eyes sought Rhoda. She was half-hidden behind the cart, her hand over her mouth and her eyes enormous. As the attacker rode off, she ran to Valeria, knelt, and slipped her arms around her sister. Fear darkened eyes brimming with tears.

"I'm all right, precious. Don't be afraid." Valeria stroked Rhoda's hair and kissed her forehead. "God has protected me." She held up the coin. "And we even have enough to get Galen's new boots."

The basket woman had scrambled away when the officer grabbed her arms, but Valeria didn't blame her. She couldn't have helped even if she'd been brave.

Now her aged friend reached out to help Valeria up. "Roman troops are like hungry wolves. I thought nothing could stop one once he started, but that tribune protected you. I never heard of such a thing."

Valeria smiled as she took her hand for some help getting back on her feet. "God sometimes uses the strangest tools to do His work. I never would have expected Him to use a tribune, but I'm very thankful He did."

"You should leave now, before they finish eating. He may not be so protective when his stomach is full."

"I still have a few more things to sell. We'll leave after I sell them. God will still protect us."

Valeria watched the tribune ride his high-stepping stallion toward the trees by the inn. An aura of power surrounded him. Her attacker had responded instantly to a single, softly spoken word. The tribune, tautly muscled and proudly erect as he rode, radiated strength. He was so full of pride in his Roman blood, so confident that he was superior and in control. He probably thought he knew more than anyone in the village, but she knew some truths that he did not. The power and glory of a man were fleeting, and only God was really in control.

Rhoda was watching, too. "Aren't they magnificent?"

The red capes draped across their shoulders, the shiny red-crested helmets, the spirited horses they rode—Valeria had to agree that the Romans looked magnificent.

Rhoda pointed at the tribune. "Especially the one with that tall red fringe on his helmet, the one at the front—just look at his horse."

Valeria fought to suppress a grin. Rhoda looked at the power and pride of a handsome man and what did she see? Only his beautiful, spirited horse. The sleek black stallion was full of energy, sporting a luxuriant mane and tail, taller than the other horses, heavily muscled and obviously expensive—a superb example of the best horses from Spain. Her father had told her how magnificent the Spanish horses were, but she'd never actually seen one before.

The stallion had been fidgeting, pawing the ground impatiently with his hoof while the purchase of her berries was being made. Frequently tossing his head but perfectly obedient to the equally magnificent man seated upon him, so relaxed and in control.

What a perfect reflection the horse was of its rider—striking in appearance, full of controlled power.

Warmth spread across her cheeks. She'd been gazing too long at the handsome Roman. No doubt he knew he could make a woman's heart flutter, but God judges by what's in the heart of a man, not by his appearance or the power he seems to have. She should do the same.

◆

The tribune and his men tied their horses to the trees by the inn and settled in at a table in the shady courtyard.

The innkeeper scurried over to take their orders, smiling with his lips but not his eyes. He'd told his daughter to hide in the house and had taken over serving as soon as he saw the Romans riding into the village.

When the young officer had grabbed Valeria, the innkeeper's teeth had clenched. He'd known her since she was a small child, and he always bought some of her produce. If only there had been time to warn her as well. He knew what to expect of Roman troops.

She'd struggled with the brute, but nothing would stop the inevitable. No one would even dare try. The innkeeper's head had snapped back when the Roman only pushed her down and threw a coin in her face. That was the last thing he'd expected. Mercy and Roman were never words he used together.

Any chance to get some Roman money was welcome, but he was no fan of the Empire or those who exerted its power. Neither he nor anyone else at the inn even considered warning the Romans about the danger along the southern road. It would be a good thing if the robbers were to attack them. There would be fewer Romans or fewer robbers or, most likely, fewer of both after the encounter. Whoever was killed, it would be a good thing as far as the innkeeper was concerned.

"What can I bring you, tribune?" He tried to make his smile look natural, but he wasn't a very good actor. Not that the tribune would care.

◆

Decimus removed his brass helmet and set it on the table. He ran his fingers through his hair, swishing them to loosen it. Too bad helmets always trapped sweat. A light breeze began to evaporate the dampness and cool him.

"Some of that stew for my men and some wine."

The innkeeper dipped a quick bow. "Right away, tribune."

Decimus flexed his shoulders and back before stretching his legs out and lacing his fingers behind his head. A satisfied sigh escaped. The aroma rising from the cooking pot convinced him that stopping at this inn had been a good choice. The food would be tasty, the company jovial, and the time off his horse refreshing.

◆

A burly man was loitering under a tree near the edge of the village square. His calculating eyes flitted on and off the Romans as they made their way through the village. It was wisest to look at them neither too much nor too little as they approached and passed by. When their backs were toward him, his gaze locked on the wooden box strapped to the packhorse. Large enough to hold a Roman payroll. A worthwhile prize—worth the risk of attacking a Roman cavalry troop. Only three officers and four cavalrymen—an easy target for a dozen robbers at the place on the southern road that was perfect for an ambush.

When the Romans dismounted and walked into the inn's courtyard, he faded back into the trees. After skirting the edge of the village so no one would notice him, he mounted his horse and headed down the road in the direction the Romans would soon be traveling.

◆

Laughter from the courtyard reached Valeria's ears, and she found herself watching the handsome Roman again. The tribune had taken off his helmet and set it on the table. With his fingers laced together and his hands resting on the top of his head, he was leaning back in his chair, a smile on his lips as he talked with his men. It was obvious he wasn't only their commander. There was real camaraderie among them. When they'd finished the last of their wine, he stood up and placed his helmet back on his head. Still laughing together, the Romans rose and sauntered over to their horses to mount up.

Valeria had just sold her last cabbage. It was time to start the long drive home. She folded her blanket and raised one hand to catch Rhoda's attention.

"Rhoda, please fetch Placida."

Rhoda hugged Bertha goodbye and ran to get the mare from where she was grazing.

The basket seller took Valeria's hand. "Be careful as you travel. I hope you don't run into the robbers."

"We'll be safe. God is our protector." Valeria squeezed her hand before walking to her parked cart.

She hooked the mare's harness to the cart shafts while Rhoda spread the blanket on the seat again and climbed aboard.

◆

As Decimus untied Astro, the big horse tossed his head and shook his mane. The left corner of Decimus's mouth lifted. "Ready for another gallop, boy?" He patted the stallion's neck.

When Decimus settled into the saddle, the horse began dancing in place, eager for speed. As soon as the others were mounted, he turned Astro toward the south and signaled the column of twos to move out.

One gentle nudge and Astro sprang forward, hitting full gallop within ten strides.

◆

Valeria slapped Placida with the reins. As she was pulling out onto the road, the Roman troop galloped by, cutting her off. The mare startled and reared. The cart tilted at a crazy angle, and Rhoda almost fell out before grabbing the seat just in time.

"Whoa, girl, whoa!" Valeria shortened her grip on the reins and arched back, using her full weight to keep the mare from bolting. Placida's hooves settled back to earth. She stood still, but her edginess kept her ears pricked, her nostrils flared, and the whites of her eyes showing.

As Valeria watched the backs of the Romans as they galloped away, her eyebrows dipped. "Cutting us off like that. Not a thought about anybody else."

Her lips tightened and she shook her head. Arrogant and selfish—that's what the tribune was. Nothing admirable about him at all, no matter how handsome he might be. Rhoda could have been hurt or even killed when he spooked the mare.

But as she watched him riding away, her anger faded. The poor tribune. He didn't realize his feeling of superiority was separating him from the most precious thing in God's creation—other people. He was missing so much by neither noticing nor caring about most of the people he saw. Still, he wasn't completely devoid of human feelings. He'd shown he could be merciful when he stopped Fabius, and he treated his men like friends.

Placida had calmed enough, so Valeria clucked to her mare. As she followed the Romans down the southern road, she chided herself. *Perhaps I judge him too harshly. Lord, please forgive me. At least he seems to care about his own kind. I know my judging him is a greater sin than his pride. I know the Way, and he's probably never even heard Your words.*

Rhoda was still watching the horses. "That black stallion is so beautiful. I'd love to have a horse like him. He'd come when I call, and I'd pet his nose and comb his mane and tail. I'm sure he'd enjoy it as much as me."

Valeria wrapped her arm around Rhoda's shoulders. "He'd look very funny if I tried to harness him with our mare."

Rhoda grinned back. "He's too big and she's too small to pull together, but I think they'd make beautiful baby horses for us to sell. I've never, ever seen a horse as wonderful as him. Maybe God made him to show just how pretty a horse could be."

Valeria nodded as she lowered her arm to take the reins in both hands again. "I loved our horses when my father used to raise them. It would be fun to have foals in the corrals again. Maybe someday. Then you could help me with the horses like I used to help my father."

Rhoda hugged her arm and snuggled against her sister as they continued down the road. "I'd love that, too."

Chapter 3

The Ambush

The Romans slowed to a trot as they entered the woods. A breeze stirred the leaves, and the sunlight made broken shadows as it shone down through the branches. Decimus was thoroughly enjoying himself. It felt good to ride through the cool quiet after a relaxing meal in the village. This was much better than traveling the river road.

As he rode alone at the head of the column of twos, the soft pounding rhythm of the hoofbeats behind him penetrated his thoughts. He raised his hand as he slowed Astro to a walk. He was alternating between periods of trotting and walking to keep the horses fresh. They had covered a good distance since sun up, but they still had a long way to go before nightfall.

About three miles from the village, the road wound down a steep hill where the forest was interspersed with large rocky outcrops. Many were taller than a mounted man, and some overhung the wagon track.

The horses had been walking for a while, and it was almost time to trot again. Decimus twisted to look behind. "Fabius."

Fabius rode ten feet back. He kicked his horse to come up beside his commander.

"The berry seller. With what we're carrying, your action was unwise. She may have been a virgin, and I don't want to be followed by a father bent on revenge for you spoiling his daughter. We should be in a town tonight where you can get satisfaction from a woman who wants your attentions."

Fabius grinned and nodded. Decimus slapped him on the back, then nudged his horse to a trot to end the conversation. Fabius fell back into his place in the column.

Actually, Decimus had surprised himself when he stopped Fabius. Army life was hard, and he usually let his junior officers find relaxation in whatever way they chose. What Fabius had planned for his lunchtime pleasure had been perfectly acceptable on previous trips. Something made him tell Fabius to stop this time, but he didn't know why. She was only a German peasant. He was not a cruel man, but he was not a merciful one, either. Mercy was not considered a virtue in Rome.

◆

The troop approached the bottom of the hill, trotting beside a tall, overhanging outcrop. Ahead the road curved and went through a narrow gap in the rocks.

The tribune should have been more alert. He should have slowed to a walk so he could listen. He should have passed through what looked like a perfect place for an ambush with his hand on his sword and his eyes scanning in all directions.

Instead, he sat relaxed on his stallion's back and led the men through at a trot. The river road was always safe. He hadn't considered the possibility that the road through the hills might not be.

It was a fatal mistake.

When the last pair of Romans was in the gap, the robbers leaped upon them, swinging their axes and swords. Two at a time they jumped the Romans, pulling them from their horses. The four at the rear were killed almost before they realized what was happening. Decimus, Fabius, and the other young officer were already through the gap. They wheeled their horses to face the attackers who were swarming them. The sound of metal on metal echoed up the hillside as the outnumbered Romans fought for their lives.

Fabius cut down two before he was felled by a sword through his neck. The other officer killed two more before he was struck down by an ax.

◆

The sword sliced into Decimus's leg before it cut into his horse's shoulder. Astro stumbled, and Decimus was pitched off as the stallion almost fell. Despite the deep gash in his calf, he managed to roll and rise into a standing position. As his attacker charged, Decimus ran him through, then pushed the body off his sword.

Two more were advancing toward him, their swords raised. One of his men lay dead behind them. Bloodlust burned in their eyes. With blood gushing from his leg, he made an easy target.

He stood facing them, his sword ready. His eyes turned to ice.

Come on, make your move. Now, while I still have strength to fight.

He'd seen enough battle wounds to know he couldn't stand much longer. Death was close, but he'd rather die fighting, taking his enemies with him.

One robber stepped forward, sword raised, and Decimus was poised to deflect his blow and run him through. Even with his lifeblood draining out of him, few could match his skill with a sword. He'd have the satisfaction of taking one, maybe two more with him as he died.

Then all went black.

◆

The robber had struck from behind with an ax. The brass helmet absorbed most of the force of the blow, keeping the tribune's skull from cracking wide open. As the helmet split under the blade, his scalp was cut, and blood gushed from the palm-width gash. With so much blood, his attacker thought he'd killed him and didn't waste his energy striking the "dead man" again.

With a war-whoop of victory, he bent over the tribune and began stripping him of valuables. The sword and scabbard were finely crafted and would replace his own. The dagger with its engraved silver handle and ivory-inlaid sheath would bring good money. Even split, the bronze helmet with the tall red crest was a worthwhile prize. The bronze cuirass that sheathed the tribune's torso was too big, but he could sell it. Another whoop came when he pulled off the gold signet ring and snatched the purse filled with Roman coins. Leaving the tribune stripped to his tunic and lying in his own blood, the robber ran to join in the looting of the other dead men.

The head of the band seized the packhorse's lead and sliced the tie ropes with his dagger. Everything tumbled to the ground. Grabbing the wooden box first, he jerked it open. Scrolls and codices! There must be something else valuable inside. He dumped the contents out. Finding nothing, he tossed the box aside with a string of curses. The rest of the pack contained only clothing and provisions.

The words rolling from his tongue would have made even a brothel slave blush. There should have been a Roman payroll. He'd lost five of his band and only had seven dead Romans and a few horses to show for it. When he saw the sword wound on the tribune's stallion, he cursed again. The best horse wasn't even worth taking. He mounted the second-best horse and called to his men.

"Get their horses and let's go. Leave that black one. It'll only slow us down."

With each one clutching his share of the loot, the remaining robbers mounted the Roman horses and rode away to the south.

Chapter 4

His Life or Hers?

Valeria started down the hill where the rocky outcrops made it easy for robbers to hide.

She glanced at Rhoda beside her. The tribune had spooked Placida, but with his troop ahead of her, at least she wouldn't have to worry about the robbers who'd killed the silver merchant.

Her breath caught as the clang of metal on metal rang in her ears, and she pulled back on the reins. Then came savage cries from men celebrating the end of battle. Her stomach knotted as she listened to the blood-curdling yells. Whoever was fighting, it didn't sound like the Romans had won.

Rhoda trembled as tears pooled in her eyes. "Is it the raiders? Are they going to kill us?" Her whisper sounded like a shout as Valeria's ears strained to hear what the robbers were doing.

Valeria held her finger to her lips, and Rhoda fell silent. Valeria flicked the reins and guided Placida off the road to a spot behind some thick bushes.

Oh, God! Please don't let them see the cart if they come up this way.

She released the shafts from the harness to free her mare. Then she led Rhoda and the mare into an area of rocks that hid them from anyone passing on the road. Hid them...unless whoever killed the Romans saw the cart and decided to hunt for its owner.

Rhoda wrapped her arms around Valeria and buried her face in her sister's dress. She clung to Valeria's waist, sometimes shaking as she shed silent tears. Valeria longed to encircle her with comforting arms,

16

but she needed to hold the halter and stroke the mare's neck to keep her calm and quiet. How ironic that Gaius had named the skittish little mare Placida.

They remained hidden among the rocks, still as death, praying and listening to the sounds of the robbers celebrating. Valeria shuddered at the laughter as they stripped the bodies of valuables. Vile cursing followed as they discovered there was no payroll money in the box on the packhorse. More cursing as they gathered up the horses. At last, the sounds of voices and horses' hooves faded away as the robbers headed down the road, taking the Roman horses with them.

After several minutes, Rhoda's frightened whisper shattered the silence. "Do you think they're gone? Can we go home now?"

Valeria forced a smile to comfort her sister, but did her eyes betray her own fear? "Let's wait a little longer. Another half hour should make it safe."

She had no idea if that was true, but she didn't want to scare Rhoda. The risk of running into the robbers was too real, but it would be dangerous to wait too long where they were. She had to get them home before nightfall. She hadn't brought a lantern to light the trail. In the dark, a cart could fall into the ravine where the path narrowed at the sharpest curve. Galen would be terribly worried if they didn't return before sundown and with good reason.

The normal sounds of the forest had returned: squirrels chattering, birds chirping. The robbers were gone, but would they return and reset the trap if she waited too long?

Valeria placed one finger across her lips and kissed her frightened sister's forehead. Then she shifted her grip from halter to reins and led them all back to the cart.

With Placida back between the shafts, Valeria slapped the reins to start the mare down the road toward the gap. If only she had asked Galen to grease the axle before their trip today! Its quiet squeaking sounded horribly loud to her now. If the robbers were anywhere nearby, they couldn't fail to hear it.

They approached the narrow cut through the last rock outcrop before the valley floor.

Valeria swallowed hard. *Oh, God! Please protect us...I'm so scared they're going to find us. If they do, at least get Rhoda away safe.*

She whispered to Rhoda, "Close your eyes and don't look until I tell you to open them. Just keep praying."

Then she guided the cart around the last curve and through the narrow passage.

A nightmare sight awaited them. She didn't want Rhoda to see the dead men lying there, bloody and mangled by sword and ax. She didn't want to see them herself, but she had no choice if they were going to get home. As they emerged from the passage into full view of the carnage, the little mare balked at the smell of blood and death. Valeria flicked her several times with the reins. She snorted but remained frozen in place. She was not going to walk past the dead on her own.

"Keep your eyes closed." Valeria's whisper felt like a shout as she scanned the surrounding forest for lurking robbers. "I'm going to lead Placida and clear the path. Remember, don't look until I say."

After handing Rhoda the reins, she climbed down to lead the horse. She leaned her forehead against the mare's cheek. "We can do this. Come on, girl."

Taking the mare's halter in hand and stroking her neck to calm her, Valeria began to lead her past the dead. The little horse shuddered and then relaxed as they moved forward.

Three bodies lay across the wagon track. Before they could pass, she'd have to move them.

Placida snorted as they stopped just short of the first Roman.

"Nothing to fear, girl. You can do this." Valeria's soft words and three stokes of Placida's nose settled her down.

"I'm letting go of the halter, so you've got her," whispered Valeria. Rhoda nodded without looking up. Valeria took a deep breath and blew it out slowly.

I can do this. She swallowed to clear the lump in her throat. *Help me do this, God.*

When she gripped the ankles of the dead Roman, she focused her gaze on his feet. She couldn't bear to look at eyes that stared but saw nothing. Tears blurred her vision, but she flicked them away. No time for weakness.

I can do this.

She dragged the body aside.

A shudder convulsed her shoulders before she dropped his ankles. One down, two to go.

Rhoda's father, Gaius, had been training Valeria to be a physician like himself when he was murdered by the raiders. She'd seen and touched death before, but this was so horribly different. Tears began to well up again. She shook her head, trying to shake off the fear...and the pity. No one in the village liked the Romans, but no one deserved to die like this.

Taking hold of the halter once more, she led the horse forward until the way was blocked again. The next man on the track was one of the robbers. A shiver slithered up her spine as she pulled him out of the way, saying a prayer for his soul. Gripping the halter again, she moved down the road to the last body blocking her path.

The final Roman sprawled across the full width of the track.

Her breath caught as she stared at the corpse of the tribune who'd bought her berries. He'd been a commanding presence, sitting his horse with such confidence. He'd been magnificent in his red cape and red-crested helmet. Now his purple-striped tunic was red with his blood. The aura of power was gone, leaving only an empty shell.

His body looked heavy. It would take all her strength to pull it off the path so the cart could pass.

"Hold the reins, but still don't look. We're almost through."

One more body, and she could drive away from the horror around her. She reached down, seized the dead tribune's ankles, and began to pull.

A crimson rivulet trickled down his calf and splattered into the red puddle on the ground below the deep gash in his leg. With a gasp, she jerked her hands back, dropping his feet. Bright scarlet swirled into the dark red.

That was fresh blood.

How could he still be bleeding? Dead men didn't bleed.

He lay face down with a jagged wound on the back of his head. His hair was matted with dark, clotted blood. He couldn't be alive.

Her palm covered her mouth, and her breathing accelerated. Maybe the blood only looked fresh because she'd lifted his leg enough to free what had pooled in the deep wound. With so much blood on him and the ground, surely he must be dead.

Valeria sucked air between her teeth. What if he wasn't?

She knelt beside him and picked up his hand. It was large and sinewy, and she was certain the dried blood on it wasn't his own. She searched for a pulse, as Gaius had taught her. At first it was hard to find. His artery felt squishy, like it wasn't full, but finally her fingertips felt something. His pulse was weak and too rapid, but it was there.

There was no doubt. This Roman was alive, but he would die soon...unless she helped him.

Valeria bit her lip as she stared at him.

Alive—he shouldn't be alive. The bloody wound on the back of his head should have killed him. So much blood from the five-inch gash on his left leg. How could he lose so much without dying?

Her fingertips lifted his dark brown hair aside to expose the cut in his scalp. It was still oozing a little fresh blood, but mostly the blood had clotted. The wound wasn't as deep as it first appeared. The ax hadn't cut into his skull.

As she knelt beside him, she rolled her eyes at the sky. *Oh, God! Why does it have to be the tribune who's alive?*

She couldn't just leave him to die by the road, but helping him would put her whole family in mortal danger. This man wore the wide purple stripes of a senatorial tribune. He was second only to the legion commander. How could a man of his rank fail to enforce the governor's decree? That was the duty of every Roman soldier, but this was the man who sent them out to hunt for Christians.

Saving the tribune's life might mean sacrificing her own. And what about Rhoda and Galen? She'd be putting them in grave danger if she brought the Roman home to care for his wounds. If he recovered, he might arrest them all.

She stared at his handsome profile. *God, do I have to try to help him? He's probably going to die, no matter what I do.*

She'd never seen a living man so deathly pale. And even if his skull hadn't cracked, was his head injured beyond healing? Even Gaius had never treated a wound like that.

He'd seemed bigger than life as he relaxed on his fidgeting stallion in the village. Up close, he seemed even bigger. She was small, even for a woman. How was she going to get such a large man into the cart? Rhoda was only nine, too small to help much.

The robbers might return and catch them if she and Rhoda stayed long enough to get him loaded. They would finish him off, and it would all be for nothing. She sucked her breath through her teeth. What would they do to her and Rhoda for trying to help him?

There were so many reasons to just drive away, but were they really only excuses?

Jesus's parable of the Good Samaritan echoed in her mind as she weighed her options. Just like this Roman, the Jew had been jumped by robbers and left to die. The Samaritan spared no effort to care for the Jew who thought he was scum.

Jesus wouldn't want her to just leave the tribune there...but she was afraid of him and for good reason. He wasn't simply a man in need who considered her beneath himself. He truly was her enemy.

Both hands cupped her face as she bit her lower lip.

Jesus's command to love her enemy—what if she obeyed and the tribune recovered? Like an injured wolf who'd been released from a trap and tended, would he turn and kill her when he was well again?

As Valeria slowly shook her head, she sucked another deep breath through her teeth.

She'd heard too many stories about the cruelty and callous hearts of Roman soldiers. This man had stopped the other officer...maybe he would spare the people who rescued him. But he was a tribune, and Roman power was never merciful.

Valeria glanced over her shoulder at Rhoda, sitting in the cart with her eyes squeezed shut. She pressed her palms against her cheeks as she turned her gaze back on him. What kind of man was this tribune? Would he put duty above all else? Would he arrest her whole family even though she'd saved him?

To avoid execution, they'd have to deny Jesus as their Lord and of-fer sacrifice to Caesar. Her brother, her sister, her...none of them would do that.

But if she refused to help her enemy, wouldn't she be denying her Lord anyway?

She shook her head again as she stared at him. This Roman des-perately needed her help, but at what cost? Her life for his? Could she willingly make that sacrifice? Maybe, but it wasn't just her life in the balance. Whatever she chose, she dragged Galen and Rhoda along with her. If the tribune showed her no mercy, they would all die.

She closed her eyes and took a deep breath. *Jesus, please! I want to be faithful, but I'm afraid of what might happen if I take him home. Not just for me, but for Galen and Rhoda. Please show me what I should do.* She opened her eyes and stared at his motionless body. *Whatever that is, give me courage to do it.*

As she finished her prayer, the tribune stirred, then lay still.

Her shoulders slumped, then straightened. No more excuses masked as reasons. There really was no choice. She would have to risk her own life and those she loved to save her enemy.

Chapter 5

THE RESCUE

Valeria stood and gazed down at him as she took one more deep breath and slowly blew it out. *If this is what You want, Lord, then I'll do it.*

She walked past the mare and laid her hand on Rhoda's arm. "The tribune is alive. We can't leave him here to die without trying to help him."

Rhoda's eyes popped open. "Like the Good Samaritan. We'll care for him, and God will make him better."

The near-smile on Rhoda's lips told Valeria she didn't understand the risk, but now was not the time to tell her. Plenty of time for that later if he didn't die on the way home.

"First I have to check all the others. Then we'll load him into the cart."

Valeria walked among the bodies, checking the eyes or pulse to see if any still lived. None did.

Back beside the tribune, Valeria rested her cheek in her palm as she stared at him. *God, how am I supposed to do this?*

Even with his deep tan, he was paler than some corpses. By God's mercy, he was still alive, but could she keep him that way?

He bled a little simply because she lifted his foot. When she tried to lift him into the cart, would the clotted wound reopen? That would kill him.

His red cape had been cast aside by whoever took his armor. She tore several strips from it and bandaged the gash in his leg.

She slipped her hands under his armpits and dragged him to the side of the wagon track. He'd looked big on his horse; he felt enormous as she strained to move him. If only Galen were there to help lift him into the cart! How was she ever going to manage that with only her and Rhoda?

God, if You want me to do this, You're going to have to tell me how.

She led Placida forward until the back of the cart was just past where he was lying.

"He's too heavy for me to lift alone. Come help me. I'll lift his shoulders. You lift his legs. Be as careful as you can with the one with the cut on it."

Rhoda dropped the reins and climbed down. The little mare stood like a statue, somehow calm as they prepared to load him into the cart.

"God, give us strength to do this." whispered Valeria. "And please keep Placida from moving the cart."

Each picked up her own end and sidestepped to carry him past the cart. He was so heavy they had to set him down and rest before trying to hoist him up and onto the bed.

Valeria arched her back to stretch her muscles. "I'm going to kneel down and lay his chest across my shoulder. Help me lift him enough so I can get under him. When I start to stand up, hang onto him so he won't slip off."

Her gaze shifted from the tribune to the cart bed and back. "If we can get his chest resting on the cart, I think I can pull the rest of him in. Let's pray that we don't hurt him more doing that."

Pushing upward with all the strength her legs could muster, Valeria lifted him. She staggered under his weight but managed to struggle to her feet with him draped across her right shoulder. She stood for a moment with her feet wide-spread, his weight bearing down on her. She wrapped her arms around his torso, fighting to keep him balanced so he would stay on her shoulder when Rhoda let go.

"Back the cart up against me and then we can push him off."

Rhoda ran forward to the mare and backed her up until the end of the cart was right next to Valeria. Together they got him off her shoulder, leaving his chest resting on the cart bed.

Valeria flexed her shoulders before she ran her fingers through her hair and pushed the strands that had fallen across her face back behind her ears. "Halfway there. God, please give me strength!"

She climbed in past him and sat down. She braced her feet against the sides of the cart, placed her hands under his arms, and pushed hard with her legs, sliding herself and him backward into the cart. One more time, and she had most of him in as far as she wanted, leaving room for her to sit between him and the seat.

She sagged against the front wall of the cart and closed her eyes for a moment. "We did it. I wasn't sure just the two of us could get him into the cart. It's a good thing Galen will be there to help us take him out."

Rhoda's brow furrowed as she stood at the end of the cart and nodded her agreement. "We got him in...but is he going to die?" Her voice quavered as she stood as if frozen, staring at him.

Valeria placed her fingers on his wrist to check his pulse. It was unchanged, weak and rapid but steady. "Only God knows, but he's still alive now. Surely God wouldn't have had us stop to help him if he wasn't going to get well. Just keep praying."

Rhoda rested her hand on his good leg as her face relaxed. "God can make him better. I'm sure He'll answer our prayers."

Valeria struggled to turn him onto his right side to keep pressure off his head wound. Then she climbed over him and out of the cart. He was a very tall man, so she had to bend his legs to get him completely in. Finally, she covered him with the striped blanket. Gaius had always said to keep injured men warm.

Her hair had fallen across her face as she strained to maneuver the large man into position for the ride home. When she pushed it back, she felt the wetness on her forehead. Her sweat or his blood?

"I don't want his head bouncing around and getting hurt more, so I'm going to sit back here and hold him. You can drive us."

She climbed back into the cart and settled into the space she'd left for herself before lifting his head into her lap. Even though the cut in his scalp had mostly stopped bleeding, he still left a blood stain on her dress.

Rhoda adjusted the blanket to cover the Roman's feet before stepping away from him. After climbing up onto the cart seat, she picked up the reins and clucked to the horse. With a lurch, the cart started down the road toward the junction where they would take the faint trail that led to their farm.

As they drove past the spot where the robbers had dumped everything from the packhorse, Rhoda whispered, "Scrolls. They must have been in his treasure box. Can I get them so he won't lose them? Maybe they were his parents', and they're really special to him."

Valeria wanted to say they shouldn't delay even a moment, but the pleading look in Rhoda's eyes stopped her. Her little sister treasured the scrolls and codices that Gaius and Priscilla used to read to her. She often took them out and read them to herself because they helped her feel close to her parents again.

"Yes, just be very quick about it. I want to get off the main road as soon as we can."

Images of what the robbers would do if they caught them swirled through her mind. It would be horrible enough to be found alone. How much worse would it be if they were caught helping the Roman?

Rhoda handed the ends of the reins to Valeria and sprang down. First, she dragged his box to the back of the cart. She strained to lift it up onto the bed.

"His box is really heavy."

"Maybe it's a special kind of wood."

Rhoda pushed the box in beside his legs and left it open so she could pack everything back into it. She gathered the dozen or so codices and scrolls, brushing the dust off each as she ran with it to the cart.

As she was picking up the last one, something rustled behind them. Both whirled to face it. Had the robbers returned?

Valeria held her breath. The bushes parted...and there stood the Roman's stallion. He had a bloody cut on his shoulder and was limping, but the faithful horse was following his master. He limped over to the cart and nuzzled the tribune.

Valeria reached out for one of the hanging reins. The cut on the stallion's shoulder wasn't very deep. It would probably heal well if she treated it. If they both recovered, the Roman would have a way to get home.

"Quick, tie this to the cart, and let's get going."

Rhoda took the stallion's reins, and he let her stroke his nose. "We can be the Good Samaritan to his horse, too."

When they reached the turnoff, Valeria eased herself out from under the tribune's head.

"Drive the cart around the bend and wait for me. I'm going to hide our tracks coming off the road."

As Rhoda drove forward, Valeria picked up a fallen tree branch. With it, she swept away the tell-tale marks of the horses' hooves and the cart wheels. Then she gathered some more branches and scattered them across the trail. That should hide it from anyone who wasn't a skilled tracker. If the robbers did return, they wouldn't find an easy trail to follow to the farm.

She ran up the trail and around the bend to where Rhoda was waiting. She climbed back into the cart and resumed her position cradling the Roman's head.

"I have him. Let's go."

Rhoda slapped the reins, and they continued the jostling trip home.

Valeria pushed back a lock of hair that had fallen across his forehead. He didn't look like a dangerous man at that moment, but no one looked dangerous when they were sleeping...or unconscious.

The tribune had protected her when he stopped his officer from raping her, but what did that really mean? He might only have been in a hurry and didn't want to wait. He might not have done it because he wanted to protect her at all. He had ridden off without even looking at her, so it seemed more likely that he was just an impatient man.

Romans weren't known for showing anyone mercy. She'd been praying desperately for deliverance, and God might have led him to do something that was totally against his normal inclination. It was probably wise to consider him a dangerous man until he gave her reason to think otherwise.

He lay so still, so pale underneath his dark tan. She felt his wrist. The pulse was still there. What a relief...maybe. How fragile this man was who'd seemed so strong and proud and...invincible when he rode into the village and bought her berries. He looked anything but invincible now. What would he be like when he recovered? If he recovered...

That thought triggered a shiver.

What if he didn't recover? Surely God wouldn't have told her to bring him home if he wasn't going to live, but what if his stirring hadn't been a sign from God that she should risk trying to help him? What if he died? What if the Romans came looking for him and thought she'd killed him? They would see his horse and know he'd been with them. What would happen to Galen and Rhoda?

She shook her head. *Stop that! Stop second-guessing whether I'm obeying God in this.* Surely everything would turn out all right, and this Roman would be grateful enough for them rescuing him that he would choose not to punish them for their faith. Still, even if he wasn't going to be grateful, she had to take care of him now.

Jesus had commanded her to love her enemy, to care for those who needed help, to pray for those who persecuted her. This had to be the right thing to do. Surely that was a sign from God as she knelt beside him on the road.

And surely God would protect them. He could change the Roman's mind about arresting the followers of Jesus. The tribune could choose not to enforce the governor's decree. Maybe he wouldn't be so dangerous after all.

Her fingertips swept across his forehead, pushing his hair back again. Even if he didn't change, Jesus always wanted His followers to love their enemies. Love wasn't just an emotion. It was doing whatever it took, no matter the cost, to help a person who needed help.

It was time to stop worrying about whether she'd made a wise decision. She had to be the Good Samaritan for this poor man. If anyone had ever needed her help, it was him. Peace settled over her as she closed her eyes and began to pray for him.

It was still another three miles to the farm, and the afternoon was almost over. Galen would already be wondering where they were. Was he ever going to be surprised!

Chapter 6

THE BROKEN ROMAN

Galen glanced out the cattle-shed door for the fifteenth time. The sun was much too low in the sky. Where were his sisters? There was always some variation in when they came, depending on how quickly Val sold her wares and whether they stayed a while to visit with friends, but it was already much later than normal, even for a slow market day. He'd heard the rumor that the raiders were waylaying travelers in the neighborhood again.

If they didn't come soon, he would get the ax and start down the path to look for them. At thirteen, he was growing taller all the time, looking more and more like a man and taking on manly responsibilities. He would soon be the man of the house and protector of the family. Val saw him growing, but to her he was still just her little brother. He didn't feel that way anymore.

Galen finally heard the creaking of the cart as he was finishing up in the cattle shed. He stepped out, prepared to tease Rhoda about staying in town so long so he would get her chores done before she got home. His tease died on his lips when he saw the limping stallion tied behind the cart and Val sitting in the back while Rhoda drove. Val looked like she was praying, and his usually cheery little sister looked grim. Galen dropped his rake and trotted toward the cart.

He was totally unprepared for what he saw when he looked over the sidewall.

"Whoa! Rhoda's always bringing home birds with broken wings or something, but a broken Roman soldier? Where did you find him?"

"That's not funny, Galen," Rhoda retorted. "We found him by the road after the robbers jumped him, just like the Jew in the Good Samaritan story. We couldn't just leave him there to die. God told Valeria we should bring him home, so we have."

Valeria shifted the tribune in her lap. "Galen, please lead the cart over by the porch. I think we can get him into my bed if we all carry part of him. He's heavier than he looks. Once we get him in there, I can start tending his wounds."

Rhoda ran to open the door, then scurried back to help carry her share of the Roman.

Galen's eyebrows rose as he scanned the soldier. "He's really big, Val. How did you ever get him into the cart?"

"I got my shoulder under him and stood up. I don't really know how I did that. God must have given me extra strength."

"We can try that again with my shoulder. I'm a lot stronger than you."

◆

Valeria was not so sure. Galen was still only a couple of inches taller than her and not filled out. But he did do the heavy work on the farm, so it might work.

"He's too broad for one shoulder, so you take his right side and I'll take his left. Rhoda can guide his feet."

Galen took hold of his legs and prepared to pull him out.

"Be careful of his left leg. I don't want the cut to start bleeding again. Just pull the right one if you can. I have to keep the back of his head from hitting anything."

As Galen pulled, Valeria supported his shoulders and slid along the bed of the cart.

Once they had him positioned with only his chest still lying on the bed, each crouched at his side, wrapped one of his arms across their necks, and stood.

Valeria struggled to support her half of him as they carried him into the cottage. God must have given her special strength in the forest. A clear sign that He wanted her to bring the tribune home. She wouldn't question her decision anymore.

Rhoda lowered his feet to the floor and pulled the covers back on Valeria's bed.

"Help me get him on his right side." Muscle fatigue had her shaking when they finally got him on the bed and Galen stepped back.

Valeria unwrapped the temporary bandage that she'd applied before moving him. As she'd feared, the cut had bled more during their trip home, but it appeared to have finally stopped.

"Rhoda, please put the kettle on to boil. I need to clean and stitch his head and leg while he's still unconscious. It will hurt too much if he's awake, so I want to hurry. He could be waking up any time."

Galen's eyebrow shot up. Valeria shook her head at him. Now was not the time for him to be joking aloud about the Roman looking much more likely to die than to wake up. She could see exactly what Galen saw, but God had told her to help the tribune. She would obey and trust Him to heal this man who'd lost enough blood to kill most people.

As Rhoda started the water, Valeria went to the cupboard for the bottle of acetum, the antiseptic mixture of vinegar and plant oils that Gaius had taught her to make. It really stung in open cuts, but it also prevented infection. She gazed at him lying unconscious on her bed. He wouldn't notice how much it hurt when she poured it on his wounds.

Valeria clipped his blood-matted hair close to his scalp with her sewing scissors. After she trimmed a patch almost two inches longer and wider than the cut, his wound didn't look so bad. As Gaius had taught her, she cleaned it thoroughly and applied the acetum before taking needle and thread to close it.

She tapped her chin with her fist. How could she bandage a wound on the back of the head? She couldn't wrap bandages around his face. Maybe she'd have to leave it uncovered and pray that she could keep it clean enough.

His leg was a simpler problem. She'd helped Gaius treat a man who'd cut his leg with his ax, so she already knew how to treat the wound in his calf.

She bit her lip as she tied off the last stitch, and a small smile tugged at the corners of her mouth. *I thank You for keeping him unconscious through this, Lord.*

What would a soldier like him do if he awakened while she was working on him? Both the cleaning and the stitching would have felt like she was trying to hurt him. A wounded animal was the most dangerous kind, and he wouldn't have known she was only trying to help him when he first awoke.

She checked his pulse. Steady and somewhat stronger. His breathing was fast and shallow. Not quite what she'd like, but not too worrisome.

Now that she had him home where she could care for him, he might survive his ordeal. He'd already survived the worst, but until he woke up, she could be sure of nothing. Only then would she know if he might live.

She straightened up as she gazed down at him.

Rhoda touched Valeria's arm. "Now can we help his horse?"

Valeria fought the sigh. She was already tired and might have a long night ahead of her if he didn't awaken quickly, but the look on Rhoda's face convinced her.

"Galen, please tell him he's among friends if he awakens and then come get me right away."

The sun had almost set by the time she finished treating the Roman. She stroked Rhoda's hair and kissed her forehead before picking up a lamp. It might be well after dark before she finished with his horse.

"We'll need a bucket of water and my medicine bag. Time to be Good Samaritans to his horse, too."

Rhoda grabbed the bucket, hurried through the door, and headed to the well for the refill. As Valeria turned to pull the door shut, her gaze fell once more on the tribune.

If he lives, God, please make him let us live as well.

Chapter 7

WAITING

The fire had burned down to embers. A faint glow appeared above the trees to the east. Valeria raised her head from the table. She'd spent the night there, listening to his breathing and praying for his healing. At last, she could stay awake no longer. She'd laid her head on her folded arms and dozed off for a few minutes.

The Roman still lay motionless on her bed. He should have awakened long before this. She'd found him more than fourteen hours earlier, but he looked no different than he had lying across the road. If he was going to recover, why was he still unconscious?

She had no experience with head injuries, but Gaius had brought his medical scrolls when he escaped from Rome. Soon it would be light enough to read. Maybe she would find some answers to her questions, some advice on what to do.

As she gazed upon the tribune's emotionless face, tendrils of unease wrapped around her. His face was deeply tanned, but his pallor was too much like the dead men by the road. His pulse seemed a little stronger and was steady enough, but his shallow breathing worried her. Twice in the night it had become so quiet that she'd checked for a pulse to see if he was still alive.

The sky brightened from gray to pink-suffused blue. Soon Galen and Rhoda would awaken and come down for breakfast. Rhoda would be disappointed that he wasn't awake yet. Galen wouldn't be surprised. Last night his mouth had been grim as he looked at the Roman. He expected the wounded man to die.

She rubbed her eyes before dragging herself to the tribune's bedside. When she placed the back of her hand on his forehead, her breath caught. Did he feel warmer than he should? She bit her lower lip.

Fever. Nothing could be worse. If his wounds infected, he would die. She sat beside him and touched his forehead again. He did feel warm, but her hands were cold in the brisk morning air. Maybe that was the problem.

There was a more reliable test.

Oh God, please don't let him be fevered. She leaned over and placed her lips on his forehead.

Galen was coming down the ladder as she sat back up.

"Val, kissing the poor man when he can't defend himself? For shame!"

She ignored his comment. "No fever, praise God. When he wakes up, he'll have passed the crisis."

Galen walked to the bedside and took her hand in his.

"Cold hands." He rubbed her small hand between his two larger ones. "I guess you'll be kissing him again until these warm up. Good thing he's unconscious. We wouldn't want him getting the wrong idea about you."

He gazed down at the Roman. "Has he moved at all?"

"No, but it hasn't been a full day, and I prayed all night."

Galen's eyes flipped from the Roman to Valeria and back. Then he shrugged as a smile leaked out.

"He might look a little better. Maybe we won't have to bury him after all. I have lots of other chores today, so that's a good thing."

"Galen! Don't talk that way with him maybe listening. He won't know you're joking like I do. If you have so many chores, you should get started." With a smile, she shoved him toward the door.

She sat down at the table again, leaned on her elbows, and rested her face in her hands. She sometimes stayed up all night as a baby was being born, but there were always other people to talk with and to share the joy of a new life coming into the world. This had been the hardest night vigil she'd ever kept.

Rhoda climbed down from the loft and walked over to the bed.

"I think he looks much better this morning, don't you? Sleeping is a good thing when someone is trying to get better."

She stepped over to Valeria at the table and gave her a big hug. Valeria kissed her forehead.

"Did you stay up with him all night?"

"I slept a little at the table. God kept him alive through the night. He's made it through the hardest part now."

Rhoda turned to look at the Roman again. "He could wake up and need you right away. I can do your chores as well as mine today so you can stay with him."

Valeria kissed her once more on the forehead. "That will be a wonderful help. Now I need to make breakfast before your hungry brother returns and complains that he's starving."

After breakfast, Valeria climbed into the loft where she kept the trunk that contained Gaius's medical writings. Scroll VII of Celsus described what to do with several kinds of battle wounds, and Scroll VIII had a section on broken skulls. His skull wasn't broken, but surely there would be something in one of those that would to help her care for the Roman's wounds.

She carried them to the table and unrolled Scroll VII. She found plenty about treating wounds from arrows and other missiles, but there was nothing about deep cuts on the back of the head. She rolled up the scroll and slid it back into its protective sheath.

She unrolled Scroll VIII and found the section on blows to the head. Lying insensible—that was exactly what he'd been doing since she found him. Celsus said that meant his skull was fractured if he bled from his ears or nostrils, but she'd seen no blood on his head except around the cut. It also said he might be bleeding under the bone even if it wasn't broken. The description of how to cut into the skull to relieve pressure...she had neither the knowledge nor the equipment to even think about trying something like that.

She glanced at the Roman. *God, what am I supposed to do? Gaius would know, but this poor man only has me to help him.*

After rolling up the scroll, she slipped it into its sheath.

She squared her shoulders. She would just keep doing what seemed right and praying for God to guide her. That was much better than what she would find in something written by men, anyway.

Back in the loft, she returned the scrolls to the trunk. She lifted a pillow from Rhoda's bed and climbed back down the ladder. She laid the pillow on the table and fluffed it. There was time to catch a little sleep before she started the morning's weaving.

Before her nap, she checked on him. She didn't like anything she saw. He was still pale as death, and he hadn't moved since she'd finished tending his wounds.

Her fingers wrapped around his limp wrist to check his pulse. Steady and maybe a tiny bit stronger. She pushed a strand of hair off his forehead and rested the back of her hand there. There was no sign that he was any closer to waking up, but at least there was no fever. *I thank You, God, for that blessing!*

She hoped she was wrong, but she had a feeling the table might be her bed for some time.

Valeria hadn't intended to sleep all morning, but she'd been too tired. How Rhoda and Galen had kept from waking her during their lunch was hard to fathom.

She pressed the heels of her hands against her eyes and ran her fingers through her hair. Then she walked over to the bed and looked down at the Roman.

He still hadn't moved from where he was lying when she started her short nap...hours ago.

Surely he should have awakened by now. When she was helping Gaius, she'd seen two men who'd been knocked unconscious, but both of them woke up within a few minutes. It had now been over a day for the Roman.

Valeria chewed her lip. What if he didn't wake up? How long would it take him to die?

No, Lord. That can't be. You told me to care for him.

She pulled back the blanket and unwrapped the bandages to check his leg. No sign of spreading redness or pus or sickening smell to show the start of infection. The bleeding had completely stopped, too. After rewrapping his leg, she leaned over to examine the cut in his scalp. Again, no sign of infection. She placed her hand on his forehead. It felt cool to the touch—no fever.

If only he would wake up.

She pushed a strand of dark brown hair back from his temple. Up close, he was even more handsome than he'd seemed in the village. He might be dangerous when he was awake, but he looked so peaceful lying there now.

But how could a man of war like this tribune be a man with a peaceful heart? Perhaps he would learn something about peace from her family...if God spared his life. Was that why God had him fall where she would find him?

Valeria returned to her loom by the window. As she passed the shuttle back and forth between the warp threads, she found her eyes often drawn to her patient. After another hour passed, he still hadn't stirred. That surely couldn't be a good thing. It was time to help him wake up.

She walked over to the bed and shook his upper arm. No response.

His muscles were firm, even with him just lying there. His upper arm was almost as big as her thigh. No wonder he was so heavy. How had she and Rhoda ever managed to lift him into the cart? God must have given her extra strength. She couldn't have moved him by herself now.

She sat on the edge of the bed and took his hand in hers. It was a large hand, a strong hand. The hand of a soldier that had spilled the blood of many men, but it still reminded her of Gaius's hand when he would reach out to help her into the cart. She'd loved how he used to lay it on her shoulder and gently squeeze to show he was particularly proud of how quickly she learned something.

Her finger traced a large vein on the tribune's right hand.

If only Gaius were here. He'd know what to do to help the poor Roman. Gaius had always known exactly what to do...

She drew her fingers across the tribune's cheek. He'd been unconscious so long that stiff bristles covered his cheek and chin. Stroking a cheek always awakened Galen or Rhoda. Why didn't it work with him?

"Please wake up." He didn't seem to hear her.

She ran her fingers through his hair several times, then let her hand rest on his bristled cheek. She tapped several times with the palm of her hand.

God, I don't know what I should do for him, but You do. Please guide me.

Two more taps on his cheek. Still nothing.

Please wake him up, and let him be grateful enough not to arrest us.

Her hand rested on his cheek as her thumb stroked it.

Surely God would protect them from him when she'd chosen to be faithful by caring for her enemy. Still holding his hand, she closed her eyes and began to pray once more.

Chapter 8

THE ROMAN MASK

Decimus awoke to find himself lying on something soft, surrounded by blackness. Where was he? In a cellar dungeon? But that wouldn't be a soft place...or warm. Someone had placed a blanket over him. Surely not a prison guard. Was he dead? No, that couldn't be. His head hurt abominably when he moved even a little. Dead men don't feel pain. He shifted as if to sit up, and he felt a stabbing pain in his leg. What was going on?

A slight rustle was followed by very soft footsteps coming toward him. His muscles tensed, ready for the attack that might be coming in the darkness. He sensed the warmth of a body leaning over him and felt hands adjusting the blanket. His hand shot out, and he grabbed the arm reaching over him, gripping it as hard as he could.

There was a sharp gasp of pain, then a woman's voice speaking Greek. "Finally, you're awake. All should be well now." She tried to pull her arm free, but the attempt was a feeble one. "Please let go. You have nothing to fear from me."

He struggled to maintain the strength of his grip, to no avail. Then he relaxed it so she wouldn't realize how weak he was, but he didn't let go. He wanted to know exactly where she was, and he couldn't see her in the darkness.

"Is there a lamp here? Light it." His voice was hard. The set of his mouth was grim. He wanted to look and sound like a man in control when the lamp was lit. He'd found that looking the part usually made it so, even when his words were not understood by those who heard him.

◆

Valeria expected him to be dangerous when he first awoke, and she was right. At first, his grip on her arm was vise-like. There would be bruises left by his fingers. It was a good thing he had no weapon within reach.

His fierce scowl and flinty eyes would make a warrior draw back. Even in his weakness, his bearing would have terrified many women. Not her; she'd been praying for God's protection.

His words were another matter. There was nothing threatening about them. She understood his Latin because Gaius had insisted she become a "well-educated lady." To do that, she had to master the spoken language, not just read it. Still, she'd seldom heard it since Gaius died. She was more comfortable with Greek, and everyone in the market town spoke the Germanic tongue.

She'd been eager to read Latin since Gaius's treasured medical writings used it, but she'd learned to speak it well mainly to please him. Who would have thought she'd need her Latin to converse with a wounded Roman tribune in her own home?

"Isn't there enough light from the fire? I can add another piece of wood if there isn't."

She watched his eyes widen when she spoke. At first, she thought her Latin had surprised him, but then a flicker of fear crossed his face before he set it to show no emotion.

Oh, no! He's blind. She bit her lip as she shook her head.

Why hadn't she considered that possibility? The blow to his head was in the right place to cause blindness. Gaius had treated a man kicked by a horse in the same place. He was blind for several days, but he did finally recover his sight. Maybe the Roman would, too...but more likely he wouldn't. Gaius told her that usually the blindness was permanent.

Physical courage—he would have plenty of that, but that wasn't what he needed to face this. For a warrior, to be blind was to be helpless. He might fear that more than death itself. Being helpless and all alone—maybe that was everyone's greatest fear.

Valeria understood that fear. Seven years earlier, she'd been alone and dying of the fever that killed her parents. Then Gaius and Priscilla came. They nursed her back to health, and they made her their daughter. They told her about God, and she became His daughter, too.

Whatever came from helping this Roman, Jesus was with her. She would never be alone, and He would give her courage to overcome her fear.

Jesus, please help him with his fear, too.

She didn't try to break free, even though it would be easy. A toddling child would be stronger than him after losing so much blood. After that first vise-like grip, his hand kept relaxing the pressure on her arm. That must be because he had to, not because he wanted to. A Roman soldier wouldn't be a gentle man and wouldn't care whether he was hurting her or not.

He didn't look frightened at the moment, but it was important for him to release her when he wanted to and not before.

She placed her free hand on his. "You're hurting my arm. Please let go. I promise I won't try to hurt you. I only want to help."

◆

The German's Latin was spoken with a pronounced accent, but Decimus didn't expect to hear gentle words in Latin if he were among enemies. She was only a woman. No threat lurked in her tone of voice. It was probably safe to let her go. His grip had weakened too much to hold her anyway. When he released her, he left his arm where he could grab her again if needed.

She sat down on the side of the bed and rested her hand on his arm. His bicep relaxed under her touch.

"Where am I?" He tried to sound commanding, but a trace of fear crept into the question.

"You're in our cottage a few miles from the main road. My sister and I found you where the robbers left you, and we brought you home to care for you. We brought your horse, too. His shoulder's cut, but he should heal. Rhoda is taking very good care of him for you. We also brought your scrolls and codices. The robbers didn't realize they're more precious than gold. Rhoda thought they might be special to you, so she gathered them and put them all back in your box. We have that here as well."

Decimus lay still, trying to remember exactly what had happened. The piercing pain in his head made it all seem disjointed. He reached back to feel the focus of it, but she grabbed his hand before he could.

"Don't touch it. You have a nasty cut in your scalp. It bled a lot, but the ax blade didn't break through the bone. I've cleaned the wound and stitched it up. It will heal faster if you don't touch it. God has truly protected you. The ax must have cut through your helmet to make such a wound. I thought you were dead when I saw all the blood. Your attacker must have, too, or he would have struck you again. You've been unconscious for more than a day. I was beginning to think you might not wake up. But now you have...so that's good."

His mouth curved down more as he listened to her.

"You also have a cut on your leg, but it's in the fleshy part and not too close to your knee or ankle. I've cleaned and stitched that, too. It should heal well enough if you stay off it for a while. You've lost a lot of blood, so you should expect to feel weak for a few days."

Decimus was silent for a long time as the severity of his injuries sank in. Unconscious for so long, massive blood loss—the robbers had almost killed him.

"How do you know all this?" He almost growled at her.

Something was very strange here. How did a German peasant woman know how to treat battle wounds like his?

"Gaius was a physician. He was training me...until the raiders murdered him. These robbers may have been the same men."

Disjointed images of the battle began to coalesce in his mind. The narrow passage through the rocks, the ambush, the sword cutting into his leg, being thrown from his horse as it stumbled, killing his first attacker, hoping the next would attack while he still had strength to kill him...

His breath came faster as he relived the battle in his mind. His eyes hardened to match the grim set of his jaw as he clenched his teeth. Then his eyebrows dipped as concern surged through him.

"My men?"

"I'm sorry...you were the only one I found alive."

Decimus took a deep breath and held it briefly before letting it out. A shadow of grief passed across his face, but again he quickly concealed the emotion. These men had reported to him, but Fabius and Aemilius had also been his friends. Men die in battle, but this was different. He should have been more alert, and they had paid for his failure with their lives.

Even a new recruit would have seen the potential for ambush among the rocks on that hillside. This was a frontier province, and Rome was not especially loved out here. The river road was safe enough, but he should never have assumed the road through the hill country would be. He should have been on guard as point rider. Their deaths were entirely his fault...and now he was alone.

He strained to see something, but only darkness pressed in upon him. The cold grip of fear seized him again—blind and alone. How long would this last? Every moment in darkness was a moment in danger. If he couldn't see, how could he read the intentions of others? How could he watch his enemies to see their weaknesses? How could he defend himself when they moved against him? How could he...fears and questions swirled through his mind.

Fear surged again as he strained to see her. This time it took him longer to erase the emotion from view.

The seriousness of his situation shook him to the core. Alone... and no one would be looking for him here, wherever "here" was. They would assume he'd taken the river road like he always had. It was a surprise inspection anyway, so it could be many days before anyone even knew he was missing. He could expect help from no one.

He swallowed hard to push back the growing panic. He was a man of action, unprepared to face life as a blind man in a world full of threats he couldn't see. Blind, hurt, alone, at the mercy of this woman who was helping him but whose motive for that was a total mystery to him—he'd never felt himself in greater danger in his entire life.

◆

Valeria watched his face, and it was quite frightening to see the cold, hard eyes and clenched jaw of the warrior until they softened into the panicked uncertainty of a blind man. Then he masked his emotional turmoil almost completely.

She'd never known anyone who could mask surging emotions as well as he did, but he didn't fool her.

Poor thing. God, please help him. He needed help to bear his pain and fear. *Please give me wisdom to find the right things to say to him right now.*

"Are you thirsty?" He nodded his head, and that triggered a grimace. "Let me prepare you a drink to help with the pain, and then you should rest. With a head wound like yours, you may have some trouble seeing well for a while. Things should get better as you heal."

His unseeing eyes were fixed on her face as she spoke, and his chest jumped with his rapid breathing. At these reassuring words, his face relaxed and his breathing slowed.

I thank You, God! That was what he needed to hear...for the moment at least.

Maybe he would regain his sight, but that might take a miracle. Maybe God would grant him one more after sparing his life in the ambush. Meanwhile, it would not help him to know the odds were against him seeing again. He needed some hope to fight his fear.

"I'm going to brew a tea that should help the pain. It may taste a little bitter, but I hope not too bad. It will help you feel much better."

She patted his arm as she rose. It jerked back at her touch.

After putting a small amount of water in the kettle so it would boil quickly, she swung the hook on which the kettle hung over the fire. Then she ground some dried herbs and placed them in a small pitcher.

She glanced at the Roman. He was lying on his side with his head cocked, trying to hear where she was and what she was doing. A scowl twisted his face.

He didn't trust her, and she couldn't blame him. He didn't understand why she would help a stranger like this. He didn't know she was a Christian who was duty-bound to care for her enemy, even when that put her in mortal danger. He wouldn't know Jesus's teachings.

If he knew she followed the Way, he'd probably think she really was his enemy planning to harm him and not trust her at all. The governor would have told him Christians were dangerous and should be purged from the Empire.

God, please change his mind. Let me caring for him help him see the truth.

Her family's future depended on him deciding not to enforce Governor Lentulus's anti-Christian decree when he finally recovered. She'd chosen to be faithful to Jesus's command to love her enemy. Surely God would protect them from the danger that he posed to them.

God, please let this end well for all of us.

The sooner he began to trust her, the more likely that would be. She began softly humming so he could follow her movements more easily, and the scowl vanished.

As Valeria ran her fingers through her hair and tucked it behind her ears, her eyes never left him.

How was he managing to bear so much and reveal so little? He had to be in great pain, but he gave no sign except a tightness around his eyes and mouth. Gaius had taught her about stoic philosophy. Perhaps he was drawing on that.

She contemplated him as the water heated. A tribune would be a brave man. Perhaps he would be fine even if he didn't regain his sight. Courage gave one strength to face the many tragedies that come with life. She'd learned that from Gaius and Priscilla. That, and also that God made living through all things possible.

Her eyes softened as she watched his emotionless features. Even a stone-hearted Roman tribune needed to know how much Jesus loved him. Was she supposed to be the messenger? Was that why God made him fall across her path and then told her to help him? Was his blindness part of God's plan to save him? *God, please show me what You want me to do for him. I'll try to do it.* Her throat tightened as the scowl reappeared. *Please don't let him kill us when I do.*

She turned toward the kettle. The water needed to be boiling to extract the medicine from the crushed herbs, so she listened for the first bubbling sound. He needed medicine as soon as possible. Pain made it hard to lie still, and moving too much could make him bleed again. He'd already lost so much blood. It would have killed a weaker man. It truly was a miracle that he was still alive at all.

Chapter 9

THE PHYSICIAN

Decimus lay with his eyes closed and focused on the German woman's quiet humming. The pain kept shouldering aside rational thought. He was desperate for any distraction, and she provided one. She was a strange woman—willing to bring home a man she didn't know and who might be dying to care for him. Why would anyone do that?

She'd spoken of a sister—a younger sister, maybe?—who'd helped her. She sounded young herself—unmarried? A married woman wouldn't bring a wounded stranger home. Her husband would be angry if she did.

But how had an unmarried woman dared to help a strange man, to bring him into her house and risk ruining her reputation? Maybe her father lived here, but a father wouldn't be any happier about it than a husband would. Besides, the only man she'd mentioned was some dead physician who'd been training her. What kind of woman trained to be a physician, anyway?

The mystery of this woman didn't stop there. It had been very dangerous for her even to stop. The robbers might still have been nearby and returned. Everyone knew what they did to unprotected women. Why would she risk her sister's life as well to help him? Even if her sister had been just as willing to help.

How had they even managed to get him here? She'd said it was several miles to the road. They must have had a wagon or a cart, but how could a woman and a girl or even two women have managed to lift him into a cart? She didn't seem very tall when she stood by the bed, and her sister might be even smaller. He was a big man—too heavy for a small woman and a girl or even two women to move easily.

She was as matter-of-fact as a military surgeon when she talked about his wounds and how she'd cared for them. Now she was brewing a tea to ease his pain. He knew many women. Not one of them could have dealt with his injuries or even been willing to try. None of them were physicians, but still...that gave her the knowledge, but what made her willing to risk stopping to help a man dying by the roadside?

Was she thinking he'd pay her handsomely for her services when he recovered? He planned to, but he must have looked like he was going to die. Dead men don't pay their physicians, so that couldn't have been her main motive.

What did this risk-taking physician look like?

That thought jerked him back to the present—his blindness and the pain.

◆

At last, the water was boiling, so Valeria swung the kettle away from the fire. She wrapped the handle with a cloth and poured its steaming contents into the pitcher. The acrid aroma of the bitter herbs filled the room as the leaves steeped in the hot water.

She sat on the edge of the bed again and rested her hand on his arm. His eyes were closed, but his breathing proved he wasn't sleeping. It was fast, like someone who'd just run a great distance or was struggling against pain or emotion. His eyelids stayed shut after her touch; maybe that was less frightening than looking into the blackness that shouldn't be there.

"The tea is almost ready. Do you think you can sit up a little to drink it?"

He nodded once and pushed with his arm into a reclining position. Gaius had told her about the sumptuous banquets with Roman aristocrats propped up on one arm as they reclined at table. He looked just like she'd imagined them. She patted his arm and rose to fetch the cup.

"It's still very hot. It has to cool a little before you can drink it. I'll hand it to you when it's ready." She sat down beside him again and held the cup while it cooled enough to be safe to drink.

The smell was pungent, and he grimaced as it struck his nostrils.

She fought a smile. He looked just like Galen when she made him take medicine. "Yes, I know it smells terrible, and maybe it does taste almost as bad as it smells, but it really will help you feel much better

when it dulls the pain. I'm sorry I don't have anything more pleas-
ant-tasting that will help."

Slowly and silently he nodded his head.

As she gazed at him, her head tilted. He didn't seem dangerous at
that moment. He was hurting and not just physically. She'd seen in the
village how his men had been his friends. The look on his face when
she told him they were all dead confirmed it. He'd suffered so much
already, and even more suffering lay ahead.

Her eyes moistened, but she blinked hard to stop the building
tears. Crying wouldn't do. He mustn't know she felt sorry for him. The
tribune was a proud man who wouldn't want her pity, no matter how
bad his condition.

It would be best if he never knew how afraid she'd been that he
would die. There were many things he'd be better not knowing, at least
not yet. How intense her prayers had been that he'd wake up as he lay
unconscious for much too long. How thankful and relieved she'd been
when he finally awoke. Most of all, how serious his head wound might
be, that his blindness might be permanent.

She closed her eyes. *Oh, God, please give me wisdom to know how to
help him. Please give this poor Roman comfort and courage.*

He was going to need both.

He lay tense and silent beside her, a frown tugging his mouth down
as she swirled the tea in the cup, trying to make it reach a drinkable
temperature faster. Finally, it had cooled enough.

"Here, try just the smallest sip and blow on it as you take it." She
took hold of his free hand and placed it around the cup. "I'll hold it for
you while you drink if you'd rather. Whatever way you prefer, that's
what we'll do."

◆

"I'll do it."

Decimus could feel the heat of the tea through the walls of the cup.
He took a very small sip. It truly was as horrible-tasting as it smelled.
He fought the overpowering urge to spit the vile mouthful out. He
scrunched up his face as he made himself swallow that first sip. A little
bitter but not too bad. She was a master of understatement.

He faked a scowl. "So now I know I can't trust your word."

She sucked her breath through her teeth, clearly shocked by his
sudden accusation that she'd done nothing to deserve. Her startled response amused him.

The corner of his mouth turned up. "It doesn't taste almost as bad as it smells. It tastes much worse."

◆

Valeria wasn't at all surprised that the tribune wanted to do it himself. He'd been a man in control. Of course he'd want to control what he still could. What she hadn't expected was for him to joke with her when he obviously felt terrible. Pain and fear weren't conducive to humor in most men. It was a promising sign.

She patted his arm as she rose. Yes, it was a very good sign that he felt he could joke with her. He must be starting to trust her at least a little.

A sense of humor should help him bear what lay ahead of him, too. Her lips tightened as she shook her head, then they curved upward. If he remained blind, he'd need a sense of humor and all the courage he could muster. Maybe he had what he needed.

"You must be feeling a little better if you're ready to insult your nursemaid."

◆

Decimus heard the smile in the woman's tone. The voice moved away from him. "I'm not sure whether it's worse hot or cold. I'll save the extra for later, and you can tell me when you drink your next cup cold."

Footsteps, a creaking hinge, the sound of a small door closing. She must be putting things away in a cupboard.

She was right that the tea would help. He'd taken several sips, and already he felt the pain beginning to subside. It was worth the disgusting taste for that effect. The tea had finally cooled enough for him to drink more quickly. He downed the remainder as fast as he could. He didn't want that horrible taste in his mouth any longer than was absolutely necessary.

"Here, I've finished."

He lowered himself to lie on the bed as he held out the cup. Her footsteps were coming closer. A sudden drowsiness enveloped him. He jerked his head up, triggering a fresh explosion of pain.

"Did you just drug me, woman?" A black scowl dragged his mouth and eyebrows down.

"Of course. All medicines are drugs, but this one is good for you. It will ease your pain and help you sleep." Two light pats on his arm. "Don't worry. You haven't been poisoned."

His face relaxed as his anger morphed into intense fatigue. His cheek settled onto the pillow.

Her soft voice came out of the unnerving darkness. "Time for you to rest. I'll stay with you until I'm sure you're well asleep. You can trust me and my family. I promise we won't harm you."

Her fingers brushed his as she took the cup. Then she tucked the blanket around his shoulders before walking away. Something, maybe a chair, scraped on the floor before she resumed humming.

The pain began to slide into the background. She was probably speaking the truth when she said she wouldn't harm him. Why would she have helped him at all if that had been her intention? This nightmare might not end badly after all, as soon as his sight returned.

He drifted off, listening to her soft melody.

Chapter 10

Help from the Enemy

Valeria stopped humming and sat quietly at the table, listening to the Roman breathe. Now it was slow, deep, steady—exactly what she'd been praying for.

Relief drew out a smile. *I thank You, God, for bringing him back from the brink of death.* Her lips tightened. *Please forgive me for being so afraid when I found him. I know he's a dangerous man, but I thank You for giving me courage to try to help him anyway. I know that's what You want, but please protect us from him when he's well again.*

She set her elbows on the table and rested her chin in her palms. The poor blind man. What would become of him if that didn't change?

God, I beg of You, don't stop with sparing his life. Give him back his sight, too, but make him see that we aren't his enemies because we follow You.

It was a battle to keep her own eyelids open, but she sat for several minutes watching his chest expand and contract. His face looked peaceful now, and his breathing remained deep and even. She could finally end her vigil.

She slipped sideways off the chair so it wouldn't scrape the floor and tiptoed to the ladder leading to the loft where Rhoda and Galen were sleeping. She'd put the tribune in her own bed in the alcove off the main room, the bed that had belonged first to her parents and then to Gaius and Priscilla. She would share Rhoda's bed until he recovered, just like she had before the raiders killed them.

After the better part of two nights and a day watching over him, she was desperate for a few hours of deep sleep. Short naps with her head on her arms or a pillow had helped. Praying for him had kept her alert when she was awake, but crushing fatigue was winning now. She'd been afraid to leave him alone in case he had a crisis and she didn't hear him in time. Now that he'd awakened, he could call her should he need her.

She took off her shoes and climbed the ladder, placing each foot against a pole so the rungs would be silent under her weight. She stepped past the rung that always creaked. She didn't want to risk waking him. At the top, she crept to Rhoda's side and lay down beside her.

Rhoda stirred and sat up. She whispered, "Is he getting better now?"

"I don't know, precious. He's awake, and I think the cuts will heal well. But that wound on his head—it's like when the horse kicked Oleg. He can't see. Oleg's sight returned, but Gaius said that was rare, that people usually stay blind from something like that. I don't want to tell him that yet. His blindness frightens him."

"You don't think he can bear being blind?"

"I'm not sure. I think he's strong and brave, but he relies on his own strength and makes his own courage. That may not be enough. He's proud and used to bending life his own way. He needs the strength from God that lets us walk through trials without breaking. He doesn't have that."

Even in the darkness, Valeria could hear the smile in Rhoda's voice. "We'll just have to teach him to know God like we do. Then he'll be fine no matter what."

Valeria wrapped her arms around Rhoda and rested her cheek against her little sister's hair. "You are so wise for someone so young. I think he feels he's all alone and surrounded by danger right now. He doesn't understand yet that we'll care for him no matter what because Jesus wants us to. Maybe God did bring him to us so we can teach him about Jesus's love."

She said nothing to Rhoda about her fear of what he might do if he regained his sight and strength without understanding that their faith didn't mean they were his enemies. Nothing would be gained by letting Rhoda share her fear.

Rhoda hugged her back. "I know how I'll be praying for him now." She pushed a strand of Valeria's hair back from her face. "You need to sleep. I'll listen for him needing something. I'll wake you if he does."

"Thank you, precious. I really am tired."

Valeria kissed Rhoda on the forehead, wriggled to settle into the mattress, closed her eyes, and was asleep in less than a minute.

Galen was the first one awake the next morning. His mouth curved when he saw Val sleeping soundly next to Rhoda. She didn't look like she'd been crying, so the Roman must be getting better. She'd have been dozing at the table again if he wasn't, or she'd have looked like she'd been mourning his death apart from God.

He crept past the slumbering girls and climbed down the ladder. As he was looking at the sleeping Roman, he put his weight on the creaking rung.

◆

Like a soldier in the field, Decimus jerked awake. A pulse of pain shot through his head as his eyes swept the blackness. Then he shut his eyelids so whoever was in the room might not realize he was awake. That seemed safer in a world filled with dangers he couldn't see.

Whoever it was finished descending the ladder, walked over to the bed, and spoke to him in Latin.

"It's good to see you back safely among the living. My sister needed a good night's sleep. Can I get you anything before I go do morning chores? A drink of water? Some bread?"

Decimus opened his eyes and turned his face toward the sound of the youth's voice. From the pitch of it, the boy might be between thirteen and fourteen. Not a grown man yet, but not a child, either.

The pronunciation of his Latin was perfect, but this youth seemed too friendly toward a stranger, too casual in his conversation to be a Roman. Why did this younger brother speak perfect Latin while his older sister had such a strong accent?

Everything about these people seemed odd, but maybe he could find out what was really going on from this boy. He shouldn't be as good at lying as an adult.

Decimus's eyes narrowed as he began to listen for any sign of falsehood in the boy's words.

"Do you know why your sister brought me here?"

"Of course. You were the man left by robbers at the side of the road."

An odd answer to a simple question. He'd hoped to find out why the sister was helping him. That statement of the obvious was no explanation. Was the boy hiding something?

"But why did she help me?"

The boy chuckled. "Val's the good Samaritan."

Decimus frowned, and his eyebrows started to dip before he stopped them. Samaritan? She didn't sound like a woman from Judaea. This boy talked in riddles.

The boy chuckled again. "Hey, if you don't know the story, I'm sure Rhoda or Val will be really glad to tell it to you."

Decimus propped himself up on one arm. The movement made his head throb, but nothing like it had last night. Time to take a different tack to get the information he wanted. "Some water would be good. Who are you?"

"Gaius Licinius Crassus, but call me Galen. We already met. But you were unconscious, so I guess that doesn't count. I couldn't believe what my sisters brought home from market day. You looked terrible, blood all over you and those bad cuts on your head and leg. Val had so much of your blood on her, she looked like she'd been in a fight, too. I was sure you'd die before the first night was over, and I'd be digging a grave yesterday. But Val was sure God had told her to bring you home to heal and that you'd live, no matter how bad you looked. I have no idea how she and Rhoda got you into that cart by themselves. You were so heavy to carry in to her bed, even with the three of us."

Footsteps retreating. A trickle of water being poured into a cup. Footsteps returning to his bedside. The boy was probably offering the cup, but he couldn't take what he couldn't see. He'd been careful to keep his eyes directed at the sound of Galen's voice, but the boy must know now that he wasn't actually seeing him. A wave of unease washed over him. The boy was probably not a threat but...

Galen picked up Decimus's hand and placed the cup in it. "Here."

Legs scraped as Galen moved something closer to the bed. It sounded like he might be sitting astraddle a chair, leaning on the back, watching him drink. Decimus felt a little foolish for thinking the boy posed a threat.

"Want some more before I go feed that great stallion of yours? Rhoda's been looking after him almost as closely as Val's been looking after you. She calls him Pegasus. He comes to that name, but she'd probably like to know his real one."

"Astro, from the star blaze on his forehead."

Decimus found himself liking the friendly young man. His sister had spoken truth when she'd assured him last night that her family wouldn't hurt him. The boy's general openness made it seem unlikely that he'd deliberately lie to him.

"Do you and your sisters live here alone?"

"Since my parents were killed in the raid on the village three years ago."

"Was this your father's farm?"

"No, it's Val's. Father became a physician when we left home because he'd always liked studying medicine. Val's the physician now. She really knows how to help people when they need her. Just look at you."

"Your Latin is excellent. That's unusual this deep in the northern provinces."

"We used to have a villa just outside Rome. I spoke it as a little child. Rhoda was too little to speak when we left there. Mother taught her, and Father taught Val after we found her."

"Found her?"

He'd been right about the boy. He was revealing a family history with peculiar details that might explain her behavior.

"This was her parents' farm, but they died of the fever. Val was really sick with it, too, when we found her lying out by the corrals. We stopped to take care of her, and before we knew it, we were family. She taught Father how to farm here. The slaves did everything at our estate in Italia. He used to say Val was one of the smartest, kindest people he ever knew. She's been as much mother as sister to us since the raid."

"How old is she?" The left corner of Decimus's mouth curved. The boy was a talker. One question and a whole story tumbled out of him.

"Nineteen, but the way people ask her for advice all the time, you'd think she was an elder."

"Is she betrothed?"

"Not yet. She hasn't met a man who could pass the test."

So she was a young unmarried woman and head of her household. With all that Galen had revealed, some of his questions were answered, but none of it explained why she'd decided to help him. That mystified him as much as it had before their conversation.

He held out the cup for a refill. Galen brought it back full and placed it in his hand again. As Decimus framed the next question to draw out more truth, rustling in the loft interrupted the silence.

Galen lowered his voice. "I hope we didn't wake them up. But if I have to be up doing chores, maybe they should be up, too."

With a chuckle, he dragged the chair away from the bed. One soft thud as the door closed behind him and Decimus knew he'd gone to tend the livestock.

He had much to think about after his talk with Galen. He drained the cup and lay down on his side to ponder what he'd heard.

A wealthy man leaving his villa near Rome and bringing his young family to a frontier province. Why would he leave such a privileged life and settle here on the small farm of a sick girl he'd treated? What had happened to his wealth? The boy said she thought a god had told her to bring him home and he would recover. She'd said a god had protected him from being killed by the ax. So much talk about a god as if he were a person who cared what happened.

He sucked air through clenched teeth as the truth struck him. He'd fallen into a den of Christians.

The tension in his shoulders radiated out into the rest of his body. For as long as he could remember, his father had despised Christians. When Father was organizing the games as part of his regular duties as quaestor, he took particular pleasure in having wild animals tear Christians apart as one of the featured events. After his elevation to praetor, he passed the harshest sentences allowed on any Christian who came into his court. As provincial governor of Germania Superior, he'd established the same policy as Pliny did in Bithynia and Pontus, executing any Christians who refused to deny their faith and sacrifice to Caesar and the Roman gods.

Decimus knew his duty when it came to Christians. Father wanted them arrested and executed for very good reasons. They were atheists who refused to even pretend to worship the emperor or the gods of Rome.

That was traitorous. Anyone could take part in the sacred rites of the state religion without believing in the Roman gods. He didn't believe in them himself, but like any true Roman, he went to their temples and offered the sacrifices to show his loyalty to Rome. The superstitious feared the gods' favor could be withheld from Rome and her Empire if the rites weren't performed perfectly. Even a slight error and the whole ritual had to be repeated. The Christian refusal damaged the perfection.

Even worse, the Christians wouldn't acknowledge Caesar as divine and swear loyalty to him as their lord. All because they claimed only their crucified rabbi deserved the title. Of course, Caesar wasn't actually a god, but he really was lord of the empire and should be served as such. If Caesar wanted worship as part of that service, Decimus was perfectly happy to perform the required acts of worship as part of his duty to Caesar and to Rome.

The Christians' refusal was a threat to the Empire that needed to be stamped out. It set an example of rebellion that couldn't be tolerated. They might question Caesar's position as lord for religious reasons, but if they got away with it, others might question it for political ones.

He'd watched many Christians die in the arena, singing songs of praise to their god rather than worship Caesar. That kind of fanaticism made them very dangerous people.

His dark scowl softened. He'd also heard good things about them. Reports were circulating of them caring for deathly ill strangers, even though they might sicken and die themselves. Galen's parents had done that for Valeria. The danger hadn't stopped them. These Christians were the same. They'd saved him from dying by the side of the road, even though they must know any soldier was sworn to enforce the governor's policy against them.

By definition, any enemy of Rome was his own enemy. But this particular set of Christians...what was he to think of them? Especially her. Why was she so willing to help him when she must know he was the enemy of her whole family? His mere presence put them all in mortal danger.

His lips tightened. There had to be some ulterior motive behind her helping him the way she was. The whole family would bear close watching. He desperately needed their help right now. They seemed willing to give it for the moment, but what the future held was another question altogether.

Chapter 11

SAFEST PLACE IN THE EMPIRE

Footsteps on planks above Decimus were followed by a soft rustling in the direction Galen had first come from. Her foot on the ladder produced a softer creak than Galen's. He turned his head toward the sound.

Soft footsteps approached. "Good morning. You look like you're feeling much better today. You met my little brother Galen?" Her fingers brushed against his as she took the empty cup from his hand.

"Yes." He paused. What was safe to say to this Christian? "He asked my horse's name."

"Rhoda will be glad to learn his real name. We don't know your name, either."

"Decimus."

"That's very short for a Roman name."

"It's long enough."

Caution was in order. It was unlikely that some woman in the hill country of Germania would know the wide purple stripes on his tunic meant he was the senatorial tribune, second in command of the legion and a member of the highest order of Romans. She probably thought he was an ordinary soldier. He'd be a fool to let these people know he was Decimus Cornelius Lentulus. His full name would immediately reveal that he was not just any Roman soldier but the son of the Roman governor who wanted them dead.

It was safe enough to tell her his first name. There were only a few first names in common usage, so many people shared his. It al-

56

ready made no sense that these Christians were helping him. Surely no Christian would help the son of the man who had decreed they should be executed, but he couldn't afford to have them stop. He needed his sight and his strength back before he could risk that.

"I'm not sure I told you my name last night. It's Valeria." She adjusted the blanket that had slipped off his shoulders when he'd raised himself up to drink. "Do you need something to ease your pain this morning?"

"I don't want to sleep now."

He needed to watch her for a while to figure out why she'd brought him to her home. She didn't seem like a stupid person who wouldn't realize he was her enemy.

The irony of his choice of words struck him. *Watch her*—not really an option for a blind man, but he could listen. Maybe his vision would clear in a few hours. Then he could rely on his eyes again and not just his ears.

"Last night I used a special mixture to help you sleep. I'll make you something for the pain only." The gurgle of water being poured into a kettle was followed by the squeak of metal on metal. A hook holding the kettle swinging over the fire?

Her voice was directed away from him. "I'm sorry it will taste just as bad as the tea last night. It's the pain killer that's so bitter."

"The pain's not bad if I don't move suddenly. I can bear it."

"I'm sure you can, but you shouldn't try. You'll heal faster if you can rest comfortably."

"Maybe later." The new tea was probably safe to drink, but if it dulled the pain, would it dull his remaining senses as well?

She was humming again, and the sound moved around the cottage. His ears focused on her movements, but he couldn't decide what she was doing while she waited for the water to boil. He wanted to know everything she did. Now that he knew she was a Christian, he couldn't trust her.

Finally, the gurgling of water rising in pitch told him she was pouring the boiling water into a small container of some kind, and he could smell the bitter aroma even from his bed—not something he wanted to drink before he needed to.

"The tea is ready. Are you sure you don't want some now?"

"Not now." He didn't want her pain killer, but he did want her answer to what he was most eager to know. "What I want is to know when I can expect this darkness to clear from my eyes so I can see again."

The long silence that followed raised the hairs on his neck like an enemy creeping up behind him. Why was she so slow in responding? She'd been quick enough to answer all his other questions. Was she trying to hide something from him? He could usually tell when a man was lying by watching his face. It was much harder just listening. With a woman, it was even harder. He was about to demand that she answer him when she finally spoke.

"Well...when Oleg was kicked by the horse, it was about a week before his sight began to return. Gaius said the deep bruises inside his head had to heal enough first. Then it took a while to be fully restored. Perhaps we'll see something like that for you. That's the only case I've seen myself, so I can't predict exactly."

The prickles on his neck subsided. He was mostly satisfied with her answer. A week wasn't that long. Longer than he would like, but he could put up with the darkness for a few more days. It would take longer than that for his leg to heal, and he couldn't really do anything until then anyway.

◆

Valeria had been truthful, but she hadn't revealed what she feared. Gaius had said the blindness would almost always be permanent. But God had already given the tribune one miracle by keeping him alive, so why not restore his sight, too? She would keep praying for another miracle.

His face had shown no emotion as he listened to her trying not to tell him too much. Was he just trying to cover his fear, like he had last night, or did he not suspect how serious his injury was? He was still weak from blood loss, and he needed to rest for several days before much of his strength would return. He'd find out soon enough, and the stronger he was when he did, the better he'd be able to bear it if God didn't choose to restore his sight.

She cleared her throat, not sure exactly how to say the next thing. "There are probably some...man things that you need to do in private. When Galen comes back in, he can help you with ...whatever."

◆

The corner of Decimus's mouth pulled upward. This young woman who wasn't fazed by blood and death had girlish modesty. Her cheeks would probably be an appealing pink...if he could see them. Well, that shouldn't be too long.

Her perception and forthright statement of his needs both amused and surprised him. Nothing much seemed to escape this woman's attention. Why did she seem so unaware of the danger a Roman soldier posed to her family of Christians?

Her footsteps came toward him. "Since you'll be with us for a while, we need to change your clothes. Galen can help with that, too. Yours need washing to remove the blood, and they're too...Roman. We'll need to fix that before anyone sees you.

"You're taller and broader than Gaius, but he was plumper. I think some of his clothes will fit well enough for now. At least the shirts should, although the sleeves will be short. The pants will too short, but that's the best we can do until I make some alterations."

Whatever she dragged from beneath the bed made a heavy scraping sound. The soft thud against the bedframe suggested a trunk. Fabric rustled as she took some clothes out of it before shoving it back under his bed.

"It would be wise to speak something other than Latin if anyone except my family might hear. Germanic is best, or Greek if you can't do that. Rome is not loved around here, and very few speak the conqueror's language really well. Your Latin is too polished. People come unexpectedly for my help, and rumors of a real Roman in the neighborhood might bring trouble."

"As you wish, Valeria," he replied in Greek. Safer if she didn't know he mostly understood what they spoke in Germanic. "Anything else?"

Curious. Why such concern about keeping anyone who posed a threat to an injured Roman from knowing he was here? Maybe he didn't need to worry about why she was helping him. All that really mattered was that she kept doing it until his sight and strength returned.

"Well, very few men here are clean-shaven like you were. You have a two-day growth now. You should let it keep growing. Galen or I can trim it for you when it grows out enough."

Decimus's laugh broke free—a deep, full-throated laugh like he'd shared with his men in the inn's courtyard.

"You would turn me into a Greek merchant." Despite his pain, he found the image incongruous and funny. A Lentulus as a money-grubbing Greek!

"I would keep you safe from unfriendly eyes until you're better."

A door hinge creaked. Galen must have returned from feeding the livestock.

Her voice turned away from him. "Stop! Do not track that mud from the cattle shed into the cottage. And we're speaking Greek to Decimus if anyone comes by. His Latin sounds too much like a Roman."

The door closed. Galen had probably stepped back outside to scrape his feet before entering. Another creak of the hinge, then footsteps of the boy coming to the bed.

Valeria's voice was directed toward her brother. "Here, Decimus needs some help with these clothes and a few other things. We want to make him look less Roman, just in case. Be careful of his wounds so they don't start bleeding again. I'm going out to collect the eggs while you help him with whatever he says."

Her footsteps moved away. The door swung on its hinges again, and she was gone.

"Planning for everything—does she always do that?" So many practical ideas for concealing his Roman identity impressed him, but were they necessary?

Galen chuckled. "She does, indeed, but it can make life really simple. I don't have to think too much myself. Now, what do you want me to help you with?"

Decimus hadn't expected to be so weak when Galen helped him into a sitting position. He had to place his hands out to both sides just to steady himself. Sitting up made his head throb, too. Even though she spoke as if she expected him to recover completely, he still felt terrible. He'd be in no shape to deal with any enemies for many days, maybe even a few weeks. Much longer than the week it might take for his sight to return. Looking less Roman probably was a good idea.

Galen's hand gripped his arm to steady him more. "Don't worry about being wobbly for a few days. It happens to everyone who loses a lot of blood, and you probably lost more than anybody Val's ever treated before. She'll probably let you stay mostly in bed for a few days, but she makes people get up at least some as soon as they can. Father thought people healed faster that way. So does she.

"You can lean on me to steady yourself until I get your crutch made this morning. Just don't put any weight on your left leg yet. I'll be in big trouble with Val if I let you tear the stitches loose and it starts bleeding again. She wouldn't want to sew you back up when you're conscious."

"She could give me more of that vile-tasting sleeping potion from last night." Decimus's nose scrunched at the thought.

"Vile—that's the right word for it. It tastes so bad I'm almost afraid to tell her when I've hurt myself. The pain has to be almost unbearable to be worse than drinking that tea."

Decimus's mouth curved as an image formed of Galen dodging a medicine cup that Valeria held. The image swirled away, and his smile faded when he could put no faces on their bodies.

Galen had helped Decimus into one of Gaius's tunics by the time Valeria returned.

She rapped on the doorframe. "Are you ready for me to come in?"

Galen's response was immediate. "I'll say yes, because I'm ready for breakfast."

The left side of Decimus's mouth twitched. Galen had a quick answer to every question. The boy's running conversation and sense of humor would be a welcome source of entertainment while his wounds were healing.

Hopefully, his sight would return more quickly than it did for that man with the horse. He was already tired of being blind.

Decimus cocked his head when the ladder rung creaked softly. Rhoda must be descending from the loft. What would the third member of the family be like, the one who'd rescued his codices and scrolls and was so fond of his horse?

The soft padding sound of her footsteps drew closer. The sweet little-girl voice was no surprise when she spoke.

"I'm so glad you're feeling better this morning. We've all been praying for you."

He stopped his eyebrow before it rose. How should he respond to that statement? He would rather not think about them being Christians because he found himself already liking Valeria and Galen.

He changed the subject. "Thank you for helping Astro. I hear from Galen that you're taking very good care of him."

"He didn't want us to take you away, so he followed us. I'm glad we brought him home, too."

Decimus just smiled. He didn't know what else to say.

A small hand rested on his arm. "I'll be right back with a surprise for you."

Her scampering footsteps headed out the door.

The tantalizing smell of breakfast filled his nostrils. He was as ready to eat as Galen. It had been almost two days since he last ate at the inn in the village. He'd enjoyed that last meal with his fellow officers—friends now lying dead somewhere in the forest because of his inattention. Again, in his mind he was back in the forest, knowing his men were dying, fighting for his own life and losing...

The door swung open, and Rhoda entered. She plopped down next to him on the bed. The sweet smell of strawberries came with her.

"I thought you'd like some more of our berries. You liked them so much in the village. Here." She placed his hand in the bucket so he could feel them, cool and damp from being washed at the well.

A jolt of recognition struck him. The woman he'd bought berries from in the village, the one he'd stopped Fabius from raping, the one whose horse he'd spooked as he galloped out of town—she was Valeria. She and Rhoda must have been on their way home when they found him.

It had made no sense that she would stop and risk her life to help a total stranger. Normal people didn't do that. At last he had a reasonable explanation for her trying to save him. She was repaying him for stopping Fabius. Risking her life to repay a debt of gratitude or honor—he would do that himself, even if the person was an enemy.

Now that he knew he'd seen her before, he tried to remember what she looked like. In his mind, he saw the striped blanket, the basket of red strawberries, the back of Fabius's helmet and armor as he crushed the woman against his chest, but he couldn't put a face on the struggling woman's body. She'd just been some vendor in a village who was nothing special. He didn't usually bother with such people, but this time...he suppressed a sigh. Why hadn't he paid more attention?

He masked his thoughts, simply saying, "Thank you, Rhoda. I like your berries very much."

Decimus enjoyed his breakfast more than he expected. Valeria had insisted that he remain in bed so his leg wouldn't start bleeding again. Her porridge wasn't the sumptuous banquet he usually ate while reclining, but it had been much better than the legion cooks prepared, well-seasoned with aromatic herbs and the perfect temperature.

Perhaps the best part had been the entertaining conversation between Galen and Rhoda. She was filled with stories about how Astro had done this and that, and Galen kept suggesting ridiculous things that she could try to train him to do when he was healed. There had been a lot of laughter. They'd even tried to make him feel part of the circle at the table by asking him for humorous Astro stories.

After breakfast, Galen went out to his farm chores, and Rhoda hurried off to take care of his horse.

He lay with his eyes closed, listening to Valeria move about the cottage as she cleaned up after breakfast. She was humming again. His head and leg both still hurt more than he'd ever thought possible, but listening to her gave him something other than the pain to focus on. He tried to keep track of where she was in the room, but he no longer worried that she might be doing something that put him in danger. She was repaying her debt of gratitude, and that meant he could trust her.

Stopping Fabius had been the right choice, even though he didn't know why at the time. It might well be that Christians were enemies of Rome, but these were not his enemies. There probably was no safer place in the Empire than in this cottage with her family while he waited for his sight to return.

Chapter 12

A WISE WOMAN

Valeria chose a task that allowed her to stay in the cottage to watch over the tribune. He'd passed the turning point when he regained consciousness, but he could start bleeding again if he moved too much and tore loose the stitches in his leg. His eyes were closed, but his head moved to catch every sound, like someone on guard duty. He needed watching to make sure he didn't do something he shouldn't.

She was adding some length to Galen's trousers today. She needed to do the same to a pair of Gaius's pants so the tribune's legs didn't stick out at least four inches past the hem. The men of Germania didn't wear tunics, and trousers that fit would make him less conspicuous.

He would soon be able to go outside using the crutch Galen was making. He needed to blend in should someone come to the cottage for help.

She glanced at him and tried not to sigh. Roman nose, Roman hair, Roman attitude of superiority. At least she could try to get him to blend in. Everything about him screamed "Roman officer." There was nothing she could do about that if someone got too close, but from a distance there was some hope.

◆

Decimus felt the mattress dip when she sat on the side of the bed. She placed her hand on his upper arm, so he opened his eyes. Everything was still blackness, but that wasn't so disturbing now that he knew it wouldn't last long.

64

"So, how are you feeling now?" A smile brightened her voice. "Are you ready for something for the pain?"

His head still hurt like someone was trying to break out with a hammer, and the pain in his leg was a brutal companion. But he never allowed weakness to show. To admit he couldn't bear the pain would be weakness.

"Galen said it's better to suffer than to drink a cup of your tea. Until I hurt more, I'm inclined to agree with him."

◆

Valeria saw the tightness around his eyes and mouth. He was fighting pain—a lot of it. Nothing hurt less, but how could she get him to drink the tea if he didn't want it?

"Then I won't make you suffer another cup right now, even though that means I must wait to find out whether it tastes worse hot or cold. I'm not willing to test it myself. There are limits to what I'll do for my patients."

His mouth curved up into a fleeting smile, but he said nothing. Stubborn man. She'd hoped joking with him would get him to volunteer to take a cup.

"I'm going to check your wounds. If they're healing properly, you'll be able to get up and move about in a day or so. Today I'll alter a pair of Gaius's pants so you can go outside."

Decimus lay still while she examined him. "Well?"

No sign of infection around either wound. God was being very merciful to this Roman. Now if He would only end his darkness.

"As good as I've seen. But you mustn't try to do too much too soon, or you'll have a setback."

His satisfied smile brought a smile to her own lips. His failure to say he'd take it easy confirmed her suspicion that he needed close watching.

"I need you to straighten out your good leg so I can see how much I need to lengthen the pants."

When Decimus complied and stretched to his full length, his foot hung over the edge. Valeria laid Gaius's pants on top of him; they came barely halfway down his calf. He was fully seven inches taller than Gaius had been. She knew he was tall, but this much surprised her. She'd need more fabric than she'd planned.

◆

Decimus could hear the smile in her voice every time she spoke to him. She had a quick wit, and it distracted him from the pain. Kind humor like hers and her brother's was unusual in his experience. The humor of his friends usually had a cruel twist.

"Will I look more like a Greek merchant in these pants?"

"No. Today we're going for the Germanic farmer look. That's equally good for hiding a tribune from unfriendly eyes."

He blanked his face to hide his surprise. So she knew he was a tribune. Well, she had seen him up close in the village when he bought her berries. A man of his height tended to stand out in people's memories. He would have preferred she didn't know, but she'd still brought him home so apparently she didn't care.

Why she didn't was a mystery. Surely a smart woman like her would know his high rank made him more dangerous to a Christian than any ordinary soldier would be. It was a good thing she was repaying him for stopping Fabius.

She was the first woman he'd ever known to repay a debt of gratitude owed to an enemy. Her sense of honor was more like a man's than what he'd seen in any of the women he'd known. The rank of your enemy didn't matter when it was a debt of honor, so he shouldn't have to worry about her knowing he was a tribune. Still, it would be unwise to say anything that could reveal he was also the governor's son. It was unclear how far her willingness to repay the debt might go.

She laid her hand on his forearm and gave it two pats. "Rest now. I'll be over by the window sewing if you need anything."

She was humming again as she moved away. He liked that habit. It made it easier for him to keep track of where she was.

Fatigue crashed down on him when she stopped talking. He closed his eyes, hoping for sleep to ease the pain, and he drifted off as he listened to her quiet melodies.

Decimus had just awakened and was trying to ignore the pain when the door opened and her footsteps hurried toward him. He opened his eyes but saw only blackness.

"Lie still and stay very quiet. Some people are coming, and it might not be safe for them to see you. I'm dropping the curtain in case I can't keep them out of the cottage." With the rustle of the curtain, she was gone, closing the cottage door behind her.

Through the open window, he heard the hoofbeats of horses coming up near the porch. There were two, maybe three riders. Were they dangerous to Valeria as well as to him? His lips tightened. He couldn't do anything to help her if they were. His shoulders tensed, as if for battle. He strained to hear what was happening outside.

"Welcome, Baldric. I hope no one in your family needs my help today."

He didn't understand all the Germanic words she spoke, but he understood enough. Her voice was cheery and relaxed, not frightened at all. His muscles relaxed as well. She wasn't in danger.

Odd. Why did he feel so protective of her? Why had he just thought more about her safety than his own?

"No, Valeria, we are all well. I bring you some news and a warning." The voice was deep and commanding.

"News and a warning?" She didn't sound quite so relaxed.

The deep voice again. "Someone ambushed soldiers on the south road at the gap. Probably dead since market day. Six Romans, five Germans—more battle than ambush. We have given all the dead burial. It is good to see the Romans die, but too bad there is robbery and murder along that road again. I think it is only robbers and not the raiders of three years ago, but I cannot be sure. The Romans may come to avenge their dead, and they will not care if they punish the innocent as well. Be careful when you go to the village next market day."

◆

Valeria was waiting for the question she knew was lurking on Baldrics lips. Baldric's piercing blue eyes missed nothing. He couldn't have failed to see Astro in her corral.

He glanced over at the corral when Astro nickered at the mare his son was riding. He focused inquiring eyes on Valeria. "A magnificent new horse is in your corral today..."

She met his gaze. "Rhoda and I had to drive past the dead from the ambush. I'm glad you gave them decent burial. We were afraid to stop for that. That horse followed us. The robbers must have left him because he's hurt."

She shifted her gaze to the horse, hoping Baldric would do the same. She wanted no questions about its owner. She didn't want to have to lie to him. "He might not heal enough for heavy work, but I think I can get him strong enough to breed. He'll make big, strong foals. If you have a mare that's ready, you may bring her to him, if you wish."

Baldric's chuckle was followed by a wide grin. "You are a wise woman, Valeria. You let nothing go to waste. Now, if you were only wise enough to marry one of my sons..."

"You have fine sons who would make the hearts of many maidens happy, but they don't follow the Way. Only that will do for me."

"Perhaps I can change your mind about that."

Valeria smiled and changed the subject. "Speaking of your fine sons, how are Olga and your new baby doing? All still goes well, I hope."

"Yes, she is well, and my son grows stronger every day. She is a good wife. Your medicines cured her, and I am grateful for that." A deep chuckle rumbled up from his chest. "And as you always say, maybe your god had something to do with it, too."

Turning his horse, he looked back over his shoulder. "Farewell, Valeria."

"Farewell, Baldric, and thank you for the warning. We'll be careful."

Valeria stayed on the porch until Baldric and his two oldest sons rode into the trees and out of sight. Then she reentered the cottage.

She pulled back the curtain to find Decimus with his eyes open and a thoughtful crease between his eyebrows.

"I see now why you don't want me looking too Roman. You are a wise woman, Valeria, even if you won't marry one of Baldric's sons."

Valeria's own mouth curved as she watched the left corner of the tribune's mouth lift into a half smile. "So my Greek merchant understands more Germanic than I thought. Yes, I am a wise woman, able to recognize a good horse and a good man. Baldric is a powerful man, respected by his friends and feared by his enemies. His father was a warrior chieftain. The men for many miles call him their leader. It's very much better to be considered his friend.

"I've known him all my life. He was a close friend of my father. His wife was dying of fever after childbirth, and I treated her. God healed her, and now Baldric counts me among his valued friends, too.

"If he knew I was helping a Roman tribune, he might question whether I belong in that group. I think you should stay quiet for a while in case he returns. You still don't look enough like a Greek merchant, no matter how hard I've tried to change you."

Although he said nothing, the corners of his mouth tipped up in a full smile.

What a relief to see his spirits improving, despite his pain and continuing blindness. It was a good sign that he was making jokes and enjoying hers. She gently squeezed his forearm. "I have a bit of work to finish outside. Rest now. I'll be back soon." Still humming, she walked out and closed the cottage door.

Decimus closed his eyes. He now had proof that she would protect him if she possibly could, and he no longer worried about her motives for helping him, even though she was a Christian. Her ability to distract him from the pain and make him smile was remarkable.

What would a woman like her consider a good man?

Decimus had been dreaming about the ambush, and he awoke with a start. Everything was still blackness, and once more his vulnerability and pain pressed hard upon him.

His ears picked up the rustling as she set down her sewing and quiet footsteps as she approached. She sat down beside him. "Do you need something?"

"No."

He wasn't expecting the light touch of her fingers on his forehead as she moved a loose strand of hair back in place. He jerked his head back. The jolt of pain from the movement made him clench his teeth and squeeze his eyes shut.

"Oh! I didn't mean to startle you." Her warm hand rested on his upper arm. "I'm so sorry I hurt you. I'll warn you before I touch your head again."

He took a deep breath and blew it out slowly. As he reached to feel the back of his head, she grabbed his hand.

"No, you mustn't touch it." She pulled his hand down into her lap and held it there. "Do you want something now for the pain?"

He took another deep breath and blew it out. "No. It's not too bad."

The pain was like waves breaking on the beach: swelling, cresting, and pulling back, only to surge again. But he didn't want to take any medicine that might dull the senses he still had.

"You're a strange man. I don't understand you. You can bear all this pain without complaining, but you're afraid to help me test what my tea tastes like cold."

The corners of his mouth turned upward but the tightness near his eyes remained. He couldn't control that. She was an acute observer. No doubt she wasn't fooled by his pretense that nothing hurt.

She continued to hold his hand in her lap and stroke the back of it with her thumb. He wished she would keep talking to get his mind off the pain. When she didn't, he chose the next subject himself.

"Valeria, what do you look like? You must be very beautiful since Baldric is so eager for you to marry one of his sons."

Her laughter had a musical quality. He liked it. "What Baldric values is different from other men. When he was young, he married Elka. She was the most beautiful maiden in the area, and she had a large dowry as well. But she was also kind and smart, and in time he grew to love her much more for herself than for her beauty. She gave him four sons and three daughters. Then she died from the fever that killed my parents.

"His grief was so deep that some thought he would never marry again, but his children needed a mother. He could have had any maiden he wanted, but he chose Olga. She's very plain and had only a very small dowry. But like Elka, she's smart and kind, and he was sure she'd mother his children well. He was right. She loves them as if she gave birth to them all. In time, he grew to love her deeply, too. That's why he's so grateful for my help when she was dying.

"He wants his sons to marry the right kind of woman, someone like Olga or Elka. He doesn't care what they look like or if they even have a dowry."

She had laid her other hand on his forearm and was casually fingering the hair there as she talked. A maiden like her had no idea how that affected a man, and he wasn't about to tell her. Her unintended caresses helped take his mind off the pain, but nothing worked as well as talking with her.

"So he wants a woman like you for his sons."

"Plain and with no dowry? Well, I do have the farm..." Her laughter worked even better than her words. "His sons are good men, but they're not for me. They don't follow the Way."

He had no response to that, and there was a short silence. Follow the way? Did that have something to do with her being a Christian? He didn't want to get into any discussions about that. He already knew enough about the Christian threat to the Empire, and he didn't want to think of her as his enemy, especially while he was so completely dependent on her. It was time to change the topic.

"You haven't answered my question."

"Oh, I guess I didn't. Well, my hair is brown, and my eyes are gray. I'm not a beautiful woman, but I'm not ugly, either. I'm very capable of attracting a man's attention...as long as I'm holding a large basket of juicy ripe berries."

She gently squeezed his forearm as she rose. Her footsteps moved away. The rustle of fabric told him she had returned to the seat by the window to resume her sewing.

Decimus forced a smile because he knew by the lilting tone in her voice that she thought she'd just made a very good joke. However, her light words struck him hard.

The most powerful man in the region looked at this woman who was not beautiful and had little or no money, and he saw someone worthy to marry one of his sons. He'd looked at her in the village and hadn't even seen her.

Even when he was ordering Fabius to leave her alone, he hadn't really looked at her. She'd risked her own life to save his, and he'd thought her so unimportant he had no idea what she looked like. That thought began to gnaw at him. It was a mistake he would correct as soon as his sight returned.

Chapter 13

A Real Family

V aleria glanced at the tribune often. He never moved much, but every time she looked at him, he had shifted slightly. His pain was too much for him to rest quietly, no matter what he said. She placed her sewing on the chair and stepped to the shelf where she'd stored the tea. She poured a cup and sat down on the bed beside him. His restless motion stopped when she placed her free hand on his arm.

"I know you're strong enough to bear the pain, but I can't bear watching you do it. Please, for my sake, will you drink a cup now?"

◆

The throbbing in Decimus's head was like a blacksmith hammering red-hot metal on an anvil. It was impossible to shut it out and rest. Crushing fatigue from fighting the pain made it even worse.

He hadn't wanted to lower his guard, but the deep concern in her voice swayed him. She'd protected him from her chieftain friend. Proof enough she'd watch over him if the medicine dulled more than the pain.

"Yes."

"I have a cup here, but I'm going to touch your forehead to check for fever first." Her fingertips brushed some hair aside before settling there.

"No fever. That's good. This tea can cool a fever, and that can mask what the fever is trying to reveal."

"So if I had a fever, I wouldn't have to drink it?"

"Galen has already been a bad influence on you. He's a horrible patient when I have to give him medicine." The lilt in her voice revealed her smile.

Her fingers swept another lock of his hair back into place. It surprised him when she did it, but this time he didn't flinch. There was something about her touching his forehead that was soothing. He liked it.

"You'd need to drink the tea even with a fever. I'd just have to watch you more closely."

His eyebrow rose. "Is that possible? I have a very attentive physician." He managed a smile.

"Well, maybe not. Some patients do need very careful watching, and I'm afraid you're one of them." The smile she returned brightened her voice. "Here, drink your tea now."

He pushed himself into a reclining position. She lifted his free hand and placed the cup in it. As he gulped the bitter liquid down as quickly as he could, she rose, walked across the room, and returned to sit beside him again. She took the empty tea cup from his hand and placed another cup in it.

"Here's some water to wash the taste from your mouth."

He handed her the second empty cup and lowered his cheek to the pillow. "I can now tell you it's much worse cold than hot."

"Well then, if I ever have to drink it, I'll be sure to brew myself a fresh hot batch." That might be a grin he was hearing.

A fleeting smile acknowledged her remark. She patted his arm and rose. "Time for you to get some rest."

That second cup was a kindness he hadn't expected. It would be good when his vision cleared. Then he could put a face to the soft voice and gentle touches.

As the pain subsided, he drifted off.

The next time Decimus awoke, the delicious smells of stew simmering over the fire and freshly baked bread teased his nostrils. Valeria was humming as she tapped a spoon on the edge of a pot. The laughter of Galen and Rhoda grew louder as they walked through the door.

Rhoda skipped over to the bed, sat down beside him, and took his hand in hers. "Astro is feeling so much better today. Are you feeling better, too?"

"Yes, I am."

His head did feel much better. It only hurt like the morning after a night of too much wine. Her tea and the undisturbed sleep it made possible had helped a lot.

"I'm glad." Rhoda hopped off the bed. "Valeria, shall I slice the bread now?"

"Yes, precious. Everything else is ready. Please set the table after you slice it. Decimus, do you feel up to joining us at the table tonight?"

"Yes."

With his head hurting so much less, he felt ready for more than lying in bed like an invalid.

"Galen, would you please help Decimus to the chair? Rhoda, please set for four."

Decimus swung his legs over the edge of the bed and stood with his arms held away from his body. He didn't feel as wobbly as he had that morning, but he was still far from normal. Galen had warned him about tearing the stitches if he put any pressure on his left leg, so he balanced on his right.

He still saw only darkness, but suddenly that darkness was swirling. Even with Galen holding his arm to steady him, he started to teeter.

"Val! Help!" Galen was struggling to hold him up on his own. Valeria was instantly at his side. Her arm wrapped around his chest closer to his waist than his shoulders. For a German woman, she was tiny.

"We've got you. Perhaps we're trying to get you up too soon. Would you like to lie back down?"

"No. I've been lying down long enough."

Galen and Valeria helped him the few steps to the chair and supported him as he sat. He rested his elbows on the table and his head on his hands until he felt steady again.

He probably should have stayed in bed for the evening meal, but he wasn't going to admit his mistake.

The rich aromas of rosemary and onions and something he couldn't identify tantalized his nostrils as Valeria dished the stew into bowls. One by one, he heard Rhoda setting the bowls on the table. Then she sat down beside him.

She picked up his right hand and placed a spoon in it. She guided his other hand to a bowl she'd placed right in front of him. No words spoken, just enough help to make it possible for him to eat. All three of them were so casual about his blindness, helping him just enough but not fussing over him. He hated the darkness, but they were trying to make him comfortable with it while he waited for his sight to return.

He'd filled the spoon and was raising it to his lips when Valeria began to speak. His hand froze halfway to his mouth.

"Father, we thank You for Your many blessings this day. We thank You for this food to strengthen our bodies and Your word to feed our souls. We thank You especially that Decimus is able to share this meal with us this evening. In the name of Your precious son, Jesus, amen."

Galen and Rhoda echoed, "Amen."

Decimus remained silent. They knew he was a Roman soldier. She even knew he was a tribune, yet they prayed to the Christian god right in front of him. What foolish boldness! He would never expose himself like that in the presence of his enemy.

The stew tasted as delicious as it smelled, and the bread was soft and chewy. For a while, everyone ate quietly. After they'd taken the edge off their hunger, the conversation began.

Galen's voice came from his left. "Decimus, I made you a crutch today. With you being so tall, it wasn't easy to find a straight branch that was thick enough and long enough, but I finally did. I made the crutch extra-long so we can cut it to the right length when Val says it's time for you to start using it."

Valeria's voice from his right. "I think that should be in a day or so at the rate Decimus is healing." Her hand rested on his for a moment and patted twice before she withdrew it. "I'm very pleased with my patient's progress."

Rhoda's little-girl voice piped up just to his right. "Astro is getting better, too. He was following me around today."

Galen chuckled. "I'd follow you around, too, if you kept feeding me bites of carrot. You'll make him fat as a pig if you keep that up."

"No, I won't. His legs are too long for him to ever look like a pig. I'm not saying you're a pig, but you eat so much sometimes. Where do you put it? I'll get the rest of the bread so you won't starve before breakfast."

Rhoda slid past Decimus. When she returned, she paused beside him and placed her hand on his upper arm. He turned his face toward her. "I'm so glad we found you in the forest and brought you home for God to heal."

Decimus blanked his face to hide his astonishment. He'd given her no particular reason to like him or want him there. Some response was required, but he wasn't sure what that should be. In silence, he laid his large hand over her small one.

Then he smiled in her direction. "You know, Astro might have followed you home even if I wasn't in the cart."

Galen slapped the table and roared with laughter. "That's excellent! You got her there!"

Rhoda laid her head against his shoulder and hugged his arm. That affectionate gesture surprised him even more than her words.

The talking and joking continued after Rhoda sat down again between him and Valeria.

Decimus cupped his chin before rubbing it. How very different this was from his family. His mother had fulfilled her marriage duties and borne his father two sons, but she had no interest in raising them. When she died ten years ago, it was as if a stranger had passed away. He'd been raised first by slaves, then by tutors. They'd always treated him with the cool respect owed the young aristocrat that he was.

His father had shown little interest in him until he was about Galen's age. Then he took great pride in Decimus's accomplishments at the gymnasium as an athlete and scholar. He introduced him to patrician society and all that involved. As the only surviving son in a senatorial family, he was expected to follow the standard course of offices leading finally to a provincial governorship, just as his father had done.

He quickly earned a reputation for his skill as a swordsman, and his unusual aptitude for military affairs made him a protégé of the commander of the legion in which he was serving. His appointment as a senatorial military tribune in a frontier legion had gratified his father, who had excelled in both the military and political phases of his own career. But their relationship was one of mutual respect, not special affection.

He'd never seen this kind of warmth and caring anywhere. Certainly not in his family or the families of his friends. The nearest to it was the family of his closest childhood friend. Titus was very fond of his little sister, Claudia, and they were both very close to their father, Publius Claudius Drusus. Publius had always shown Decimus more affection than his own father ever had, treating him like a son and always being there with a listening ear and sage advice when he needed it most. But their older brother Lucius was an aloof, selfish man, and their mother had divorced Publius and abandoned her children to marry into a politically powerful family, so even that family couldn't compare to this one.

These Christians might not be related by blood, but this was family as it should be. It felt good just to be around these people. They occasionally asked him a question to include him in the circle. He kept his answers short. For the most part he sat in silence, enjoying the warmth of their words and laughter.

He finally propped his elbows on the table and rested his chin in his hands. Fatigue was winning the battle, but he didn't want to say anything and have to leave the family circle.

Valeria's hand rested on his forearm. He turned his face toward her.

"You look tired, Decimus. Time for you to rest. Galen, would you please help him get ready for the evening? Rhoda and I will clean up."

Decimus dozed for a few minutes after he lay down, but he wasn't sleeping deeply. He awoke when someone—Galen maybe?—spoke his name, but he didn't open his eyes. There would have been no point in opening them, anyway. All he saw was black. Then Valeria's voice penetrated the darkness.

"Dear Father, I thank You for letting us find Decimus before he died in the forest. I thank You for showing me what I needed to do. I thank You that he didn't bleed to death, as I feared he would. I thank You for the miracles of the healing You have given him so far. Please continue healing him. I especially ask You, in Your mercy, to give him another miracle and restore his sight. If You choose to let him remain blind, please help him bear it. I pray this in the name of Your precious son, Jesus."

"And, Jesus, help him come to You. Amen." Rhoda's sweet voice finished the prayer.

His eyebrows started to dip, but he relaxed them to hide his thoughts. This was no formal prayer to a distant deity. They were talking to their god as if he were a person in the room. Talking about him.

What did Valeria mean about helping him bear it if he remained blind? Did she expect that? His stomach knotted at the prospect. Hadn't she told him it might be a week or so, but his vision would return? Had she been lying to him? His throat constricted, and he swallowed hard.

Tomorrow, when Galen and Rhoda were not around, he would make her tell him the truth.

He didn't let them know that he was awake, that he'd heard. He listened with his eyes closed while Galen and Rhoda climbed into the loft and told each other goodnight. Popping sounds from the fireplace told him Valeria was banking the coals for the night. Then her footsteps approached his bedside. She tucked the blanket around his shoulders to keep him warm against the growing night chill. Footsteps moved away from him. As she climbed into the loft to join Rhoda and Galen, she stepped past the creaking rung so she wouldn't awaken him.

As if he could sleep after what he'd heard! He lay awake in the darkness for a long time, brooding over what he might hear tomorrow.

Chapter 14

HOPE IN THE DARKNESS

The next morning, Valeria sensed something was different about the tribune. He hadn't joined them at the table, and he hardly spoke a word. Even when they tried to include him in their conversation, he was mostly silent and curt when he did speak.

After breakfast, Rhoda stayed in the cottage to help Valeria spin some spring wool into yarn. When her little sister tried to get him to talk about Astro, his answers had been clipped and cold.

He slept much of the morning, but his eyes remained closed even when he awoke. His clenched jaw and downturned mouth discouraged any attempt at conversation. The brooding dip of his eyebrows was a little frightening. Each time Valeria looked at him, she saw the dangerous Roman tribune lying there, the one who bruised her arm when he first awoke.

He hadn't seemed dangerous when she sat on the bed chatting with him yesterday. He'd actually seemed rather friendly and appreciative of the care she was giving him. At supper last night, he'd seemed relaxed and even glad to be with them.

Valeria ran her hand through her hair before cupping her face in her hands. Worry lines formed between her eyebrows as she contemplated his sleeping form. Time to wake him for lunch, but which man would she find when she woke him? The man glad to have her help or the tribune who didn't trust her?

The tribune knew they were Christians. What if that coldness in his voice revealed a hostility that would make him arrest them when he recovered? That is, if he recovered his sight. If he remained blind, he posed no danger to them. She could take him down to the river road and leave him with someone who'd get him back to the legion. He'd never be able to tell anyone where they lived.

Despite the risk, she prayed for his sight to return each time she looked at him.

Decimus refused to join Valeria and her family at the table, choosing instead to eat his bread and cheese reclining on the bed. Then he feigned sleep until he heard Rhoda and Galen leave. Light footsteps and rustling fabric told him Valeria had moved to the window and was probably preparing to sew. His opportunity to force the truth out of her had come.

He swung his legs off the bed and sat up. The sudden movement made his head spin, but he steadied himself with both arms until everything settled. This was not a conversation to have lying down and looking weak.

◆

"Valeria. Come here."

There was that commanding tone of voice the tribune had used the first time he spoke to her. Not what Valeria wanted to hear.

She walked over and stood in front of him. "Can I get you something?"

"I have a question, and you will answer me with the truth. The whole truth."

The short hairs on her neck quivered as she watched the grim line of his mouth. He was frightening when he set his face that way. "Of course. What's the question?"

He took a deep breath before continuing, obviously steeling himself for what she might say. "Am I going to see again? Don't tell me what happened with the man kicked by the horse again. I want to know what you really think is going to happen...to me."

So that was why he'd withdrawn. Not anger with her, only worry about his future. A wave of relief surged through her, followed by a deeper concern.

Why did he decide to ask so soon? It would have been so much better if he'd waited a few more days. He was still so weak from blood loss. But it wasn't physical strength that he needed most to face her answer.

His face was set in that grim look of an angry soldier, but she felt the fear underneath. He had asked, so he must be told. She wouldn't lie to him.

"I don't know."

"I know you don't know, but what do you expect? Truthfully. Don't lie to me again."

"I haven't lied to you."

"You haven't told me the whole truth. That's the same as lying. Tell me now. Not what you think I want to hear, but the truth."

A scowl twisted his mouth as he accused her of lying. She saw the dangerous tribune who had grabbed her arm in his darkness. She didn't want to see the frightened man when she told him what she feared. She closed her eyes.

God, please give me wisdom to pick the right words. Protect him from fear and despair. When she looked at him again, the angry look was gone. He sat in stony silence, waiting for her to speak.

She sat down beside him. "I really don't know whether your sight will return. I can only tell you what Gaius told me when Oleg was blinded by the kick to his head." She took a deep breath before continuing. "He said that what happened to Oleg was very rare, maybe even a miracle. Usually, someone blinded by a head injury like that would stay blind."

His jaw clenched. He'd been sitting upright beside her with his hands resting on his knees, facing straight ahead, like a soldier facing the enemy before the first assault. Blind—that final word changed everything. It sucked the strength out of him. He bent over, rested his elbows on his knees, and covered his face with his hands. He took several slow, deep breaths.

Then he spoke so softly she could barely hear his words. "If I had my sword, I'd finish it now. Better dead than blind."

She slid from the bed, knelt in front of him, and took his hands in hers. She drew them away from his face, and replaced them with her own. He remained hunched over, leaning on his elbows with his hands hanging limply by his knees. As she cradled his face in her hands, she tilted it upward until his face was close to hers.

The defeat and despair in his eyes before he closed them pierced her heart. This was exactly what she'd feared would happen to this proud man who'd always depended on his own strength. She rested her forehead against his and closed her eyes.

God, please give me the right words to say to him now. Taking a deep breath, she moved back enough to look at his closed eyes again.

"No. Don't talk about killing yourself. Don't even think it. It's too soon to lose hope. God has already done so many miracles for you. The ax could have split your head open. We would have driven by you if you hadn't fallen right across the wagon track. You could have bled to death before we got you home. You might have never awakened from the blow to your head. Your wounds could have infected and killed you. Every one of these has been one of His miracles. God can surely do one more miracle and restore your sight."

◆

Decimus snorted and a sneer twisted his lip. The Roman gods weren't real. Just something used to control the thinking of weak-minded men. Why should he believe her god was any different?

He pulled back from her hands. "Why would your god want to do that, even if he could?"

She cradled his face again and stroked his cheek with her thumb. He didn't pull away. "Because He loves you, Decimus."

"Why would he or anyone else love me now? A blind man is useless. A blind man has nowhere to go. No one wants him. Death is better." Bitter despair colored his voice.

"That can't be true. Your wife and children will want you even if you're blind."

"I have no wife and children."

A sigh welled up from deep within him. It shouldn't have been that way. His father had arranged the ultimate political marriage, but the girl had died of a fever just before he was going to marry her when he was sixteen. They had agreed to wait until Father could arrange another equally good political alliance. All their plans...it was all for nothing now.

◆

Valeria's heart ached for him. He truly was alone...except for her family.

"But you don't have to worry about going anywhere. We want you here with us, whether you can see or not. You can stay with us as long as you need to, and we'll be glad to have you here. But we still don't know if your sight will return. It's too soon to tell. Don't lose hope yet."

He opened his eyes again and stared into his darkness. The anguish in them was beyond anything she'd ever seen. She lifted one hand from his cheek and pushed a strand of hair back from his forehead before cradling his face in both hands again.

"Please don't give up. God really can heal you, and we don't know yet if He will. It's too soon. I can't believe that He would have me rescue you without intending only what's best for you. I haven't given up hope. You shouldn't either."

Again, she pushed the loose strand of hair back before laying her hand back on his cheek. *Please, God! Pull him back from the hopelessness that's crushing him. Please let my words reach him.*

"You're only a woman. You don't understand. I'm a soldier. I'm not afraid to die." His words wrenched her heart. He was like a wounded animal lying helplessly in a trap, waiting for death to release it.

His words were once more almost too quiet to hear. "I don't know how to live as a blind man."

Her thumb stroked the thick stubble on his cheek.

"We don't know yet if you'll even have to. It really is much too soon to tell. And even if you do, we'll help you figure out how to do it. You aren't alone. Please don't give up like this. I couldn't bear it if you killed yourself."

Tears were swimming in her eyes as she gazed at him for what seemed like ages, praying for God to give him courage and hope. If he died now, if he killed himself, he would be lost for all eternity. She already cared about this poor man whom God had told her to rescue, and the thought of him being eternally lost tore at her heart.

◆

Decimus longed to see her face, to read what was really going on in her head. Was that a tremor in her last words? Was she crying? No, not possible. No one could care that much after so short a time.

So many of her words and actions befuddled him. She'd picked him up from the side of the road and brought him home. That more than repaid any debt of honor for him stopping Fabius. Besides, paying an honor debt to an enemy didn't mean you had to care about him as a man. He was still your enemy. Once that debt was paid, you could treat him as your enemy again.

She wasn't doing that. Her voice sounded sincere, like she really cared what happened to him, like she would actually grieve if he died. Either she was a great actress, or she was really crying. But why should she care that much? He'd done nothing to earn any deep affection from her, nothing to earn any affection at all, for that matter.

His loyalty was to Caesar and the Empire. She was a smart woman.

Surely she knew he was the mortal enemy of Christians like her. Didn't she realize that she and her family might be better off if he died? So why was she saying everything she could to make him want to live, blind or otherwise?

He so wanted to believe what she said about his sight returning, but how could he? Her god would have to be real to do anything. What proof was there of that? Even if he was real, why would any god care about the suffering of one man?

And even if the Christian god did care about his own worshipers, why would he care about a Roman sworn to destroy the people who do worship him? A man who'd overseen executions of people who refused to deny him to save themselves?

Still, she sounded so sure when she spoke about her god saving him from dying and even loving him.

She wasn't a silly woman. Except when she was talking about her god, everything she said and did was sensible and practical. Maybe there was some truth in what she was saying.

He knew battle wounds. He should have died in the forest like his men. Maybe her god really had performed miracles for him to be alive. Maybe he would do one more, even for a Roman like him.

And what if there is no miracle? Why did she say she wanted him with her, even as a blind man? It made no sense, but she and her whole family kept treating him like a friend instead of an enemy. They couldn't possibly have taken better care of him if he'd been a member of their own family. They really did seem to be glad he was with them even like he was, so maybe he did have someplace to be, no matter what happened.

Besides, the man with the horse took more than a week to see again. Maybe she was right. Maybe it was too soon to give up hope.

◆

Relief surged through Valeria as she watched the black despair fade and a glimmer of hope return. She rested her forehead against his again. *Oh, thank You, God, for pulling him back from his dark thoughts of death before they destroyed him. Now just one more miracle...please let him see again.*

He straightened up, so she rose from her knees and sat beside him. As had become her custom, she placed her hand against his upper arm to reassure him that she was there.

Please help him. Please give him courage and hope.

◆

84

Decimus reached across his chest and covered her hand with his. He took a very deep breath, held it, then released it slowly. He didn't understand it, but somehow he felt stronger when she was near. He could bear the darkness, at least for a while. He could wait to see what would happen. He could kill himself later if his sight didn't return and he decided being blind was more than he could bear.

"As you wish, Valeria. I'll wait, and we'll see if your god will do one more miracle."

She didn't answer, and he couldn't see her response to his words. He only knew that she still sat beside him, and somehow that gave him the courage to wait and see.

They sat for a long time with his hand resting on hers. At last, Valeria broke the silence.

"Time for me to finish lengthening Gaius's pants so you can go outside tomorrow when you try out Galen's crutch, and time for you to lie down for a while. You'll want to be rested and ready for supper."

He lowered his hand as she rose.

"You know, we really are glad to have you with us." He didn't smile, but he nodded his head. He almost believed her.

She patted his arm and returned to her sewing by the window.

The last of his energy left with her, and he lay down on his side.

She was right about him needing to rest. She was usually right about almost everything. If only she could be right about his sight.

Chapter 15

The Good Samaritans

Decimus had just awakened when he heard the laughter as Galen and Rhoda came toward the cottage. Rhoda's light footsteps skipped into the room, but Galen's tromping feet stopped before entering.

"Look, Val." His voice boomed. "I remembered to wipe off the cowshed mud before you told me. Aren't you impressed?"

Valeria almost whispered. "Shhh. He's still sleeping."

Galen's voice dropped to a murmur. "Sorry."

"Galen, do you have something Decimus can do with you tomorrow? I think he's strong enough to leave the cottage for a little while, and he's the kind of man who needs to do something useful. Something that won't hurt his leg or take too long so it won't tire him. He's still weak from the blood loss and needs to rest."

"Tomorrow? No. He's—"

Blind. That bitter thought stripped off the thin veneer of hope she'd given him before he slept. *Blind and useless.*

"got those stitches in his leg. What I'm doing tomorrow could tear his leg up. Day after tomorrow, he can help me. I have lots of things he can help me with as long as he doesn't mind doing farm work. It'll be good to have help from someone with arm muscles almost as big as mine."

"But his arms are at least twice as big as yours." A short chuckle followed Rhoda's protest.

A scuffling sound was followed by a soft squeal.

"Stop it, Galen. Put me down. You're going to drop me on my head."

"Hey, my arms are plenty big enough to swing you like a bell."

Giggles erupted. "Stop it! I'm not a bell."

"Hush, you two. You'll wake him. Here, use those big muscles to get us some fresh water. Supper is almost ready." Scolding words but a laughing tone.

Decimus almost smiled himself.

A draft passed over him as Galen opened the door and headed for the well, but nothing could chill the new warmth in that room.

Galen's response had shocked him. Valeria had assured him they wanted him with them, even if his sight never returned. It was impossible to believe she could mean it. He would have sworn that he'd only be a useless burden, but maybe he was wrong. Galen was actually eager to have his help.

He'd never thought a blind man would be good for anything. The only blind men he'd seen had been beggars at the side of the road, and he would rather die than be the object of other men's pity. Galen seemed to think a blind man could be a farmer or at least a farmer's helper. Valeria must think that, too, or she wouldn't have asked Galen to find something for him to do. If he could actually do something useful, perhaps the future wouldn't be so pointless after all.

"Rhoda, would you please wake Decimus?" There was that smile in her voice, as if no dark shadows hung over the future.

Rhoda skipped over to the bed and sat down beside him. She nudged his shoulder, but he didn't stir.

"Time to wake up, Decimus." No movement. She shook him gently. "Decimus?"

She shook him once more, this time harder, but still he didn't stir. "Decimus, are you all right?"

She shook him hard, enough to wiggle his entire chest. Nothing. "Valeria, he won't wake up. I think there's something wrong."

His arm shot out and wrapped around her waist, pinning her to him. She squealed in surprise, then giggled as she wriggled and squirmed, trying to free herself from his muscular arm. Even in his weakened condition, he was much too strong for her to break free, but she kept trying as Valeria laughed at the sight.

A huge grin split his face as he held the giggling, squirming girl in his carefully laid trap.

◆

For the first time since Valeria saw the trickle of blood on his leg in the forest, she was almost certain he would make it. She opened her mouth to speak as she watched the two of them wrestling on the bed. Then she closed it. She wouldn't spoil his pleasure at being alive by warning him to be careful of his stitches.

◆

Decimus was sitting on the edge of the bed when Galen returned.

Water sloshed in the bucket as Galen set it down. "Ready for me to help you to the table, Decimus?"

He stood, keeping his weight off his left leg. "I can get there myself if you'll point the way."

"Want to lean on me or the crutch? Val will skin me if I let you rip your stitches."

"The crutch." Decimus held out his hand and waited for Galen to place it against his palm.

Galen placed Decimus's free hand on his shoulder to guide him. "This way."

He inhaled deeply as he lowered himself onto the chair. Supper was bread and stew again. The savory aroma wafted around him. Rhoda placed his left hand against the hot bowl and slipped a spoon into his right. This time, he waited to begin eating until after Valeria had said her prayer.

As he scraped the last morsels from the bowl, Galen's fingers touched Decimus's forearm.

"Val told me you get one more day of rest before I can put you to work. I hope you won't mind helping me out. I promise I won't work you too hard to start with."

Decimus smiled broadly. "I've never been afraid of hard work. It's much better than doing nothing."

◆

His words drew Valeria's smile. It was good to see how the prospect of doing something useful had brightened his outlook. It had been a stroke of genius to have him help Galen so he'd feel like a man instead of a worthless beggar. She'd talk with Galen later about what she thought he should and shouldn't do right now.

The conversation, as always, was relaxed and happy. Valeria kept a close eye on him. He seemed content, like he enjoyed being part of her family circle. To see him now, it seemed silly to have worried so much about whether he would enforce their execution.

The sun was soon low in the sky, and supper time was over. Galen helped Decimus prepare for evening while she and Rhoda cleared the table and cleaned the dishes.

◆

Decimus was reclining on the bed when he heard the legs of furniture sliding on the floor. They were gathering at the table again for their evening prayers. It still amazed him that they would worship the Christian god as if there were no Roman officer lying on the bed listening to them.

Someone opened a cabinet door near the foot of his bed, then closed it. Rhoda spoke. "It's my turn to read tonight, and I know exactly what I want Decimus to hear."

Her footsteps, then something set on the table. A soft rustling—she was turning pages of a codex.

Rhoda cleared her throat. "Jesus said, 'A man was going down from Jerusalem to Jericho, when he was attacked by robbers. They stripped him of his clothes, beat him and went away, leaving him half dead. A priest happened to be going down the same road, and when he saw the man, he passed by on the other side. So too, a Levite, when he came to the place and saw him, passed by on the other side.

"But a Samaritan, as he traveled, came where the man was; and when he saw him, he took pity on him. He went to him and bandaged his wounds, pouring on oil and wine. Then he put the man on his own donkey, brought him to an inn and took care of him. The next day he took out two denarii and gave them to the innkeeper. 'Look after him,' he said, 'and when I return, I will reimburse you for any extra expense you may have.'

"'Which of these three do you think was a neighbor to the man who fell into the hands of robbers?' The expert in the law replied, 'The one who had mercy on him.' Jesus told him, 'Go and do likewise.'"

The cover of the codex closed, and her feet shuffled against the wooden floor as she turned toward him. "Did you like that story? Jews wanted nothing to do with Samaritans in those days. That makes him helping even more special. Valeria and I got to be the Good Samaritan for you."

He froze his face as the shock wave passed through him. The parallel between the story and what had happened to him was too perfect. He would have preferred to say nothing, but he felt Rhoda's eyes on him. She was waiting for an answer. "You read it beautifully."

He heard the slight rustle as she turned back to the table. Valeria's voice came to his ears, "Father, we thank You for..." She and Galen and

Rhoda continued, alternating among themselves as they praised and thanked their god for many different things and asked his help for others, but Decimus wasn't listening to them anymore.

His mind focused on the day of the ambush. He was the man who'd fallen into the hands of robbers and been left to die. Galen told him as much during their first conversation. Galen had even said she was the Good Samaritan when he asked why his sister had stopped to help.

Decimus had convinced himself that Valeria rescued him out of gratitude for him stopping Fabius. That made total sense to him...but it was totally wrong. She and Rhoda had rescued him solely because their god said they should. It didn't matter that he was a Roman tribune duty-bound to enforce his father's decree against Christians. They'd willingly risked death to help their sworn enemy just to obey their god's command.

More amazing, they didn't even seem to care that he might kill them. They'd done nothing to hide that they were Christians from him. They prayed for him out loud and often. They truly believed their god listened to their prayers.

He'd bet anything that they would never deny their Jesus and worship Caesar. Faced with that choice, they'd die like the Christians he'd watched in the arena, singing and praising their god as they were cut down.

The way they were caring for their enemy—that shook him to his core. He'd been so certain that Christians should be exterminated as a threat to the Empire. The longer he was with these people, the more he was torn between his loyalty to Rome and his gratitude for them caring for him. And they weren't just caring for him. They actually seemed to like him. They seemed to enjoy having him with them. Were they his enemies or his friends?

Valeria—she was unlike any woman in his wide experience. What made her so brave and wise and so unfailingly kind? It couldn't all be because she followed the Christian god.

He ran his hand through his hair. She'd become important to him. She'd kept him from dying by the road three days ago. She'd managed to pull him out of the pit of despair today. Somehow, he felt better able to face a frightening future when she was nearby. There wasn't anything about her that he didn't like...except her being a Christian. That actually bothered him a lot when he thought about it, so he tried not to.

He'd never met another woman who intrigued him like she did. More than ever, he longed to remember what she looked like.

Chapter 16

GAIUS'S WAY

Valeria banked the fire and turned to check on Decimus before climbing the ladder to join Galen and Rhoda in the loft.

Her breath caught. He wasn't lying down as she expected. Instead, he sat on the edge of the bed, a shadowy, slumped shape in the dying firelight. His elbows rested on his knees, and his face was buried in his hands.

Her hand shot up to cover her mouth. Was he contemplating suicide again? Would he hunt for a knife after she climbed into the loft?

She walked to his bedside. "Is something wrong?"

"No...well...yes." He lowered his hands, but he still faced the floor. Then he raised his head, but his sightless eyes only stared past her into his darkness. "But there's nothing I can ever do about it."

"What is it? Maybe I can help."

Decimus ran his fingers through his hair. "I'm sorry for how it was in the village. Something that didn't matter to me then truly matters now."

He drew a deep breath, as if the words hurt to speak. They probably did. A tribune wasn't the kind of man she would expect to apologize for anything.

"I can't remember what you look like. I've tried, but I just can't. I never really looked at you, at least not to actually see you. And now I'll never know what the woman who saved me looks like." He dropped his head again.

"Well, then I guess I was wrong."

91

His head tilted as he directed blind eyes toward her voice.

Her smile brightened its tone. "I thought I could at least attract the attention of a man if I had a bucket of ripe berries, but then I guess I wasn't actually holding the berries..."

His mouth drooped. "I mean it. I wish I knew what you look like." Obvious regret softened his voice. Joking about it wasn't making him feel any better.

She knelt in front of him and took his hand. "You don't need to feel bad about not remembering me. You had no way of knowing then that you would ever see me again."

She rolled her eyes. Why did she say "see"? The sadness in his eyes seemed to deepen at that word. This wouldn't do. He mustn't start thinking that being dead was better than being blind again.

"Anyway, we can fix that now. Gaius taught me a very useful skill. If you close your eyes so there's nothing to distract you, you can see with your fingertips."

His eyebrows dipped as his head drew back.

"No, really. It works. I've done it many times. Give me both your hands."

He made no move to give her the second one, so she picked it up. He let her position them, palms together, between her own.

"Now the secret is to touch what you want to see very, very lightly with just the tips of your fingers. I'll show you."

His hands dropped back onto his knees when she released them. She placed the fingertips of both her hands on his forehead, then closed her eyes.

With a feather-light touch, she traced the shape of his eyebrows. "Your eyebrows don't quite match because you have a small scar here on the outer corner of the right one."

She continued moving her fingers downward, tracing one fingertip along the bridge of his nose. "You have a lump right here on the side of your nose. I think you must have broken it at least once."

Her fingertips slid down along his nose to his mouth. The corners were twitching. "Stop laughing at me. This really does work."

◆

Decimus caught her hands and stopped her. It felt too much like she was caressing his face. He might be blind, but he was still a man, and the tingling touch of her fingertips skimming across his skin heated his blood in a way he was certain she didn't intend. It was best to stop her now.

Her voice was bright, almost playful. "Now it's your turn. Start at my forehead and work your way down my face, touching all of it. By the time you reach my throat, you'll be able to picture in your mind what I look like. Use both hands or you'll only see half of me, and that wouldn't be a pretty picture at all."

She leaned against the edge of the bed between his knees to steady herself. He felt her closeness, and that warmed his blood, too. Then she lifted his hands and placed his fingertips against her forehead.

"I'll try to stay perfectly still until you finish. I'm closing my eyes so you can feel everything."

Decimus began slowly, tracing her hairline. He fingered a strand of hair. It felt silken between his fingertips. Then he traced the fine arched shape of her eyebrows. They felt perfectly matched to him. His fingers skimmed over her eyelids and felt her thick, long lashes. He drew one finger down the bridge of her small, straight nose. Her cheekbones felt high, and they slanted upward.

She was right. He was forming a picture of her in his mind. As he began feeling the softness of her cheeks, the tips of his right fingers touched a raised welt just below her cheekbone. He jerked his hand away.

Her voice was soft. "You can touch it. You won't hurt me. It's a very old scar. I did warn you that I wasn't a beautiful woman." She placed his fingers back on her face. "Keep seeing me."

"What did this?" He traced the length of the scar with his index finger. It was about an inch long and forked at one end.

"I was thrown from a horse."

He raised one eyebrow, but it quickly settled back into place. By now, nothing about this woman should surprise him.

"How did that happen?"

"When I was young, my father bred horses. I was his only child, so I helped him like a son would. We had a beautiful stallion. He wasn't as big as Astro, but he was just as spirited. Of all our horses, he was my favorite. The only problem was he spooked easily. I was riding him one day when a rabbit jumped from under a bush and ran between his legs. I wasn't paying close enough attention, so when he reared, he threw me. I landed in the bushes by the side of the ravine. They stopped my fall and probably saved my life, but one of the branches tore my cheek. I was ten at the time."

"No wonder you can recognize a good horse."

"Astro could be a great stud. I expect Baldric to bring one of his mares to him. He raises horses, and he has some truly beautiful ones. I'm sure he'll want to improve his herd with Astro." She sighed. "Father would have wanted to breed our mares to him, too."

He tilted his head. The wistfulness in her voice as she spoke of her father was followed by a few seconds of silence. When she spoke again, the brightness was back.

"If it weren't for that stallion, I would have died when I was twelve. My parents had already died of the fever. I was lying in the cottage, burning up with fever, too. I was sure my time was near. I couldn't bear the thought of the horses dying from lack of food and water, so I dragged myself out to the corrals and opened all the gates. It was the last thing I did before I passed out. God used the horses to get me out in the yard where Gaius and Priscilla would find me."

He'd lowered his hands to rest on his knees on either side of her while she was telling him the story. She picked them up and placed his fingertips back on her cheeks just below the scar.

"I've closed my eyes again. Don't stop touching. You need to finish seeing my face."

His mouth curved into a smile until he turned it off. He needed no encouragement to caress her silken skin again. He traced first the upper curve of her soft, full lips, then the lower one. They were smiling, just as he expected. He slid his fingertips along her jaw, under her chin, and across her upper throat. His right hand finally came to rest with his thumb lying along the bottom of her jaw and his fingers lying on her cheek with the scar. He left them there, stroking her cheek with the side of his index finger.

The corner of his mouth tipped up. Looking at a woman's face this way was much more satisfying than using his eyes. Her skin was as soft as any he'd ever caressed, and the scar added an interesting texture as he slowly slid his finger across it.

Best of all, he now had a face to go with the kind voice and gentle touch. Gaius's way of seeing might well become his favorite, even if his sight returned.

◆

Valeria opened her eyes. Why was he leaving his hand on her cheek for so long?

Maybe he was having a hard time figuring out what her scar looked like. It did make her stand out from other women. Even a blind man couldn't help noticing it. It was vain to care about that, but she still did sometimes. Well, she'd warned him she wasn't beautiful. She took his hand and made him stop.

"Can you picture what I look like now?"

"Yes, and for the second time I've caught you in a lie."

"What do you mean?"

"You told me you weren't a beautiful woman."

She rested her hand on his forearm and stood. "I can see I'm going to be living with two hopeless teases for a while. You and Galen make quite a pair."

He looked so much better with his lips turned up in a smile instead of down in a frown. What a relief to have him joking with her. The deep shadow of sadness was gone, at least for now. He no longer seemed likely to try to kill himself before morning.

Her words had a charming lilt. Why was she laughing at him? Decimus had meant exactly what he said.

He listened to her footsteps as she walked away from his bed. He wasn't expecting her to suddenly turn and walk back to his side. He didn't jump much, but it startled him when she laid her hand on his shoulder.

No trace of teasing colored her voice. "Please don't have any regrets about what you did in the village. I want you to know how very thankful I am that you were there. I know you don't understand yet, but God used you twice to save me that day. If you hadn't cut us off and galloped ahead, Rhoda and I would have been the first ones through the gap where the robbers were waiting."

He reached across his chest and placed his hand over hers. Then he interlaced their fingers and gently squeezed. He didn't want to think about what the robbers would have done to her and Rhoda. Strangely, he was glad he'd gone through the gap ahead of them.

She squeezed back. After a moment, she withdrew her hand.

"Good night, Decimus. Rest in peace."

He stretched out on the bed, and she tucked the blanked around him. Two soft pats on his shoulder, and she left his side.

He listened to her climb the ladder and lie down to sleep.

Valeria lay in her bed, praying for Decimus's sight to return and thanking God that he was in much better spirits and feeling hopeful again.

◆

Decimus lay on his bed, thinking about a kind-hearted, beautiful woman with silky brown hair that framed a face with fine arched eyebrows, high cheekbones, soft lips with a smile constantly upon them, and laughing gray eyes—too bad she was a Christian.

Chapter 17

THE NIGHT CALLER

The pounding on the door jerked Decimus from his deep sleep.
A young girl's voice—was it Rhoda's? "Valeria! Come help us!"

He sat bolt upright, straining to understand what was happening. Quick creaks of the ladder. Footsteps approaching.

Valeria's hand gripped his upper arm. Her lips brushed his ear as she whispered, "Lie down and be very quiet. Someone has come for my help."

The curtain rustled as she dropped it to hide him from view.

A bolt slid back, and light footsteps scurried in.

"Papa sent me to get you right away. Mama needs you really bad. The baby started coming early. Mama's having horrible pain, and she feels so hot. Papa's scared she might be dying. I ran as fast as I could, but it's taken me so long to get here..."

"I'll come right away. Sit here by the hearth and warm up while I get ready. We'll take my mare so we get back to your mama as soon as we can."

A scraping sound told him Valeria had moved a seat near the fire for the girl. The rung creaked as she climbed back up the ladder.

Decimus kept his breathing slow and silent. Only the curtain separated him from the little girl as she wept.

◆

When Valeria came back down, she wore an old pair of Galen's trousers under her dress. She would be taking the shortcut over the top of the hill where the brush was thick, and she wanted to protect her legs.

"I'm almost ready, Elsa. I just need to gather a few things."

After she carefully wrapped several small jars of herbs, powdered minerals that could slow bleeding, and some of Gaius's medical instruments, she put them all into a tie sack that she slung across her chest.

"Let's go help your mama."

Decimus felt a rush of cool air as they hurried out the door and closed it behind them. Through the window, he heard her shrill whistle to call the mare.

The little horse nickered. Trotting hoofbeats and her running steps meshed as she brought the mare back to the porch where the girl waited, still crying softly.

"Elsa, calm down. You'll have to sit behind me and wrap your arms around my waist. Can you do that?"

The crying girl managed a weak "yes."

"When I get on, I want you to step on this stool and climb on behind me. Then hang on. We'll be back to your mama before you know it."

He heard some rustling as they mounted. Then the sound of cantering hooves faded quickly into the distance.

He couldn't say exactly what, but something in Valeria's voice disturbed him. She was trying to hide something from the girl so she wouldn't be too frightened.

He remembered the mare. She was a small cart horse, not a riding horse. If Valeria was going to ride double on a cart horse, she must have thought it vital to reach the mother very quickly. She must be afraid of what she would find when she got there.

Decimus awoke to the sounds of Rhoda getting ready to make breakfast. Valeria must not have returned. The bed creaked as he raised himself up on one elbow.

"Good morning." Rhoda moved the curtain aside and hopped up on the bed beside him. "Do you know where Valeria went?"

"A girl about your age took her to help her mother have a baby."

Rhoda's breath caught. "Was it Inge?"

"No. Elsa."

"That's Inge's oldest daughter. That's not good. It's too soon for

Inge's baby to come. We've been praying for her for weeks. She had a terrible time with her third baby. I hope everything turns out well even with the baby being early."

The cottage door swung open. Galen was back from feeding the livestock. "Val took the mare but not the cart. She must have been in a big hurry."

"Oh." Decimus felt Rhoda tense beside him. "I guess I'll have to do Valeria's chores today. I don't think she'll be back very soon."

"Well, you make good enough bread. Your stew's not so bad the pig turns down what's left over, so I guess we'll be fine for one day."

There was a short silence before Rhoda answered. "I'm going to get some eggs." The door opened, and Rhoda's footsteps faded away as she crossed the porch and stepped off.

Galen directed his voice at Decimus as soon as she closed the door. "You don't have to start helping me until tomorrow. Today is baking day. Rhoda knows how to do everything, but it's hard for her to knead all that dough. She and Val usually do it together. Would you mind helping her with the kneading? I know it's not what you'd call "man's work," but she could use your help."

"Soldiers often do their own cooking. I'll help her."

"Just don't tell her I asked you."

Decimus's eyebrow rose at Galen's desire to help his little sister without her knowing. He teased her all the time about almost anything.

"Besides, if the bread turns out as good as Val's, I don't want to have to admit she did a superb job all by herself."

The corner of Decimus's mouth twitched up. Galen wanted to help her, but he couldn't resist the tease.

Breakfast was much quieter than usual. Rhoda didn't speak much, and even Galen couldn't get her laughing.

After Galen left, Decimus returned to his bed and lay down to rest until Rhoda needed him. He listened to her moving around the cottage as she cleaned up after breakfast. Finally came sounds of her placing several things on the table. The sound of a spoon scraping the side of a bowl told him it was time to make his offer of help.

"Rhoda, I'm tired of doing nothing. Is there something I can do in the cottage today? Perhaps I could help with the bread making. You can teach me what I need to do."

"That would be a huge help. I still need to do all Valeria's work in the garden, too." She walked over to give him a big hug and bring him back with her to the table.

Later, as he stood beside her kneading the large lump of dough, it felt good to be useful to someone again, even a little girl.

Decimus was alone in the cottage when Valeria finally returned. Her steps were slow as she walked to the table. She set something heavy down. Then silence filled the cottage as she just stood there, saying nothing.

Her silence was disturbing. Something was very wrong. He stood and hobbled toward the table. His outstretched hand found her arm. Then he reached across her body for her second arm and turned her to face him.

"Valeria?" Silence. "What's wrong?"

"I was too late." She spoke so softly he could barely hear her.

If only he could see her face so he would know what she was thinking. In his darkness, he reached out to try Gaius's way of seeing. His hand had just found her cheek when a tear trickled onto his fingertip.

She made no sound, but she was crying. He drew her into his arms. For a moment, she just stood there, her cheek resting against his chest. Then she wrapped her arms around his back and clung to him as sobs shook her body. The river of tears soaked into his shirt.

The last thing he expected was for her to crumble like this over the loss of her patient. Soldiers and physicians both dealt with death, and it wasn't always possible to win. She was in the wrong profession if she got this upset when a patient died.

Would her heart be so torn if he killed himself? She'd tried so hard to convince him not to that he was sure the answer was yes. She'd sounded like she was about to cry that afternoon. Maybe she actually had. This flood of tears was proof she really meant it when she said she couldn't bear it if he did. He didn't want to cause such pain for her, so he hoped it would never come to that.

It felt good to hold her in his arms, to give some comfort to the woman who'd done everything she could to comfort him. He laid his hand on the back of her head and held her close until the shaking stopped and the flood subsided.

He'd never been called upon to console anyone before. He lived among men who chose to conceal whatever grief they had. He should say something, but what?

"I'm sure you did everything that could be done."

"You don't understand." Valeria whispered into his chest.

"Tell me so I will understand." He kept his arms wrapped around her, and she made no effort to move away from him.

"Inge almost died when she had her third daughter four years ago. Gaius used everything he knew to save her, and he warned her that trying to have another baby would probably kill her. But she wanted above anything to give her husband a son, so she decided to try once more. She had problems from the beginning, so Rhoda and I visited often. Inge and I became close friends. I've been telling her about Jesus. She'd started asking me questions, but she wasn't quite ready to follow the Way. When I got there last night, she was burning up with fever and frantic. We both knew she was dying."

Silence and a single jerk told him she was fighting tears again.

A deep breath, and then she continued. "I told her again how much God loves her, how Jesus died for her, and what awaited her if she chose to believe in him. She was staring wildly at me, gripping my hand so hard, and then she looked past me. One smile...and she was gone. But I don't know for sure if she heard me. I don't know what she chose. She may be lost forever...when she didn't have to be."

❖

Valeria felt him stiffen, so she lifted her head to look at his face. Dipping eyebrows, a frown, the confused look in his eyes—he was both puzzled and disturbed by what she'd just said. In her own distress, she'd told him much more than he could understand or even handle. He was a Roman tribune. He knew nothing about following Christ— the love, the joy, the peace. He didn't know how empty his own life was without Jesus. He couldn't possibly understand why death apart from Jesus was such a tragedy but death when you follow him is not— even death in a Roman arena or by a Roman sword.

She pulled away and stepped back. She took a deep breath and slowly released it. *God, please give me the right words to say to him now.*

When she spoke again, her voice was calm. "I wasn't able to save her, but I fulfilled her deepest desire. I took her new son from her womb when she died. He's small, but he seems very strong. They have goats for milk, and I'm sure Elsa can be a good mother to him. I was gone so long because I was teaching her what she must do to care for him."

❖

Decimus stood listening to her in utter amazement. He was a soldier, accustomed to brushing aside the horror of death and fighting on until the battle was over. She was no soldier.

He'd never seen anyone cry over a friend like she had in his arms. She'd been upset to the point of tears when he was drowning in despair and talking about ending it all, and he was almost a stranger. He'd never known a heart more tender than hers.

How could she have watched her friend die and then cut her open to save her baby?

◆

His wide eyes and raised eyebrows told Valeria she'd only succeeded in changing Decimus from puzzled and disturbed to incredulous. Not at all what she'd intended, but she wasn't sure what else to say to him. Maybe it was just time to stop talking.

"I've kept you standing on your leg much too long. You need to rest it." She placed her hand against his chest. "Thank you for listening. It helped to tell someone. I'm sorry I got your shirt wet. Now I need to go help Rhoda finish my chores before supper."

She took his hand in hers and squeezed, and then she left the cottage to find Rhoda.

◆

She was right, as usual. Decimus had blocked it while he held her, but the pain in his leg pressed in on him again. He sat down heavily on the chair beside the table. He ran the fingers of both hands through his hair. Then, as was his habit when relaxing or thinking deeply, he laced them together and rested his palms on the top of his head. He remembered only at the last moment to keep them away from the cut.

A puzzled frown dragged his mouth down.

What on earth had just happened? She'd let him console her in her deepest grief. To be allowed to see her so exposed—he'd never expected that level of trust. For her to give it to him...well, it was deeply gratifying. She'd cared for him in his time of greatest need. It felt good to be allowed to care for her, too.

But how could she be weeping like that in his arms and within moments be apologizing for soaking his shirt with her tears? The tears hadn't even been because her friend had died but over whether she had chosen to believe in the Christian god before she did.

He felt the wet area of his shirt. She was right. He didn't understand her at all.

Supper was much quieter than before, and Decimus didn't like it. The usual gaiety was missing. Valeria gave thanks and spoke a normal amount although her voice was missing its usual lightness, but Rhoda said almost nothing. Galen was trying to brighten the mood, teasing Rhoda to get her to laugh, but he wasn't succeeding. Finally, Rhoda began to cry.

"Please, Galen, stop. Elsa and her sisters just lost their mother. I remember how much it hurt when Mother was killed, and I don't feel like laughing tonight."

There was scraping when Galen pushed back his stool, footsteps as he walked around the table, and rustling as he wrapped his arms around his sister.

"I'm sorry, Rhoda. I remember, too."

Galen stood between her and Decimus. Her voice was muffled by his shirt as she clung to him. "I wish I knew that Inge chose Jesus. Then I could tell Elsa something that would help make it hurt less."

Decimus fought to keep his eyebrows down and his mouth shut. How could choosing to believe in the Christian god have any effect on how much losing someone you love hurt? Rhoda and Valeria both thought it did, but that made no sense whatever.

Valeria stood. "I think it would be good to have prayer time earlier tonight. Galen, would you help Decimus while Rhoda and I clean up?"

◆

Decimus lay on his bed as they gathered at the table. Valeria was the reader. The pages of the codex turned until she found what she was looking for. She took a deep breath, let it out slowly, and began to read.

Her voice quavered as she began, but it steadied as she read on. "Jesus said to her, 'I am the resurrection and the life. Whoever believes in me, though he die, yet shall he live, and everyone who lives and believes in me shall never die. Do you believe this?' She said to him, 'Yes, Lord; I believe that you are the Christ, the Son of God, who is coming into the world.'"

She closed the codex. After a moment of silence, she began their prayers.

"Jesus, we come to you with heavy hearts tonight because of the death of our dear friend, Inge. I know she was almost ready to follow you. I saw her fear approaching death, but I also saw her beautiful, peaceful smile as she crossed the threshold. I ask that, in your mercy, her smile was the sign that she had chosen you and was meeting you for the first time. I pray for her family in their time of deepest grief and that they, too, will find peace knowing you."

She continued, giving thanks and praying for him and for others. Galen and Rhoda added their prayers.

"We pray all this in Jesus's name. Amen."

Rhoda spoke immediately after the amen with a lightness that shocked him. "She smiled! I'm certain she was meeting Jesus. She's with him now."

Valeria's peaceful reply was no less shocking. "Yes, precious. I'm certain she is, too."

Galen and Rhoda had climbed into the loft. Decimus heard Valeria step out onto the porch, but he couldn't tell what she was doing. Was she out there grieving for her friend? Did she need to find consolation in his arms again? Would she welcome it if he offered? He would welcome the chance to hold her again if she needed him to.

Before he could decide whether to go out to check, she came in. The bolt slid into place, and footsteps approached. She would adjust his blanket before she climbed into the loft.

He was lying with his eyes open. It had been a disturbing day in this house of Christians.

She rested her hand on his upper arm. "Good night, Decimus. Rest in peace."

No trace of tears in her voice. Just the calm, soft voice that he found strangely soothing. If he hadn't known better, he would have sworn it had been just another day for her.

"Good night, Valeria."

The rung creaked as she climbed into the loft, and the cottage became quiet.

Valeria lay in her bed, giving thanks for Inge's smile that had revealed her choice and praying for Decimus. If only his sight might return and his heart might find God as Inge's had.

♦

Decimus lay on his bed, wondering how it was possible for these

Christians to think about death so differently than he did and marveling at the peace it seemed to give them.

Chapter 18

A Fair Price

Decimus awoke with a feeling of anticipation. He didn't know what Galen had in mind, but it didn't matter. It would be good to be out of the cottage and doing anything useful.

Valeria was humming by the fireplace as she scraped a spoon along the wall of a pot. The aroma stirred his appetite. He'd gagged down his share of the breakfast porridge dished up by army cooks, but she managed to use a variety of herbs to turn the otherwise plain meal into something quite delicious and different each day.

He'd no sooner swung his legs over the edge than her footsteps approached his bedside.

"Good morning. How are you feeling today?"

Her tone was light, pleasant—normal for her. Any sadness she might have from her friend's death was well concealed, from him at least. Her friend was just as dead now as she was when he held her sobbing in his arms. How could there be no detectable trace of yesterday's grief in her voice this morning? Sometimes these Christians truly baffled him, especially when all he could do was listen. Maybe there would be signs of more normal grief if he could see as well.

"Better. I have an excellent physician."

"That's not difficult when she has such a good patient."

She patted his arm before handing him the crutch. He hobbled to the table as she returned to the fireplace.

The soft creak of the ladder and skipping footsteps announced Rhoda's arrival even before she hugged Decimus's arm.

"Good morning. I hope you're feeling much better today."

"I am." He rested his hand on the side of her head before she went over to the fireplace to help Valeria.

Amazing. Just like her sister, the tears of last night had been replaced by the cheerfulness of this morning. These Christians just weren't normal people in how they reacted to death, and he wasn't making much progress in his attempts to understand them.

Galen came in from feeding the livestock. "It sure smells good this morning, Val. I'm starving." He plunked himself down at the table next to Decimus. "Ready for me to start putting you to work? I'm glad Val is finally willing to let you out of her sight."

"He still needs to take it easy, Galen, so don't plan on working him too hard or too long today. I don't want him doing something he shouldn't."

Decimus's lips tightened. "I can judge myself whether the work is too hard and whether I should do it."

There was an edge on his voice. He'd never liked it when his tutors had been overprotective when he wanted to try something. He didn't need her to be mothering him even if she only did it out of concern for him. Being blind and still weak didn't mean he was a child who couldn't think for himself.

She patted his arm twice. "I'm sure you can."

Her response was too patronizing, but he let it pass without comment. He wasn't going to let anything spoil this first chance to be a man again even if he couldn't see.

Rhoda carried the bowls to the table and handed them out. Valeria gave thanks as usual, and the time of happy conversation followed.

Breakfast was soon over, and Decimus was eager to start working.

Galen placed Decimus's hand on his shoulder and led him out of the cottage. "I have the perfect thing for us to work on today. I need to repair the stall fencing in the cattle shed. You can hold the rails in place while I tie them with leather bindings. The whole job shouldn't take us more than two hours."

In the shed, Galen positioned Decimus and placed a rail in his hands to hold while Galen wrapped the bindings.

A smile lifted the corners of Decimus's mouth. This was a good first choice for them working together. Even in his weakened condition, the railings were light enough that he had no problem holding them in place. He was far from his full strength after losing so much blood, but the strength he had was enough for this task. He could easily keep his weight off his left leg as well.

Galen liked to talk, and his conversation was often funny. Decimus was thoroughly enjoying himself as they worked.

◆

Valeria was working in the garden just past the cattle shed when Rhoda came running over. "Baldric is coming with Otto and one of his mares."

"Tell Galen to keep Decimus in the cattle shed so Baldric doesn't see him, and tell them both to be quiet."

Rhoda hurried into the cattle shed and came back out with Galen behind her.

Valeria's lips tightened at the sight of Galen. He and Otto were the same age and good friends. He was always eager to spend time with Otto, but he should have stayed in the shed. He shouldn't have assumed Decimus would be fine alone.

Otto waved, and Galen returned the greeting. Too late now to send him back in without arousing suspicion. Valeria sighed. Hopefully Rhoda had told Decimus silence was essential and he'd do a better job of obeying than Galen.

She walked over to the back side of the corral where Astro was drinking at the water trough. As Baldric rode toward them, leading the mare along the corral fence, the big stallion tossed his head and flared his nostrils. With a snort, he headed toward the mare, keenly interested.

Baldric and his son rode up beside Valeria and dismounted. "I come to take you up on your offer. He is a beautiful animal. Of course, I will give you something for this."

When she was twelve, nothing had fascinated Valeria more than watching her father strike a deal. He always seemed to enjoy it immensely. She would have let Baldric breed his mare for free, but since he was offering to pay...

"Let's consider what might be fair to both of us. He is truly a magnificent animal, as you say, and we can both see that he's eager to perform. But he's unproven as a stud, so I can't in good conscience charge you a high fee up front when we don't know what will come of the breeding. I'd like to rebuild my father's herd, but for that I'll need more than just my one small mare. I need her for work, too, so I'm not sure I want to breed her, especially to such a big stallion."

She paused and rubbed the back of her neck before making her offer. "You have many mares, and some of them are not important to you. What do you say to breeding three of your best mares with him, and when they're with foal, I would take in payment one of your least important mares. Three fine horses for one ordinary one seems a fair deal to me."

Laughter exploded from Baldric. "That is a proposal like none I have heard before. You are still your father's daughter, no matter what else the physician taught you. I will make you a counter offer. If you will marry one of my sons, I will give you three of my best mares as your own."

Now it was Valeria's turn to chuckle. "Your sons are such fine men that no woman would ask to be paid in horses to marry them. I would find your offer irresistible if my husband didn't have to be a man who follows the Way."

"Would five mares change your mind?"

Valeria chuckled again. "No, that's not negotiable."

◆

Decimus stood motionless, listening to their exchange. One corner of his mouth turned up. It was a very bold proposal, but the way she said it made it sound so reasonable, even when it wasn't. She was asking a very high price for the services of a horse that wasn't even hers. Still, taking care of Astro did give her the right to use him. Baldric had described her well when he called her a wise woman.

The more Decimus knew of Valeria, the more he could understand why Baldric was so eager to get her as wife for one of his sons. She was more than wise. She was kind and playful and pretty, at least according to Gaius's way of seeing. He'd never known her equal.

He'd been standing a long time, and his leg hurt. When he reached down to massage it, his hip bumped the crutch that he'd leaned against the wall. As it fell, his blind attempt to catch it only caught air.

Decimus rolled his eyes as the clatter of a falling stack of pails announced his presence that she'd tried so hard to hide.

◆

Everyone turned toward the racket in the cattle shed.

"I'll be right back." Galen left Otto and trotted into the shed. Decimus stood with his arms extended, trying to balance on his good leg. Galen almost laughed at him. He'd never seen such a big man looking sheepish, like a kid who'd just done something foolish.

Galen stood on tiptoes and whispered in his ear. "Don't worry. I'll explain the noise."

He handed Decimus a milking stool and helped him sit down so he wouldn't bump into anything else. Then he went back to the corral.

"Not a problem, Val. I left something standing that I shouldn't have, but nothing's broken."

They all turned back to the corral to continue the negotiations.

◆

Baldric rubbed his chin as his eyes drifted from Valeria to the stallion and back again. She was the daughter of his best friend. Her father had been dead seven years, but she had earned his respect and affection in her own right. He owed her the life of his beloved wife, and that was a debt nothing could fully repay. Giving her a mare to restart her herd would be a good way to thank her.

"There is merit to your proposal. I accept. Otto, put the mare in the corral, and we will see whether that stallion can start earning Valeria her mare."

Chapter 19

A New Perspective

Baldric was smiling as he and Otto mounted their horses. "The stallion traded his dead owner for a much better one. Perhaps he knows that." His smile broadened. "Even hurt, he is already doing his part to earn you a mare. I will leave my mare here to be sure she does hers. I or one of my sons will come for her in two days."

Valeria grinned. "I'll look forward to seeing you then. Farewell, Baldric."

"Farewell, Valeria." Baldric reined his horse away from her and kicked him into a trot.

After he and Otto disappeared into the trees, Valeria led Galen back into the cattle shed. Decimus was still sitting on the stool. His head hung down, and his shoulders slumped as fatigue enveloped him. Clearly, he'd taken on too much for his first time out of the cottage.

"You've done enough work for your first day, Decimus. Time for you to quit and come back to the cottage for a rest."

Galen took Decimus's hands and helped him to his feet.

Decimus turned his face toward her. "Not yet. Baldric interrupted us before we could finish. A task shouldn't be left until it's completed." The firmness in his voice signaled that he expected no argument.

Valeria's eyebrows rose. She hadn't expected a stubborn response to her perfectly reasonable statement. She caught Galen's eye and flicked her head toward the door to get him to tell Decimus to quit.

"We can't work on this much longer, Val. I need to go to the upper meadow for a while. We can finish here tomorrow. I'll bring Decimus back to the cottage when we're done for the day."

"Good. I'll have something for you to eat when you're through."

Galen grinned at the prospect of food.

She left them to their work. As she headed toward the cottage, she pursed her lips and shook her head. What a stubborn man he was!

She probably should have expected that. A Roman tribune would be accustomed to people doing exactly what he told them, and only the commander of the legion and the provincial governor could expect to give him orders and have him obey them. She would have to rely on persuasion rather than telling him what to do like she did with Galen and Rhoda.

He would need watching when he helped Galen. That stubbornness might make him push himself too hard too soon, but that same trait would help him survive if his sight didn't return. Stubbornness and determination usually went hand in hand, and determination could get someone through difficult times.

She was stubborn herself when it came to doing what she knew was right. There couldn't be two more different people than a Roman tribune and her, but in one thing they were kindred spirits. She understood his determination to finish what he started.

◆

Galen patted his stomach. "I'm hungry, so let's get back to work. I think we have time to get one more rail in place before lunch. Then I have to go to the meadow."

He moved Decimus and slid the rail into place before placing the tribune's hands in position to hold it steady while he wrapped the leather strips to hold it there.

"Finished." Galen handed him his crutch and placed Decimus's free hand on his shoulder to guide him as they walked together toward the cottage. "I'm sure glad Val decided you were ready to work. It's too hard trying to balance the rail and tie it in place by myself."

"It's good she did. I couldn't stand sitting around doing nothing for much longer. That's no way for a man to live."

Galen chuckled. "Probably not, but sometimes I think it would be nice to try it out. I'll never get the chance with so much to do around here. You may end up wishing Val hadn't told me we could work together."

◆

Valeria sat on the porch, waiting for them. Decimus leaned heavily on his crutch as he hobbled toward her. He was exhausted and hurting, but a smile lit his face as he talked with Galen. He'd done something worthwhile today, even though he was blind. It was worth him being tired and sore for him to feel useful again. To see him now, she would never have known he'd been ready to kill himself only two days ago.

She met them by the door. "Don't forget to wipe the cowshed mud off your feet."

"Don't I always, Val?" A big grin split Galen's face.

"No, but you're getting much better. Besides, I was really reminding Decimus." She rested her hand on his arm. "I'm only just starting to train him."

He smiled down at her. "Some of us aren't trainable."

"You don't know how good a trainer I can be."

◆

Decimus could hear her smile. He assumed she was joking. She certainly couldn't be thinking it was her place to train a man like him to do anything.

When Valeria passed around the lunch of bread and cheese, Decimus savored each bite. It was good to be doing something again that could make a man hungry.

Then Galen headed out the door to go do whatever it was he did in the high meadow. What was up there that kept Galen so busy? He would ask later.

He hobbled over to his bed and lay down. As his head hit the pillow, deep fatigue wrapped around him. Time to rest for a while. His leg hurt much more than it had when he got up that morning, but he didn't care. It had been a surprisingly good day so far.

Galen probably had made the task easier than normal because he couldn't see, but it had been real work worth doing, and he was satisfied. It was good to know that a blind man actually could do more than beg.

◆

Valeria heard his breathing slow and deepen. She tiptoed to the edge of the bed to gaze at him. A slight smile curved his lips. He looked so different from the deathly pale tribune who lay there unconscious only a few days ago. She'd been so afraid for him then, but God had answered all her prayers. To see the contented smile as he slept, one would never know that she'd been begging him not to kill himself only two days earlier. God had been so gracious to this poor Roman. Now if only He would restore the tribune's sight.

She tiptoed to the door and looked back one more time before heading out to the garden. Her smile grew as her gaze lingered on him. Her fears about bringing him home seemed foolish now. There was nothing dangerous about him. He would never arrest them. He actually seemed to like them, and a man like him could never choose to cause their deaths. God had been merciful to them all.

Rhoda was gently shaking his arm. "Decimus? Ready for supper?"

Decimus swung his legs off the bed and sat up. With his hands resting on top of his head, he arched his back.

"Ready, and it smells delicious." It was amazing how a little work could give a man an appetite.

Rhoda handed him the crutch, and he hobbled to his chair.

He expected to enjoy more than just Valeria's tasty stew. Supper had become his favorite time of day. Her family found such pleasure in simply being together while they ate. The way they included him in their conversation and laughter was as satisfying as the food.

Valeria again gave thanks for the food and for him being with them to share it. A smile tugged at his lips. When she spoke those words, she really meant them.

"Thanks for letting me have Decimus help today, Val. We already got a lot done, and we should finish fixing the railings tomorrow."

If he had any doubt left, Galen's enthusiasm was enough to convince Decimus that the boy considered him a genuine help in the cattle shed.

"I may not pass as a Greek merchant, Valeria, but with Galen training me, I'll soon pass as a Germanic farmer."

"I'll have to see whether you can convince a visitor before I decide whether Galen is doing a good job."

He liked the teasing lilt in her voice.

Galen's knuckles punched his shoulder. "I'm glad to have the chance to train you. I've been doing the work by myself for too long. Wait until you see all the other jobs I have for us."

With each passing day, Decimus felt more certain these people really did want him with them, even though he was a blind Roman tribune. Valeria had spoken the truth when she told him he didn't have to worry about having someplace to go even if his sight didn't return.

He couldn't understand why their Jesus required his followers to care for their enemies. By their very nature, enemies should be destroyed, not rescued. That these Christians kept choosing to treat their enemy like a friend still amazed him, but he'd become used to them doing it. He'd even reached the point where he looked on them as friends rather than enemies himself.

His father would be appalled by his new attitude, but he didn't care. These Christians had stopped to help him when he was their enemy dying by the side of the road. They'd saved his life, and now they treated him like a member of their family. There was no way such people could be a threat to the Empire like his father had always told him. They couldn't be a threat to anyone.

Supper was soon over. Decimus reclined on his bed as they gathered at the table again. It was Galen's turn to read. When he finished, Valeria began their prayers.

"Father, we thank You for this day, and especially that Decimus is feeling so much better. Please continue his healing, and we ask especially that You restore his sight. We thank You..." The prayers continued with Galen adding his thanks for Decimus having recovered enough to help him and Rhoda giving thanks for Astro's healing.

There was probably no god listening to them, but it was gratifying that they cared enough about him to include him in their prayers.

An ironic smile curved his lips. So many things had changed in the last few days. He'd been a powerful man in control. Now he depended on the help of others. He'd gone from fear and despair over the loss of his sight to simply trying to do what he could with what he still had and finding satisfaction in doing it. He'd learned that the people he'd believed to be his enemies were really his friends.

Galen and Rhoda had climbed into the loft and were silent. Decimus expected to hear Valeria climb the ladder as well as he lay on his bed. Instead, her footsteps disappeared through the door, and she pulled it shut behind her. She was gone at least four times as long as he expected. What could she be doing alone outside for so long?

Finally, the door opened and closed, the bolt slid into place, and footsteps approached his bedside. She pulled the blanket up around his shoulders and tucked it snuggly around him.

"Good night, Decimus. Rest in peace."

"Good night, Valeria."

She patted his arm. Footsteps moved away from him, the rung on the ladder creaked, and quiet descended upon the cottage.

Valeria lay in her bed, thanking God that this man who'd been so close to death only a few days earlier was now well enough to help Galen. If only God would do one more miracle and restore his sight.

♦

Decimus lay on his bed, thinking about how satisfying it was to do something useful again and how good it felt to be treated like he was part of this family. He still hoped his sight would return, but even if it didn't, life with these people would be worth living.

Chapter 20

THE LIGHT RETURNS

The rung creaked under Galen's weight and woke Decimus. Galen's whispered greeting of his sister drove away the last vestige of sleep. He'd been facing the wall, but he rolled over as Galen closed the door.

His eyes were still closed, but something was different.

A brightness that he hadn't seen for a long time made his eyelids seem red, not black. When he opened them, he saw Valeria by the fireplace, stirring the porridge. He blinked twice. Then an enormous grin split his face.

How he'd longed for this, but he'd decided it would never come. Valeria kept telling him this might happen. She never lost hope even when he did.

To see her first was exactly as it should be. To tell her first was exactly what he wanted.

"Valeria."

"Yes, Decimus?"

"Come here. I want to see your face."

She stirred the porridge one more time before she turned and walked toward him. He'd never seen a more beautiful sight.

"I know I wasn't memorable enough for you to see me in the village, but I did think you saw me the other night."

She stopped right in front of him. He knew she was short from the day he held her as she cried. She barely came to his chin. Still, she was so capable at everything that he hadn't pictured her as the diminutive woman with a dance-like walk who now stood within arms' reach. A playful grin lit her eyes as she took his hands.

Then she closed her eyelids and placed his fingers on her forehead before he could say anything. "Maybe you'd better look at me again to make sure you can remember."

She surprised him, but he welcomed this chance to touch her face again. Gaius's way of seeing had let him form an image of her in spite of his blindness, but he'd enjoyed it at least as much for the pleasure of caressing her face.

He fingered the strand of hair that had fallen across her forehead, stroking her skin with the back of his fingers at the same time. Gaius's way of seeing was even more enjoyable when he could see her with his eyes as well. He traced the arch of her eyebrows and continued along her temples until he tucked a loose strand of hair behind her ear. Much more gold than brown, and it cascaded down her back almost to her waist. It framed her face just as he'd imagined.

He traced the soft curve of her upper lip with one finger as he watched her smile like she was enjoying his touch. It was amazing that the image of her that his fingertips had created was so close to her true appearance. She really was a beautiful woman.

He caressed her cheek, tracing her scar with his forefinger. He liked the feel of it, but her smile dimmed as he touched it. Despite all her joking about not being pretty, she was sensitive about how she thought the scar looked. There was no need for that. It didn't diminish her beauty at all.

The corner of his mouth curved up. Her smile brightened again as he caressed her cheek and slipped his fingertips under her chin. He drew them down her neck before lowering his hands.

It was wise to stop. She attracted him too much, and that was not what she intended when she placed his fingers on her face. She was his physician, not his entertainment.

"I find Gaius's way of seeing most enjoyable, but it can't tell me that your hair is more gold than brown..." Her eyes sprang open. "Or that your eyes are more blue than gray."

"Oh, Decimus! You can see again!" She threw her arms around his chest and hugged him so tightly he couldn't take a breath. Her whisper reached his ears. "Oh, thank You, God! Thank You so much for this miracle!"

He wrapped his arms around her and lifted her from the ground.

She weighed almost nothing. It really should have been impossible for her to get him into her cart.

She stepped back when he let her feet touch the floor, but he left his hands on her upper arms. She rested her palms against his chest. Her eyes were glowing, and a joyful smile added to the brightness.

"Rhoda! Come quickly! He can see again!"

Rhoda came scurrying down the ladder and wrapped her arms around both of them. "I knew God would hear all our prayers. Can I go tell Galen, or do you want to surprise him yourself?"

He laughed, deep and full-throated. It was impossible not to. "Go tell him."

Rhoda grabbed Valeria's shawl from the peg by the door and ran out to find Galen.

He heard Galen bounding across the porch and saw him burst into the room.

"Rhoda told me you could see, but I wasn't sure she wasn't just teasing. My life is going to get so much easier now that Val will let you help me with everything."

"Not everything. His leg isn't healed, and I don't want him to tear the stitches doing something too hard."

Galen groaned, then his grin broke through. "I thought it was too good to be true."

Rhoda had gone to collect eggs. Galen had gone to finish his chores before breakfast. Decimus sat with the chair tipped back, his fingers laced and his hands resting on the top of his head. It was his favorite position for relaxing, and he felt totally relaxed as he watched Valeria stirring the porridge over the fire.

She moved like a dancer, and she was very light on her feet. No wonder he'd found it so difficult to figure out where she was when she wasn't humming.

She turned from the fire, and his smile drew one of her own. "Can I get you anything?"

"No. I was just thinking what a pleasure it is to watch a beautiful woman make my breakfast."

She stirred the porridge again. "I'm not sure where I can find one for you to watch."

"No need to look. I already have one."

She peered around the room as she carried the cups from the shelf to the table. "Where is she? I'll invite her to breakfast."

"I mean you."

"If you think so, then I guess your sight isn't as completely restored as I'd hoped."

He rocked the chair forward and placed his hand on hers as she set the cups down. His eyes locked on hers.

"Valeria, you are a very beautiful woman."

◆

Valeria gasped as she snatched back her hand. His eyes gazing into hers—they looked like he really meant it. But he mustn't! He was the total opposite of what she could accept in a man.

He was a Roman tribune. Rome had declared her the enemy. No Roman officer could expect to have a Christian woman without someone finding out. She was not a woman to be had by any man without first becoming his wife, and she would never marry a man who didn't follow the Way.

She was the tribune's physician and friend, but nothing more. Nothing more would ever be possible.

Still, she felt the full compliment of a wealthy, powerful, handsome man saying she was beautiful, even if he couldn't really mean it. He would have known many women. Some of them must have been real beauties; no scars on their faces to ruin that.

Her cheeks and even her ears felt hot, and she dropped her eyes as she took another step back.

◆

Decimus kept his eyebrows from rising. Why had his words upset her? All the other women he knew were eager for his compliments, even when they knew he didn't mean them. He meant this one, but he'd frightened her by saying it. How was that possible? How could telling a woman she was beautiful ever be frightening?

So many things about her weren't what he expected from a normal woman, but the last thing he expected was this fearful response to a simple compliment. He didn't want her afraid of him. What could undo what he'd just done?

A moment's thought, and he knew. She'd laughed and accused him of teasing after he'd seen her Gaius's way. If she didn't like his truthful compliments, she could consider them a tease.

He tipped back in his chair, stretched out his legs, and crossed his arms. "I'll have to rethink my opinion of Baldric."

She raised her eyes. Her eyebrows dipped as her head tilted. "Why is that?"

Curiosity, not fear. Much better.

"I thought him wise for wanting you in his family for your kind heart and skill with horses. Now that I've seen you, I think the most powerful man in the region may simply want the most beautiful woman as wife for one of his sons."

◆

Valeria saw the smile playing on his lips and the twinkle in his eye. She'd misunderstood him. He was only joking. He had no romantic thoughts about her. She'd been silly and vain to even imagine that he might.

"Galen's been a bad influence on you. He's turned you into a tease. I don't know how Rhoda and I are going to put up with two of you."

She patted his upper arm as she walked past to go back to stirring the porridge.

◆

Decimus's mouth tipped up into a crooked smile. It had become her habit to touch his arm to signal the end of a conversation. It had been a comfort in the darkness. It was a pleasure in the light.

He wove his fingers together and placed them on his head. She was comfortable with him again, and he wasn't going to risk that by paying her too much attention...at least not when she would notice.

He watched every move as long as she was looking away from him. Whenever she turned, he shifted his gaze out the cottage door so she wouldn't suspect. Everything about her fascinated him, but he wasn't fool enough to let her know that. She wasn't ready to hear what he really thought of her.

His smile faded. He wasn't completely sure what he thought of her himself or what he might want to do about it. There was still that problem of her being a Christian in a province where his father had declared it illegal.

It was probably best if he just enjoyed their playful conversations and her gentle touches and didn't think past that. Surely he could think she was smart and kind and beautiful without it having to lead to anything.

Chapter 21

Watching

Decimus had known Galen and Rhoda were coming by the laughter that accompanied them. Now he would get to see their grins as well. His own lips curved into a smile at the thought.

Rhoda came in first, swinging the egg basket. She carried it to a set of shelves where flour and other cooking supplies were stored. As she turned to the shelf holding the bowls and spoons, she looked over at Decimus and smiled. Such sweetness in that smile. Such kindness in the many times that she'd guided his hands in the darkness to his spoon and bowl. She was so much like her sister.

She carried the bowls to Valeria, then brought the spoons to the table. After placing his on the table in front of him, she hugged Decimus's arm before returning to her sister. Valeria stroked her hair and kissed her on the forehead before handing her two bowls filled with steaming porridge.

The sisterly love between them made it hard to believe they weren't born sisters. These Christians really did know how to love each other regardless of blood ties. They'd made a family out of strangers, and they'd even pulled an enemy into the circle and made him feel like family, too. Decimus would never have done that, but he was glad they had.

After placing his bowl in front of him, Rhoda sat down on the bench to the right of his chair and gave him her sweetest little-girl smile.

Galen had remembered to wipe his feet before coming in, which drew an appreciative smile from his older sister. He sat down on the stool to the left of Decimus as Valeria carried the other two bowls to the table.

After she set Galen's bowl down, Valeria pushed some stray hair back off Galen's forehead and patted his upper arm. That was exactly how she touched him, but Decimus was certain it didn't affect Galen the same way.

Valeria sat down on the bench with Rhoda and bowed her head. Decimus waited to begin eating until after she had given thanks.

The porridge was delicious, but that wasn't what made this breakfast so special. Who would have thought simply seeing the people at the table could bring such pleasure?

Galen was so obviously Roman. His hair was the same dark brown as Decimus's own with the same waviness and loose curls that tended to fall onto his forehead. In fact, Galen looked very much like he had at the same age, except he'd been a lot taller. They could have been brothers.

Rhoda had wavy brown hair that framed her face and drew attention to the smiles that were almost always on her lips. Her light brown eyes sparkled with warmth whenever she looked at him and smiled, which was often. He would have enjoyed having a little sister like her.

As much as he enjoyed watching Galen and Rhoda, it was Valeria who captured his full attention. He'd spent hours wondering what she looked like. He'd imagined that someone as kind as she was must have a beautiful smile and warm, gentle eyes. His imagination had not done her justice.

She truly was a beautiful woman, no matter what she said. The scar did nothing to make her less attractive. There was so much life in her eyes. Her love for her family filled them with a radiance he'd never seen in anyone else. When she joked with him, they sparkled irresistibly. She was so quick to smile, and each one drew a smile from him. How could he ever have failed to notice her in the village?

When breakfast was over, Decimus was eager to work. Galen rose from the table and stretched.

"So, Val, can I have Decimus help me with anything I want today?"

Decimus stood and grabbed his crutch.

"No, but he can help a little as long as you don't do anything that's going to hurt his leg or tire him. He still needs to rest, and I don't want that cut to open and bleed again. All he should do today is help you finish the rails in the cattle shed."

Galen grinned. "I'll be careful with him."

Maybe caution was appropriate, but Decimus's lips started to tighten before he relaxed them. He didn't like being mothered now that he could see again. He was a grown man who could decide for himself what he should do. Physician or not, she wasn't going to keep him from helping Galen. He wasn't willing to lie around like some rich Roman matron.

Decimus hobbled out the door behind Galen. "So, what will you have me do today?"

Galen looked back over his shoulder. "The same thing you did yesterday."

Decimus masked his surprise. So Galen hadn't made the job easier for a blind man. "It should go faster today now I can see."

Galen shook his head. "I don't think so. I was the slow one yesterday, and I wasn't planning on trying to hurry it up today. I'd rather do it well than fast."

Decimus nodded as he smiled. That was his philosophy as well.

After about half an hour, Valeria walked to the shed to check on whether Decimus was overworking himself. She was quite sure she would find that he was. She'd wanted Galen to give him something to do when he was blind and feeling useless. It had cheered him up and given him hope, just as she'd expected. Now that he could see, she would prefer that he rest and not risk hurting himself.

They were just finishing up as Galen tied the last rail in place. Decimus looked satisfied but tired. He had done more than enough today. It was time to rest.

She picked up his crutch and handed it to him. "It looks like you boys have finally finished. That's good since it's time for my patient to take a break and rest." She rested her hand on his arm. "I'll walk you back to the cottage."

"Whatever you say, physician. I put myself in your hands again." A smile played on his lips as he looked down at her.

"Very wise of you. We'll get you healed much faster if you do."

She walked beside him as he hobbled slowly back to the porch. Just before they entered the door, his gaze locked on the bench. He turned toward it.

"I'd rather sit out here and watch than lie down inside."

She would have preferred that he lie down for a while, but he'd already seated himself on the porch bench. Something about his eyes declared his intention to stay there. She opened her mouth to tell him it would be much better for him to lie down instead of sitting on the porch; then she closed it. She'd never persuade a man like him to go inside when his sight had just returned. After so long in darkness, who wouldn't want to enjoy the view outside?

She moved a stool over and raised his leg to rest upon it. He placed his other leg on the stool as well and leaned back in that now-familiar pose with his hands resting on top of his head. He held her gaze as he grinned. "The view is much better from here."

"Will you rest and not try to do something you shouldn't?"

She wasn't so sure that he wouldn't.

◆

"I'll do whatever you say, physician, as long as I get to enjoy the view." Decimus smiled at her teasingly, but she didn't seem to pick up on his meaning.

She patted his arm. "I'm going to work in the garden now. Just call if you need my help for anything."

As he watched her walking toward the garden, he was glad he'd chosen to stay on the porch. Any view of her was much better than any other view he could imagine.

Just sitting on the porch watching while everyone else had something to do was harder than Decimus had expected. He wasn't a man who enjoyed being idle. Still, they didn't let him get lonely. Rhoda came over often to see if he needed anything and usually hugged him before she left. Galen used his breaks for a drink as an excuse to talk with him for a few minutes, too. Valeria was keeping an eye on him from the garden. He watched her most of the time, so he saw her frequent glances in his direction and her occasional wave.

It seemed too long until she finished her garden work and came back to the cottage to start supper. She handed him his crutch as her lips turned up in a smile that seemed alluring to him even though she didn't mean it to be.

"I hope you enjoyed the afternoon. There's still time to rest before supper, if you want." The hopeful look in her eyes was more effective than a command would have been.

"Lead the way, physician."

He followed her inside and lay down on the bed just to please her.

Without her to watch, staying on the porch had lost much of its appeal anyway. As his whole body relaxed, a huge yawn stretched his face. How could he have become so tired just sitting on the porch? Still, it had been a much better choice to spend the day watching instead of sleeping. A man could get bored almost to tears just lying around with nothing to do and no one to watch. He was still weak from losing so much blood, but he was feeling stronger every day. He didn't need to be coddled.

Valeria didn't talk to him much. She probably hoped he'd take a nap before supper, but his eyes were never closed when she glanced over at him. Why would he want to sleep when he could watch her?

Soon the delicious aroma of her stew filled the cottage.

Valeria walked to the cottage door. "Rhoda! Galen! Supper's almost ready."

Rhoda skipped into the room after she'd washed up, and Galen was not far behind.

The family gathered around the table with Decimus sitting between Rhoda and Galen in the chair that had become his assigned place. Valeria began their supper by giving thanks for the food and especially for the return of his sight. Again, the conversation was filled with good-natured humor and affection for each other. They seemed almost as glad as he was himself that his sight had returned. He felt more at home than he could ever remember. He was going to miss being with them when he returned to the legion.

Decimus lay on his bed as they gathered for their evening prayers. It was Valeria's turn to read.

"As Jesus and his disciples went out of Jericho, a great crowd followed him. And behold, there were two blind men sitting by the roadside, and when they heard that Jesus was passing by, they cried out, 'Lord, have mercy on us, Son of David!' The crowd rebuked them, telling them to be silent, but they cried out all the more, 'Lord, have mercy on us, Son of David!' Stopping, Jesus called them and said, 'What do you want me to do for you?' They said to him, 'Lord, let our eyes be opened.' Jesus in pity touched their eyes, and immediately they recovered their sight and followed him."

She closed the codex and rested her hands on its cover as she bowed her head.

"We thank You, Jesus, that You still heal the blind. We praise and thank You for all the healing that Decimus has received, and especially for Your miracle in restoring his sight." She continued praying, with Galen and Rhoda joining in.

Decimus listened in silence. Valeria obviously believed his sight returning was a miracle from her god, but it could just as easily have been the natural course of events. The man had recovered from the horse's kick about as fast.

Still, he was glad these Christians had found him and decided they would risk bringing a Roman tribune home. They would probably have done it even if they'd known he was the son of the governor. He would have died by the road without their help. He would have killed himself if she hadn't talked him out of it.

The stories about Christians risking their own lives to help the sick during outbreaks of plague were probably true. He'd never believed people would do that for strangers before, but now he did. No one but Christians would have bothered with him, either. Whether her god had power to do miracles or not, he still owed her everything.

Decimus was on the verge of sleep when Valeria stepped out onto the porch alone. His eyelids were leaden, but he forced them open. No sleep for him until he was sure she made it back into the cottage for the night.

First there was silence. Then he heard her singing. The melody was hauntingly beautiful, more beautiful than any music he'd ever heard, but he didn't understand even a single word. He lay transfixed by the sound until she stopped and entered the cottage. She closed and bolted the door, then walked over to the side of his bed.

In the dim light of the dying fire, he could see her face. Her eyes and smile were almost luminous as she gazed down at him. She pulled the blanket up over his shoulders, like she had every night since he'd been there. Her fingers pushed back the strand of hair that had fallen over his forehead, just like she did all the time for Galen. The shock coursed through him when she leaned over and kissed his forehead, just like she so often did to Rhoda.

"Good night, Decimus. Rest in peace, and know that God loves you."

She patted his arm and climbed the ladder into the loft, still humming that haunting melody.

Valeria lay in her bed, praising and thanking God for the miracle of Decimus's sight returning, praying for the continued healing of his body, and praying especially that his heart would be open to everything God wanted for him.

◆

Decimus lay on his bed, thinking back to when all had seemed hopeless. It was a good thing Valeria had talked him out of killing himself. She'd told him how her god loved him and would restore his sight. He hadn't really believed her, but now he could see again. He was a strong man, and he might have survived his injuries and regained his sight naturally. Then again, maybe she was right, and there was something special about the Christian god.

Chapter 22

FIRST MEETING

Decimus awoke as Galen opened the door to go feed the livestock. The sunshine streaming in revealed Valeria coming down from the loft. There was no better way to start the day than seeing her smile as she walked over to his bedside. He swung his feet to the floor.

"How's my favorite patient feeling this morning?" She pushed back the stray lock of hair that had fallen onto his forehead.

Her fingertips touching his face sent quivers down his spine. Did she have any idea how much that stirred him? Did she enjoy it as much as he did? Or was it just a habit? She did it all the time to Galen as well.

"Better each day and ready for another delicious breakfast prepared by a beautiful woman."

"Well, you'll have to settle for breakfast prepared by me instead." Valeria patted his arm. "You and Galen are quite a pair. He says everything tastes delicious and devours anything I put in front of him. You give me compliments even though the food and the cook are plain."

His gaze followed her as she stepped to the fireplace and laid the fire. She started humming as she poured some crushed grain into the porridge pot and added the water and herbs.

The food might be plain; the cook was anything but.

After breakfast, Decimus contemplated Valeria from the cottage window. She was standing beside the corral watching Astro and the mare. Baldric or one of his sons would be coming for her later that day, but his stallion had already succeeded. If he stayed long enough, Astro would earn Valeria the promised mare.

Galen had gone to the high meadow for the morning. That was too far and too steep a trail for him to try yet, so Galen had gone without him.

Decimus was tired of staying inside. A few minutes of conversation with her would enliven even a boring morning. With his crutch under his arm, he hobbled over to join Valeria at the corral.

A fleeting smile greeted him. "You really shouldn't be out here until after they get the mare."

"Don't you think I look enough like a Greek merchant now to pass casual inspection? I promise not to speak Latin and give myself away."

The twinkle in her eyes and the broad smile his words brought to her lips drew a smile in return.

"No, I don't, and neither do you. Baldric is no fool. He would spot you as a Roman the moment he saw you, and he wouldn't greet you with pleasure."

The hoofbeats behind him punctuated her prophetic words. It was too late to avoid the encounter.

Baldric himself cantered out of the woods as she finished speaking. Valeria spun to face him. Decimus leaned the crutch against the rail and turned in slow steps, favoring his left leg even though he tried not to.

Baldric reined in not ten feet from Decimus.

"Why is there a Roman here?" Baldric's Latin had a rough Germanic accent made even more harsh by the anger simmering beneath the words. A scowl twisted his face as he fingered the sword at his side.

Valeria sidestepped closer to Decimus. "Rhoda and I found him near death after the ambush. We couldn't leave Decimus there when he needed our help, so we brought him home to care for him, just as Jesus commands. He's healing well and should be able to return to his legion before too long. God has been very merciful."

Baldric eyed the crutch. His brows lowered further as he took in the calm, confident expression Decimus had assumed. Show no fear to an enemy, even when injured and unarmed—but don't start the fight with a better prepared opponent. He'd taught his junior officers the same...before he got them killed.

Decimus sized up Baldric as well. He was a big man, as tall as himself and heavily muscled. He sat his horse like a man in control, much like he had before the ambush. Valeria had said he was a powerful man. He could see the truth of her statement.

Baldric's fingers wrapped around the hilt of his sword. "Valeria, go into the cottage. I would be alone with this Roman."

◆

The coldness of Baldric's gaze and the grim set of his mouth as he glared at Decimus ramped up Valeria's heartrate. Her eyes widened when his forearm tensed as he tightened his grip on his sword.

"My home is a sanctuary for anyone who needs my help. I won't let any harm come to someone under my care. I'll stay here."

Three steps placed her between the two men.

Baldric swung his right leg over his horse's neck and slid off. "And his great stallion is also under your care. You are wise to get some use out of him while his owner recovers. Perhaps that will take long enough for me to bring my other two mares."

A wry smile appeared on his lips, and the tension was broken. He placed his sword hand on her shoulder as he looked down at her. "You need not worry, Valeria. I will do nothing right now to hurt this man that you have worked so hard to save. I only want to speak with him alone. Then I will come talk with you before I take my mare."

She laid her hand on top of his and squeezed it as she looked up at him with an affectionate smile. "I always trust your word, Baldric. I'll be in the cottage." She smiled at Decimus as well before walking away.

◆

The big German swung around to face Decimus with a scowl and ice in his voice.

"Roman, if you think Valeria has no man to protect her so you can treat her as you wish, you are a fool. She has been under my protection as if she is my own daughter since the physician died. She will marry one of my sons when she is ready. Anyone who tries to harm her will answer to me."

Decimus kept his eyes locked on Baldric's. "You have my word as a Roman that I won't harm her."

Baldric's lip twitched before he spat on the ground between them. "That is worth less than nothing to me. Romans are thieves who take what they want—women, horses, whatever—without paying or caring who they hurt. I have seen no Roman honor that would make me trust your word."

Decimus was a master at not letting his thoughts show, and he needed every bit of skill he had to keep his face passive. Baldric's insult inflamed him like oil on glowing coals, and he normally would have struck down anyone who questioned his honor so insolently. But he was unarmed and in no shape to fight even a youth. Baldric was built like an ox.

He was not a reckless fool, so, for today at least, he must let the insult pass.

"Then I give you my word as a man who knows he owes her his life."

Baldric fixed a glowering stare on Decimus, his head tipped as he took his measure. Decimus returned his stare, calm and unflinching. The silence stretched out longer than a man lacking Decimus's self-control would have been able to stand.

"I will take your word...for now." Baldric extended his arm. Decimus responded in kind, and the two men grasped each other's forearms.

Baldric strode toward the cottage, then turned back toward Decimus. "If you break your word and hurt her, I will hunt you down and kill you."

◆

Valeria couldn't make out their words, but she saw them grasp forearms in agreement over something. Their meeting had gone much better than she'd expected.

Baldric entered the cottage. He stood before her with his arms crossed and a grim set to his mouth.

"Valeria, I know your kind heart, but taking in this Roman was foolish...and dangerous. Roman soldiers are not men who can be trusted. Right now he is weak. He may seem like a friendly farm dog, but when he is strong, the wolf will return."

"I know Romans can be dangerous, especially since we follow the Way, but we had no choice but to bring him here. Jesus commands us to love our enemies. I couldn't leave him there to die when I might be able to save his life. God told me I should help him, and He'll protect us."

"Relying on your god might not be enough to stop a Roman soldier. I told him that you are like a daughter to me and under my protection. I hope that will be enough to keep him from hurting you."

She laid her hand on one of his crossed arms. "That means more to me than you'll ever know. I am truly grateful."

He uncrossed them and patted her hand. "Grateful enough to make it true by marrying one of my sons?" The corner of Baldric's mouth lifted as his eyes softened.

Valeria's eyes crinkled as she returned his smile. "If one of your sons becomes a follower of the Way, I would consider it a great honor to become your daughter-in-law."

◆

As Baldric and Valeria walked out of the cottage and toward the corral together, Decimus saw them both smiling. It was a relief to see that his presence hadn't damaged their friendship. Baldric's chilling glance swept over him as the German entered the corral to get his mare. Valeria resumed her place standing beside him at the rail.

Baldric led the mare out of the corral and mounted his horse.

"Farewell, Valeria. I will bring my other mares soon."

"Farewell, Baldric. I look forward to seeing you, as always." An airy tone accompanied her warm smile.

Baldric focused icy eyes on Decimus, who calmly returned the fixed stare. "Remember what I said, Roman. I will be watching."

Decimus nodded once without speaking.

Baldric wheeled his horse and cantered off, leading his mare.

Decimus watched Baldric until he disappeared into the trees. It was a sure bet the big German was planning to return often and unexpectedly to make sure he was keeping his word. It was what he'd do himself.

Valeria rested her hand on Decimus's upper arm. "Well, that went much better than I'd feared it might."

"Baldric has restored my high opinion of him."

"I'm glad. He's a very good man. He's watched out for us like family ever since Gaius was killed. I'm glad you had a chance to meet him. What did you talk about?"

Decimus placed his hand over hers. "How he will kill me if I hurt you."

Valeria's eyes widened as her free hand shot up and covered her mouth. "Oh, Decimus!"

"Don't worry. I won't give him any reason to do it."

Her hand dropped. "I know. He warned me that Roman soldiers are dangerous men, but I told him you weren't dangerous to us."

He chuckled. "Baldric is right, but so are you."

Her happy smile and warm eyes were proof that she believed him.

Chapter 23

NEVER MORE AT HOME

Decimus lounged on the porch bench, enjoying the warmth of the morning sunshine as he watched Rhoda stroking Astro's nose. His high-spirited stallion sought attention like a puppy whenever she came near. He'd sold two stable slaves in Mogontiacum because Astro had been too much for them to handle. A smile tugged at the corner of his mouth as he pictured Valeria at that age riding her father's stallion. She'd have no trouble with Astro, either.

His gaze drifted across the farmyard in time to see Galen start down the trail from the high meadow. Maybe after lunch they could work on some chore together. He was tired of resting and ready to do something useful with his time.

As Galen approached the porch, Decimus stood and put his crutch under his arm. "So, what's the afternoon project?"

Galen shook his head as he washed up for lunch. "Sorry. It's taking longer than I thought it would in the meadow. I have to go back up after lunch."

Not what Decimus wanted to hear. "Will you be up there all afternoon?"

He turned as footsteps came up behind him.

Valeria slipped past him and rested her hand on the post holding up the porch roof. "It will be better for your leg to rest today. Besides, I have sewing to do, and I'd like your company."

Rhoda came skipping up to the porch. "I like your company, too." She smiled up at him before going through the door.

After lunch, Valeria brought her sewing and joined Decimus on the bench. He sat with his leg propped up on the stool, sometimes watching her sew, sometimes watching Rhoda with Astro, sometimes watching the breeze make the leaves at the top of the trees dance.

If he couldn't be doing something with Galen, sitting with her beside him was a pleasing alternative. Her fingers moved swiftly, making the stitches so uniform and placing them so precisely. There was something soothing about it. She didn't speak much, but she was humming one of the melodies that had helped him relax when he lay in darkness and pain.

What a difference between then and now. He'd been suspicious of everything she said and did when he first awakened to the darkness. Now there was no one in the world he would trust more. What had been almost unbearable pain had become mostly fatigue from the loss of blood, and that wouldn't last much longer. He felt stronger every day.

Her hands kept making the tiny stitches, but his gaze drifted to her face. Serene, with a smile constantly on her lips. The quiet humming continued as she worked. Stitch after stitch until suddenly her needle paused midair. Her smile brightened as she turned her face toward him.

"You've been very quiet. I know you're bored, but a day of rest really is better for your leg."

"Sitting next to a pretty woman is never boring."

"Perhaps so, but you have to settle for my company."

"I can't think of anything better."

"Then I guess you don't have a very good imagination."

Her eyes sparkled during their exchange and made her even prettier.

Decimus enjoyed these playful conversations, but did she only see him as an older Galen, teasing her about being attractive but never meaning a word of it? What was it going to take for her to admit to herself that she attracted him?

The afternoon passed more quickly than he'd expected. Valeria finally gathered up her sewing and rose. "Time for me to start supper."

He'd been leaning back with his hands resting on top of his head while he gazed off into the distance. He straightened and reached for his crutch to follow her into the cottage.

She patted his shoulder. "You don't have to come in yet. I'll call you when supper is ready."

With a warm smile, she turned and walked through the door.

As much as he hated to admit it, spending the day resting had been a good idea. He felt almost back to normal, other than the pain in his leg. That was mild enough now that he hardly noticed it when he wasn't putting weight on it. Then it still hurt a lot, but even that was starting to get better.

How long would it take for his leg to heal enough for him to ride a long distance? How soon would Astro be able to carry him and the gold back to the capital?

It was his duty to return as soon as possible, but he had to admit he was in no hurry. The family villa near Rome was luxurious, but this simple cottage was by far the pleasantest place he'd ever stayed. Watching Valeria and talking with her was endlessly entertaining. He was not a patient man, but he would have no trouble waiting this time.

Decimus was looking forward to another family supper with its jokes and laughter and warm affection. He was not disappointed. Rhoda passed out the stew and Valeria asked for God's blessing. Then the conversation began.

"Galen, what are you doing in the high meadow, and how far is it? If it's not far, I'm healed enough to help you there."

"That's where the grain field is and a sheep fold. I'm repairing the fence that keeps the sheep out of the grain. It's not so much that it's far as it's steep and rocky. Val's right to keep you from going up there yet, at least until you don't need your crutch anymore."

Valeria reached across the table and touched the back of Decimus's hand. "I'm glad you didn't take Decimus with you today, Galen. It was nice having his company for the whole day."

"But one day sitting around is more than enough." Decimus turned from Valeria toward Galen. "What can I do tomorrow?"

Galen directed a big grin at Decimus. "I need to repair the cattle shed roof tomorrow. That will be much easier with your help."

Decimus smiled back as he nodded his agreement to the proposed task. It felt good to be included like a valued member of the family. Who would have thought a Roman tribune could feel more at home with a group of Christians in a small cottage than he ever had in his father's villa or the governor's palace?

Decimus lay on his bed as they gathered at the table. It was Galen's turn to read. Then Valeria began their prayers.

"Dear Father, we thank You for Your many blessings, but especially we thank You for how You've brought Decimus to us and how much You've healed him so far. We ask You to continue his healing. We thank You..."

She continued her prayers with Galen and Rhoda adding their own thanksgivings and requests. Decimus couldn't imagine himself talking to a god like it was a person with him in the room, but it no longer seemed odd that they did.

Galen and Rhoda climbed into the loft after their time of prayer, but Valeria went out on the porch for longer than he liked. What could she be doing out there every night?

Finally, she stepped through the door and bolted it. She came to the side of his bed and tucked the blanket around his shoulders, just like she had when he was blind. Her fingers pushed a strand of his hair back in place as she smiled at him. "Good night, Decimus. Rest in peace."

"Good night, Valeria." His eyes followed her every movement as she climbed the ladder.

Valeria lay in her bed, thanking God that she had obeyed Jesus and brought Decimus home to care for him. Once more she asked God to continue healing his body and, more importantly, to give him the desire to learn about Jesus before he had to leave them.

Decimus lay on his bed, thinking about how good it felt to be here with this family. He'd be sorry when it was time to leave. He'd almost died, but he expected no lasting problems from his wounds. He might have a limp for a while, but that was nothing. He owed everything to Valeria, and she was never far from his thoughts. Her laughing eyes and gentle smiles played in his mind until he drifted off to sleep.

Chapter 24

NOT JUST HIS PHYSICIAN

Decimus awoke to the sound of Valeria softly humming as she stirred the porridge. She turned from the fire as Rhoda slipped her arms around her.

"Good morning, precious." Valeria stroked Rhoda's hair and kissed her forehead before they shared a big hug.

One of Valeria's hugs—he'd like that himself.

He swung his legs to the floor and stood up. This morning his leg didn't feel so bad. Valeria was watching him, so he picked up his crutch but didn't use it as he limped to the chair.

Galen scraped the mud off at the door before taking his place at the table. "Sure smells good, Val. I'm starving this morning, so I hope you made a lot."

He turned to Decimus. "I've got the perfect project for us this morning. The cattle shed has a few leaks in the roof. I hate to keep climbing up and down to get things when I work on a roof, so maybe you can hand them up to me while I crawl around up there."

"Sounds good to me." Decimus was feeling stronger every day, but his leg still hurt more than he'd admit to Valeria if he put too much weight on it. He needed the crutch if he walked more than a few steps. Galen's project should cause him no problems.

Valeria turned from the fire to fix her gaze on him. "Just be careful that you don't overdo it."

His lips tightened until he relaxed them. She meant well, but he really didn't need a mother. She should have realized that by now.

"I'm a good judge of what I can and can't do."

"I'm sure you are, but be careful anyway. I don't want you to tear your stitches and start bleeding again."

Valeria had seen already that knowing what he ought to do and actually doing it were not always the same thing for Decimus. He would try to do more than he should, and Galen wouldn't be any good at keeping him from doing it. Men were such stubborn creatures. Would Galen grow into a mulish man like this one? Galen's grin as he watched their exchange was not reassuring on that point.

After breakfast, Galen climbed up the ladder and onto the roof of the shed. Decimus stayed on the ground to hand supplies up to him. From his vantage point, Galen was the first to see Baldric and Otto approaching. He slid down to the edge of the roof and jumped off.

He called toward the cottage, "Hey, Val! Baldric's here with his mare." Then he trotted over to talk with Otto.

Decimus limped the few steps to the corral and leaned his arms on the top rail. All of Baldric's horses that he'd seen so far were impressive animals, and this mare would be the pride of many Roman stables. Breeding his mares with Astro should improve Baldric's herd even more.

Valeria came from the cottage and met Baldric by the corral gate. "She's a beautiful animal. She and Astro should make a magnificent foal."

Decimus stopped watching the mare and started watching Valeria. She'd told him the night his fingers first saw her face that she'd loved working the horses with her father. She was almost glowing at the prospect of Astro earning her a mare. The bright sparkle of her eyes and the big smile on her lips brought the same to his own.

Each day he appreciated more how smart she was, how thoughtful of others, how kind...how beautiful.

Valeria continued watching the two horses nuzzling each other, but Baldric was watching Decimus watch Valeria. He did not like what he saw.

"Your Roman is looking much stronger."

"I'm very pleased with how he's healing. God has been so merciful. He still gets tired quickly, and his leg still bothers him a lot, but he never complains."

"When will he be leaving?"

"I'm not sure. With his leg the way it is, he wouldn't be able to ride very far, but he is well enough to help Galen as long as he's careful and doesn't work too long. He gets restless when he isn't doing something useful."

"He needs to leave soon. I do not like what I am seeing, Valeria. He looks at you now like you are a woman, not just his physician."

She fought a smile. "I don't think so. I haven't noticed anything different in how he treats me from how he treats Galen and Rhoda. He does like to tease. He's really a lot like Galen, except older."

"You are letting your kind heart fool you. You always look only for the good in people. He is not the friendly farm dog you think he is. He is strong again. The wolf is close to the surface. He gave me his word that he will not hurt you, but I do not know if that word can be trusted."

She placed her hand on Baldric's forearm. "I am grateful that you're so concerned, but please don't be. I don't think he's dangerous, but if he is, God will protect me."

"So will I." With a grim set to his mouth, Baldric walked around the corral to talk with the Roman.

◆

Decimus stopped watching Valeria and turned his attention to the approaching Baldric.

There was a flinty set to Baldric's face and coldness in his eyes. Decimus stood erect and turned to face him squarely. This was not likely to be a pleasant conversation.

"You are looking much stronger, Roman."

"Valeria is an excellent physician."

"I have warned her to be careful of you, but she does not think you are dangerous. I know better. I see how you are looking at her, and I do not like it."

"I gave you my word that I won't hurt her."

"See to it that you do not. I will do as I promised if you do."

"I would protect her with my life. She's in no danger from me."

◆

Valeria didn't like what she was seeing as she watched their conversation. The two big men stood staring at each other, almost mirror images with their arms crossed and jaws clenched. It was time to break it up before it went past talking.

140

She hurried around the corral to stand between them.

"It's time for lunch. Baldric, will you and Otto join us today? I'd be so pleased if you will."

Her tactic worked. The confrontational stares were broken as each turned to look at her. She got Decimus's crutch from where it leaned against the cattle shed. Then she walked between them with a hand on each of their arms as they went to the cottage for lunch.

The conversation at lunch was lively, or at least the conversation between Galen, Otto, and Rhoda was. Baldric said almost nothing and spent most of the time watching Decimus with a scowl on his face. Decimus spent almost as much time watching Baldric, but his face had a relaxed expression. Except for his eyes—they were cool and alert.

Valeria didn't enjoy lunch at all as she watched the two men watch each other.

Finally, Decimus stood. "It was delicious, as usual. Galen, let's get back to work. Your sister may want to visit with Baldric more." He nodded once to acknowledge Baldric as he placed his crutch under his arm and headed for the cottage door.

Galen punched Otto's shoulder and grinned his goodbye before he followed Decimus outside.

◆

Baldric rose as well. "It was a good lunch, Valeria. We must leave now, but I will be back in two days for the mare. You be careful of that Roman."

Valeria laid her hand on his arm. Warmth filled her eyes as she smiled up at him. "It's always such a pleasure to have you come by. Please don't worry about me. I'm sure he's not dangerous anymore."

Baldric patted her hand before he turned and walked out the door with Otto trotting behind him. Perhaps she was right about the Roman, but he still wasn't happy about the way her patient was looking at her now.

When they'd mounted their horses, Baldric rode over by the shed. From his superior vantage point on the tall horse, he looked down at the Roman. His glare was cold, and his frown colder still.

"Remember I am watching, Roman."

Her Roman looked unperturbed as he nodded once in response.

Baldric wheeled his horse and rode out of the farmyard. He still wasn't sure what to make of the Roman, but he would keep a close eye on him for however long it took for her patient to heal and leave.

Chapter 25

WHICH ENEMY TO LOVE

It was late afternoon. Rhoda was standing by the corral scratching Astro's head. The big horse snorted and looked toward the trail where it emerged from the trees. She turned to see what had caught his attention.

A strange man was walking toward her. His eyes were scanning the farmyard, as if he was looking for something or someone in particular. Something about him made Rhoda's stomach flutter, so she scurried toward the cottage. The man followed her.

Rhoda stood on the porch and kept watching him as she called through the window. "Valeria, a man I don't know is coming."

◆

Valeria came out of the cottage and walked toward him. They both stopped halfway between the corral and the cottage.

"Welcome. Do you need some help?"

"Yes, but I need a man to help me. Call your father or husband."

Something about his eyes triggered prickles at the back of her neck. He kept looking around the farmyard rather than directly at her. What was he looking for? Decimus?

She started to bite her lip but forced herself to stop. "Are you sure? Perhaps I can help you with what you need."

His hand shot out and grabbed her arm. Before she could pull free, his other hand slipped behind her neck and grabbed a handful of hair.

He began pulling her towards him. "Perhaps you can, if there's no man around."

A bolt of fear raced through her. "Please let me go. You don't want to do this."

With a cruel laugh, he threw her to the ground and was instantly on top of her. She tried to roll sideways from under him, but he pinned her arms and laughed again.

Rhoda screamed as she ran toward them. She pounded on his back and tried to pull him off. He clutched Valeria by the throat with one hand as he struck Rhoda in the head with the other, knocking her away. As Rhoda lay sprawled on the ground, he turned his attention back toward Valeria.

❖

Decimus and Galen were working on the back side of the cattle shed. Decimus was handing some wood up to Galen when Rhoda's terrified scream tore into him. He flung the wood aside and raced toward the sound.

As he rounded the corner of the shed, he saw the man on top of the struggling Valeria. The world turned red as rage engulfed him. He sprinted toward them, oblivious to the pain in his leg. He grabbed the man and jerked him off, hurling him to the side as if he weighed no more than a child. Then he stood between Valeria and her attacker, breathing hard.

The man staggered to his feet and pulled a knife. Swinging it menacingly, he uttered a string of curses. Then, with the knife raised, he charged.

Decimus stepped forward to meet him, catching the man off guard. As the man tried to bring the knife down, Decimus grabbed his arm. With the expert skill of the well-trained warrior, he twisted the arm downward, driving the knife into the man's own heart. He pulled the knife out and tossed it to the side as the dead man crumpled to the ground.

Turning back to Valeria, he dropped to his knees beside her. His wounded leg throbbed, but what was a little pain when she needed him?

He wiped his hand on his pantleg to remove any blood and placed it on her cheek. "Everything is fine now. I killed him."

❖

Valeria sat motionless on the ground, staring at his calm eyes. Everything most certainly was not fine! A man lay dead less than ten feet from her. The wolf had exploded from within the friendly farm dog, killed so effortlessly, and completely vanished as quickly as it had appeared, before he could even kneel down beside her. How could he offer her even a trace of a smile when he'd just killed a man?

He did it so easily, and it was as if it meant nothing to him that the man was now dead. He had done it to protect her, and the man was trying to kill him as well. The attacker gave him no choice, but every human life was still precious to God, no matter what a person had done. How could he feel no regret that he'd had to kill? What kind of heart lived inside this man who had become her friend?

She swallowed hard.

Baldric was right after all; Decimus was a very dangerous man.

◆

It took some painful effort for Decimus to get back on his feet. Kneeling hadn't been a good idea. He took Valeria's hands and helped her stand. Then he wrapped his arms around her. She was trembling, so he pulled her closer. She stood with her cheek pressed against him, her forearms resting against his chest. At least she wasn't crying. He remembered well what her tears felt like when he held her this close.

He worked his fingers into her hair as he rested his cheek on the top of her head.

◆

Valeria could feel the beating of his heart. At first it was slowing down, but as he held her, it began to beat faster. That shouldn't be. The crisis was over. It couldn't be beating faster—unless something else was exciting him.

She pushed against his chest to free herself. He resisted, then let her push back to arms' length, although his hands remained on her arms. She stepped back, and he let her go.

She felt his gaze locked upon her, but she didn't look at his face. She didn't want him to see how shaken she was by his killing the man and caring no more than if he'd swatted a fly. He mustn't see the fear in her eyes.

She reached out one arm toward Rhoda, who dashed to her side and wrapped her arms tightly around her. She buried her face in Valeria's dress and began to cry.

Valeria took Rhoda's face gently in her hands and assessed the damage. There was a bruise beginning to form on her temple where the man had struck her, but she was otherwise unhurt.

"Hush, precious. It's over now." Still not looking at Decimus, she held Rhoda tight, stroking her hair.

Decimus stood where she'd left him, immobile.

With her left arm around Rhoda, Valeria began walking the two of them toward the cottage. She paused as she passed Decimus and rested her hand against his upper arm, but she didn't look at his face.

"Thank you."

◆

Decimus reached to place his hand on hers, but before he could touch her, it was gone.

She had walked past him, her arm still around Rhoda. "Let's go get cleaned up, precious, and then we can start supper."

As they crossed the yard, Decimus watched them, motionless and silent as a statue. He'd learned to suppress fear during battle, but he'd never felt fear surge through him like it had when he saw Valeria struggling under the man. He'd felt no pain as he ran to save her. He'd been consumed with rage at the man who tried to hurt her. Nothing had mattered except protecting her.

His eyes remained riveted on her until they entered the cottage and closed the door.

He stiffened as the truth struck him. He, Decimus Cornelius Lentulus, senatorial tribune of the XXII Primigenia and son of the provincial governor, was in love with this Christian woman. By his father's own decree, she should be arrested and executed. By the loyalty he'd sworn to Caesar, he should carry out his father's decree. As tribune, he knew his duty, but that didn't matter anymore. As a man, he would never be able to betray this woman who'd saved him...this woman he loved.

He reached down and massaged his leg, which kept throbbing now the crisis had passed. Then he stood immobile, staring at the door through which she'd disappeared.

Galen kept glancing at Decimus's face as he stood six feet to the left. Decimus had never seen him quiet for so long. Finally, the boy could stand the silence no longer.

"It looks like I'm going to have to dig a grave because of you after all."

Decimus's gaze remained fixed on the cottage door. "Bring two shovels. I'll help you."

He didn't move until Galen came back with the shovels and his crutch.

"Father and Mother and Valeria's parents are buried behind the cottage. I think maybe behind the cattle shed. The ground is soft there."

Decimus nodded and grasped one leg. Galen took the other, and they dragged the dead man to where the earth was soft.

The man's purse hung from his belt. Decimus removed it and handed it to Galen.

"Put this someplace safe. Valeria may need the money later, but now is not the time to give this to her."

Galen nodded without speaking. He started digging, but when Decimus tried to drive the shovel into the ground, a sharp pain ripped through his calf. He hobbled over to a fallen tree, where he sat and pulled up his pant leg. A trickle of blood—his stitches had pulled loose.

"You'll have to dig it alone. I can help fill it back in."

He ran both hands through his hair before he rested them on top of his head and sat there frowning while Galen dug the grave. She was already upset with him about something. He could imagine how unhappy she would be with him tearing his stitches when she'd tried so hard to keep him from doing exactly that.

He looked more closely. It wasn't bleeding very much. Maybe he wouldn't have to tell her if it stopped.

After Galen climbed out of the grave, Decimus rose and took one step. The ripping pain told him to stop.

"You'll have to finish alone. My leg won't take it."

He couldn't put any weight on his leg without sharp pain, and the bleeding hadn't completely stopped by the time Galen threw the last shovel of dirt on the grave.

He would need the crutch. Decimus's mouth turned down as he anticipated what she would say when he told her he'd reopened his leg wound.

Galen trotted on ahead. His words drifted out the open door. "Val, he tore his leg up. He's bleeding again."

A sigh escaped. At least he wouldn't have to tell her himself.

When Decimus hobbled through the doorway, leaning heavily on his crutch, Valeria was ready for him. She had a bowl of clean water and some bandages. She still didn't meet his gaze. She only looked down at his leg.

"Sit down on the chair and let me see it."

He obeyed without speaking and pulled up his pant leg.

She sucked her breath between her teeth. "Oh, no."

◆

Valeria knelt at Decimus's feet to survey the damage. First, she carefully washed the wound. After she'd cleaned away the blood, it didn't look so bad. He'd bled where the stitches had pulled, but the cut had healed enough that the wound hadn't fully re-opened. She wouldn't have to re-stitch it. It should be enough to bandage it well for the night to stop any bleeding.

She looked up at him and gave him a weak smile. "It's not so bad, but you've probably set your healing back at least a week, if not more."

His eyes were intense as he gazed down at her. "That's a very small price to pay to protect you."

She looked quickly away and focused again on his leg.

"The acetum's going to hurt, but I have to clean it."

"Do what you must."

He sucked air between his teeth as she trickled the herb-laced vinegar onto the wound. She finished by wrapping it with clean bandages.

"That will have to do for now. Try not to put any weight on it tonight. Rhoda, would you please get a bowl of clean water for him to wash his hands? I don't want him walking any more than he has to right now."

◆

As she stood to return to the fireplace to finish cooking, Decimus's throat tightened. She didn't touch his arm like she always had before.

Galen and Rhoda had already climbed into the loft. Decimus sat on the edge of his bed, watching Valeria bank the fire. She'd been unusually quiet during supper after she offered thanks for the food, and she'd avoided looking at him. Rhoda read from their scriptures, and, for the most part, Galen led the family prayers.

Valeria was deeply troubled about something, and that something had to do with him.

The night was cool, and she picked up her shawl before she stepped out on the porch. Decimus grabbed his crutch and followed her. She was sitting on the bench, so he sat down beside her.

"You shouldn't have come out here. You should stay off your leg."

Maybe she spoke only out of concern for him, but "you shouldn't have come" still cut. Her words hurt even more than her trying not to look at him. What had he done that had driven her away?

She sat in silence beside him, twisting and untwisting the fringe of her shawl around her finger, still not looking at him.

"Valeria, what's wrong? Is it something I've done?"

She kept twisting the fringe and said nothing. He took her hand to stop her. She still didn't look at him, but at least she didn't try to pull her hand away.

After a long silence, she spoke. "You frightened me today." She covered her mouth, then slowly pulled her hand down. "I knew it from the beginning, but I'd forgotten that you were so dangerous."

Her words shocked him. "What do you mean?"

"You killed him so easily, and it was as if his death meant nothing to you."

"He was trying to hurt you. I'm glad I killed him."

She flicked her eyes up to his face, then looked down at their hands again. "That's what frightens me. I know you're a tribune, but you've become my friend. I forgot you were such a dangerous man. I wasn't expecting you to act like a Roman." She paused. "Gaius told me all about Rome...the arena...the bloodlust, how life is held so cheaply, how people are killed for entertainment."

It was all he could do to keep his jaw from dropping. "Why would he tell you that? Rome is so much more."

"He wanted me to know what I might have to face someday if I chose to follow Jesus."

Decimus was dumbstruck. Many times he'd been with friends at the arena, cheering as gladiators fought to the death, watching as Christians were torn apart by lions. His father had organized many games during his service as quaestor in Rome, and he'd often gone to the games with Father even when he was a boy. He'd never considered whether it was right or wrong to enjoy such things. It was simply the Roman way.

But Galen and Rhoda might have been among those killed by the lions if their father hadn't fled to the frontier. Even now, they and Valeria could be in the arena if he chose to enforce his father's decree against them.

"But I would never hurt you...or Galen or Rhoda."

"I know...And I am thankful that you were here to rescue me. It's just...I didn't expect it to be so...so easy for you to kill. I'm sorry he's dead."

His eyebrows shot up at those words, then lowered. "And if I hadn't killed him, would you be trying to nurse him back to health right now? Surely not."

"I'd have to. Jesus never said I could pick and choose which enemies to love."

His jaw started to drop, but he stopped it before she saw. Outwardly he was calm, but inwardly he was incredulous beyond words. The man had tried to rape her, maybe kill her, yet she would have taken care of the brute…just like she took care of him. Can't choose which enemy to love? Had she thought he was a dangerous enemy when she stopped to help him? She was too smart not to know he was. Had she cared for him because she had no choice as well? Love an enemy—what did she even mean by "love?" This love that her god commanded—it wasn't the emotion that he called love, of that he was certain.

At least she knew he would never hurt her, that he was no longer her enemy. She'd even called him her friend. That was something good that came from this mess.

Would she ever consider him more than a friend?

His realization that he loved her—loved her as a man loves a woman—that shook him. The last thing he'd wanted was to fall in love with a Christian, but he couldn't help himself. Could she love the man who used to be her enemy? Love him the way he defined love? Love him as a man, not a friend?

He didn't know what to say, so he sat in silence with her hand wrapped in his.

Finally, she rose, still holding his hand. "I'm very tired. You must be, too, and you need to rest your leg. Let's go in."

She led him through the door, holding his hand until she reached the ladder. "Good night, Decimus. Rest in peace."

She left him standing there as she climbed into the loft.

A chill passed through him. She wasn't going to draw the blanket up around his shoulders and tuck it in, as she had done since the first night. What else would she no longer do now he was once more dangerous in her eyes?

Valeria lay down beside Rhoda and began her nightly prayers for Decimus. He'd become a precious friend to her, but the coldness of his heart shocked her. His body was healing, but his soul had so far to go.

Decimus lay awake on his bed for a long time, wondering how he could be so much in love with a woman when he didn't understand her at all. Did she think him too dangerous to ever want a future with him now? And why did the first woman he'd ever loved have to be a Christian? Even if they both wanted it, what future could there possibly be for a Roman tribune and a woman that Rome wanted to kill?

Chapter 26

JOINING THE CIRCLE

Decimus was in battle, and it felt good. His sword moved effortlessly as he cut down his opponents, one by one. He'd just dropped another one when he heard someone behind him. He turned and in one fluid movement drove his sword into the heart. Too late, he looked to see who it was.

Valeria. He threw his sword aside and caught her as she fell. Her blood spread out in an ever-increasing circle on her chest. As she lay dying in his arms, she reached up and pushed a strand of hair back from his forehead. Eyes filled with love gazed into his as a peaceful smile replaced a grimace of pain. Her eyes began to glow with a brightness like he'd only seen that night after his sight returned.

She whispered, "I forgive you. Don't grieve for me." Her gaze left his face as she looked past his shoulder. Her smile grew brighter. "Jesus..." She lifted her hand, reaching for something he couldn't see, and then...

She was gone. He rocked on his knees as he cradled her lifeless body against his chest. "NO!"

Decimus jerked awake. Galen and Valeria both stood beside his bed.

He hadn't killed her! Relief flooded through him as he gazed upon her worried face.

"It was only a dream." She sat down on the bed beside him. Her fingertips pushed a strand of hair back from his forehead. It was wet with perspiration. "Are you all right now?"

"Yes." He'd never seen anything more wonderful than her sitting beside him instead of lying dead in his arms. "I dreamt of battle."

Her eyes brimmed with compassion. She pushed the errant strand back again and ran her fingers slowly through his hair several times.

"Well, it's over now. You're safe here. Would you like me to stay until you get back to sleep?"

"I'm not a child, Valeria."

"Quite so." She smiled at him as she patted his arm and rose. "Let's go back to bed, Galen."

Galen climbed into the loft ahead of her. When she was halfway up the ladder, she paused to look at Decimus.

"Good night, Decimus. Rest in peace."

Rest in peace. How was he going to do that tonight?

The Roman soothsayers claimed their dreams foretold the future. He wasn't sure he believed them, but if there was any truth to what they claimed, what could his dream mean? Was Baldric right and somehow he was going to hurt her horribly? That was the last thing in the world he wanted to do, but would he do it anyway?

It was a long time before he finally drifted off to sleep.

Everything seemed back to normal at breakfast. Valeria was looking at Decimus and smiling like she used to, and Galen and Rhoda were teasing each other.

Decimus's leg still hurt more than he intended to admit to Valeria, so he wasn't going to help Galen finish the roof. She wanted him to rest it as much as possible, and he was planning to do exactly what she asked today.

The others headed out to work, leaving him alone with his thoughts.

He ran one hand through his hair as he sat on the edge of his bed. What did Valeria really think of him? Did she have any feelings toward him, like he had toward her? She told him yesterday that she thought of him as her friend, but that wasn't enough.

It pleased and excited him when she touched him, especially when she pushed some hair back from his forehead. The light touch of her fingers made his skin tingle and heated his blood. But she did that to Galen's hair all the time, so she probably didn't mean anything by it.

In fact, the way she talked with him, the way she touched him—it was like he was an older version of Galen. The night she'd kissed him on the forehead—it was as if she were kissing Rhoda. She'd offered to sit with him after the nightmare, like she would with Rhoda or Galen, as if he were a younger brother in need of comfort.

He'd been a fool to turn down her offer. Even having her sit with him in silence was better than not having her close by. But she seemed oblivious of his feelings toward her. She certainly gave no sign that she felt the same about him.

When he'd taken her in his arms yesterday, she'd pulled away, but that might only have been because she was upset about him killing the man. Whenever he tried to tell her how much she attracted him, she treated it as if he was joking. Did she even see him as a man, or was he just the newest member of her family, an older brother to Galen?

Rhoda walked in carrying a basket of vegetables from the garden. He hadn't expected her, and his thoughts were showing before he masked them.

"Decimus? Is something wrong? You look sad."

An artificial smile lifted his lips. "I'm just tired."

She walked over and took his hand. "No, you're not, but I know what will fix that. Will you read to me?"

Her request surprised him, but he was ready to focus his mind on something different for a while. "I'd be glad to."

She climbed into the loft and came back with a scroll. "My parents read this to me when I was little."

He took the scroll from her hand. "Aesop's Fables?"

She nodded and hopped onto the bed beside him.

He smiled a genuine smile at her. "I read these, too, when I was little."

She beamed as she snuggled over against him. She rolled the scroll to reach one of her favorites and handed it to him. He put one arm around her, and she laid her head against his chest. He began to read aloud, and she followed along as he read.

◆

Valeria entered the cottage to find Rhoda nestled against Decimus. How natural the two of them looked together. It was almost as if she was watching Gaius reading to Rhoda again. Decimus looked up at her, smiled a relaxed, contented smile, and continued reading. Rhoda looked so happy cuddled up against him. When he finally was well enough to leave, they would all miss him terribly. She was almost glad he'd delayed his departure by tearing his stitches.

It was a typical supper, with delicious food and happy conversation. Then it was time for their evening prayers, so Decimus left the table and lay down on his bed. Suddenly Rhoda stood beside him. When he looked up at her face, she took his hand.

"It's my turn to pick the reading tonight. Will you come read it to me?"

She invited him with such a hopeful smile. He glanced at Valeria. She looked almost as hopeful as Rhoda. He hesitated, then swung his legs off the bed.

Why not? He enjoyed reading aloud, and it would make both Valeria and Rhoda happy. He stood and let Rhoda lead him to the chair.

She brought the codex from its special place in the cupboard at the end of his bed. After spreading a red cloth on the table to protect it, she turned to a page in the back half.

"I want this one tonight. It's one of my favorite parables."

She crawled into his lap and snuggled in like she had earlier that day. He put his arm around her and began to read.

"So Jesus told them this parable: 'What man of you, having a hundred sheep, if he has lost one of them, does not leave the ninety-nine in the open country, and go after the one that is lost, until he finds it? And when he has found it, he lays it on his shoulders, rejoicing. And when he comes home, he calls together his friends and his neighbors, saying to them, 'Rejoice with me, for I have found my sheep that was lost.' Just so, I tell you, there will be more joy in heaven over one sinner who repents than over ninety-nine righteous persons who need no repentance.'"

As he finished, he glanced at Valeria. Her face shone with her brightest eyes and warmest smile. It had been worth reading just to make her so happy. As he closed the codex, she began their prayers. "Dear Father, we thank You..."

Decimus held Rhoda in his lap while the three of them thanked their god for various things and asked him for his help and blessings. As always, Valeria gave thanks for him being with them and prayed for his continued healing. He still didn't understand how they could treat a god like a personal friend, but he was glad he'd joined them at the table, if only for how happy it had made Valeria. Perhaps he would make a habit of it.

Decimus lay on his side, watching the cottage door. Valeria had gone out on the porch to spend a few minutes alone after banking the fire and before going to bed. It had been a long time since she walked outside, much longer than usual. Had something happened to her?

He rose from the bed and followed her onto the porch.

"Valeria? Is anything wrong?"

She was leaning against the post, gazing up at the night sky. Even in profile, he could see the droop of her shoulders and the absence of her usual smile. Without turning toward him, she replied. "No. I was just remembering."

"Remembering what?" He moved over to stand close beside her.

"Standing here with Gaius in the summer, watching the falling stars together. There's one now."

She shivered. The night was already chilly, and she hadn't brought her shawl.

"He used to put his arm around me to keep me warm, and we would stand here for the longest time, just watching the stars and talking." There was a long pause. "It's been three years this month since the raiders killed him. I know he's with Jesus in heaven, but I miss him so much sometimes."

Decimus never wasted a strategic opportunity. "My arm is usually reserved for Rhoda while we're reading, but she won't mind if I use it to warm you up tonight." As he spoke, he leaned his crutch against the post, wrapped his arm around her shoulder, and drew her to his side.

He half expected her to pull away. Instead, she gave him a grateful smile and almost snuggled into him. She'd never let him get so close when she wasn't crying. How could he keep her there?

A streak of light revealed the solution. "There's another one. I'd like to watch them for a while, too."

They stood together in silence for many minutes. She was counting the falling stars. He was acutely aware of her breathing in and out, relishing the warmth and the closeness as he enfolded her in his arm.

Finally, she sighed. "Time to go in." As she stepped away, she turned to face him. "What is it about Roman hair?"

She pushed a stray lock back from his forehead and ran her hand slowly through his hair to keep it from falling back. His blood heated and surged. He fought to keep the desire out of his eyes.

"You and Galen are a pair when it comes to letting it fall onto your face." Then she handed him his crutch before she walked through the door ahead of him.

His lips pursed. How ironic. She would let him put his arm around her as long as she thought it was like holding Rhoda, and she would touch his face only in the way she would touch her little brother. That was more than he'd expected, but it was much less than he wanted.

At the foot of the ladder, she smiled as she pushed the wayward strand back from his forehead again. "Good night, Decimus. Rest in peace."

"Good night, Valeria."

He watched her climb the ladder. It felt so good when she touched his face, even if she was only thinking of him as a brother...for now.

Valeria lay in her bed, thanking God that she'd found him alive, thinking about how nice it was having him as part of her family circle, and praying that his willingness to read Jesus's words would turn into a desire to follow him as Lord.

Decimus lay on his bed, wondering what it would take for her to see him as a man who loved her instead of a grown-up version of Galen and pondering what he should do about it if she ever did.

Chapter 27

A Good Brother

Valeria was already cooking their breakfast when Decimus awoke. He rose and limped over to the chair.

Her eyes narrowed as she gauged how his leg was doing when he put his weight on it. He was moving like he had before he hurt it trying to dig the grave, so it must be at least a little better. But even if it wasn't, he would tell her it was much better and not to worry about him.

"So how are you feeling today?"

"Ready to work with Galen again. The day of rest helped."

"I want you to take it easy today. Too much too soon is always a bad idea. You've had a major setback."

"I might be tempted to take it easy if I can spend the time watching a beautiful woman."

The smile that was playing at the corner of his mouth and the twinkle in his eyes triggered the same in response.

"I'm sorry we haven't found one for you yet. I know a good hostess should try to give a guest what he wants, but you'll have to settle for me."

He brought the tease out in her, just like Galen always did.

"You must be the best hostess around here since you're exactly what I want."

"Then I don't know why you keep asking for a beautiful woman if I'm all you want."

The grin he gave her was as big as her own. Joking with him was such good fun.

Rhoda came in with the basket of eggs and Galen right behind her.

"Hope you made a lot this morning, Val. It smells great, and I'm starving." He grinned as he settled onto his stool.

She pushed a strand of his hair back from his forehead as she placed a steaming bowl in front of him. "You make it so easy to cook. You'll eat anything and say it's good."

She glanced at Decimus. How best to keep him from doing too much today?

"Are you working in the high meadow again? If so, we'll be glad to keep Decimus company this morning."

"I was planning to work on—" Galen stopped with his mouth open. "Right. I'm going to the high meadow." He grinned at Decimus. "Sorry. I guess you'll have to put up with these two this morning."

◆

Decimus saw through her attempt to manipulate what he'd be doing. Normally, her being too protective would have irritated him, but today he was willing to let it pass. It probably would be better to have another half-day of rest for his leg.

"It's no sacrifice to watch a pretty woman instead of working. I can handle that."

He looked at her to see if he made her blush, but she only smiled like it was one of Galen's jokes.

Rhoda almost bounced on the bench. "Can you read me more fables after I get my chores finished?"

The corner of his mouth pulled up as he nodded. That wouldn't be as much fun as watching Valeria, but making Rhoda happy was a good way to spend a morning, too.

Decimus was sitting on the porch bench, watching Astro, when Galen began washing his hands for lunch.

"What are you doing in the high meadow?"

Galen shook off the water before grabbing the towel by the porch washbasin. "I'm repairing the sheep pens."

"That sounds like what we did in the cattle shed."

"It's not much different."

Decimus leaned back and laced his fingers atop his head. What Galen was doing sounded like something he could help with that afternoon. He didn't feel like resting the whole day, even if Valeria was convinced he should.

After lunch, Valeria spotted Decimus following Galen toward the path that led to the high meadow. Her lips tightened. Galen should know better than to take him up that trail yet. It was steep and rocky and no place for someone who needed a crutch to help him walk. He was sure to do something to make his leg worse, maybe even start the bleeding again. If he really hurt it, how would they ever get him back to the cottage?

She hurried to catch up with them.

"Where are you two going?"

"Galen needs help fixing the sheep pens. It's easy work, and I've rested enough."

Galen's eyes flicked from her to Decimus and back. "Val, I told him I could manage myself, but he really wants to come help. He says his leg is much better."

She put her hand on Decimus's arm.

"That trail is steep and slippery, even with two good legs. You need to wait a few more days before you try it, or you'll undo all the progress you've made. I'll help Galen with the pens today."

◆

Decimus stopped his lips from tightening. She didn't need to be such a mother hen, but she was probably right this time. He wasn't that surefooted using the crutch. His leg didn't hurt much as long as he wasn't using it to lift something. Then it bothered him a lot. Maybe climbing a steep trail was too much like lifting.

"All right, physician. I'll follow your instructions...today at least."

She smiled and patted his arm. "That's good. Let's go, Galen."

His gaze stayed locked on her until they disappeared over the top of the hill.

Decimus was reading by the window when Valeria returned from the high meadow.

"You look like you've had a restful afternoon."

"A well-written history is as good a way as any to pass the time when there's nothing else to do and no pretty woman to watch. I'm glad Rhoda rescued my scrolls and codices."

She smiled at him and nodded. "I don't often have time during the day, but I love reading, too."

She'd ignored his comment about her being pretty. Disappointing. He'd expected a playful exchange with her claiming she wasn't beautiful and him insisting she was.

She took her comb from the cupboard at the foot of the bed and sat down at the table.

"There's always a good breeze in the high meadow. I forgot to braid my hair before I went up." Her first attempt to pull the comb through met with fierce resistance.

He smiled at the opportunity before him. She would have to loosen the tangles by hand before she could begin to comb it. As she started to work the snarls out with her fingers, Decimus walked over behind her.

"Rhoda would help you do that, but since she isn't here, let me help."

She turned and smiled up at him. "That would be nice."

He picked up a tangled section. Beautiful hair, lustrous and thick. For days, he'd wanted to work his fingers into it, to feel its silky softness. This was the perfect chance to run his fingers through it, to play with it as he removed the snarls. Asking her to let him substitute for Rhoda had been a stroke of genius. No reason why she shouldn't let the "extra brother" do her sister's job.

The first section wasn't as tangled as it looked, and he soon had it flowing loose and free.

"You're good at this. Have you untangled the hair of many women before?"

"No. Only Astro's tail."

The laughter that shook her shoulders was musical in his ears. "So now I'll know when you tease me about having the softest hair you've ever untangled that you only have Astro's tail to compare it to."

Decimus let her laugh at him. It was true that hers was the first woman's hair he'd untangled, but he'd played with the hair of many women before her. He could honestly say hers was the finest in his extensive experience, but she wouldn't believe him.

"Do you have any sisters, Decimus?"

"No. I had an older brother, but Tiberius died when I was only four. I don't really remember him."

"That's too bad. You would have made a wonderful brother."

Her comment frustrated him. There was nothing brotherly about his feelings for her. Still, he did enjoy running his fingers through her hair, and she wouldn't allow that if she thought of him as a man instead of a brother. For the moment, he'd settle for what left her comfortable, but it couldn't come soon enough that she'd see him as the man he was rather than the brother she imagined him to be.

When the clean-up after supper was finished, Rhoda opened the cupboard and lifted out a codex and the cloth for their evening prayer time. Cradling it in one arm, she reached out to Decimus with her free hand as he sat on the edge of his bed. He took it and let her lead him to the table.

"It's Valeria's turn to pick tonight, but she won't mind if you read."

She handed the codex to Valeria and spread the cloth on the table in front of him.

Valeria beamed. "I would love to have you read what I choose."

He settled into his chair, and Rhoda crawled into his lap and snuggled in. He wrapped his arm around her and waited for Valeria to show him what she would have him read.

A special glow lit her eyes as she looked up from the codex and fixed her gaze on him. The last time he saw her that happy was the day his sight returned. Why him reading made her so happy mystified him, but he was willing to do anything so simple that could bring her such pleasure.

He cleared his throat and began. "...And I tell you, ask, and it will be given to you; seek, and you will find; knock, and it will be opened to you. For everyone who asks receives, and the one who seeks finds, and to the one who knocks it will be opened."

Rhoda whispered, "That's Jesus talking to the people who were thinking about following him."

Valeria touched his hand where it was resting on the codex.

"Thank you." Her smile was radiant.

"Father, we thank You today..." As she began praying, he settled back in the chair with both arms wrapped around Rhoda. There was a strange sense of peace around the table when they were praying. He couldn't quite figure out why sitting there felt so good, but he would be willing to do this every evening. He'd made Valeria happy, and something that he couldn't explain made it feel so right to be sitting there while they prayed.

Rhoda and Galen were already in the loft when Valeria finished banking the fire and headed for the porch. She paused in the doorway and turned her gaze on Decimus, inviting him with her smile to join her. He followed her out the door and stood beside her at the edge of the porch.

"I'm glad you're joining us for prayers." Her eyes sparkled as she smiled up at him.

What could he say that would keep that beautiful smile on her lips?

"I enjoy reading. I'm glad Rhoda asked me to start."

He'd chosen his words well. Her smile remained as she took his hand and squeezed it before turning to gaze at the stars.

It was another chilly night, so he moved closer to her to place his arm around her. "Warm enough?"

She leaned into him as he pulled her against his side, and she wrapped her arm around his waist.

"Yes." Her deep, contented sigh drew his smile. After a few minutes of watching stars, she moved away from him, taking his hand in hers as he lowered his arm. She led him back into the cottage and released his hand at the ladder.

"Good night, Decimus. Rest in peace."

"Good night, Valeria." His eyes followed her into the loft. Bright stars on a cool night and his arm around her—the perfect ending to a good day.

Valeria lay in her bed, thanking God that Decimus's healing continued and that he was happy to be learning more about Jesus.

◆

Decimus lay on his bed, thinking about how much he'd enjoyed every quiet moment with her: untangling her hair, watching the stars, holding her close to his side.

Chapter 28

JUSTICE

It was market day, and Valeria had already loaded the vegetables into the cart. Now she was making breakfast.

Decimus sat at the table with the chair tipped back and his hands resting atop his head. "Galen and I are going to start a new project."

She turned from the fireplace to look at him. "What are you planning to do?"

He rocked the chair back onto its legs. "I can never repay you for all you've done, but I want to do something. If you're going to raise horses, you'll need a stable for your broodmares and new foals. It's a two-man job, and Galen and I should have time to complete it before Astro's healed enough to carry me back to Mogontiacum."

Her eyebrows shot up at his suggestion. She hadn't thought of him as a man who knew how to build things, only as a wounded soldier who needed her help to get better. It sounded like an excellent way for him to hurt himself again.

"That's too much to ask of you."

"You're not asking. I'm offering, and it's not too much at all. I've overseen the construction of army camps. I know exactly what it will take to build the stable. There are plenty of the right type and size of trees in your woods, and I can teach Galen all the skills he doesn't already have."

Her lips parted to tell him not to do something so likely to hurt him, but the set of his jaw told her he was already determined to do it. Nothing she could say would persuade him not to.

He crossed his arms. He was expecting an argument from her, but instead she smiled.

"It's a wonderful idea."

Galen came through the door and sat down by Decimus. "Did you tell her?"

"Yes, and we'll start work on it tomorrow. Today we'll finish up in the cattle shed."

As Valeria handed out the porridge to everyone, she found herself looking at Decimus differently. She'd been so used to thinking of him as the wounded tribune who needed her help. He was actually a complex man of many talents. He wasn't helping Galen anymore. He was directing what the two of them did together. Funny she hadn't noticed that before.

The drive to the village had been uneventful. Valeria unhitched the mare and left her to graze in the green as Rhoda ran over to greet Bertha—a typical market day.

She pulled the basket from the cart, balanced it on her shoulder, and strolled to her usual spot. Before she could even spread out her blanket, the old basket maker's broad smile arrested her.

"Valeria! Have you heard? The problem of the robbers on the southern road is over."

"That's very good news. What happened?"

"I never dreamed I would say this, but we have the Romans to thank. It was very clever, what they did. A few days ago, a man came through talking about his master being a wealthy merchant who'd be traveling with a wagon caravan through here yesterday. He seemed drunk, and he kept talking too much at the inn. We all thought him very foolish. Now I think he was hoping the robbers had a spy listening.

"Yesterday two boxed-in wagons with only drivers and two guards drove through the village. When they passed through the gap, the robbers attacked them. But the wagons were full of soldiers, and they killed the ringleader and all but two of the robbers. They escaped into the woods, but only two shouldn't be ambushing travelers any more now their leader is dead."

Valeria's smile was as broad as her elderly friend's. What a relief to know the road she traveled so regularly would no longer be stalked by the robber band. Then her smile dimmed. Two had escaped. For a moment, that made her uneasy. They might have headed in the direction of her farm. Still, God was their protection, and Decimus was at the cottage with Galen. There couldn't be any real danger.

Galen and Decimus were in the cattle shed when two men walked out of the lane through the trees into the farmyard.

Astro whinnied, and Galen stepped over to look out the door. "Two men. I'll go see what they want."

Decimus would have told him to wait, but Galen was out the door before he could say anything. He peered out the small window facing the corral. Something wasn't right about those two, something sinister in the way they walked and the way they scanned the whole area. Then he saw the swords that hung at their sides.

One of them was his own.

His gut clenched. Galen was walking into mortal danger that he had no reason to expect and no way to handle.

Decimus slipped out the back window of the shed and slunk through the trees, trying to stay out of sight as he circled behind the buildings. He stopped where he was still concealed by the cottage wall. He strained to hear their conversation.

He had no weapon, and there were two of them. It was impossible to get into the cottage unseen to get the sword he'd noticed in the trunk of Gaius's clothes. He would need the element of surprise if things turned nasty.

◆

The robbers stood by the corral as the youth walked toward them.

"I know that stallion. It's the one we left behind. Looks like he's healed enough to be worth taking now. I don't see anyone to stop us except that boy."

The second robber grinned. "That's the same as no one at all."

◆

Galen could hear their low conversation but couldn't make out the words. He smiled as he greeted them. "Welcome. Can I help you with something?"

The leader put his hand on his sword and surveyed Galen. "I'd like this horse."

"He's a beauty, but he's not for sale."

"I wasn't planning on buying him." The sword slid from its scabbard, and the sunlight glinted off the blade. "And I'll take any silver and coin you have as well."

Galen's eyes saucered as he froze by the corral. The second man had moved between him and the cottage to block his escape. His hand rested on the pommel of his sword.

As Galen shifted his gaze back and forth between them, he caught a glimpse of Decimus in the shadows against the cottage wall. Time to stall.

"We don't have any silver, and we barter for everything. We don't have anything you'd want."

"Then we'll just take the horse." He held the sword in position, ready to kill, and took a step toward Galen.

Galen's escape was blocked behind, so he dropped to the ground and rolled under the lowest rail into the corral where Astro was pacing.

A string of curses sprang from the robber's lips. "Big mistake, boy. You want games? I'll play with you a while, but you won't like it."

The robber vaulted into the corral and grabbed Galen's sleeve as he was stumbling to his feet. Galen twisted down and out of his shirt, leaving the robber holding it as he scrambled away. He was almost clear when the robber grabbed his ankle and jerked, planting his face in the dirt.

◆

The second robber stepped over to lean on the rail of the corral while he watched the show.

A cruel chuckle escaped sneering lips. "He was going to kill you quick. Now you'll suffer before he does."

It was the chance Decimus had been waiting for. He sprang from his hiding place and reached the corral before the second robber even realized he was coming. With one quick twist, he broke the man's neck.

With the dead man's sword now in his hand, he vaulted into the corral. As he landed, his left leg buckled, and he staggered as he fought to regain his balance.

The first robber turned from Galen to Decimus. A mocking laugh rumbled from his chest as he grinned at Decimus's clumsiness. An arrogant sneer twisted his lips as Decimus hobbled toward him.

"Come on, farmer. Do I kill you first or your boy?" He moved forward, waving his sword. "Come on. What do you want?"

"I want my own sword back and your blood for the death of my men." Decimus flexed and twisted his wrist, swinging the sword in a tight arc to get the feel of it as he assumed a fighting stance.

The robber's eyes flared with fear. "Tribune!"

With a limping lunge, Decimus was upon him. Metal on metal rang out four times before he drove his sword into the robber's heart. Decimus pushed the body off the sword, then wiped the blood off on the dead man's shirt.

Galen sat, shirtless, in the dust of the corral. His eyes were enormous as he stared at the two bodies lying on the ground before him. He was silent, a strange condition for him. Decimus held out his hand and helped him to his feet.

"You did well, Galen. Quick thinking. Better than most men." He slapped Galen on the back, then wrapped his arm around Galen's shoulder to steady him.

"I almost got myself killed. What will Val say?"

Decimus contemplated the two dead men.

"We'll bury them before she and Rhoda return, then say nothing. They would never feel safe here again if they knew what just happened." *And I don't want her to know I killed two more men today, even if it was to save her brother.*

"I'll get two shovels. Thanks...for saving my life." Galen looked deadly serious—the first time Decimus had ever seen him that way.

"It was worth the effort. It would be boring around here without all your jokes." He tousled Galen's hair and got a weak smile in return.

It would be some time before Galen got over what had just happened. He seemed more like a man, less like a boy than he had at breakfast, and in some ways, Decimus was sorry to see it.

He bent over the dead robber to reclaim his sword and scabbard. His own purse hung from the robber's belt. When he looked inside, he found his gold signet ring. He would hide the purse and swords somewhere in the cattle shed where Valeria wouldn't see them. What she didn't know wouldn't grieve her.

Valeria glanced around the farmyard as she drove the cart to its usual place by the corral. Why hadn't Galen come to meet her like he usually did? There was no sign of Decimus, either.

Her lips tightened as she shook her head. They were probably in the high meadow. Galen should have known better than to take Decimus up there to help him. Decimus should have known better than to go. His leg wasn't ready for such a long walk and a climb up so steep a trail. She would talk with the two of them later about making better choices. Foolish boy and stubborn man—the perfect recipe for Decimus hurting his leg again.

As she was unharnessing the mare before turning her loose to graze, a movement in the woods caught her eye. Galen and Decimus were walking toward her. Decimus turned to Galen like he was saying something, and they both dropped whatever they were carrying. As they got closer, it was obvious he was limping worse than he had that morning.

Valeria set her fists on her hips. "Galen, what have you had him doing with you?"

"I'm sorry, Val. I didn't mean to have him do something to hurt his leg. It's just that ...well...we didn't mean to... we just ended up..." He looked at Decimus as he struggled to find the right words.

Decimus put his hand on Galen's shoulder. "Stop. I'll tell her."

Valeria's eyebrows dipped. "Tell me what?"

He took a deep breath before answering. "I killed two men, and we were burying them."

◆

The anger in her eyes morphed into sadness and cut into Decimus. "I'm sorry..."

He looked away from her, fixing his gaze on the cattle shed so he wouldn't see her deep disappointment in him. He had no regrets that he'd killed two such men, but he was sorry that she knew he had. The death even of these murderers would touch her heart. He would have given almost anything not to have to tell her, but he wouldn't lie to her.

"He had to, Val. It was two of the robbers from the ambush. They were going to steal the stallion, and they were about to kill me when he stopped them. It was my fault for walking up to them without thinking."

◆

Valeria's gaze focused on Decimus's face as he stared into the distance. He seemed genuinely sorry this time. Perhaps God was changing his heart.

She stepped close to him and touched his arm. She offered him a weak smile when he turned his troubled gaze to her face.

"Thank you for saving my brother. Come inside, and let me see what I can do to repair the damage you've done to your leg."

◆

167

Valeria finished applying some liniment to relieve the soreness of Decimus's strained calf muscles. The heat from the liniment and her massage of the sorest part made his leg feel much better.

Decimus had been silent while she worked, thinking about what had almost happened to Galen and why.

"Valeria, I need to talk with you about Galen."

Worried eyes locked on his as her breath caught. "They didn't hurt him, did they?"

"Not today, but they could have. He's almost a man now, and there are things a man needs to understand and know how to do. There are things he needs to learn that you can't teach him."

He paused, fearing she would not like what he was going to say. "He was almost killed today because he didn't see the danger. He needs to learn how to defend himself. That means how to see and avoid danger...and how to use a sword. If his father were alive, he would teach him these things. I can teach him much of what he needs to know before I leave."

Her eyes clouded. "I don't want him to think fighting is good."

"I don't think you need to worry about that. He follows your god as devotedly as you do. He's not going to want to become a soldier like me. I saw Gaius's sword in the trunk. I'm sure he knew how to use it to protect his family. Often just being prepared for trouble keeps trouble from happening. I'll teach Galen to be prepared for trouble, not to start it."

◆

Valeria stared at the ground. As much as she hated to admit it, what he was saying made sense. She looked at his face. His eyes were intense as he waited for her response. He only wanted to do what he thought best for Galen.

How could she ever hope to teach her brother what he needed to know as a man? She didn't even know what all that might be. Decimus didn't follow the Way, but she trusted that Galen loved Jesus enough that he could learn how to fight without wanting to. Perhaps Decimus was right. She could trust him to do what Gaius would have done.

"Teach him what you think he needs to know."

◆

Decimus nodded once, then smiled with satisfaction. He'd been afraid she would deny his request. Now he would have the chance to do something truly valuable for her family before he had to leave.

The suppertime laughter and conversations were over, and tonight Decimus stayed at the table for prayer time. It was Galen's turn to read, but he made his selection and handed the codex to Decimus. Somehow he'd become the official reader, but he didn't mind. It delighted Valeria, and he was willing to read whatever she wanted to have that effect. Joining them made Rhoda happy, too. She curled up in his lap while he read, and snuggled in his arms as he continued to hold her while they prayed. Her father probably held her the same way before he was killed.

"Father, we thank You for protecting Galen and Decimus today. We pray for the souls of the men Decimus had to kill, that You would deal with them in Your mercy." Valeria continued to pray with Galen and Rhoda joining in. "We pray all this in the name of Your precious son, Jesus."

Galen and Rhoda echoed her amen.

When Valeria headed out to watch the stars, she paused at the door. She held out her hand as she smiled at Decimus. Her invitation was irresistible. He limped over and wrapped her hand in his. She walked ahead of him to the bench and sat down.

"I think we should sit tonight. Your leg had a hard day."

Decimus settled in next to her. "Not so bad, really. I can stand at the edge of the porch. The view's not as good from here."

"But the company is just as good." It startled him when she rested her head against his shoulder, but he masked his surprise. He let go of her hand and put his arm around her. She sighed contentedly and slid a little closer to him. "I love this time of night."

"Me, too."

Her hair was lying across her shoulder right by his fingers, so he started playing with a strand. Soft. Silky. A smile curved his lips as he imagined lying with her head resting on his chest, her hair spreading out across his skin.

They sat together for a long time. Finally, she rose and took his hand. "Time to go in."

She led him through the door and paused at the foot of the ladder. Once more she pushed a loose strand of hair back from his forehead.

"Good night, Decimus. Rest in peace." She took a step up the ladder.
"Good night, Valeria."

Valeria lay in her bed, thanking God that Decimus had been there today to protect Galen and that he seemed happy to join them for the reading and prayers. Surely he was starting to hear God's call.

◆

Decimus lay on his bed, remembering how soft her hair was as they sat together in the dark, his arm around her as they watched the stars.

Chapter 29

THE TEACHER

As the breakfast conversation began the next morning, Decimus turned toward Galen.

"Valeria and I talked about what happened yesterday. I'm going to teach you some things about defending yourself that your father would have if he were here. We'll start your sword lessons after lunch."

Galen's brows shot up. "Really? Otto's father is teaching him now, and I was wondering how I'd ever learn." He grinned. "I bet I'll have the better teacher."

Decimus reached across the table and tousled Galen's hair.

"You might not think so after you see what a demanding teacher I can be."

It felt good to know that Galen thought so highly of him. It felt even better to know that he would be doing something of value for this family. The debt he owed was beyond what he could pay, but at least he could teach Galen part of what he needed to know as a man.

After swallowing his last spoonful of porridge, Decimus rose.

"Let's get to work. I want to get the trees cut down. Then we'll cut the trunks into the right lengths for the walls before lunch."

Valeria pursed her lips. "That seems like a lot to do after what you did to your leg yesterday."

A wry smile tugged at the corner of his mouth. "With both of us working, it's a reasonable goal. We can get everything cut today, and tomorrow we'll use the mare to drag the logs up by the corrals. We can start building by tomorrow or the day after." He shifted his weight off his injured leg. "Don't worry, Valeria. I know exactly what's needed, and what we're going to do won't hurt my leg as much as you seem to think."

Her lips parted, as if she was about to protest. He raised his hand to stop her.

"Perhaps, but try to be careful anyway."

With lips pressed together to keep from laughing at her persistence and a shake of his head, Decimus headed out the door.

◆

Galen brought two axes from the cattle shed, and he and Decimus headed into the woods. Soon Valeria could hear the thwocks of ax blades cutting into tree trunks, followed by the crash of falling trees. After she heard the last tree fall, the thwacks continued as the axes cut the fallen trees into the lengths needed for the walls of the stable.

Perhaps she didn't have to worry about Decimus doing too much for his leg today. As long as she heard the axes cutting into wood, he would be mainly working with his arms, not his legs. His chest was broad, and his upper arms almost as big as her thigh. He was in superb shape for work that needed upper body strength, and nothing about his injuries in the ambush should be a problem there. Perhaps, as he said, there wasn't any reason for concern.

◆

As the work progressed, Decimus started to wonder whether Valeria might have been right. Cutting down one tree wouldn't have been a problem, but the walls of the stable were going to need more than a dozen, and the roof added to that number. He had to keep shifting his weight from his right leg onto his injured left to properly swing the ax while they were cutting down the trees.

Cutting the logs to length after the trees were down made him keep his weight evenly distributed between both legs. While that wasn't as hard on his leg as bending and lifting, he soon found it getting sore. It didn't hurt so badly that he couldn't do the work, but the pain was a constant reminder that he was far from completely healed.

He massaged it frequently, and that seemed to help, but it didn't solve the problem. In fact, the more logs he cut, the less it did help. When he took the last swing with his ax, he sucked in a deep breath and blew it out slowly.

His leg was throbbing as he and Galen started their walk back to the cottage. Still, if he concentrated on how he was walking, he could keep from limping so badly that it would make Valeria think he'd done too much and fuss over him. The ax work was finished, so his leg would have a chance to recover during the afternoon. He was only going to be training Galen, and that should be easy.

After lunch, Decimus took Gaius's sword out of the trunk and drew it from its scabbard. He flexed and twisted his wrist to check how it handled. It was well balanced and had a comfortable grip. It would be a good sword for Galen to learn with, even though it was more work of art than weapon. Both sword and scabbard had intricate engravings on them, and the scabbard was even decorated with some jewels. The whole set had been very expensive. Galen had told him during their first conversation that his father once had an estate outside Rome. From the look of the sword, it might have been a large one.

He was about to close the trunk when something purple at the bottom caught his eye. He flipped back the shirts lying on top of it. There lay a tunic with the narrow purple stripes worn only by the Roman equestrian order. Since membership in that order required a personal fortune of at least 100,000 denarii, Gaius must have been a wealthy man before he left everything behind. What had Galen said his full name was?

Decimus's eyebrows rose as he remembered. Licinius Crassus. That family had produced several consuls during the Republic, and Marcus Licinius Crassus had ruled Rome in the First Triumvirate with Julius Caesar and Pompey before his death in battle. His wealth was legendary. Why would a rich aristocrat with such a family tree abandon Rome and all he owned to follow the Christian god? That was beyond understanding.

He shook his head as he closed the lid. He would never make such a choice himself.

Decimus's sword was also well balanced and fit naturally in his hand. He was glad he'd recovered it. It had been specially crafted for him by a master swordsmith, but it was a soldier's weapon with clean lines and no frills. He draped the narrow strap attached to the scabbard across his chest, and handed Gaius's sword to Galen. "Take this, and let's go start your lessons."

Baldric and Otto were bringing the third mare. They'd almost reached the edge of the trees when they heard the metallic ring of sword striking sword.

"Stay here." Baldric left Otto with the mare and trotted into the farmyard with his sword drawn. He pulled back on the reins when he saw it was only the Roman and Galen sparring. He watched as the soldier stopped to demonstrate a defensive move, then had Galen try first to attack and defeat it, then to use it while he attacked. The Roman's skill was impressive and his way of teaching effective. These were moves he would like Otto to know.

He turned as he slipped his sword back into its scabbard. "Bring the mare."

◆

Decimus heard Baldric call and stopped. "Go. Visit with your friend. We can do this after he leaves."

Galen handed his sword to Decimus and trotted over to join Otto, who was about to let the mare into the corral with Astro.

Decimus sat down on the tree stump that served as a stool by the corral and massaged his leg. He'd started the lesson already sore after the morning's ax work. The quick footwork of a sword fight was more stressful on it than he'd anticipated. His leg was really hurting now. He was glad of the break while Galen talked with Otto. Maybe he would wait until tomorrow to resume the lesson.

◆

Baldric rode over by the Roman and dismounted.

"I see you are putting your time to good use, Roman. Galen is handling his sword well for a beginner. The moves you were showing him, I would like Otto to learn."

Her Roman tilted his head as he looked up at Baldric. Baldric could never quite read what was going on in his mind. He was too good by far at concealing his thoughts when he wanted to. One more thing Baldric did not like about the man.

"I'd be glad to teach them both if Otto wants to join us."

Baldric's head tipped once to show his appreciation. He did not like her Roman, but he would gladly use him to teach Otto the skills he was teaching Galen. He was definitely good with a sword.

He looked toward the boys. "Otto, Galen. Your teacher is waiting for you." With another silent nod toward the Roman, he turned to join Valeria on the porch where she was sewing.

"Welcome, Baldric. I'm glad to see you've brought your third mare."

"Your Roman's stallion is doing a fine job for us both. Perhaps I should bring a fourth."

Valeria smiled in anticipation of the mare that would soon be hers. "You certainly may if you want to. No extra charge. Astro's proving to be as good a stallion as I thought he would."

Baldric's lips twitched up to acknowledge her offer as he joined her on the porch bench. He would take her up on it if the Roman and his horse stayed long enough.

"I see you have asked your wolf to train your puppy."

"I didn't ask. He suggested it. He said a man needs to know how to protect his family. He promised to teach Galen only how to defend, not to start a fight."

Baldric fixed his gaze on the Roman. He seemed to have developed a real concern for Valeria's family. He should have thought himself to tell her that he would train Galen like he was training Otto now.

"So you will be getting something of value from both your Roman and his horse."

Baldric sat on the porch in silence, watching the Roman train the two boys. He was superbly skillful with the sword. He would be a deadly opponent in a real fight. It was good to have this chance to observe him, to watch for weakness in his fighting style. So far, he had seen none except a slight lack of balance due to his weak leg, and that would soon be gone. However, the more he saw of the Roman, the less likely it seemed that they would end up fighting. He no longer expected him to do anything to hurt Valeria or anyone else in her family.

The Roman's limp was getting worse. His leg was obviously hurting. He sat down on the stump to massage it and began to talk to the boys about how to read the intention of an opponent.

Baldric's attention locked on what her Roman was telling them. He talked about watching the eyes and the mouth to see if they showed the same emotion. He counseled them to watch the hands to see if they were sweating from fear. He warned them how fear could make a man more likely to try to hurt you before you could hurt him, and that made him unpredictable. He told them how showing your own fear could make someone decide you were an easy target.

He described how important it was to seem confident but not threatening, how they should try to appear strong even when they were weak because appearing weak brought out the bully in cowards. Baldric had seen these things in the Roman's own behavior the first two times they met.

The Roman told them how a man who couldn't control his temper was still like a boy no matter how old he was and how losing your temper gave your opponent an advantage in a fight. He said real men didn't have to prove anything by being cruel. These were good things for Otto to hear. Baldric had not thought about telling such things to Otto himself, although they were all true and important for a man to know.

Baldric glanced at Valeria and caught her watching him watch the Roman. She looked happy. Probably because she wanted him to like her Roman, or at least respect him. He could give her part of what her kind heart wanted. He did respect the Roman's swordsmanship.

The afternoon was almost over when the lesson ended. Baldric rose and squeezed Valeria's shoulder. She rested her hand on his and smiled up at him. Then he turned his attention back toward the swordsmen.

"Otto, get my horse."

Otto trotted over to get both horses from where they were tied to the corral. Baldric stepped off the porch and walked over to the tired, hurting man.

"So, Roman, what time do you start the lessons tomorrow?"

◆

Decimus was shocked at such a question coming from Baldric, but he didn't let it show. Still, he was genuinely pleased that Baldric saw value in what he'd been teaching. The big German was a man whose respect was worth having.

"After lunch. Galen and I have some work to do in the morning."

Baldric swung himself into his saddle. "Otto, time to go. We will come back tomorrow."

Otto mounted his horse and waved at Galen as he followed his father out of the farmyard and into the trees.

Valeria left the porch and walked over to Decimus. As he stood up, his leg almost buckled. He'd seriously overworked it with the training on top of the soreness from the morning.

Her lips tightened when she saw the twitch at the side of his mouth that revealed his pain when he first stood.

"Galen, would you please get his crutch? I think it's near his bed."

As Galen headed for the cottage door, she looked at Decimus with lowered brows and shook her head.

"You shouldn't do this tomorrow. You've hurt your leg again."

"Baldric is bringing Otto back, and he's not a man I care to disappoint." *Or show any weakness.*

"I'm sure he'll understand. I won't let you do too much and hurt yourself again."

He looked down at her with an irritated half-smile. Her statement was out of line, but as he gazed into those caring blue eyes, his irritation vanished.

"I'll make that decision, not you. You can't give me orders, and I won't let you persuade me not to do it." He pushed a loose strand of hair behind her ear, then drew his thumb along her jaw line before holding her chin for a moment.

"I'm not Galen."

◆

When Decimus released her chin, he smiled at her in a way that made Valeria feel strangely warm. She hadn't expected his gentle touch or the warmth in his eyes that confused her. Something about the way he was looking at her made her feel strange, like there were little butterflies in her stomach.

"Besides, it doesn't hurt as much as it did yesterday, and some of your liniment and a good massage fixed that. Nothing can make a man feel better than some attention from a pretty woman." The odd look was gone, and his joking eyes had returned.

"I'm not sure I believe that, but let's go in. I'll try to fix you again."

Galen came trotting over, carrying his crutch. Decimus positioned it under his arm and waited for her to take the first step.

She glanced at the man limping beside her. It was odd. Even though he needed the crutch, there was something about him that reminded her of the tribune on his stallion, strong and in control.

Chapter 30

STALLIONS

At first Decimus wasn't sure which felt better, the heat from the liniment or the feeling of her hands massaging his sore muscles. As she continued, he was certain it was her hands.

"If you keep overdoing like this, you're going to set back your recovery by at least a week."

"That doesn't sound so bad to me. I'm going to miss having such a pretty woman make my breakfast every morning." He kept the joking tone in his voice.

"I may be prettier than your typical army cook, but that's not much competition."

"You have no idea what a sacrifice it will be to make that change." She was looking at his leg as she massaged it, so she didn't see the regret that crossed his face as he spoke.

She finished the massage.

"Seriously, you can't keep overworking your leg like this without risking permanent damage. Can't I persuade you to cancel the lesson tomorrow?"

"No." The finality with which he spoke that word should have silenced her...but it didn't.

"Well, at least you can take it easy in the morning rather than doing something with Galen that will tire out your leg before you even start the lessons."

Her lips parted as if a thought suddenly struck her. "I also want you to let me try something that my father used to do for the horses."

He raised one eyebrow as his head tipped.

"No, really, I think this might help. We had an old stallion that hurt his leg. It was very slow healing, and it seemed to bother him a lot. Father wrapped it with cloth strips to support the muscles, and it really helped. He could walk around like it wasn't hurting at all. I can wrap your leg before you start training the boys."

She was looking at him so hopefully. What she was asking didn't seem like a bad idea.

"That sounds reasonable. Maybe that will solve my problem like it did for your stallion. Did he heal faster after that?"

"Well, yes and no. He felt so much better that he tried to jump the corral fence to get to a mare. He didn't quite clear the top rail. When he fell, he broke one of his legs. Father slit his throat to put him out of his misery."

Decimus exploded with laughter. When he finally stopped, he took her hand in his.

"Whatever you do, don't tell that story to Baldric. I don't want him to get any ideas about putting me out of my misery if I try to vault into the corral and fail."

He started laughing again, and it was so contagious that she laughed along with him.

He stood up and placed his crutch under his arm.

"You have persuaded me to take it easy until lunch tomorrow. I'll go tell Galen that I won't be working with him in the morning."

He offered his hand and helped her to her feet. As he limped toward the door, he paused and turned to face her. He didn't even try to mask his thoughts.

"Who's to say that stallion wasn't wise to risk everything to gain a beautiful mare." His usual joking tone returned as he stepped out the door. "I'm certainly not going to blame him for trying."

◆

Valeria moved so she could watch him through the door as he hobbled toward Galen. He had such a delightful sense of humor sometimes. It was impossible not to smile when he got going with a joke. His grin could light up a room. It was amazing how much more handsome a man was when his eyes were sparkling as he laughed.

When he'd paused at the door, there was that look in his eyes that put butterflies in her stomach. He was the only one who'd ever had that effect on her. She would miss it all when he left.

179

Decimus was more than ready to eat as soon as Valeria finished asking the supper blessing. Between the work in the woods and the sword lessons, he'd worked up an appetite almost as big as Galen's. Valeria loved feeding her family food they enjoyed. Tonight, his appetite was sure to draw smiles from his pretty cook.

When the conversation began, Galen was almost bouncing.

"Otto and I both had so much fun today. I was right about you being a great teacher. Baldric thought so, too. I'm glad he's bringing Otto back tomorrow."

"I'm glad you think so. You two are good students, and it's working well to have you learning together." He glanced at Valeria. "Your sister thinks I overdid it on my leg today, and I have to admit she's right. I'm sorry you'll have to work without me in the morning if I'm going to teach you in the afternoon."

Galen grinned at him. "I'd be willing to do the work of three to have you teaching me to use a sword."

Valeria smiled at him, too. "It's good to have you here to teach Galen. I don't know how he'd learn without you."

Decimus's mouth curved up in a smile that reflected hers. By building the stable and training Galen, he was repaying part of his debt to her family. Honor demanded that, but affection, not honor, had become his reason for everything he was doing.

After supper, they gathered for prayers. Tonight, he came to the table without anyone inviting him. Everyone assumed he would read the scripture, which was fine with him. It was Rhoda's turn, and she selected something before she climbed into his lap and snuggled in. When he glanced at Valeria while he read, her eyes were glowing again. As he held Rhoda in his arms while they prayed, his head tilted. Something he never expected had happened. He now enjoyed their prayer time almost as much as he enjoyed supper.

Valeria had gone out alone to watch the stars appear. He followed her and placed his hands on her shoulders as he stood behind her.

She turned her head to smile up at him before she turned her gaze back to the sky. "They really are beautiful, aren't they. It's so peaceful this time of night. I love the sound of the crickets and the breeze in the leaves."

"I never took the time to look at them before you pointed out their beauty."

"Gaius and I always loved doing this. It's nice to have someone to share it with again." She shivered.

"You're getting cold. Let me warm you up so we can watch a while longer."

He stepped forward against her and wrapped his arms around her waist, drawing her close to him. "Warmer?"

"Yes. Thank you." She rested her small hands on his large ones as she stood there, contentedly watching as the fainter stars began to appear.

He was content, too. She was letting him hold her close without being frightened by him or pulling away. It was his great good fortune that Gaius had taught her to love the evening sky. He might get to do this every evening until he had to leave. It was something he would look forward to all day tomorrow.

Finally, she lifted his hands away from her waist. She kept holding one of them as she turned to go into the cottage.

"Time to go in." She led him through the door and released his hand to place hers on the ladder.

"Good night, Decimus. Rest in peace."

"Good night, Valeria." He remained by the ladder until she disappeared into the loft.

Her wrapped in his arms and enjoying it—it had been a good night already.

Valeria lay in her bed, thanking God for Decimus becoming like part of her family and for his willingness to read God's word. Even more fervently, she prayed for him to decide that he wanted to follow the Way like they did. If he did, maybe he wouldn't have to leave when he finally healed.

◆

Decimus lay on his bed, remembering how good it felt to feel her heart beat as he held her in his arms and imagining what it would be like if she could grow to love him like he loved her. There was still the problem of her being a Christian, but he could figure out how to deal with that if she would only decide she loved him.

Chapter 31

THE WHOLE STORY

After breakfast, Decimus restrained a frown as he watched Valeria braid her hair. She was going to work with Galen in the high meadow until lunchtime. No chance for the stiff breeze to give him an opportunity today.

Valeria had taken Rhoda aside, probably to tell her to make sure he didn't try to do something that might hurt him. He let a smile escape. She was subtle how she tried to keep him from doing too much, but he knew most of her tricks now.

By mid-morning, all he'd done was sit on the porch and watch Rhoda with Astro. He'd promised Valeria he would rest his leg, but it was hard to sit doing nothing. He was bored almost beyond endurance when Rhoda walked over to keep him company.

She sat down beside him on the bench and took his hand. "Would you like to come inside and read to me?" She smiled up at him, an unusual glint in her eyes. "You can read me my most favorite of all."

His mouth curved into a smile as he looked down at her. "Certainly. We have plenty of time before lunch, so pick whatever you like, and we can read it all."

She led him by the hand to the bed and patted it to indicate where he should sit. He was expecting her to climb into the loft to get her scroll of fables. Instead, she walked to the cupboard where they kept the codices. She took out the one she always picked when it was her turn and carried it to him. Then she hopped up on the bed next to him and laid it in his lap. She opened it to the first page and looked at him expectantly.

"This is my favorite writing about Jesus. Luke wrote it, and he was a physician like Father." She snuggled over against him, and he wrapped his arm around her as he began to read.

"Inasmuch as many have undertaken to compile a narrative of the things that have been accomplished among us, just as those who from the beginning were eyewitnesses and ministers of the word have delivered them to us, it seemed good to me also, having followed all things closely for some time past, to write an orderly account for you, most excellent Theophilus, that you may have certainty concerning the things you have been taught.

"In the days of Herod, king of Judea, there was..."

Most of Decimus's own library were histories. It shocked him to find that their religious codex started off like it was a history. Like the best historians, this Luke described gathering information from eye witnesses so he could write an orderly account of the events. The codex's finely crafted literary style made it enjoyable to read. The author had been a well-educated man and a skillful writer.

As he read, it surprised him that so many of the events were fixed in time relative to real men that he'd read about in other histories. But the events themselves were stories about their Jesus, who was supposed to be a god who took human form to ransom people from having to face the just punishment for what they'd done wrong.

That didn't make sense to him. There were many stories about how the Roman gods sometimes took human form, but they always acted like selfish people who happened to have special powers. He'd never heard of any god who created people to love them and sacrificed himself to save them from the punishment they deserved.

He didn't believe any of the stories about the Roman gods. They were merely part of Roman culture, not something real that intelligent people would believe strongly enough to die for them in the arena. If the Christians believed the stories in this codex were true, that could explain why they were so willing to die rather than deny their god. It could explain why Valeria didn't seem to care about what might happen to her when she obeyed her Jesus's teaching and brought him home to care for him when he was still her enemy. It also could explain why she was more concerned about her friend Inge choosing the Christian god than about her dying.

There was a lot about this Christian god that he needed time to think about. He wanted to understand Valeria, but that was impossible unless he understood her faith in her god.

◆

When Valeria walked into the cottage to start making lunch, Decimus was finishing the story about how Jesus rose from the dead and showed himself to his followers after being crucified. Rhoda was snuggled against Decimus, and he was so totally immersed in the codex he was reading to her that he didn't immediately look up. Valeria's heart leaped when she heard the words in his deep, rich voice.

Thank You, God! Thank You for Rhoda finding the perfect way for him to learn Your whole story. Please take the seeds being planted right now and grow them into true faith for him.

She had watched God heal his body. How she longed to see God save his soul!

◆

Decimus suddenly realized someone had come into the cottage and looked up. He didn't know how long she'd been there, but she looked so happy watching him read, just like she did when he read in the evening. Her face was extraordinarily beautiful when she was that happy.

He read the final sentence and closed the codex. Rhoda lifted it off his lap and placed it back in the cupboard. Then she came back and hugged him. "Thank you so much for reading it all to me. I love hearing the whole story at once." He stroked her hair as she continued to hug him.

"I enjoyed it, too." As he spoke the words, his eyebrows rose. Strange as it might seem, he meant them.

Chapter 32

LESSONS

Lunch was finished, and Baldric and Otto would arrive soon. Valeria brought some long strips of cloth from the loft to wrap Decimus's leg before the training session.

She tipped her head and contemplated him as she tried to decide how to proceed.

A half-smile played on his lips. "Do you want me to sit or stand while you do this?"

"Father always wrapped the stallion's leg while he stood, but there really wasn't a choice. I'm thinking the muscles might be more relaxed if you're sitting, and that might be better."

He sat on the edge of the bed and pulled his pant leg up as she knelt at his feet. She began from his ankle and wrapped up to just below his knee.

"I don't want to wrap it too tight, but it won't help if it's too loose. You'll have to tell me when it just feels snug. This is the first time I've tried this, so we may have to adjust it some later."

"I would hope you haven't had a lot of practice doing this for a man. I'd like to be the first for you."

Her eyes snapped up to look at his face. Sometimes she didn't know how to interpret what he said. Sometimes he sounded serious, like he truly meant what he was saying, and other times she could easily tell from the tone in his voice that he was joking with her. This was one of those times that she wasn't sure. But his eyes were looking at her with that usual twinkle, so he must just be joking again. He was a confusing man sometimes.

"There, stand up and see if it feels better when you walk."

He rose and walked to the cottage door, then back to her.

"This is the best it's felt since I've been here. Yet again I am amazed by your knowledge and skill, physician." He picked her up and swung her around in a circle. "It's never felt good enough for me to do this before."

She chuckled. "And you shouldn't be doing it now. Put me down. You're twisting your leg too much."

"It doesn't seem so to me, but whatever you say, physician. I'll try to be a good patient, at least until after the training session." He set her down.

◆

A lock of hair had fallen onto Decimus's forehead as he was spinning around. She pushed it back into place and ran her fingers through his hair, trying to get it to stay. This had become his favorite of all her habits. She didn't even say anything about him and Galen having such similar hair. That was even better. Maybe she was beginning to see him as something other than an extra brother in the house. That thought spawned a grin.

Galen stuck his head in the cottage door. "Otto's here."

Decimus donned his sword. "Time to see if I can do as well as the old stallion did."

Baldric had just reached the cottage as Decimus walked out the door. They nodded at each other in passing as Decimus stepped off the porch to go join the boys. Galen and Otto were already practicing some of the moves he'd taught them the day before. Their grins and laughter promised the eager attention of his students on their second day of lessons.

◆

Baldric relaxed on the bench beside Valeria while he watched the swordplay. He was by far the best swordsman in the area, but he had already learned a few things himself watching the Roman. He and Otto could practice the sword skills later, and he would teach his older sons some of the new moves he had learned. It was definitely worth his time to have brought Otto back today.

"Your Roman is moving much better today, like his leg is hardly hurting. I am surprised after seeing how sore he was yesterday."

"I wrapped his leg like Father did for the old stallion. It seems to be working well."

"I remember that stallion, the one that broke his leg trying to reach the mare."

"Don't tell Decimus that you know that story. He thought it was hilarious how it ended, but he told me not to tell it to you."

"Was he afraid I might get ideas about how to deal with him?"

Her head snapped back as her eyebrows rose. "Why, yes. How did you know?"

He chuckled. "Your Roman and I understand each other a great deal better than you realize."

It was a warm afternoon, and the exercise had her Roman and the two boys sweating. He was showing them some things to do when two men were attacking at once, with them being the attackers and him defending. The longer Baldric watched, the more his admiration for the Roman's skill grew.

It was a good thing that he and the Roman would never have to fight. He might have been able to defeat him, but he wasn't sure. They would probably both have ended up badly hurt or dying.

He had seen enough to know the Roman posed no physical danger to Valeria or her family. Emotional danger was another thing.

The way the Roman looked at Valeria—Baldric did not like it. The Roman clearly saw her as a desirable woman, but the attraction was not just physical. He might be in love with her. Valeria was the kind of woman who could make a man fall in love without even trying. She probably would not even realize she had done it.

She treated him like a brother, not a man who stirred her emotions. It needed to stay that way. The Roman was destined to leave soon, and Baldric did not want to see her heart broken like his had been when Elka died.

When Rhoda stepped out the cottage door, Valeria turned toward her. "Rhoda, would you please get a bucket of water and take it to the boys? They need to take a break and cool down."

Rhoda got the bucket and two dippers and skipped off towards the well.

◆

Decimus saw her coming back. "Time for a break, boys."

He slid his sword into its scabbard. Then he rested his hands on the top of his head while he arched his back to stretch and relax it. It had been a good session. The boys were both having a good time and learning fast, and his leg was hardly bothering him at all. He could understand how a stallion might forget he was hurt when his leg was properly wrapped.

Rhoda offered him the first dipper of water, and he took a long, cool drink. Then he poured the rest on his head. When Rhoda offered the two dippers to the boys, they each took a deep drink, then flung the remaining water on each other. Suddenly it turned into a water fight, with each scooping water out of the bucket to fling at the other as fast as they could and Rhoda squealing as she got soaked in the process.

Decimus stood smiling at the horseplay until Galen flung a dipper of water on him. With a laugh, he scooped the bucket out of Rhoda's hands and dumped the remaining contents on Galen's head. Galen stood there sputtering and laughing with everyone else.

◆

One corner of Baldric's mouth pulled up as he watched the boys' antics and Decimus's revenge on Galen. "I can see why you might think he is a friendly farm dog. He keeps the wolf on a tight leash."

"Yes, he does."

Valeria's gaze swung from Baldric to Decimus. It was a good thing Baldric didn't know about the man who attacked her or the two robbers. She didn't want him to keep thinking Decimus was dangerous, even though she knew he was. There was a wolf there, but he would never hurt her or the ones she loved.

Baldric rose and walked over to Decimus.

"It was good training, Roman. I am coming tomorrow to get the mare. Are you planning sword lessons again?"

"I have enough worth teaching for one more day."

"I will bring Otto. After lunch?"

"Yes."

Baldric nodded his head and turned toward Otto. "Time to go."

Otto went to fetch the horses as Baldric and Decimus stood calmly looking at each other. Valeria walked over to join them. Their silence didn't make her nervous like it had the other day. She only wanted to say goodbye to Baldric.

"It's been good having you visit. You're more than welcome to bring another mare if you wish."

Otto handed his father the reins, and Baldric mounted. He smiled down at Valeria. "I intend to. Farewell, Valeria."

"Farewell, Baldric."

As he turned his horse, he looked down at Decimus. "Tomorrow, Roman."

Decimus nodded once in response "Tomorrow."

Baldric and Otto trotted away.

Valeria stood close to Decimus and crossed her arms as a smile spread across her face.

He glanced down at her. "Why are you looking so happy?"

"I think Baldric is starting to like you." He raised one eyebrow.

"No, really. I can tell. He said that you and he understand each other. I don't think he wants to kill you anymore."

The corner of Decimus's mouth rose. "Well, that's progress."

"I didn't tell him the story about the old stallion, but he remembered it. It was funny how he knew you might think it would give him ideas about what to do to you. That's when he said you understood each other."

Decimus rocked with laughter. "Maybe it's not so much progress after all."

Valeria looked up at him. "What's so funny?"

He pushed a loose strand of hair behind her ear. "Your kind heart amazes me sometimes. You really don't understand men."

He'd taken hold of her hand and was gazing down at her with that odd look. Her ears felt warm. There were those butterflies again.

She turned her eyes away, and he released her hand. "I must admit you were right about the wrapping. My leg hardly hurt at all. I've fared much better than the old stallion, but then I didn't lose my head and go after something I shouldn't. So, do we leave my leg wrapped or not?"

"I think we should unwrap it and rewrap it tomorrow. I think I can trust you not to do something to hurt it for the rest of the evening."

He chuckled. "Probably, but you have my permission to tell me to stop if you think I am. I might even do what you tell me."

"I would hope so. I'm only trying to help you heal."

"Ah, Valeria." A smile played on his lips as he pushed the loose strand of hair behind her ear again and drew his thumb along her jaw as he took his hand away. There was an odd warmth in his eyes as he gazed at her. She felt a little warm with him looking at her that way. It was time to change the subject.

"Time for supper. Let's go in."

She was acutely aware of his presence as he walked beside her into the cottage.

As Valeria headed out for her evening of star-gazing, she stopped and turned toward him. A smile and an outstretched hand drew Decimus to her side. She led them to the edge of the porch for the widest view of the sky.

"I want to thank you."

"For what?"

"For being so good to Galen. You were right about training him. I've tried so hard to make up for them having no father or mother, but I'm only their sister. I can never do for Galen what Gaius would have. He needs an older brother for that, not a sister."

The corner of his mouth twitched before he answered.

"Any man would be proud to have him as a son. I enjoy teaching, and Galen's an excellent student."

His answer started with a trace of that edge that she sometimes heard when she told him what to do, but it was gone when he finished. Valeria glanced at his profile and saw a slight smile. Maybe she'd imagined his irritation.

"I'm glad to do anything I can to help your family."

The warmth in those words emboldened her to ask what she longed to know.

"You made Rhoda very happy today reading all of the gospel by Luke to her." Her heart beat a little faster. "What did you think of it?"

"I enjoyed reading it to her. The writer was skillful. His Greek was beautifully crafted, as good as any in my collection."

That wasn't her question. She turned and looked up at his face.

"I was really asking what you thought about the story."

◆

Even in the moonlight, Decimus could see the eagerness in her eyes. How he answered the question obviously mattered a great deal. What answer would make her happy?

"I found it intriguing. I'd like to know more."

Her face lit up, which drew his smile. He'd found exactly the right answer to please her.

"We're fortunate that Gaius was a wealthy man. He was able to buy copies of both the writings of Luke and the gospels written by Jesus's apostles, Matthew and John. They're all in the cupboard. You can read them any time you want to. The one by John is my favorite. He tells us so many of the actual words and thoughts of Jesus. That's the one you should read to learn more."

She bubbled with excitement at the possibility that he would read it. He didn't want to disappoint her and see those bright eyes dim.

"That's what I'll have to do."

Her eyes glowed even brighter when he spoke those words. Now he'd have to read it, or she'd be disappointed. Well, it was a small price to pay to make her so happy. She put such store in the words that her Jesus was supposed to have spoken that reading them himself should help him understand her better. Besides, if the Greek was as well-crafted as that in the writing by Luke, it would be an enjoyable read.

She turned around to look at the stars again. When she shivered, he put his arms around her and drew her against him like he had yesterday.

"Warmer?"

She smiled up at him and laid her arms on top of his. "Yes, thank you."

They stood like that for many minutes, watching the faint stars grow brighter. Holding her close against him stirred his blood and made him feel warmer, too. He would be happy to do this all night if she'd let him.

"Time to go in."

She'd spoken the words much too soon for him. She led him by the hand to the base of the ladder. Before she climbed up, she pushed a stray lock of hair back from his forehead.

"Good night, Decimus. Rest in peace."

"Good night, Valeria." Even in the faint glow from the banked fire, her form as she climbed out of sight was beautiful in his eyes.

Valeria lay in her bed, thanking God that he'd enjoyed reading Luke and was eager to learn more about Jesus. She would be looking for a chance to have him read all of John. Surely then he would understand and be drawn to follow Jesus like she did.

Decimus lay on his bed, thinking about how good it felt to hold her in his arms and how she meant more to him every day. He would like to have her with him for the rest of his life, but he hadn't yet figured out how that would be possible as long as she was a Christian.

Chapter 33

MUTUAL UNDERSTANDING

Decimus was surprised by how good his leg felt when he got up the next morning. For the first time since the ambush, it didn't hurt while he put no weight on it. Valeria's idea about wrapping his leg had been a stroke of genius. He walked over to the table and leaned against it, stretching his legs out as he stood right behind her, waiting for her to turn so he could tell her.

She'd been stirring the porridge. As she stepped back from the fireplace without looking, she tripped over him. He caught her as she lost her balance and swung her away from the fire. Then he continued to hold her as he smiled down at her.

"Careful there. I don't want my beautiful cook getting burned making my breakfast."

◆

Valeria felt the heat sweep across her cheeks and ears as he held her.

"You need to make more noise so I'll know you're there. You're much better off with a good cook like me than a beautiful one."

"It's a good thing I have both." He made no move to release her.

"Let me stir the porridge if you don't want your breakfast burned."

His broad grin and twinkling eyes were too close for comfort. "I like holding you. Some things are worth letting the porridge burn."

She blushed even deeper. He was only teasing, but he still gave her butterflies when he looked at her like that.

"Well, I don't want my own porridge burned, so it's time for you to let me go." She pushed gently against his chest, and he released her.

◆

Rhoda descended from the loft and came over to give them both hugs. Valeria kissed her on the forehead, and Decimus once more wished it was his forehead she was kissing. It would be even better if she was kissing his lips.

Galen came through the door. "I'm starving. Smells really good, Val."

"You're lucky Decimus didn't make me burn it this morning."

Galen sat down. "Even burned sounds good to me right now."

Decimus walked over to his chair as Rhoda carried the steaming bowls from Valeria to the table.

Valeria gave thanks and turned to Decimus. "What are you boys going to be doing this morning?"

Decimus rubbed his cheek. Using the term "boy" to refer to him—that truly bothered him. It meant she was thinking of him like a brother, not a man. It frustrated him that she still felt that way, but he answered her question anyway.

"We're going to bring the logs from the woods."

"How's your leg feeling this morning?"

"You did an excellent job wrapping it yesterday. It feels good. The mare is going to do all the real work, so you don't have to worry."

"I guess that doesn't sound too hard."

His lips twitched as he suppressed the grin. She was fighting the urge to tell him what to do, and this time she stopped herself. He was a man who knew his own abilities. It was good to see she'd finally figured that out.

When they finished eating breakfast, Galen harnessed the mare, and they headed into the woods. One by one, they dragged the logs to the construction site and arranged them ready for assembly. The job was completed well before lunchtime, and Decimus had a chance to rest for a while on the porch.

He lounged on the bench with his legs propped up on the stool and his hands resting on top of his head, watching Valeria work in the garden. He never tired of watching her. It didn't get much better than this, except when he was making her blush while he joked with her or, best of all, when she was standing in his arms while they watched the stars.

◆

Valeria glanced over at the porch to make sure he was resting. He was leaning back with his hands atop his head, but he seemed so different from the tribune she'd watched in the village. The tribune had been dangerous. The man on the porch was her friend.

Such a handsome man, especially when he was so relaxed and smiling at her. In fact, he seemed to be doing that every time she glanced his way. Her cheeks warmed each time. At least he was far enough away that he wouldn't see her blushes. They always brought out the tease in him.

Valeria decided to make lunch a little early so they could be finished before Baldric and Otto arrived.

Galen ate as much as two people again. "Excellent lunch, Val. It really filled me up."

She pushed some stray hair off his forehead.

"I'll take that as a compliment, even though I think you'd be happy with anything as long as there was enough of it."

Decimus smiled that smile that made her feel funny. "It isn't the quantity or even the quality that makes it an excellent lunch. It's the beauty of the cook."

"Then I guess that means I have no chance to serve you an excellent lunch."

"No, it means that lunch will be excellent no matter what you serve."

His voice sounded like he was joking, but his eyes had an intensity that made her feel off balance. A sudden heat spread from her cheeks to her ears, and that turned his teasing smile into a full-blown grin. It was good that Rhoda and Galen started talking so she could focus on their conversation rather than the warmth of his eyes.

Galen finished first. "Otto and Baldric should be here soon. I'm going to watch for them."

Valeria started clearing away the remains of lunch. "After you let Baldric's mare into the corral, come get me."

Galen was halfway out the door, but his backhand wave acknowledged her request.

"Are you ready to prepare me for battle?" Decimus turned in his chair and pulled up his pant leg.

"Not for battle, I hope. Only for teaching." She began to wrap his leg, beginning at his ankle again.

"I'm glad your father taught you what to do with a stallion with a bad leg. It's come in handy for me."

"Yes, but be sure you don't try to do something foolish just because it doesn't hurt as much." As she finished, she looked up at his face to find a smile playing on his lips and an especially warm look in his eyes.

"There. That should do it." She placed her hand on his knee for balance as she stood up. His smile became broader.

Through the window came the sounds of the approaching horses and Galen greeting Otto. Decimus stood and hung his scabbard strap across his chest.

"Time to see if I can get Baldric to like me even more than he already does or at least make him less eager to try to kill me."

She slapped his arm.

"You're making fun of me, but just wait. You'll see that I was right about him starting to like you."

He chuckled as he stepped out the door.

Galen and Otto were already sparring. Baldric was still mounted, watching them with a relaxed smile. Her Roman walked up to him and rested his hand on the horse's neck.

"It's another good day for a lesson. Before you leave, we should give them a show."

Baldric looked down at him. He was not sure why the Roman wanted to spar with him, but he was willing to test their relative skill in a friendly contest.

"A good idea, Roman. I am sure they will learn something of value from it."

The Roman stepped back from the horse, drew his sword, and saluted Baldric with it. "All right, boys. Time to begin."

Baldric tied his horse to the corral rail and joined Valeria on the porch bench to watch and maybe learn. The Roman was a natural-born teacher. The boys were totally focused on the mixture of explanation, demonstration, and practice that was his teaching style. Otto was already a much better swordsman than he had been only two days ago. The Roman had been right when he said he had at least three days of things worth teaching.

When he had taught the boys the last move for the day, he turned toward the porch and saluted with his sword. Baldric stepped off the porch and strode over to him.

He drew his sword from its scabbard. "Time to show them how grown men do it."

Again, her Roman saluted him with his sword and assumed a fighting stance. "You attack, I'll defend. Then we'll switch."

Baldric's first strike was lightning swift, but the Roman was ready and parried it easily. With a speed and ferocity that drew gasps from the boys, Baldric struck again and again, each time being skillfully blocked or deflected by the Roman's sword. The sound of metal on metal echoed from the buildings as the Roman was repeatedly forced backward under the force of his blows.

"Switch."

Her Roman began his attack. Baldric was equally skillful in blocking the rain of blows from his sword, but he knew the Roman was holding back. He wasn't using some of the deadlier moves that he had seen him show the boys. Instead of forcing Baldric backward, he was forcing him to turn in a circle, letting the boys see the thrust and parry from different angles. His admiration for the Roman's skill grew still more. It was a very good thing they would not be fighting for real.

◆

Valeria's heart beat faster and faster as she watched. It didn't look like a game to her. One of them was going to get badly hurt or killed if they continued. Finally, she couldn't bear to watch any longer. She stepped from the porch and approached the fighting men.

"Please! Stop now. Before someone gets hurt."

Decimus backed off and wiped some sweat off his forehead.

"We're only sparring. We're both good enough that this is perfectly safe." He prepared to attack again.

She stepped close and placed her hand on his sword arm. He looked down at her pleading eyes.

"Please stop."

His eyes softened as he smiled down at her, and he stood up straight. He placed his free hand on hers as he slid his sword into its scabbard.

"That's it." He turned to the boys. "The show is over for now."

Decimus offered his arm to Baldric. "The best match I've had in a long time. It's a good thing we won't have to do this for real."

Baldric met his gaze and clasped his arm. "My thoughts as well, Roman."

Rhoda carried the bucket of water with two dippers to them. Each took a deep drink, then poured the remainder on their heads. Decimus placed his hand on Rhoda's hair and smiled at her as he put the dipper back into the bucket.

◆

Baldric saw the glowing smile he got in return. The Roman was like a brother to Galen, and Valeria...well, she treated him like a second brother, too. Too bad this Roman had ever come. There would be three sorrowful hearts left behind when he returned to his legion.

Baldric hadn't missed how Decimus looked at Valeria when she pleaded with him to stop and how readily he responded to her request. The wolf was, indeed, on a very short leash, and she held the end of it, whether she knew it or not.

He had no doubt the Roman was in love with her. She didn't seem to realize it, and she didn't seem to be in love with him...yet. She still treated him like an older Galen, but how much longer could that last? There would be at least one deeply wounded heart when the Roman had to leave. That departure needed to come soon enough that Valeria wasn't deeply hurt as well.

"Otto, get the horses." He fixed his gaze on her Roman, but there was no hostility in it. "It has been an interesting three days, Roman. You have trained my son well."

"I think both boys are better from having trained together." The Roman's mouth curved into a satisfied smile.

The last three days had given Baldric some respect for him, and the Roman appeared to appreciate hearing it. He should. Baldric's respect wasn't bestowed without good reason.

He mounted, then looked down at the pair of them.

"Farewell, Valeria. I will be returning with the fourth mare."

"Farewell, Baldric. I hope it's soon. I always enjoy your company."

He looked down at Decimus without even a scowl. "Roman."

Her Roman dipped his head. "Baldric."

◆

As the pair rode away, Decimus turned toward Valeria. "I hope you still have some of that liniment. I asked you to prepare me for battle, but you only wrapped my leg for teaching. It wasn't quite enough."

Her lips tightened as Valeria shook her head. "I knew it wasn't a good idea to be fighting like that."

"It was necessary. I told you I wanted to make him less eager to try to kill me. I needed to fight him in practice so he wouldn't want to fight me for real. He is good. Very good. Good enough that if we fought, he might be able to kill me if I held anything back. I would have to kill him first, and I don't want to hurt anyone who's important to you. Now he knows I could kill him, and we'll never have to fight."

She stared at him with huge eyes and one hand over her mouth. He pushed a strand of hair behind her ear.

"Don't look at me like that. He fought me for the same reason. He wanted me to know he was good enough to kill me if I hurt you. He and I really do understand each other."

She gazed into his intense eyes that were totally focused on her own. He was right. These two men who were so important to her really were a lot alike.

"Well, now that's settled, I guess you can work on trying to get him to like you more." She patted his arm. "Let's go find that liniment."

Decimus's leg felt much better after the liniment and a good massage. Valeria certainly knew how to make a man feel better when his muscles were hurting. Being with her was enough to make a man feel better in every way that mattered.

He stretched out on his bed and watched her prepare their supper. She was humming as she stirred the stew. She glanced over at him and smiled, but he couldn't tell if it was a smile for a brother or a man.

When she stepped to the cottage door to call Galen and Rhoda, he rose and took his seat at the table. Rhoda skipped into the house, looking over her shoulder at Galen and giggling. Galen entered and sat down by Decimus.

"That match between you and Baldric was amazing. Can we practice some every day until I get that good?"

"We can practice, but it takes years to get that good. You and Otto have both made a good start. You should keep working on your skills with each other."

Galen grinned at the prospect. Decimus glanced at Valeria. Her teeth bit her lip as she looked at Galen.

"Just make sure you both remember that swords are meant for defense and not for starting trouble." He looked at her again, and she smiled her approval of his reminder.

After the clean-up following supper, the family gathered for prayers. Rhoda snuggled against his chest as he began to read what Galen selected. It was something from Rhoda's favorite, so he recognized it. "But I say to you who hear, love your enemies, do good to those who hate you, bless those who curse you, pray for those who abuse you. To one who strikes you on the cheek, offer the other also, and from one who takes away your cloak do not withhold your tunic either. Give to everyone who begs from you, and from one who takes away your goods do not demand them back. And as you wish that others would do to you, do so to them."

He glanced at Valeria. She wasn't going to have to worry about Galen misusing his sword training.

Valeria smiled her warmest smile at him and began their prayers. "Thank You, Father..." Rhoda curled up in his lap again as they prayed. Once more he felt the peacefulness he couldn't explain, and he was content.

As Valeria stood at the cottage door, she held out her hand. He walked to her side, and she led him out to the edge for the best view. He stepped close behind her and drew her against him. He hadn't waited until she seemed to be getting cold, and she seemed perfectly happy to snuggle against him right away. She rested her arms on his while she absent-mindedly played with the hair on his forearm. They stood in companionable silence for several minutes.

"Valeria, I've been wondering. You're Germanic, not Roman, but you have a Roman name."

"When I decided to follow Jesus, I was born again as a new person. I asked Gaius to give me a new name. He and Priscilla chose Valeria because it means strong. They thought it described me much better than the name my parents gave me."

"What was that?"

"Alba."

"But Alba means white. That suits you, too. You're so bright and pure."

She chuckled. "You're thinking like a Roman. Not everything is Latin. My parents were Germanic. Alba means elf. I didn't want to be called Elf anymore when I left my old religion and the old ways."

"Why did they call you elf?"

"My mother chose it. She wanted a son, and she was terribly disappointed when I was born. She never treated me like she wanted me. I was a tiny baby, but she had a very hard time giving birth. I was the only baby she ever had. I think she always blamed me for that. Having many children, especially sons, is a measure of worth for women here. If Father blamed me, he never let me know. Working with the horses made us close. I was both son and daughter to him."

Decimus nodded. "My mother had no interest in raising her children, and my father and I were never close when I was growing up."

"I'm sorry. I've been blessed with two good fathers, and Priscilla was everything a mother should be. I've tried to mother Galen and Rhoda like she did."

He rested his cheek on the top of her head.

"You're a wonderful mother."

She flexed her shoulders and settled back against his chest. The heat from her body radiated toward his heart. He held her a little closer.

What if you were the mother of my own children? It was a satisfying thought.

"I've seen how you are with Rhoda and Galen. You'll be a wonderful father someday." The corner of his mouth rose. Father, not brother.

After several more minutes watching the stars while wrapped in his arms, she stepped away from him and took his hand. "Time to go in."

As was now her habit, she held his hand until she reached the ladder.

"Good night, Decimus. Rest in peace."

"Good night, Valeria."

He watched her disappear into the loft before lying down.

Valeria lay in her bed, thanking God that he had blessed her with Gaius and Priscilla as her second parents so they would lead her to Jesus. If only Decimus would be open to her leading him to Jesus, too.

◆

Decimus lay on his bed, thinking about what a wonderful mother she would be and wondering whether he would be the one who would father her children someday. Just how would a tribune marry a Christian? The marriage ceremonies he knew all involved worship of the Roman gods. She wouldn't do that. Well, he'd figure it out later if he decided to ask her and she accepted his proposal. There must be some way.

Chapter 34

A Different Kind of Danger

Decimus had slept well, and he hadn't awakened as early as usual. When he finally did wake up, Galen was standing by Valeria, watching her stir the porridge.

"I think I'm going to need an extra bowl today, Val. We're going to be working really hard on the stable, so I'd better eat a big breakfast."

She pushed back the hair that always seemed to fall onto Galen's forehead.

"You always need an extra bowl no matter how hard you're working. It makes the cook feel truly appreciated."

Decimus stretched and walked over to the fireplace to join them. "A beautiful cook should always know she's appreciated."

"I wouldn't know about that, but a good cook does like to know when someone likes her food."

◆

Valeria pushed back the stray hair from Decimus's forehead, too. When she did, his eyes changed from joking to intense. The half-smile that tugged at the corner of his mouth made her cheeks feel warm. She spun and stirred the porridge, and she heard him walk away from her to take his seat at the table.

After breakfast, Valeria stood in the doorway and watched Decimus limp along the far side of the corral with his hand on Galen's shoulder. She couldn't hear his words, but they pulled a peal of laughter from Galen.

Today he would be teaching Galen the next steps in building a log stable. They had all the logs cut to length and laid out parallel to the final wall positions. The first round of logs was in place to make the start of the four walls with a door in one of them. She could already see what the shape of the stable would be.

She carried her sewing to the porch bench. She tried to focus on her needle, but her gaze kept drifting to the tall man across the corral. Decimus had spoken the truth when he said he knew exactly what was required to build the stable, and he was teaching Galen so many things. He was so patient as he explained how to figure out where the notches needed to be and then showed Galen how to shape them with the hand ax so the logs would lock together just right.

Watching him work was pure pleasure. He had his back to her, and he'd just finished chopping the notch into a log. Now he was standing with his fists on his hips watching Galen make the next notch. Except for his injured leg, he was so strong. He made it all look so easy. It was fascinating how his arm muscles bulged when he was using the ax or moving the logs into place. Even when he stood still, like now, she could see how muscled he was under the shirt that fit his shoulders snuggly.

He must have felt her gaze. When he began turning to look back at her, she looked down at the sewing in her lap. She blushed at the thought of him discovering she'd been watching him and thinking about how strong and handsome he was.

When she looked up again, Gunther had entered the farmyard, clutching his arm. He was not one of her favorite people. He was well known for his drunken revelry, his bragging, and his total lack of respect for women. Still, he looked like he was in pain, and she would never refuse to help someone.

He walked over to the edge of the porch. "I need help with my arm."

Pain twisted his mouth as he cradled his right arm with his left. He might be a notorious liar, but this time he was speaking the truth.

"I see that. Come with me." She led him into the cottage. "Sit at the table and let me look at it."

"Must I take my shirt off? I'm not sure I can."

Her nose twitched at the thought. "You don't need to. I can see your shoulder is dislocated."

She didn't have the strength to pull his arm out far enough for the bone to slide back into the socket, but Galen should be strong enough.

She stepped to the cottage door and called out to Rhoda. "Would you please get Galen? I need his help right away."

◆

Decimus and Galen had just finished lifting a log into place when Rhoda skipped over to them.

"Galen, Valeria needs your help in the cottage right now."

Galen shrugged at Decimus and trotted toward the cottage.

Since they were taking a break, Decimus decided to go to the cottage as well. Nothing could be more refreshing than some conversation with Valeria.

He froze in the doorway. A man sat on the chair while Valeria stood beside him. Galen stood next to her, getting ready to pull on the man's arm. The way he was cradling it, Decimus could tell the shoulder was dislocated.

The man took one look at Decimus, and his lip twisted into a sneer. "Well, Valeria, so you have a man living with you. That's something no one would have expected, but I guess you're no different from all the women I've had. This will cause quite a stir in the village."

"He's only my patient, Gunther. Nothing more. He'll be leaving as soon as he heals enough."

Gunther's chuckle had a cruel edge. "No one is going to believe that. I certainly don't. He doesn't look hurt to me."

Decimus limped a few steps into the room and stopped. He crossed his arms and stood with his gaze fixed on the leering face.

He knew such men. This one would enjoy spreading the lie in the village. Men like him didn't like virtuous women, and he would enjoy dragging Valeria down.

Gunther's eyes darted away, unable to meet Decimus's steady gaze as he stood there in silence.

He limped over beside Gunther. "Let me fix his shoulder. I know exactly what needs to be done."

He seized the arm and began to move it slowly as he fixed an icy stare on the man's sneering face. Gunther drew in his breath with a hiss at the sharp pain that movement caused.

"Do you know Baldric?" Decimus edged his words with ice.

Gunther nodded, scrunching up his face when the pain increased as Decimus moved the arm farther.

"And you know Baldric was a good friend of Valeria's father, that he looks on her almost as a daughter?"

Gunther blinked faster and swallowed hard. Decimus moved the arm farther. Beads of sweat popped out on Gunther's forehead as he gritted his teeth.

"Do you know what he would do to a man who spread lies and ruined the reputation of one of his daughters?" Gunther flinched and blanched. Decimus moved the arm farther still. "It would not surprise me if he killed him."

Gunther's whole body began to tremble. Both pain and fear brought tears to his eyes.

"I would never say anything to anyone to even suggest that Valeria is not a fine woman in every way."

Decimus kept increasing the pull on Gunther's arm.

"Stop! I'll never say anything."

"I'm sure you won't, since Baldric would hear of it and hunt you down." Decimus put his lips next to Gunther's ear and whispered, "And if he doesn't, I will."

As he spoke the last word, he pulled hard on Gunther's arm and popped the bone back into its socket. Gunther screamed in pain.

Decimus stepped back. He crossed his arms and locked dagger-eyes on Gunther. "Now pay the physician what you owe her."

◆

Gunther fumbled with his purse and began to open it.

"There's no charge." Valeria's eyes flipped from one man to the other. Gunther needed to get out of there fast before Decimus did anything else to him.

Decimus uncrossed his arms as if he was going to take a step toward Gunther.

"Go, and remember what I told you."

"I'll never say anything!" Gunther scurried out of the cottage before Decimus could move toward him.

Valeria's lips tightened and her eyebrows lowered as she faced Decimus with her hands on her hips.

"You deliberately hurt him."

"No more than was necessary to make my point. It always hurts to pop a shoulder back in place. I really have done this many times. I just did it a little slower than usual."

"You didn't have to do that. No one would have believed him if he told them those things about me."

He stepped close and looked down at her.

"People are always eager to believe the worst about a good person. Even more so when she's beautiful as well as kind." He pushed a strand of hair behind her ear before stroking her cheek once with the back of his fingers. "I couldn't let him hurt you when I could easily prevent it."

He spoke gently. His eyes that had been so hard as he manhandled Gunther had softened as well. She couldn't stay mad at him.

"Well, I guess I should thank you for protecting me, even when I don't agree with how you did it."

◆

Baldric was just riding into the farmyard when he saw Gunther running toward him. Baldric's mouth and brows pulled down when he saw the fear on his face. He moved his horse to block Gunther's path and glared at him.

"What are you doing here?"

Gunther held his hands up in front of him. "I only came to get my shoulder fixed. I would never do or say anything to hurt her. You have my word."

"Make sure you don't." Baldric had no idea what that was about, but he moved his horse to let Gunther pass. He would find out from Valeria.

He tied his horse to the corral railing. Galen and Decimus were walking out the door as he reached the porch. Valeria was right behind them.

Decimus tipped his head. "Baldric."

"Roman." He scowled. "What has happened here?"

"I took the liberty of making Gunther a promise for you. I was certain you would have told him yourself that you would kill him if he tried to damage Valeria's reputation."

Baldric raised one eyebrow and the scowl vanished, replaced by something that was closer to a smile. "I would have. We understand each other well, Roman."

Decimus nodded once, then turned to Galen. "Let's go see how much more we can get done before lunch. We'll leave Valeria to enjoy Baldric's visit."

As they walked toward the stable, Decimus tousled Galen's hair and rested his hand on his shoulder.

Baldric lowered himself onto the bench, and Valeria sat beside him.

"Your wolf has become very protective of you."

"I know. He's become like a member of the family. He's the big brother Galen never had before."

"Being so protective only makes him dangerous in a different way."

Valeria's head tilted. "What do you mean? How can that be?"

"You think he is becoming part of your family, another brother like Galen. He is not. He is a man who looks at you as a woman, not a sister. Someone is going to get hurt because of it."

Her eyes widened before she shook her head. "I don't think that's possible. He often jokes about me being a beautiful woman, but I'm sure he doesn't mean it. He jokes with Galen and Rhoda all the time, too. It's just his way."

Baldric shook his head slightly. She was determined not to see what was so plain to him. The Roman loved her, but he was destined to return to his legion soon. He needed to heal and leave before she committed her heart to him. The safest thing was for her to keep seeing him as another brother.

"You know him much better than I do." He shrugged to make her think he was agreeing with her, but his disagreement could not have been more complete. He would say no more that might open her eyes to the Roman's real thoughts.

As Baldric watched her Roman giving instructions to Galen about the next part of their task, a better idea for protecting Valeria struck.

"Your Roman is a good trainer of swordsmen. Does he know what he is doing with the stable for your future horses?"

"Very much so. He's teaching Galen many things I never knew."

"Then I will have Otto come to learn from him again."

Valeria's eyes brightened. "I know Galen would enjoy that, and I'm sure it would be a big help. Decimus has a habit of doing more than he ought to with his leg not completely healed. Some tasks require two people, and he won't let me help with the things he shouldn't be doing yet."

Baldric fought a wry smile. Of course he wouldn't. A man like either of them would rather risk injury than let a woman do his work. She really didn't understand men.

He stood to go. "I will speak with your Roman about Otto. I expect we will be back tomorrow."

He mounted and rode over where Decimus and Galen were working on the stable wall. He sat relaxed, leaning on his horse's neck, as he gazed at Decimus until the Roman turned toward him with an inquiring look.

"It looks like you know what you are doing, Roman."

"I've built things before. It's just a matter of thinking about what to do before you do it."

Decimus's head tilted as he straightened and squared his shoulders. Where was this conversation going? Baldric never spoke just to hear himself speaking.

"I would like Otto to come and learn. You might teach this as well as you do sword fighting."

Galen's eyes brightened at the thought of his best friend joining them. "I like that idea. It would be fun."

Decimus masked his amazement at the request. Surely Baldric knew as much or more than he did about building. He didn't need any help training his son. But it would be a huge help to have another person working with them, especially with the heavy lifting that made his leg hurt, even with Valeria wrapping it. With both Galen and Otto working, he wouldn't have to do as much of that.

He focused on Baldric's face, trying to understand why he might be making the offer of help. Probably because Valeria had said how much she worried about him hurting himself.

"We'd be glad of the help."

"Then he will be here tomorrow. When should he come?"

"We start first thing after breakfast."

Baldric nodded. As he turned his horse to leave, he looked back at Decimus. "Tomorrow, Roman."

"Tomorrow, Baldric."

Baldric wore a satisfied smile that the Roman couldn't see as he rode away. If Otto helped and the Roman didn't delay his healing with a new injury, he would be leaving soon. He could be gone within two weeks. The sooner the better if Valeria was to be spared from losing a man she loved. For the moment, this was the only thing he could do to keep her Roman from hurting her. It had better be enough.

Decimus was seated by Galen at the table, more than ready for supper. He rubbed the back of his neck before flexing his shoulders to loosen the tired muscles. They'd worked hard, and the walls were now above their knees.

He'd found it necessary to stop in the early afternoon. His leg hurt from all the lifting, but Valeria had wrapped it well before they began. It wasn't as bad as it might have been. The liniment and her massage had relieved most of the soreness. Otto would be there to help tomorrow, and having an extra worker would lessen the stress on his leg considerably. He was glad Baldric had volunteered him, whatever his motive.

As he watched Valeria fill the bowls by the fireplace, contentment filled him. There was no place he would rather be than sitting at this table with this family, watching the kindest woman in the world make his supper. He even enjoyed their prayer time when his reading made her face so radiant.

Rhoda set his bowl in front of him. He stirred it slowly as the steam rose and the savory smell teased his nostrils. Life at the moment was good. He was in no hurry to return to the legion and leave these people behind.

He especially didn't want to leave the woman who fired his heart and imagination, and he still hadn't figured out how it would be possible to take her with him if she wanted to come. He didn't want to think about that, so he turned to focus his attention on Galen teasing Rhoda while he waited for Valeria to start supper with her prayer.

No sounds came from the loft. Valeria stood at the cottage door, waiting for Decimus to join her for their nightly star gazing. Her welcoming smile as she took his hand to lead him to the edge of the porch filled Decimus with desire to hold her close and kiss her, but she wasn't ready for that...yet.

He still wasn't sure whether she saw him more as a brother or a man, but she was responding to him as a man more than she had been. It was getting easier to make her blush. Sometimes all it took was looking at her a certain way to bring the pink to her cheeks.

He wrapped his arms around her and drew her close again. She leaned back into his chest and sighed contentedly. She played with the hair on his arms as she gazed into the distance. Those lightly moving fingers sent barely suppressed shivers of desire coursing through him.

A falling star streaked across the sky, and Valeria pointed at it. "I like that one. It's always surprising where they start and where they disappear. I like trying to guess about the next one."

She wiggled a little to adjust her shoulders against his chest.

He rested his chin on the top of her head. "The unexpected things in life are often the best."

How good she felt in his arms. Ironic that an ambush had led to a night like this. He pushed back the thought about how few might be left. He'd almost fully recovered. He'd have to leave her soon, at least for a while.

"We certainly never expected someone like you. Galen and Rhoda both love having you here."

"What about you?"

"Of course I do. I'm so thankful God let me find you alive. You've become my dearest friend. I'm surprised you even asked."

Dearest friend. It wasn't the description he'd hoped she'd use. "You're very special to me, too."

She sighed contentedly. After too short a time, she stepped away from him and took his hand. "Time to go in."

At the foot of the ladder, she pushed the stray hair back from his forehead. "Good night, Decimus. Rest in peace."

She began to climb. "Good night, Valeria." The radiant smile she gave him in response was the perfect ending to his day.

Valeria lay in her bed, thanking God for this wonderful man who had become her best friend and asking God to open his heart to receive Jesus.

♦

Decimus lay on his bed, wondering when she'd be ready to tell him her best friend had become the man she loved. He tried not to think about what her being a Christian would mean for the future of their love when it was time for him to leave.

Chapter 35

COMPETITION

The next morning, Valeria tousled Galen's hair as she walked past him to the fireplace. He was beaming. "Today's going to be good with Otto here. Maybe we'll have time for some sparring. How long do you think it's going to take us to finish the stable?"

Decimus cupped his chin before drawing his fingers down his cheek. "With three of us working, I would expect two more days on the wood construction and maybe two more for the thatching."

"That fast? Then I'm really glad Otto is coming."

Valeria refilled Decimus's bowl for the first time and Galen's for the second. "I am, too."

Her gaze caught Decimus's as she returned to the table and placed one bowl in front of her brother. "I still think lifting all those logs can't be good for a leg that's not completely healed."

As she placed Decimus's bowl in front of him, he caught her hand.

"When a man has a beautiful physician who knows what to do with liniment and massage, it's amazing what he can do even with a bad leg. Is there anything you can't heal, Valeria?"

A crooked smile played on his lips, and his eyes had that intense look that got to her every time. Her cheeks blazed pink, and he grinned at his success. He was worse than Galen when it came to being a hopeless tease.

"We both know very well it's God who does the healing, not me. You still need to be careful not to do too much."

She tried to pull her hand away from him, but he held it for a few seconds before he let her go, grinning at her the whole time.

After breakfast, Valeria carried her strips of cloth to Decimus, who sat on the edge of his bed. When she knelt at his feet, he rested his hands on his knees and leaned toward her.

"Wrap your stallion well before he goes to work."

Valeria made the first loop around his ankle and pulled it snug.

"I will, but I expect you to be more sensible than the old stallion." She kept wrapping. "If this starts loosening while you're working, I want you to tell me right away so I can fix it."

She looked up at his face to see if he was listening to her instructions. A crooked smile played on his lips and his eyes held that warmth that was so unsettling. Her cheeks felt warm. Why did the blood always rush to her cheeks when he looked at her like that? Teasing, teasing man. She looked quickly back down at his leg and finished the wrapping.

"There. That should do it for you."

He stood up and offered his hand to help her to her feet.

"Thank you, Valeria. There can't be many men like me with their own physician who is both skilled and beautiful." He pushed a loose strand of hair behind her ear and stroked her cheek twice with his thumb before lowering his arm.

"Since you don't even have one, you're probably right."

Having him to joke with made the morning seem brighter, even if he did make her blush so much. How she would miss that when he returned to his legion.

He paused as he walked out the door, turning around to smile at her before he went to join Galen at the stable. That smile gave her butterflies, too.

Decimus and Galen had just finished notching a log and were preparing to lift it into place when Baldric rode into the farmyard. He had Otto and another young man in tow.

The troop rode over to the stable, where Otto dismounted and turned his horse into the corral. Baldric and the other man remained mounted.

"I see breakfast ends early here. Tomorrow Otto will come sooner to learn from you, Roman."

"I don't know how much he'll learn that you haven't already taught him, but we'll be glad to have his help."

Decimus scanned the second man. He was tall and muscular with a mane of blond hair brushing his shoulders and a neatly trimmed beard. He looked enough like Baldric that it was a safe bet he was Baldric's son. He was about Valeria's age.

Baldric turned his horse, and the two of them headed toward the cottage.

Decimus's brows dipped. Baldric had come to visit with Valeria. Having his older son along was disturbing. What was the big German up to?

◆

Valeria was finishing the clean-up in the cottage when Rhoda popped her head in the door. "Baldric and Adolf are coming."

"Really? I knew Otto was coming to help build the stable, but I didn't expect so much company so early in the day."

Valeria walked out onto the porch to meet them. "Baldric, Adolf, it's good to see you both."

Adolf dismounted, but his father didn't. "It's good to see you, too, Valeria. It's been a long time since we talked, and Father thought this would be a very good day for the three of us to come."

He seemed unsure of what to say next, but Valeria ended the uncomfortable silence. They'd played together often as children, and they'd been good friends when her father was alive.

"It has been a long time. Let's sit for a while, and you can tell me what you've been doing."

She settled on the bench and motioned for him to take the stool. Adolf looked at his father, who indicated with a movement of his head that he should sit on the bench next to her instead. He sat where his father wanted.

Adolf chose one of her favorites as his first topic. "I've been gone a lot taking some of our horses to the border towns to sell, and I've seen some amazing things..."

◆

Once he got started, Adolf loved to talk, so Baldric rode back over by the stable to watch the builders work.

He lounged with one hand resting on his horse's rump as he watched her Roman directing the boys. He hadn't built anything since

Otto grew big enough to help, so all the techniques the Roman was teaching were new to his son. Just like the sword lessons, the Roman explained, then demonstrated, and finally corrected as needed as Otto tried to do something himself. Even though Baldric's goal was to make sure the Roman left sooner rather than later, it was good for Otto to join the work crew. He would know how to build something himself when the Roman was through.

Baldric shifted his gaze from the construction to the pair on the porch. The corner of his mouth curved up. Valeria was leaning toward Adolf as they talked together. A peal of laughter reached Baldric as she rocked back from his son. A promising sign that their childhood friendship might rekindle into courtship.

Twenty was the usual age of marriage in Germania, and they were both of an age to be choosing their marriage partner. Adolf was a good son, and Valeria would be the perfect wife for him. He should have had Adolf start courting her sooner instead of having him gone so much selling the family horses.

He shifted his gaze to the Roman and caught him watching the pair as well. Her Roman did not look happy. Good. He should not be thinking Valeria might be his alone. With any luck, spending time with Adolf would divert her attention from the Roman before she gave her heart to him.

A satisfied smile tugged at the corner of Baldric's mouth. His plan might be working.

◆

Decimus found his attention divided between the work on the stable and Adolf sitting on the porch with Valeria. He couldn't hear what they were saying, but he could see the conversation was animated at times. Occasionally he heard her laugh at something Adolf had just said.

He felt Baldric's eyes upon him, and he turned his own back on the rising wall. He was not going to give the big German the satisfaction of seeing how much Adolf's flirtation bothered him. Adolf was handsome, and Valeria obviously enjoyed his company. Baldric would encourage her to consider him as her future husband.

He didn't want any young man in her life except him.

The walls of the stable were almost chest high on Decimus, so it was getting hard for the boys to lift the logs high enough. He suppressed the urge to grin.

"The wall is getting high enough that we need extra help. Otto, go ask your brother to come help us lift the logs into place. He looks strong and almost as tall as me."

Otto trotted off toward the cottage.

◆

Valeria had just finished laughing at one of Adolf's funny stories when Otto reached them.

"Adolf, Decimus needs you to come help us. We need someone taller than me and Galen to get the logs up in place."

Adolf grinned. "So the Roman needs my help?" He glanced at Valeria. "Well, if he isn't strong enough to do the work alone, I guess I'll just have to help him. I'll be right there."

He took Valeria's hand as he stood up. "Looks like I'm needed. We can talk more later." He squared his shoulders and strode toward the stable.

Valeria watched him go. She'd enjoyed their conversation. He was as much fun to talk with as he'd been when they were children. He was growing into a very nice man.

Adolf reached the stable, and she watched Decimus explain what they were going to do. The contrast between the two men was striking. Adolf was still so young. Decimus was a grown man in every way that mattered.

Valeria fingered her chin. Funny that she hadn't noticed that before.

She'd been thinking of Decimus like he was another brother, but she'd been viewing him all wrong. He had a playful sense of humor that made him seem like an older Galen, but he was an intelligent man who appreciated poetry and history and silence while contemplating the stars. He never tried to show off like boys who are almost men do, even though he was handsome, smart, and strong.

He'd become her dearest friend, and he enjoyed their friendship, too. He was constantly joking about her beauty. All those playful exchanges were such fun, even when he made her blush more than she wanted to. But he didn't mean any of it.

If he really meant the compliments, it would be a problem because he wasn't a Christian...at least not yet. He was showing real interest in Jesus's teaching, but he still wasn't a believer, although she prayed he would be before he left. She would never give her heart to a man who didn't follow the Way, but she could certainly enjoy his company as her dear friend until he finally had to leave.

Her smile dimmed as she watched Decimus and Adolf hoist a log into place. He was almost healed. He would soon be returning to his legion. It would be hard to say goodbye when that time came. He'd become a member of her family, and Galen and Rhoda were going to miss him terribly, too.

◆

With Decimus's crew of four, the walls went up quickly. He had the boys cutting notches in the logs still on the ground while he and Adolf notched the logs already built into the wall where the boys were too short. All four of them lifted each log into place.

Adolf was a good worker. Even though Decimus's original goal had only been to thwart his pursuit of Valeria, the German's help made a big difference. At the rate they were working, the walls would be completed by early afternoon, and they would be starting on the roof before the end of the day.

Decimus turned to see what Valeria was doing. Her eyes met his, even across the farmyard, and she lifted her hand in a quick wave.

She wasn't watching Adolf at all. His mouth curved up in a satisfied smile.

◆

Baldric didn't try to suppress his smile, either. The Roman had outmaneuvered him. He had watched Decimus watching Valeria and Adolf. The Roman had tried to hide it, but Baldric could see it truly bothered him that she was enjoying Adolf's company. Enlisting Adolf's help was a clever way to break up their conversation without seeming jealous.

Since Adolf had been drafted into the work crew, Baldric rode over to the cottage and joined Valeria where she sat alone on the porch.

"Your Roman has given me many reasons to visit you lately. I am glad."

A warm smile lit her eyes. "It really has been nice having you and your sons visit so often. I'm glad Adolf came with you this morning. It's been a long time since we talked. He's such a nice young man. He still makes me laugh like when we were children."

That was not the response Baldric wanted. She should have found Adolf's first attempt at courtship exciting, not just entertaining.

"He is a good son. He will make a good husband."

◆

Valeria took a deep breath. A husband for her? She didn't want to encourage that expectation.

"I'm sure he will someday. If he was a follower of the Way, I would consider him a good husband myself when he finishes growing up."

She stood. "I have many people to make lunch for today. I'd better start. The work crew is going to be hungry."

Chapter 36

SOMETHING IN COMMON

There were too many people to fit in the cottage for lunch, so Valeria and Rhoda turned it into a picnic under the trees. Galen and Otto ate like only teenage boys can, devouring their first servings of bread and cheese quickly and coming back for seconds and thirds. They decided to practice their sword fighting after they finished, so they moved over by the cattle shed where they wouldn't disturb the adults.

There was very little conversation among the men. Baldric never said much, so his silence was to be expected. The only common interest that Decimus and Adolf had was Valeria, and they certainly weren't going to discuss her with each other.

When it appeared that everyone had finished eating, Decimus rose.

"Adolf, ready to get back to work? We've almost finished the walls. Then we can start framing the roof. I'd appreciate your help with that. The boys are willing workers, but it's a job that needs the skill and strength of grown men."

◆

Baldric's lips twitched. The request had been phrased in a way that Adolf couldn't refuse. The Roman had once more made sure that Adolf would be helping him and not visiting with Valeria. He had seen through the attempt to introduce a rival and had turned him into an assistant instead.

Since Valeria had already told Baldric she wasn't interested in Adolf's courtship yet, he had no objection to his son helping to build her stable. She would remember his effort later when her interest in him might change.

It was late afternoon as Adolf and her Roman put the last part of the roof framing in place. All that remained was to thatch it, and that wouldn't require the help of his sons.

Baldric rose from the porch bench where he had been keeping Valeria company as she sewed. "Time for us to go."

"Thank you for bringing Otto and Adolf to help with the stable. I thought it was too much for Decimus and Galen to do, but it almost seemed easy with so many hands working on it."

Baldric rested his hand on her shoulder. "After your Roman leaves, Adolf will be glad to help with anything that needs a man's strength and skill."

Valeria rose as well and placed her hand on his arm. "You and your family are such good friends to us, and I can't tell you how much I appreciate that."

He patted her hand. "And you can count on us remaining so."

◆

Decimus stood close to Valeria as she waved at Baldric and his sons as they rode away.

"It was so nice of Baldric to bring his sons to help you and Galen. I can't believe how fast you all got the stable up."

He glanced down at her lovely profile. What did she really think of Adolf? He couldn't ask too directly about Baldric's handsome son. She shouldn't think he was jealous.

"He brought Otto to help us, but he brought Adolf for you. I'm surprised he was able to tear himself away from such a pretty woman and spend his day working with us instead."

"Since I'm not a pretty woman, it wasn't as hard as you might think. He and I were friends when we were children. He always made me laugh then, and he still loves to tell funny stories. He and his father are so different in that, but he'll grow into a good man, too."

A satisfied smile tugged at Decimus's lips. She saw Adolf as an entertaining childhood friend who was not yet a man, so he wasn't a rival for her affection...at least not yet.

But how close was he to capturing her heart? There were promising signs. A raised eyebrow, a crooked smile...almost anything could make her blush. He'd even caught her watching him like a woman watches her man.

She kept treating his compliments as a joke, and he wasn't sure how to change that. It was hard to be patient, but speaking his true feelings too soon carried the risk of frightening her away. Still, it might not be long now.

Decimus cupped his chin and rubbed his cheek. He couldn't wait too much longer. Soon his leg would be healed enough for the ride back to the legion, and anything between them had to be decided before he left. He still hadn't worked out how to deal with him being a tribune and her being a Christian, but there must be some way.

He would figure it out in time.

It had been a long day of hard work on the stable, so Decimus shared Galen's ravenous appetite at supper. After Valeria gave thanks, her stew was devoured by both. The silence while everyone ate gave Decimus time to think.

It was just like Baldric to bring his son to court Valeria right in front of him. The big German never made any effort to conceal his dislike or his concern that Decimus might do something that would hurt her. Getting Adolf to work on the stable had kept him away from her, at least for today. Adolf did seem to be a good man. She obviously enjoyed his company, so there was a real possibility that Baldric's plan might succeed, given enough time.

His eyes kept drifting to Valeria as he ate. She was a remarkable woman—so kind, so clever, so capable, so pretty. Everything a man would want in a wife. Baldric saw it, he saw it, Adolf probably saw it, too.

Valeria watched her brother shoveling stew into his mouth. "I'll have to make a bigger pot if you two are going to be working so hard every day."

Her head swiveled toward Decimus, and her breath caught.

An earnest look darkened his brown eyes, like a smoldering fire trying to burn free. She blushed deeply and looked away. The way he was looking at her stirred up the butterflies again. The sensation was not unpleasant, but it always made her feel off balance. Why did he have that effect on her? No one else ever had.

The table had been cleared, and they gathered for prayers. Rhoda spread the cloth and opened the codex in front of Decimus. She'd chosen a reading from her favorite again.

Decimus began as soon as she snuggled into his lap. "Why do you call me 'Lord, Lord,' and not do what I tell you? Everyone who comes to me and hears my words and does them, I will show you what he is like: he is like a man building a house, who dug deep and laid the foundation on the rock. And when a flood arose, the stream broke against that house and could not shake it, because it had been well built. But the one who hears and does not do them is like a man who built a house on the ground without a foundation. When the stream broke against it, immediately it fell, and the ruin of that house was great."

He glanced down at the sweet girl with her head resting against his chest. She'd picked a good reading for the day they were building the stable. He'd built enough to know how important the foundation was. Her Jesus was right that what a man did, not just what he said, built the foundation of his life.

He looked up at Valeria when he finished. His reading always evoked those glowing eyes and that beautiful smile. That was the best part of reading aloud, whether he agreed with what was written or not.

"Father, we thank You..." Valeria began their prayers as he held Rhoda in his arms. An aura of peace enveloped the small group at the table. How good it would feel to stay together like this forever, with Valeria's family being his family as well. As he watched her praying with her eyes closed, there was a glow about her that filled his heart with love for her. If only she would love him back.

Valeria stood with her hand on the doorpost, waiting for him to come to her side so they could watch the stars together. She looked back over her shoulder as she walked out ahead of him. His eyes held that look that gave her butterflies again. Having him nearby like this made her feel so satisfied, like everything was just as it ought to be.

She stopped at the edge of the porch where the sky stretched out above them. He wrapped his arms around her waist and stepped up against her, holding her close to keep her warm. She loved him holding her like that. It made watching the stars so cozy, so peaceful. It was even better than when she used to watch them with Gaius.

"Thank you for teaching Galen so many things. You've been like a father to him. I can't believe how much you all did on the stable today. I never dreamed you could almost build the whole thing in two days."

Decimus's heart skipped a beat. Father, not brother. Finally, she was thinking of him as a man. She certainly made him feel like one as she rested against his chest, letting his arms envelop her with an intimacy he'd scarcely thought possible a few days ago.

"We still have the thatching to do, but that should only take a day or so."

Her soft sigh lifted, then lowered his arms. "When you're working all day, I miss your company on the porch."

"I'll take more breaks tomorrow. Working on the stable can't compete with sitting next to a pretty woman."

"I'm glad that you're willing to settle for me instead." She turned her head to flash a smile at him.

It took concentration to keep the fire from his eyes. She'd be looking for laughing eyes that meant he was joking like she was. Except he wasn't joking, and it was getting harder to pretend he was.

They stood together in silence, listening to the breeze in the trees, watching the stars. He couldn't remember ever being more content. She was almost ready to hear his true feelings for her. Not tonight, maybe, but soon. Before he had to leave.

Finally, she turned in his arms and pushed a strand of hair back off his forehead. "Time to go in."

She led him by the hand to the ladder. Halfway up, she paused to smile down at him. "Good night, Decimus. Rest in peace."

"Good night, Valeria." He didn't move from the foot of the ladder until she disappeared into the loft.

Valeria lay in her bed, thanking God that Decimus enjoyed being part of her family and praying that he would soon decide to follow Jesus, like they did. She wanted to know that he was no longer lost before he had to leave.

Decimus lay on his bed, reveling in the thought that she now saw him as a man and eager for the opportunity to tell her that he loved her. Time was getting short, but the way she was looking at him now, he was almost certain that she would tell him she felt the same. Then they could plan a future together.

Chapter 37

KEEPING A PROMISE

Decimus found himself in an exceptionally good mood when he awoke the next morning. He opened his eyes to see Valeria cooking at the fireplace. There was no better way to begin his morning or to end his day than by watching her.

The bed creaked as he shifted his weight. She turned, and her smile lit up the cottage. Maybe today would be the day he would tell her his true feelings. He'd know the right time when it came.

He swung his legs off the bed and stretched as he stood up. A pleasant surprise—he wasn't tired and his leg was barely sore even though he'd worked hard all day yesterday. Almost back to the way he'd been before the ambush.

He settled into the chair to watch her stir the porridge.

Rhoda came bouncing in from gathering eggs. After she placed the basket on the shelf, she skipped over to the table, pausing to hug his arm before she went to Valeria to help pass out the bowls of porridge.

Galen paused to wipe his feet. "Smells really good this morning, Val. I'm starved, so I hope you made plenty." He sat and turned toward Decimus. "Do you think we can finish the stable today?"

"We can finish most of the thatching, but there might be some left for tomorrow."

As Valeria placed his bowl in front of him, Decimus trapped her hand. "Nothing makes food taste better than having it delivered by a beautiful woman."

◆

The smile that gave Valeria butterflies played at the corners of his mouth. She couldn't stop the heat that radiated up from her neck to her cheeks and ears. Why did he make her blush so much even though she didn't want to?

"I'm sorry you have to rely on my skill as a cook to make the food taste better. We still haven't been able to find a beautiful woman to serve you."

"That's your opinion, but certainly not mine."

There was that look in his eyes again. Her cheeks flamed even more.

"It's not a good idea to disagree with the cook. You never know what she might put in your food."

"That's something I'm willing to risk." He squeezed her hand and finally let go of it.

As they ate breakfast, she felt him watching her even when she wasn't looking at him. Try as hard as she might, she couldn't keep from blushing when she felt his eyes.

❖

As Decimus and Galen walked toward the stable after breakfast, Decimus jumped when the punch hit his upper arm. He turned to find Galen fighting to keep a straight face.

Her brother bumped him with his shoulder. "You sure know how to make Val blush. You're much better at it than me, but you have an advantage. She really likes you."

Decimus fought a smile himself. Galen had noticed. Proof that he wasn't misreading her. "Probably not as much as I like her. She's a very special woman."

A huge grin split Galen's face. "I would sure like to have you as a brother, but are you ready to pass her test?"

Decimus grinned back. "If I'm not now, I soon will be."

Galen punched his shoulder as his grin got even bigger. Decimus tousled Galen's hair in response.

Galen punched him again. "There's no better life than following Jesus."

Decimus's eyebrows scrunched. Where did that come from? Valeria and Rhoda were always saying something about their god, but it wasn't something Galen usually did, even though he believed in the Christian god, too.

Before he could respond, Otto emerged from the trees.

"Otto's here! I didn't know he was coming to help with the thatching." Galen trotted off to greet his friend.

With three people working, they made rapid progress. By lunchtime, they'd finished almost three quarters of the roof. The cheese and bread that Valeria served her work crew under the trees was enough to fill up even two ravenous teenage boys.

Galen had just swallowed his last bite of cheese when he started grinning at Decimus.

"I need to work in the high meadow this afternoon, but Otto can help me. Why don't you stay and keep Val company?" His grin got bigger. "I'm sure she won't mind."

Decimus nodded his approval of the plan as he worked to stifle a grin himself.

Valeria tousled Galen's hair. "That's a good idea." She cast a quick glance at Decimus. "I still think climbing that steep trail isn't good for a leg that's not completely healed."

The boys headed toward the meadow trail, leaving Decimus to help her gather up what was left from lunch.

As they walked into the cottage, she gave Decimus one of those smiles that filled her eyes with sparkles. A teasing smile, even though she had no intention of it teasing him. Not that way, anyway. How could an innocent smile make a man's blood run so hot? No flirtatious Roman courtesan could hold a candle to this pure German maiden who'd captured his heart without even trying.

"I'm glad we'll have your company this afternoon. Rhoda and I are going to cut up carrots to dry for our winter stores. Maybe you could read to help the work go faster?"

Read to her. That wasn't exactly what Decimus had in mind, but he was willing. Nothing made her happier than him reading her religious codices, and nothing made her eyes more brilliant. Watching her would be enough to make it a good afternoon.

Rhoda walked into the cottage with a basket of freshly washed carrots. Her eyebrows popped up, then she beamed.

"Decimus is going to read? Let's have him read your favorite. He already read me mine."

Valeria went to the cupboard and took out the copy of the gospel written by John. He sat down on the bed after she handed it to him.

He'd told her he'd read it that night on the porch. This would be as good a way as any to fulfill that promise.

"In the beginning was the Word, and the Word was with God, and the Word was God. He was in the beginning with God. All things were made through him, and without him was not any thing made that was made. In him was life, and the life was the light of men..."

The more he read, the more he was bothered by what he was reading. This was very different from the well-crafted history he read for Rhoda. There were so many images and allusions that he found confusing and even disturbing. When he read about Nicodemus coming at night, he agreed with the Jewish leader that it was impossible for a grown man to be born a second time.

There were all the statements by their Jesus about being dead unless you believed in him and about how you couldn't die if you did. He'd never seen a man who couldn't die.

When he got to the part about not being able to have life unless you ate his flesh and drank his blood, that shocked him. No wonder a lot of his followers left when he said that. It sounded like cannibalism to him, but it was impossible for more than a handful of people to eat a single person, so he couldn't mean exactly what he said. He must have meant something different, but what?

The writing style was different from that of Luke, but one thing was the same. Both claimed the death of one man could be a sacrifice that would save everyone who believed in him from punishment for everything they'd done wrong. How could the death of one man do that?

If he was a god like he claimed, maybe it could, but no god would willingly let himself be tortured to death like that. Decimus had watched many men die on Roman crosses. No one would ever choose that deliberately. It made no sense at all.

Every time he glanced at her, he found that radiant smile and those glowing eyes. She loved this codex, and she loved having him read it to her. But why?

There must be some meaning that escaped him, or she wouldn't love it like she did. Maybe he'd get her to explain it to him later.

Valeria and Rhoda had finished cutting and were spreading the slices on some cloth-covered frames before taking them out to dry in the sun. He stopped reading and rose to help them carry the frames outside.

He'd read about a third of the codex, and that was already more than he wanted.

Valeria stood beside him with her eyes still glowing. "Can you see now why this is my favorite?"

He wanted to give her the answer she wanted, but he couldn't. He couldn't see why at all.

"It's very different from the one by Luke. I need you to explain several parts to me. I'm sure I'll understand then."

A joyous smile lit her face.

He'd found what she wanted to hear, but something pricked at Decimus's conscience. He hadn't actually lied, but he hadn't told the full truth, either. He hadn't enjoyed her favorite like he had Rhoda's history. He didn't want to think about any of the disturbing parts. It left him feeling strangely off balance, but he wasn't quite sure why. He was sure he didn't like that feeling.

He didn't want her to explain it to him, but she wouldn't forget that he'd said he did. It was equally certain she wouldn't be content until he finished reading the entire codex.

He suppressed a sigh. He didn't want to read the rest, but maybe it would help him understand her more, even if he couldn't understand her god.

Chapter 38

REVELATION

Supper, as usual, was filled with relaxed conversation and laughter. Then it was Valeria's turn to choose the reading. Rhoda opened the cupboard and took out the codex by John.

Valeria shook her head. "Tonight, I want Matthew, precious."

That drew a smile from Decimus. Luke's beautifully written history was his favorite, but Matthew was a good alternative. Anything but John. He'd read more than enough of John today, even with it exciting her most radiant smiles.

When Decimus stepped onto the porch behind Valeria, his heart rate ramped up. He willed it down. To move too soon, to speak too soon was never a wise maneuver, in war or love. It was going to be another perfect evening on the porch—cool enough that he would have to hold her to keep her warm and no clouds so she would want to watch the stars for a long time.

A good omen for his plan to finally tell her how he felt about her. At the right moment, that is, but that moment was so close. His many days of patience were about to gain him the prize.

From the way she looked at him now, he was certain she saw him as a man. A man who stirred her blood like she stirred his. Every blush confirmed it.

At the edge of the porch, with her head resting against his chest and his arms wrapped snuggly around her, he'd never felt so alive. Her every breath was in perfect synchrony with his own. Again, he had to will his heart to slow. Too soon for her to sense his excitement as she snuggled against his chest with contentment and absolute trust.

He rested his cheek against her hair. "You're quiet tonight. Any reason?"

"No, today was almost perfect. It was wonderful having you read while we worked." She wiggled her shoulders as she nestled against his chest. "And watching the stars like this is the perfect ending to a lovely day."

He shifted his arms to hold her a little closer. No resistance. She was welcoming his affection, just as he'd hoped. Her fingertips traced small circles on his arms. Again, he willed his heart to slow down.

They watched the last trace of color disappear in the west as the fainter stars gradually appeared in the eastern sky. The moon had risen, bathing them in silver and casting shadows. Finally, she stepped away from him to go in. As always, she took his hand, but this time he didn't move when she started to walk.

The time to reveal his feelings had come.

She turned to face him. "Ready to go in?

"Not yet. There's something I've been wanting to say to you." He laid his hand on her cheek and traced her scar with his thumb. "You think this scar keeps you from being beautiful. It doesn't. It only makes your face more interesting. The scars that can take away beauty are on the inside, not the ones you can see. There's nothing but beauty and kindness inside you."

He traced the scar again. "You are the most beautiful woman in the world to me."

◆

Valeria focused on his eyes as he spoke. They blazed with an intensity she'd never seen before. Blood rushed to her cheeks, and her eyes jerked away from his. She said nothing. She had no idea what to say. She'd never expected him to speak such words except as a joke. They sounded as if he truly meant them.

So many times he'd told her she was beautiful, but he never seemed serious. Well, almost never. There had been that one time the morning his sight returned, but then he'd returned to joking with her right away, so she thought she'd misunderstood him.

◆

Decimus took her silence as a sign to continue. He cradled her face in both his hands and tilted it upward. Stepping very close, he lowered his lips to hers as he slid his arms around her and drew her against him. She kissed him back, her arms wrapping around him and her body melting into his embrace. He pulled her even closer, and his kiss became deeper, more impassioned. His hands caressed her back. He felt her tremble as she responded to his arms, his hands, his lips. Everything he'd desired for so long was finally within his reach.

Without warning, she stiffened and pulled back. Fear filled her eyes. He slid his hands from her back to her arms, but he didn't let go. She was still trembling, but it was no longer from pleasurable excitement. She placed her hands on his chest and pushed herself farther away from him. The fear in her eyes shifted toward panic.

Impossible! How could he have so misjudged what her response would be?

Every blush said she was ready and wanting to hear what he just told her. He'd been certain she wanted him to draw her into his arms, to caress her, to kiss her. How could that have frightened her?

He silently cursed himself for moving too soon, too fast.

Her lips trembled. "Please stop. We mustn't. You've become my dearest friend. We can't go any farther than that. This...this just can't be."

It took all his willpower to push down his desire for her, but he stepped back and took both her hands so she wouldn't turn and run from him. "I'll do anything you want, whenever you want me to. Nothing more. I'm sorry...I thought you wanted me to..."

◆

Valeria had teetered at the edge of the precipice and barely pulled back. She'd never imagined how it would feel to be in his arms, to feel his hands caressing her back as his lips played with hers. It was exquisite. She wanted him as much as he wanted her, but it was impossible. It must be.

The panic was gone, but waves of sadness surged through her. He could never understand the anguish ripping her heart as she faced the truth. She'd fallen in love with this man who didn't follow the Way. She hadn't even realized she was falling until that kiss, when it was too late. How could she have let her heart be so unguarded?

How could she have failed to see he was falling in love? Baldric had warned her, but she hadn't believed him. The special looks in his eyes, the warmth of his smiles, the way he touched her face. She should have seen they revealed feelings that were much more than friendship.

All that joking about her being a beautiful woman—he'd never meant it as a joke at all.

What if his love made him ask her to marry him? How was she to keep from hurting him terribly when she had to reject him because he didn't follow the Way? What if her rejection made him no longer want to learn about Jesus?

His face blurred. A tear escaped to trickle down her cheek.

He stopped it with his fingertip and swept it away. "Let's just sit on the bench and watch the stars for a while. Don't go in because I thought more than friendship was possible. I thought you felt the same as I do. I never meant to hurt you. I never will."

She let him lead her to the bench. As they sat there, a few tears fell onto her lap, making small circles of wetness in the cloth of her dress.

She longed to tell him she loved him...but she couldn't. She shouldn't speak those words. She must not let him know. He might ask her to marry him, and she could never marry a man who didn't love Jesus even more than he loved her.

◆

Decimus longed to take her into his arms again, to comfort her from whatever he'd done that brought her such sadness, but that would only make things worse. He didn't know what to say, so he said nothing as he held her hand in both of his so she wouldn't stand and walk away.

They sat in silence for a long time.

Finally, she spoke. "We'll forget what happened tonight. We can be as we were before. You mean too much to me for this to...change how I feel about you. It's getting late, and I know you and Galen have work planned for tomorrow. Time to get some rest."

She held his hand and led him through the door. She released it as she stood by the ladder to the loft. "Good night, Decimus. Rest in peace."

As she climbed, she looked down at him. She was fighting against tears, but a few escaped as she gazed into his eyes.

He wasn't doing much better. As skilled as he was at concealing his emotions, he still couldn't mask his regret and longing.

"Good night."

He had hurt the woman he loved. His night would be neither good nor peaceful.

230

Valeria lay in her bed, her peaceful world shattered by her love for a pagan, pouring her heart out to God.

◆

Decimus lay on his bed, tormented by the thought that he'd hurt her, afraid that he'd ruined any chance he had of getting her to love him, and agonizing over how he'd failed so completely to understand the woman he loved.

Chapter 39

The Way We Were

The pale moonlight cast vague shadows in the loft. It had been several hours since Valeria climbed the ladder, and she was no closer to sleep than when she first closed her eyes.

She lay on her back, forcing herself to take slow, even breaths. The last thing she wanted was for Rhoda to awaken and ask what was wrong.

She'd known her share of loss and grief. First Father had died; then Gaius and Priscilla were murdered. She'd learned to push past the pain with Jesus's help until it didn't hurt so much anymore.

But this...it was so different. She loved a Roman who didn't love God, and Decimus loved her, too. But what if that love must end in nothing? She'd promised her Lord she'd only marry a man who loved Him like she did. What if Decimus never decided to follow the Way? What if she must lose him, too?

God, is there hope for us? I know he's pagan now, but he's happy to read Your word. He's content to listen to our prayers. I know he's starting to hear You calling him. Can't You open his heart faster so he'll decide to love You and want to stay here with us?

He'd been missing for so long. Everyone he knew must think he's dead. He wouldn't have to go back to his legion.

Will he stay if I ask him? Can we be man and wife? But what if he won't follow You and he asks me to marry him? I can't follow him into his Roman world. Galen and Rhoda and I would be killed for belonging to You.

A tear trickled across Valeria's temple and into her ear.

I can't let him know I love him. Not until he loves You enough to turn from Rome and stay.

Two more tears joined the first. *I love You, Lord. More than anything...even more than him.*

She swept the tear tracks away with her fingertips.

But I love him, too, and I don't want to lose him.

Memories of the pain on Decimus's face haunted her. What if her rejection of his affection ended his interest in Jesus? What if he thought she didn't care? He needed to know he was still her dearest friend, even if she had to hide her love. Then his heart might stay open to hearing and coming to Jesus. Everything depended on that.

Please, Lord. Tell me what I must do.

Sleep eluded Decimus, and he was still wide awake as the darkness began turning to gray.

What would the day hold? Would she avoid him? Would she turn her face away from him, refuse to look at him like she had before when he frightened her? Would she act as if nothing had happened, as she said she wanted before she left him last night? Was that possible, even for the most forgiving heart he'd ever known?

Someone was moving in the loft. Galen was always the first one up, but he usually didn't awaken until sunrise. Why would he be up so early today?

Decimus didn't want to talk to anyone, but Galen could never resist speaking some cheery greeting. He turned and faced the wall so he could pretend to be asleep when Galen headed out to do chores.

He froze when the rung creaked. A slight rustle, then the soft sound of footsteps approaching his bed. A hand rested on his upper arm.

"Decimus? Are you awake?"

He rolled onto his back so he could look at her. She was only a silhouette blocking the dim gray light coming through the window.

She drew a deep breath before speaking. "I'm sorry about last night. I didn't mean to hurt you like that."

Her voice wrapped around him in the near-darkness, just as it had when he was blind. He couldn't believe what he was hearing. She was apologizing to him when he'd been the only one to blame!

She sat on the edge of the bed and took his hand in hers. Her thumb traced arcs on the back of it. Each stroke erased more of his fear that he'd lost her.

"All those times you said I was beautiful—I thought you were only teasing, so you surprised me. I'm sorry if I made you think I wanted you to kiss me. I should have said something quicker. Then you wouldn't have misunderstood."

She pushed a strand of hair back from his forehead. "Tomorrow we'll be just as we were before that kiss."

It was so good to feel the tingle that trailed her fingers again, even if she didn't mean anything by it.

"Whatever you want, Valeria, that's what we'll be."

She patted his arm as she rose. It was too soon, but any time with her so close was more than he'd expected.

He could scarcely believe what just happened. With a few words and gentle touches, she'd given him hope and another chance. All the tension of the night drained out of him as he watched her climb back into the loft.

Tomorrow might be a good day. He closed his eyes and drifted off to sleep.

Decimus overslept after lying awake for most of the night. Valeria was already cooking breakfast when he finally opened his eyes. Anticipation and apprehension battled within him. Today would be the test of whether she really could forgive him for kissing her before she was ready.

She turned from the fireplace. "Good morning, Decimus."

Her smile seemed almost like the smile she usually greeted him with in the morning. Almost, but not quite.

He rose from the bed and headed toward his usual place at the table. As he limped toward her, their eyes met, and she turned to stir the porridge. His stomach tightened. She turned more quickly than she usually did, as if she was reluctant to keep her gaze fixed upon him.

Galen came in from his morning chores as Rhoda was climbing down from the loft. She skipped over to give Decimus a hug before she went to Valeria to get the hot bowls of porridge.

"Does that ever smell good, Val." Galen sat down next to Decimus. "So what are we doing today?"

"We should finish thatching the roof this morning. Then you can pick something."

Decimus stirred his porridge, waiting for Valeria to join them and ask the blessing. He didn't look at her.

It wasn't going to be the same, and he didn't want to see that mirrored in her eyes.

◆

Valeria had intended to act as if last night never happened, but she wasn't succeeding. Every time she looked at Decimus, the memory of his arms around her, his lips touching hers, drove her heart rate up. She'd promised him they'd be just like they'd been before the kiss. She needed to keep that promise, no matter how hard it might be.

As she walked past him, she rested her hand on his shoulder. He turned his face toward her with uncertainty in his eyes. She smiled down at him and pushed a strand of hair back from his forehead. When she touched his face, the uncertainty changed to relief.

She moved past him then and took her place on the bench with Rhoda sitting between the them. After she asked the blessing, they all began to eat.

◆

After breakfast, Decimus and Galen resumed their work thatching the stable. There was only a small area left to cover, and they only needed a couple of hours to finish it. They were almost finished when Baldric and Otto emerged from the trees with the fourth mare. Galen climbed down and trotted over to talk with Otto while Baldric let the mare into the corral with Astro.

Decimus climbed down from the stable roof and leaned on the top rail of the corral as he watched Astro nuzzle the new mare.

Baldric rode over and dismounted. He moved into place beside Decimus. His hands gripped the rail as he watched the horses, too.

Decimus's shoulders tensed. Why such unexpected attention? Private conversation with Baldric usually involved a promise of death if he hurt her.

Silence stretched out between them until Decimus started the conversation.

"You have many beautiful horses, Baldric. It's generous of you to give her one."

"I told you when I found you here that she is like a daughter to me." He turned and faced Decimus directly. "Because of that, I must ask something of you."

Decimus snapped his gaze on Baldric's face. Baldric never asked directly for anything. His requests always took the form of a statement of fact or a command.

There was a grim set to Baldric's mouth but no fire in his eyes.

"You must return to your legion soon, and you cannot take her with you. Do not do anything that would leave her with a wounded heart."

Without speaking, Decimus nodded. Had he already done just that?

Baldric held Decimus's gaze for many long seconds before nodding once in return.

"Tell Valeria I will see her in two days."

◆

Baldric remounted and rode to where Otto was talking with Galen. "Stay and help finish the roof."

He trotted across the farmyard and entered the trees. As he rode deeper into the woods, his stomach tightened. The Roman had not said anything in response to his request. Always before, he had insisted he would never do anything to hurt her. Did he say nothing because he thought he might be about to? Or maybe he already had.

Had he awakened her interest in him as a man instead of a brother? Did he think she was in love with him?

There was no future for them. There was a decree against the Christians in the province; a Roman soldier could never make a Christian his wife. Would the Roman take his request to heart and leave before it was too late?

The three of them finished the thatch work just before lunch. That was only because Otto had helped. Decimus had been distracted watching Valeria and Rhoda in the garden as he tied each bundle of thatch to the thin crossmembers of the roof.

Valeria had another basketful of carrots to prepare for drying, and he was not one to waste an opportune window.

He didn't like her codex by John, but he needed to do something that she would especially enjoy. Nothing would please her more than him volunteering to read from her favorite while they worked. Galen could have Otto help him. Right now, he wanted to spend as much time with Valeria as possible.

As they finished lunch in the cottage, Decimus seized his opportunity.

"I saw you pick all those carrots from the rooftop. Would you like me to read while you work on them?"

Valeria's beaming face was exactly what he expected.

"That would be wonderful. You were just getting to some of my favorite parts when we stopped yesterday."

Galen grinned at Decimus and triggered a smile in return. "Sounds like a good idea to me, too. Otto and I can go work in the high meadow."

Decimus knew the value of an ally, and he had one in Galen. It might seem like an odd way to court a woman, but her brother knew nothing would please Valeria more.

The afternoon found Valeria and Rhoda cutting carrots and Decimus reading from the writings of John again. Some parts of it made more sense than what he'd read yesterday.

He liked the story about Jesus healing the man born blind. It would be impossible not to follow the man who had given him his sight, no matter what the rulers told him. Blindness was something he understood too well, and although he wasn't convinced, Valeria was certain that his sight returning was a miracle from her god.

Raising a man from the dead after four days was beyond what he found normally believable, but if her Jesus really was a god, it could be possible.

The Jewish Sanhedrin did exactly what he expected. Any ruler would be worried when Jesus entered Jerusalem with the crowd hailing him as king. Nothing would draw a Roman reaction faster. But with such a response from the people, why did Jesus immediately begin telling his followers that he had come to Jerusalem deliberately to be killed?

He was suddenly aware that Rhoda was standing in front of him.

"Ready to help us take the frames out?"

Valeria beamed at him. "If you want to stay and finish reading, Rhoda and I can take them all. You're almost to the best part."

Decimus stared at her. The best part? How could the crucifixion of a man anyone cared for be the best part?

He blinked to break the stare and masked his amazement. "I'll help take them out. If it's the best part, I don't want to hurry through it."

Valeria's glowing eyes confirmed the wisdom of his choice of words. He was in no hurry to finish her book, but reading it had proven less disturbing than he expected. He'd be willing to read the final pages to her later.

After supper, prayer time followed what had become the regular pattern. Decimus read what Galen had selected, and he sat quietly holding Rhoda during the prayers. But something was missing. That sense of peacefulness and contentment was gone, and he didn't know what he could do to get it back.

Galen and Rhoda were quiet in the loft by the time Valeria finished banking the coals. As she headed to the porch, she paused in the doorway. Then she stepped back into the cottage and took her shawl from the peg where it always hung. She smiled at him before she stepped out into the darkness, but she didn't hold out her hand and wait for him.

Decimus's shoulders sagged. She'd taken her shawl. There would be no reason to put his arm around her. But maybe that was best since he wouldn't be faced with the temptation to draw her close and kiss her like he did last night.

He followed her onto the porch. She was already sitting on the bench, gazing into the distance. She'd made sure there'd be no temptation by sitting instead of standing at the edge.

He sat beside her, and she smiled at him as she took his right hand and placed it in her lap. She laced the fingers of her left hand with his while she traced one of the veins on the back of his hand with her right forefinger.

He watched her fingers as she continued to caress his hand with her fingertips and the side of her thumb. It felt so good, but he wished she'd stop. It made it harder for him to resist taking her into his arms. It made him think about how much he was missing holding her close with her hands resting on his arms, her fingers playing with his hair.

"Look. There's a falling star." He turned his eyes to the sky and tried to focus his attention on something other than her only sitting beside him instead of standing in his arms.

If only he could put his arm around her shoulder and draw her closer, but she wasn't ready for him to do that...not yet. Tonight, he had to settle for having her hold his hand. He'd been afraid last night that even this would no longer be possible. Time to be patient and wait for her feelings of friendship to grow into love. There was still a little time left before he had to leave.

They sat in silence, watching the stars for many minutes. Finally, she stood.

"Time to go in."

He stood as well, torn between relief that she still wanted him to spend this quiet time with her and regret that he was no longer holding her in his arms while she did.

He followed her to the foot of the ladder. She paused and turned to face him.

"Thank you for letting us go back to the way we were. I couldn't bear to lose you as my dearest friend."

"I want us to be whatever you want."

She began to climb. Halfway up she paused again. "Good night, Decimus. Rest in peace."

"Good night, Valeria." He watched her climb into the loft and disappear.

Valeria lay in her bed, thanking God that she'd been able to show Decimus how important he was to her without revealing her love. If only he would choose to follow Jesus so she wouldn't have to hide her love any longer!

◆

Decimus lay on his bed, wondering what he could possibly do to make her want his love as well as his friendship.

As he fretted about their future, his whole body jerked. A wrenching thought tore through him. They might have no future, even if she decided she wanted one. In his contentment living with her family and with his eagerness to win her love, he'd lost perspective.

He wasn't free to follow his own desires. He was a Roman tribune on track to become quaestor, praetor, and provincial governor, like his father before him. He had a duty to family and Rome that he must fulfill.

Baldric understood the problem; that was why he'd asked him not to hurt her.

Would he be forced to make a choice between duty and love?

Could he climb to the political summit without marrying noble Roman blood with the right political connections? Not many had done it before him. But there were some, and he was already excelling without a political marriage.

Surely he could figure out some way to satisfy both. He could make sure there was a future for them, if only she would tell him she loved him.

Chapter 40

ALMOST

When Galen came back from his chores the next morning, Decimus was sitting at the table, smiling at Valeria. He turned as Galen closed the door.

"What do you say, Galen? Don't you think we have the most beautiful cook who ever made a delicious breakfast for her men?"

"I guess so. I know it's delicious, and I'll let you decide if she's the most beautiful." He grinned at them both.

Valeria slapped her brother on the shoulder as he walked past her to the table. "You're no help. Don't encourage him."

She handed two bowls to Rhoda and carried two over herself. When she placed one in front of Decimus, he captured her hand.

"I don't need much encouragement."

She blushed when he flashed her the teasing smile before letting her go.

As Galen scraped the last of his third serving of porridge out of his bowl, he turned to Decimus. "I still have work to do in the high meadow. Want to come help today?"

"Sounds like a good idea. I've been curious about what it looks like up there for a long time."

◆

Valeria didn't think it was a good idea at all. "It's a hard climb."

"It can't be any harder than building a stable, and that wasn't a problem."

The twitch at the corner of his mouth betrayed his irritation. Stubborn man—he ought to know she was only watching out for his own good.

Then his face softened. "But I will let you wrap my leg. That works well for this stallion."

The smile he flashed at her made her blush. The twinkle in his eyes said he was joking, but the warmth in them revealed the love behind the joke. He needed to decide to follow Jesus soon. It was getting harder to keep from showing how she felt.

"Then I'd better do it now so Galen can get a whole day's work out of you."

The heat of his gaze warmed her neck as she knelt in front of him with the wrappings. "That should do for now. We can check it when you come down for lunch."

"Thank you, physician. I don't know what I'd do without your services."

He followed Galen toward the door, but he paused to grin at her before he stepped outside.

As lunchtime approached, Valeria kept her eye on the meadow trail. She needed to see for herself whether the climb had been too much for his leg. He would tell her it was fine even if it wasn't.

She set her sewing aside as Decimus came into view. He favored his leg, but he and Galen were talking and laughing as they walked toward the porch. Probably no harm done.

"Hey, Val! Hope you made us a big lunch. I'm starving again!" Galen grinned at her as he washed his hands before going in.

"Don't worry. I know how to feed my hungry men." She patted Galen's arm and went in ahead of them.

Decimus followed her to the table. "Your men appreciate all your effort."

As she placed the bread and cheese in front of him, he placed his hand on hers. She didn't pull it away as she smiled at him. "I know."

After a good day's work in the high meadow, one thing was clear to Decimus. His leg didn't hurt any more climbing up and down the hill than it did when he was just sitting. As much as he hated to admit it, his leg was no longer a good excuse for staying. But was Astro a reason?

He drifted over to the corral and leaned on the rail. Valeria's deal with Baldric was fulfilled; his stallion had earned her mare. Astro had just finished with the fourth mare and for the moment was ignoring her. He'd performed as if his shoulder had never been cut.

If Astro was ready to carry him back to the capital, it was his duty to return. Every time he moved his scroll box, its weight proclaimed the hidden legion gold. In his head, he knew he was duty-bound to return that gold and resume his post as tribune as soon as possible. In his heart, he wasn't sure how he'd ever be able to leave this place and these people, especially the woman who'd so completely captured his heart.

His leg would be strong enough for the long ride in a few days. Was Astro ready to carry his weight?

He got Astro's bridle from the cattle shed. One whistle, and the big stallion sauntered over. Astro bumped Decimus with his head, and he rubbed the star blaze. He entered the gate and stroked the stallion's neck before he slipped the bit into his mouth and pulled the bridle into place.

His leg wasn't quite strong enough for mounting Astro from the ground, so he led him out of the corral and over to the stump. Astro shook his head and looked expectantly at him as he stepped up on the stump, seized a handful of mane, and swung his right leg across the stallion's back. He settled into position and turned Astro's head away from the corral as he nudged him into a walk.

Everything seemed normal as he walked Astro to the edge of the trees. There Decimus turned and urged him into a trot. The horse's gait was unbalanced as he favored his left shoulder. Decimus reined in and dismounted.

As he led Astro back into the corral, relief flooded through him. The stallion wasn't healed enough to ride.

He patted Astro's neck before removing the bit from his mouth. "Not yet, boy. Looks like you get a few more days with Rhoda spoiling you."

I get a few more days, too.

He wanted to be certain she loved him before he left. He didn't want to leave her at all, but it was impossible to stay with his duty to return the legion's gold.

These Christians had shown him a kind of life that he'd never imagined and that he really wanted, and for a while he'd forgotten who he was and what duty required of him. He had to take the gold back to Mogontiacum as soon as possible, but then he would find some way to reconcile duty and love.

Valeria glanced out the cottage door as Decimus was leading Astro to the stump. A knot formed in her stomach as she watched him mount and ride to the edge of the woods. Where was he going? Was he leaving now? When he turned and tried to trot back, the knot relaxed. He was only testing Astro's recovery, and clearly the stallion wasn't healed enough for them to leave.

As Decimus limped back into the cattle shed to put the bridle away, her stomach clenched again. He couldn't leave yet, but he was thinking about it.

Her shoulders drooped. He was a Roman tribune. He'd always planned to return to his legion.

Then she straightened. It couldn't be God's plan for him to leave right now. He was learning about Jesus, but he hadn't decided to follow him yet. Surely that must be the reason God had her find him and rescue him. Surely he couldn't leave before that happened. When it did, then she could tell him she loved him, and maybe he would stay. Maybe he would choose his love for her over his devotion to Rome.

Decimus ran his hand through his hair as he waited for their prayer time to start. Rhoda went to the cupboard and brought back the codex by Luke. She grinned at him as she climbed into his lap. "Is there something you'd like to read tonight? I'll find it for you."

His eyebrow rose at the question. Odd, but he actually had something he wanted to read.

"I'd like that story you read when I first came, that one about the man who was robbed and the Samaritan."

Rhoda beamed. "That's one of my favorites, too."

As she turned to the right spot in the codex, Decimus glanced at Valeria. Her beaming smile and sparkling eyes proclaimed her own delight with his choice.

He cleared his throat and began. "A man was going down from Jerusalem to Jericho..." As he read the story, gratitude that Valeria had stopped for him flooded his heart. She hadn't merely saved his life. Because of her, he understood what it meant to love.

"'Which of these three, do you think, was a neighbor to the man who fell into the hands of the robbers?' He said, 'The one who showed him mercy.' Jesus said to him, 'Go and do likewise.'"

Valeria placed her hand on his as he finished. "You can't imagine how glad we are that Rhoda and I did what Jesus told us. We all love you, Decimus."

Her eyes sparkled as she squeezed his hand.

He looked deep into her eyes, then at Galen and Rhoda. "I love you all, too."

He hadn't meant to say that. He'd never said that to anyone before, but it felt so good to say those words to the three people who meant the most to him in the whole world.

Valeria began their prayers. "Father, we thank You so much that You brought Decimus to us and that You've given us a chance to know and love him. We thank You also..."

As he held Rhoda in his arms while they continued their prayers, he felt the peacefulness and contentment again. He would miss this so much when he had to leave.

Galen and Rhoda had climbed into the loft. Decimus sat on the edge of his bed, watching Valeria bank the fire for the night. When she finally walked to the door, she took her shawl from the peg.

He suppressed the sigh. She was still making sure he wouldn't need to hold her in his arms, but it was probably wise for her to help him avoid that temptation. He wasn't entirely sure he could restrain himself if he held her too close.

When she smiled at him and held out her hand, he rose quickly and joined her.

With their fingers intertwined, she led them to the bench again. They sat for a long time in silence, her small hand enveloped in his large one.

Finally, he turned to face her. "I must tell you something."

She turned toward him with an expectant but slightly apprehensive look on her face. He took that as permission to continue.

"Last night, you said I was your dearest friend. You probably know this, but I feel the same. There's no one in the world more important to me than you."

He wanted to tell her right then how much he loved her, that she was the woman he wanted to spend the rest of his life with. But a declaration of love instead of friendship might frighten her as much as his kiss had.

He stopped the sigh before she heard. He probably shouldn't tell her he loved her anyway. He must leave soon. She would never understand how he could say he loved her and then leave to fulfill his duty to Rome.

He half expected her to blush and look away, but his earnest gaze held her eyes transfixed. He took a deep breath and plunged ahead.

"When you don't care deeply about someone, you take what you want for your own pleasure and don't care what that might do to them." He looked down at her hand in his. "I've done that too many times." He raised his eyes to hers again. "But this is different. When you really care, you take only what she gives freely when she's ready to give it. Our friendship is like that. I can wait until you tell me what we are to be. More than anything, I want to make you happy."

He was sure that was love in her eyes as he revealed his heart to her. There was no trace of fear, and she didn't turn away. Her gentle smile was almost a caress.

How he'd longed for this moment, but was it wrong to ask for her love when he couldn't stay, even though he hoped to return and take her with him?

She laid her hand on his cheek, and he placed his on top of hers to hold it there.

"Oh, Decimus. You're not ready for us to become what you want us to be, but I hope you will be very soon."

His head tilted. What did she mean, that he wasn't ready? He was ready for anything, everything with her—when he'd discharged his duty.

Did she know he would have to leave soon to return the gold? He was afraid to ask. Anticipation of something painful merely prolonged the suffering, and he didn't want to cause her pain any sooner than he had to.

◆

Valeria wanted to tell him right then that it was because he didn't follow Jesus, but something stopped her. She didn't want him to pretend just so she could love him. It had to be real, or it was no good. It also had to be soon. She wasn't sure how much longer he would stay, but it wouldn't be long. He wasn't the kind of man who would abandon his duty without good reason. She closed her eyes so he wouldn't see how much that thought distressed her.

She finally opened her eyes and lifted their hands from his cheek. "Time to go in."

She led him back into the cottage. At the foot of the ladder, she pushed a strand of hair back from his forehead. "Good night, Decimus. Rest in peace."

She was halfway up the ladder, but she paused when Decimus spoke.

"Good night, Valeria."

The mixture of eagerness and uncertainty in his eyes tore at her heart. She'd tried to keep the quaver from her voice, but did he hear it anyway?

Valeria lay in her bed, praying with every fiber of her being that he would choose to follow Jesus before he had to leave and while she was still strong enough to resist telling him she loved him. Just as fervently, she asked for the strength to let him go if he chose not to stay.

◆

Decimus lay on his bed, almost convinced that she loved him already, wondering what it would take for her to admit it, and doubting whether he should try to get her to since he had to leave. He'd never shirked his duty, but how could he bear to leave her even to fulfill his duty to return the legion gold? He tried not to think about whether any future was possible for a tribune and a Christian, even if she confessed her love.

Chapter 41

DUTY AND DESIRE

Decimus had not slept well...again. Thoughts about leaving her soon had plagued him until exhaustion finally silenced them. She'd almost finished making their breakfast when he awoke.

Galen was already back from doing his early morning chores. "About time you woke up. I was hoping you'd come with me to work in the high meadow again."

Decimus glanced at Valeria, but she said nothing and gave no sign of objecting. She must know he'd healed enough to go.

"Sounds good to me." Good to be away from the farmyard, away from where he'd keep seeing her and being reminded of what he was about to leave.

◆

Valeria was leaning on the rail of the corral, watching Astro and Baldric's fourth mare...for the most part. Her gaze kept drifting to Decimus where he leaned against the wall of the new stable, waiting for Galen to get some tools from the cattle shed. It drifted, but she didn't let it linger. That hurt too much.

Her eyebrows popped up when Baldric rode out of the trees leading another horse. The mare was as splendid as the ones he'd already brought.

"Baldric, is your herd really so fine that this is one of your least important mares?"

He chuckled as he slid from his horse and tied the mare's lead to the top rail of the corral.

"You have a good eye for horses. She is not one of the least import-ant. I chose her because she is ready to breed to your Roman's stallion before he leaves. I want you to have one of his foals. If it is a colt, you should have a good stallion to build your herd. We can discuss trading her for a different mare later if you decide you do not want her."

"She's so beautiful—how could I not want her? This is way beyond a fair price, and I probably shouldn't take her...but I will. I know you know how grateful I am for this."

She stroked the mare's neck. "Too soon Astro will be leaving."

◆

The sadness in her voice caught Baldric's attention.

She was looking across the mare's back to where the Roman was standing on the far side of the corral. He knew that look; it had been his own as he watched his Elka slipping away and there was nothing he could do to save her.

He placed his hand on Valeria's. "Tell me what is making you so sad."

She looked up at his face. Her eyes glistened.

"You were right about him. He loves me as a woman, not just a friend. I see it now in how he looks at me. I hear it in the tone of his voice. I thought he was joking when he told me I was beautiful so of-ten, but he meant it every time."

Baldric stiffened, and her eyes widened. "Oh, he never did anything he shouldn't, so don't be angry with him. I didn't even realize it was happening, and I never meant to, but I've come to love him as a man. I know he must leave soon. I don't want him to go, but I can see there's no future for us. I know how much you loved Elka and how you love Olga now, so I know you understand. I love him with all my heart, but I mustn't try to get him to stay, even though I want him to so much."

"So he has hurt you after all." Baldric frowned as he watched her struggling to hold back her tears.

She gripped his arm with both hands.

"Please don't try to kill him. You'll both end up hurt or dead, and that would break my heart. You were right that he's dangerous." She paused. "I've seen the wolf kill, but he only did it to protect us."

Baldric's head snapped back. "He killed here?"

"He killed the last two of the robber band when they were trying to kill Galen." She looked down at the ground. "And he killed a man to rescue me."

Baldric's look softened. The Roman had spoken truth when he said he would protect her with his life.

"So he told you about our first conversation. No need to worry, child. I do not want to kill him. You could never love him if he had not kept his word to me. Does he know you love him?"

"No, and he must never know. I can't marry him; he doesn't follow the Way. He mustn't think he should ask."

Baldric's eyebrows shot up as he stared at her. So many times she had told him that was why she couldn't marry one of his sons. He had not understood before how serious she was when she said it.

"Well, your Roman must leave soon and return to his legion. That will be for the best. He will never know what you are giving up and what he is losing."

She released his arm and hung her head. Her gaze was fixed on the ground where her toes drew lines in the dust.

He wrapped his arm around her shoulder and drew her into its protective circle. "I know too well what it is like to be left by the one you love. Believe me that your heart will heal in time." He tilted her chin upward until she was looking at him. "When it does, and if one of my sons is a follower of your Way, I would still be proud to have you as my daughter-in-law."

He truly understood…and cared. Valeria's quivering smile told him she knew it.

Baldric took his mare from the corral and mounted. He watched Decimus watching Valeria across the corral as he leaned back against the wall of the new stable with his arms crossed.

"I will speak with your Roman before I leave."

Valeria's eyes widened, and she laid her hand on his leg. "What are you going to say to him?"

He patted her hand and smiled down at her. "Nothing you told me. Just something he needs to hear. I will not hurt him."

He nudged his horse and trotted around the corral. As he approached, the Roman uncrossed his arms and moved away from the wall. He still favored his left leg and stood so he kept his weight off it.

Baldric dismounted and stepped close. He turned his back so Valeria would not see his face and spoke softly. "When will you return to your legion?"

The Roman met his steady gaze and kept his voice low as well. "I should be able to ride well enough in a few days, but Astro's gait was too unsteady when I tested him yesterday. I'll go when he's able to carry me back to the capital. I don't know when that will be."

Baldric nodded once. "I have brought Valeria her mare to start her herd, but she will need a stallion. It would be good if you gave her yours. It is a small payment for saving your life. When you are ready to ride, send Galen to me, and I will give you a horse big enough to carry you."

"Your offer is almost acceptable. I'll gladly leave my stallion with her, but I'll only borrow your horse until I can return it or pay for it. Agreed?" Her Roman offered his arm to close the deal.

Baldric eyed him thoughtfully, then grasped his forearm. "I will have a horse ready for you."

He remounted and looked down at Decimus. A corner of his mouth turned up slightly. "Perhaps there is Roman honor after all."

Decimus nodded slightly to acknowledge the compliment and almost smiled in return.

As Baldric turned his horse, he looked back over his shoulder. "Farewell, Roman."

"Farewell, Baldric."

◆

Valeria's gaze never wavered from them. Although she hadn't heard their words, she saw how they clasped arms and almost smiled at each other. The two men who were most important to her were no longer enemies. If there had been enough time, they might even have become friends.

Galen came from the cattle shed with the tools and handed some to Decimus.

As they headed up the trail, the only sign that Decimus had once been lying in her cottage near death was a slight limp. That might never go away completely. It was obvious to her and probably to him that he was healed enough and it was time to leave. It was good that he'd be working in the meadow where she wouldn't keep seeing him and being reminded of what she was about to lose.

For Decimus, supper was bittersweet. Life with this family, the love and laughter at this table, had revealed the emptiness of his life before the ambush. He was torn between his desire to stay and his duty to return, but he really had no choice. He was a Roman tribune who would fulfill his duty, not a child who would satisfy his own desires.

He tried to act as if everything was the same as before, to conceal the growing sadness, but would even his skill at hiding his thoughts be enough?

◆

Valeria wasn't fooled by his cheerful mask. He was withdrawing from them, preparing to leave.

In the beginning, she'd only planned to take care of him until he was healed and could go back to his legion. Now she'd give anything for him to become a follower of Jesus and remain with her for the rest of their lives.

Her heart ached for him to stay, but her head knew that he would go.

The table was cleared, and they gathered for prayers. It was Valeria's turn to pick.

His eyes were expectant as he waited for her to make a choice.

How many more nights would they have Decimus with them? What did he need to hear before he had to go? She needed exactly the right thing for him to read. *Jesus, guide me. Please, reach him before it's too late.*

She found the place in the codex by John, and handed it to him.

Rhoda snuggled in his arms as he began to read. "Just as the Father has loved Me, I have also loved you; abide in My love. If you keep My commandments, you will abide in My love; just as I have kept My Father's commandments and abide in His love. These things I have spoken to you so that My joy may be in you, and that your joy may be made full.

"This is My commandment, that you love one another, just as I have loved you. Greater love has no one than this, that one lay down his life for his friends. You are My friends if you do what I command you. No longer do I call you slaves, for the slave does not know what his master is doing; but I have called you friends, for all things that I have heard from My Father I have made known to you.

"You did not choose Me but I chose you, and appointed you that you would go and bear fruit, and that your fruit would remain, so that whatever you ask of the Father in My name He may give to you.

"This I command you, that you love one another."

◆

Decimus's eyes sought Valeria's face as he finished. Her eyes were glowing, but were those tears in them?

She laid her hand on his where it rested on the edge of the codex. "Always remember, Decimus. Jesus loves you."

She bowed her head and began their prayers. "Father, we thank You..."

He gazed at her face while she prayed. She knew he was preparing to leave. Would she try to get him to stay? How would he ever be able to leave her if she begged him not to go?

As Galen and Rhoda settled into their beds in the loft, Valeria finished banking the fire. She took her shawl from the peg before stepping onto the porch.

When Decimus followed her, he found her already sitting on the bench. As he sat down next to her and took her hand, he would have given anything for them to be standing one more time at the edge of the porch with his arms around her. Was she thinking the same?

They sat for a long time in silence, bathed in silver moonlight, staring at the stars.

She spoke first. "You've been quiet tonight."

"Sometimes there's nothing you can say." He turned to face her. "Sometimes a man has to choose to do what he doesn't want because it's the right thing to do."

She was gazing into his eyes. Hers filled with a sadness that reflected what must be in his own. She slowly pushed a strand of hair back from his forehead.

"We must always choose to do what's right, no matter the cost."

Relief flooded through him. She understood. She would do her best to make it easier for him to fulfill his duty. She wouldn't beg him to stay.

Finally, she rose and led him back into the cottage. As she stood at the base of the ladder, she laid her hand on his cheek. "Rest in peace."

His chest felt like an iron band was constricting his heart. She hadn't said good night like she always had before. As she climbed the ladder, the lump in his throat kept him from telling her good night as well. It wasn't going to be a good night for either of them.

Valeria lay in her bed, begging for enough time for Decimus to choose Jesus before he had to leave, for something to happen that would lead him to make the right choice while there was still time. If he didn't choose Jesus, there was no future for them even if he wanted to stay.

◆

Decimus lay on his bed, wondering how he would be able to say goodbye when it was time to leave, wondering if it was possible to promise that he would return, wondering if it was right to ask her to be waiting for him if he did.

Chapter 42

THE ROMAN RETURNS

For the first time since the ambush, Decimus was leaving the farm. It was market day, and he'd decided to accompany Valeria and Rhoda to the village. His leg had recovered enough for him to ride, and he was duty-bound to take the gold that still lay concealed in his box back to the legion. Baldric would lend him a horse that could carry him the distance, so it was time to leave. He needed to learn the way to the village. From there he knew which way to go.

He sat on the cart seat next to Valeria while Rhoda rode in the back. The trail from the farm to the road ran along a deep ravine through which a stream flowed.

He craned his neck to peer past the thick brush on the wall of the ravine to the stream below. Somewhere along here, Valeria's cheek had been torn when the stallion threw her so many years ago.

The quiet gurgle of the water as it flowed past the small boulders in the streambed was a pleasant accompaniment to Rhoda humming to herself, but he couldn't enjoy it today.

The cart pulled onto the main road and headed north. Soon the rock outcrop with the narrow gap where the robbers had waited loomed ahead.

"We found you right there." Rhoda pointed to a spot on the road in front of them.

Decimus looked at the spot, then at Valeria. The warmth of her smile belied the shadow in her eyes. "And we're very glad we did."

As they passed through the narrow gap, the ambush swirled

through his mind. His stupid inattention, his men dying because of it. If he could bring them back, he would. But the ambush had been a gift for him, not a tragedy.

He glanced at her sitting so quietly beside him. There was only a trace of a smile on her lips. He was a master at hiding his emotions, but she'd broken through his mask in a way no other had. He couldn't keep his imminent departure off his own mind, and she knew something was wrong.

He was duty-bound to return to the legion and take the gold—but he didn't want to leave. With her and her family, he'd found happiness and contentment like he'd never known before. The thought of leaving her was wrenching. He loved her with an intensity that was beyond what he'd ever imagined possible. She didn't love him like that now, but she was beginning to love him and she might grow to love him as much as he loved her...in time.

If he left now to fulfill his duty, would he ever be able to return to her, to find out if there was a future together for them? Could there even be a future for a Roman tribune and a Christian wife? Was it too dangerous for her if he asked her to leave this place of relative safety and go with him into the Roman world where Christians were the enemy to be destroyed?

Valeria guided her cart to its usual place and climbed down to unhook the mare. Rhoda jumped out and led Placida over to the grassy area where she could graze, then ran to find Bertha.

When Valeria turned to get the basket of vegetables, Decimus was ahead of her. He swung the basket up onto his shoulder. How like a man. He wouldn't let her carry anything while he was still there.

She shook out her striped blanket and spread it in her usual place by the basket seller. After Decimus set the vegetable basket down on the blanket without speaking, he headed toward the trees along the edge of the stream that ran through the village.

The basket seller stared at Decimus as he limped away. "Isn't that the tribune who helped you?"

Valeria concentrated on arranging her produce. "Yes. Rhoda and I found him near death after the ambush and nursed him back to health."

"But he's a Roman officer. What about the governor's decree? Isn't he supposed to arrest you and take you all away?"

"I don't think he will. But even if he does, Jesus commanded us to love our enemies. We had to help him."

"Oh, Valeria. I hope you're right. I would hate to see the Romans hurt you."

She squeezed Valeria's hand and got a warm smile in return.

◆

As Decimus gazed across the meadow toward the edge of the woods, several flashes of red among the green caught his eye. He stood erect and raised his hand to his forehead to block the sun's glare. A troop of a dozen mounted Romans emerged and trotted across the meadow.

Decimus stepped to the edge of the trees and stood with his fists on his hips, watching their approach.

When they were within hailing distance, he called out to the leader. "Cassius Severus."

Cassius reined in. "Who are you that you know my name?"

Decimus stepped out into the bright light of the road where Cassius could see him clearly.

"Lentulus!" Cassius slid from his horse and pounded Decimus on the back. "The legate declared three weeks after you vanished that you must all be dead. Your father was deeply grieved. He'll be amazed to learn that his grief was premature when we reach the capital. What happened to you?"

"An ambush in the woods. I was left for dead." He waved his arm toward the vendors. "That vegetable seller found me and nursed me back to health at her farm. She's a physician."

"A young woman like that a physician?" Cassius stared at Valeria.

"People do strange things so far from Rome. I must return to her farm before we go to the capital. There was gold concealed in my box of scrolls, and it's still there.

As Cassius scanned her, an appreciative fire lit his eyes. "She's a pretty little thing even with that scar." A sly smile appeared on his lips. "You've been living with her a long time. She'd be a pleasure for any man to take. Did you enjoy her?"

Disgust flared Decimus's nostrils and tightened his lips. "I was near death for two days after she found me. You question my honor to even suggest I would do that to my physician after she saved me."

At Decimus's rebuke, Cassius shrugged. "I meant no insult. No one would ever dare question your honor, Lentulus."

Decimus nodded to acknowledge the apology. A wry smile appeared as he remembered his first meeting with Baldric. He knew one man who wasn't afraid to question his Roman honor.

◆

Valeria glanced toward the tree where Decimus had been loitering. He was no longer there. Her breath caught when she saw him walking toward her, smiling and talking with a Roman officer who was staring at her. It was obvious they were friends. A chill hand gripped her heart.

As they walked past the vendors, Decimus didn't look at her. She understood and didn't try to speak to him.

He didn't want her to say something that would reveal to his friend that she was a Christian.

◆

As they walked by the horse sellers, Decimus saw a tall man who looked like a younger version of Baldric. "I need to buy a horse. Do you have money?"

Cassius's gaze snapped on him at that question. "Of course, but why buy it? Just take what you need."

"No, I'll pay a fair price for the animal. I don't want to be thought a thief."

Cassius raised his eyebrow but took his purse from his belt and handed it to Decimus.

"I'll repay you when we reach my father."

He summoned one of the soldiers and placed a stack of coins in his hand. It was more than what the horse was worth.

"Buy that large chestnut for me. Tell the seller that he must tell the owner the physician's Roman is buying it and that he's certain he's paying a fair price. He must also tell him that the agreement has been fulfilled."

The soldier saluted and went to buy Baldric's horse. Decimus and Cassius walked on toward the inn.

◆

Rhoda had been playing with Bertha, but she now stood beside Valeria. "Who is Decimus talking to? Why didn't he say something to you? Is something wrong?"

Valeria's headshake was small and quick. "I don't think so. He knows that officer. These Romans are dangerous. I think he's trying to protect us. He doesn't want to risk me saying something that would make them realize we're Christians. Don't say anything to any of them. Stay close to me, and let me do all the talking."

Rhoda's eyes widened as she slid her hand into Valeria's. She'd almost forgotten that Romans were dangerous.

◆

Once again, Valeria watched Decimus eating with a Roman soldier who was his friend. His full-throated laughter drifted across the inn's courtyard as he and the officer joked with each other. He laced his fingers together, placed his hands on top of his head, and leaned the chair back, just as he'd done so many times at home.

She'd loved to watch him do that as a smile lit his eyes, but it was different now. She turned her eyes away before the tears formed.

When they finished, Decimus rose and strode toward the vendors.

He stood at the edge of her blanket, looking down at her with a sober expression. "Gather your things. We're heading back to the farm now." The words were spoken crisply as a command in Latin.

As he towered over her, she tipped her head back to gaze on his face. She couldn't read it. It was wearing the Roman mask that she'd seen when he first regained consciousness. She turned to the basket seller and handed her the remainder of her produce. "Please sell these for yourself. I have to leave now."

◆

The troop headed across the meadow with Decimus riding at the head of the column beside his friend. Valeria and Rhoda followed in the rear.

Rhoda had been silent as they hooked the mare to the cart and began their journey home. Now she turned to Valeria with worry in her eyes. She leaned close to Valeria's ear and whispered, "What's happening? Is Decimus going to leave us now?"

"I think so. He's a Roman officer. I always knew he wouldn't be able to stay."

Rhoda hung onto Valeria's arm and laid her head on her sister's shoulder. Her voice quavered. "I don't want him to go."

Valeria stroked Rhoda's hair and nodded twice. "I know, precious. I wish with all my heart that he could stay."

They were halfway through the woods toward the ambush point when the soldier riding in front of the cart spoke to the man next to him. "I'm glad I ended up on this patrol. Governor Lentulus will be very grateful when we bring his long-lost son home. He may give us a special reward for this."

An ice-cold hand squeezed Valeria's heart. Decimus was the son of the governor? No wonder he'd refused to tell her his whole name. No wonder he'd been such a proud man, so sure of being in control when she first saw him.

But she'd seen him change so much. He could be gentle and kind. He'd seemed content, even happy, to be with Galen and Rhoda...and her.

She swallowed hard, but it wasn't enough to clear the lump in her throat. She never meant to, but she'd fallen in love with a Roman officer. Even worse, he was a son of one of the ruling families of the Empire, raised in pride to assume positions of power. He would never be able to leave that behind to follow Jesus. His own father was even the one who'd decreed death for anyone who did.

He'd fallen in love with her, but when he left, that would be the end. She had no hope of any future with him. An aching sadness filled her as she fought against the tears.

❖

Decimus tried to pay attention to the conversation with his friend, but he found his thoughts inexorably drawn to the woman on the cart sixty feet behind him. He'd planned on a few more days with her. Now he would have to leave immediately. There was still so much he wanted to tell her, but there would be no time to say it.

Maybe that was better after all—better that he leave before she decided she loved him. He was destined for political prominence serving Rome; he would probably never be able to return. It would probably be better for her if he never did.

❖

Valeria tried to look at anything but his broad shoulders and the scar mostly hidden by his wavy hair as he rode so erect at the front of the column. Even without his red-crested helmet and polished armor, he was once again the proud Roman tribune. He'd told her already that he must do his duty. He would leave today, and she would never see him again.

That was probably the best for both of them. There would be no more risk that he would ask her to marry him. She would never have to hurt him by rejecting the man she loved for the God she loved even more.

The creak of the axle and the thuds of many hooves filled her ears but couldn't drown out the silent cries of her breaking heart. It was the longest six miles of her life.

Chapter 43

LOVE TRIANGLE

Valeria released a half-held breath when Galen was not in the farmyard. Thank God, he was working in the high meadow. She wouldn't have to worry about him saying something that would put them all in danger before she could warn him.

She stopped the cart by the porch.

With eyes swimming in tears, Rhoda looked toward the corral where Astro was pacing. "He'll leave with Decimus. Can I go say good-bye to him?"

Valeria nodded, and Rhoda trudged over to the corral. The big stallion came to the railing and hung his head down so she could reach it easily. She scratched his blaze, then she wrapped her arms around his neck. He nuzzled her, confused by her sadness.

◆

The troop rode around the corral and stopped by the water trough. After the men dismounted and watered their horses, they relaxed under the trees.

Decimus entered the cattle shed and returned with Astro's saddle and trappings. With a flick of his hand, he summoned a soldier to put it on Baldric's horse.

He drew his hand across his beard, "Cassius, give me your razor. I need to take care of a few things in the cottage, and then we can go."

Cassius took his razor from his kit and handed it to Decimus. "Take your time. We can wait until you're ready."

As he walked toward the cottage, Decimus paused and looked at Rhoda. He turned and walked to her side.

"Astro's not fit enough to carry me in battle anymore. It would be better for him to stay here and make big, strong foals with your mare. I give him to you." He laid his hand on her shoulder and squeezed.

Her eyes brimmed with tears as she tipped her head back to look up at him. "Thank you! I'll take good care of him until you return."

Her voice was almost a whisper, but he still heard it crack.

Without answering, he turned and strode toward the cottage. When he entered, he closed the door behind him, lest someone walk in unexpectedly and hear something that might expose her as a Christian.

Valeria was sitting at the table when he entered.

"I need my own tunic now."

◆

Without speaking, Valeria climbed into the loft and lifted it out of her trunk where she'd stored it. Even though she'd tried her best to clean it, it was still stained with his blood. She clutched it to her breast and took a deep breath before climbing back down the ladder. She found him taking the scrolls out of his box and laying them on the bed.

"I've given Astro to Rhoda. I'm leaving these for you and Galen. Do you have two strong tie sacks that I can keep?"

In silence, she went to the cupboard and took out several so he could select the ones he wanted.

He chose two of the strongest. "These will be fine."

He carried the now-empty box to the table. He reached inside and pressed two secret releases. The top of the box lifted away, revealing a hidden tray. Beneath several sheets of papyrus lay gold coins and grain to keep the gold from jingling and betraying its presence. He slid the papyri into the first sack. Then he lifted the gold pieces out and divided them between the two sacks before tying their cords together.

"The robbers were right. We were carrying gold. As you once said, they didn't realize that a box of writings might be the real treasure."

She only nodded. She hadn't spoken since he entered the cottage. She couldn't trust her voice not to quaver and betray her surging emotions.

◆

Her silence cut into Decimus.

"Would you get me some water? I need to shave." She went out, closing the door behind her.

His thoughts were turbulent, like ocean waves crashing and swirling around jagged rocks. Why didn't she speak? He needed her to say something that would start the conversation about them and the future. At the same time, he dreaded where it might lead.

He wanted to thank her and tell her what his time with her and her family had meant to him. As much as he longed to, he couldn't ask her to be his wife. He could see the extreme difficulties of such a marriage for a man like him and the mortal danger to a woman like her.

His duty and destiny were to progress up the course of offices to become quaestor, then praetor, then governor of a province, as his father had done before him. He was already advancing early as the son of a senatorial family and the favorite of the legion commander. He only had three years left as a tribune, and then what?

He'd been fooling himself. He couldn't have a Christian wife unless she could conceal her faith. He was certain she couldn't and even more certain she wouldn't even if she could. Even his own father would want to kill her when he discovered she was a Christian.

And how could she ever continue to love a man in charge of the games where watching men die was the main entertainment? That was an unavoidable part of the duties of his next office as quaestor.

He would find some way to explain it all—why he had to leave her even though he didn't want to, why it would be better for her if he did—if she would just say something. With her silence, the door to that conversation remained closed because he was afraid to open it himself.

Maybe that was for the best. He would leave, Baldric would get her to marry Adolf, and that would be the end of it. She would be safe, and knowing that would temper the pain of losing her to another man, even a good man like Adolf.

◆

By the time Valeria returned from the well, Decimus had changed into his short Roman tunic and had his sword hanging at his side.

She sat down at the table as he began to shave. She tried to fix her gaze on the bowl of water where he swished the blade to remove the clinging hair, but she couldn't keep from glancing at the face that had become so dear to her. With each stroke of the razor, more of the Roman tribune appeared. Finally, all that remained of her Greek merchant was the slightly lighter shade of his cheeks where the beard had protected them from the sun.

He sat for some time, twirling the razor in his fingers. She knew he was waiting for her to say something, anything, but she clung to her silence.

Finally, he stood and looked down at her. She kept her gaze locked on her clasped hands. He mustn't see how much it hurt to watch him prepare to leave. She couldn't hold back the tears if she looked into his eyes. Her voice would betray her if she tried to speak. She didn't want to make it any harder for him than it had to be.

◆

Decimus had dreaded what she might say when it was time for him to leave, but her silence cut into him far deeper than anything she could have said. He could stand it no longer; it was time to go.

"I'm a tribune of Rome. It's my duty to return to my legion. I've sworn my loyalty to Caesar, but I won't betray you and your family as Christians. You mean more to me than...anything." He turned on his heel and strode out the door.

Decimus draped the gold sacks across his horse's withers. He led the animal to the stump by the corral and was about to mount when he froze.

He couldn't do it.

He couldn't leave her like that.

"Wait a moment, Cassius. I must speak with the physician."

He left the mounted troop by the corral and strode back to the cottage.

◆

Valeria was stone still, staring at his bed. Never again would she see him sitting there, smiling at her with those laughing eyes. Soon she would hear the troop leave, and with the fading hoofbeats, the last hope for a future with him would fade away.

He'd wanted her to speak, but she couldn't. She wasn't strong enough to say goodbye without betraying her love for him, and that would be wrong for both of them.

She spun when she heard his limping footsteps on the porch. Her heart began to race. His body blocked the light as he stood in the doorway, every inch the Roman tribune again.

He stepped inside and closed the door. With a few quick steps, he crossed the room to her.

"Why won't you speak to me?"

She fixed her gaze on the floor and shook her head, unsure that she could keep her composure if she spoke. Why did he have to come back into the cottage? What could she possibly say that wouldn't hurt him?

He placed his hands on both her arms and held her at arms' length. "Look at me."

She feared it would tear her heart apart, but she couldn't resist fixing her gaze upon him for what would be the last time.

"There's something I must say to you. The ambush, my wounds, my time of blindness—I'm glad they happened. Without them, I wouldn't have found you. I don't want to leave you behind. Come with me and be my wife. If you're careful what you say, I can protect you from the decree against you Christians."

Valeria had been staring into his eyes. At those words, she blanched and shifted her gaze to the floor.

"I can't." Her voice was scarcely above a whisper as she fought to mask its quaver.

"Is it Galen and Rhoda? They can come with us. I care about them, too."

"It's not that..." Valeria swallowed hard, struggling to hold back the tears.

He cradled her chin in his hand and lifted it, forcing her gaze back to his face. He pushed a strand of hair behind her ear, then rested his thumb along her jaw as he caressed her scar with the side of his index finger.

There was so much love in his eyes, and that love became a whirlpool pulling her deeper and deeper until she was drowning.

His voice caressed her when he finally spoke. "Then what is it? I can fix whatever it is so you can marry me. You love me, don't you?"

Her eyes stung with unshed tears as she raised her hand and rested it on his cheek. A lock of hair had fallen across his forehead, and she pushed it slowly back into place.

Her voice caught, but she forced out the words she had never wanted to say. "Oh, Decimus. I do love you, even more than you can ever imagine, but I can't marry you. You don't follow the Way. I love you more than life itself, but I can never deny my Lord so I can be your wife. No matter how much I love you, I love Jesus more."

◆

Her words were a dagger impaling Decimus's heart.

Impossible! How could she say she loved him, then reject him and choose her god?

A flash of shock followed by unspeakable pain and then anger surged within him.

Then, like the night when he regained consciousness, he set his face to show no emotion—his hard Roman mask. He shoved her away, and she fell backward onto his bed.

"Then stay here with your god." Reaching into the sack of coins hanging on his belt, he took out six and tossed them on the table. "That should be enough to pay for your services, physician."

Without looking at her again, he spun and strode out of the cottage.

◆

In clipped Latin, Valeria heard him bark to his friend, "I've paid the physician what I owed her. Let's go."

The jingle of bridles, then the soft thuds of horses' hooves as the troop trotted away. Valeria sat on the edge of his bed, buried her face in her hands, and wept hot tears.

◆

Galen had returned from the meadow in time to see Decimus go back into the cottage. He skirted the corral to avoid the mounted Romans and joined Rhoda. They were standing together by Astro as the troop passed with Decimus in the lead. Although Rhoda waved, he rode past looking straight ahead, not even glancing in their direction.

Galen stood for a moment, staring at Decimus's back as he urged his horse into a canter and the Roman troop disappeared into the trees.

"What was that all about?" He turned back toward Rhoda for her answer, but she was already running toward the cottage.

Rhoda burst through the door. "Valeria! What happened? Are you all right?"

She knelt by her sister and saw wet circles where Valeria's teardrops had hit the floor.

Valeria's face was still buried in her hands. Rhoda caressed her sister's hair. "Valeria?"

"Oh, Rhoda! I just hurt him so!"

"What happened?"

Valeria dropped her hands and looked at Rhoda, anguish in her tear-filled eyes and her body jerking with barely suppressed sobs. She drew a deep, shuddering breath before she could speak.

"He asked me to marry him, but I can't. He doesn't follow Jesus. I prayed so hard that he'd join us, and I thought he was beginning to understand. But there wasn't enough time. And now he's gone, and it will never happen. He's lost. Lost to Jesus...and lost to me."

Her chest jumped as more tears escaped. "I shouldn't have told him I loved him. I never meant to, but the truth just came out. The look in his eyes when I told him I couldn't marry him, that no matter how much I love him, I love Jesus more—it was like I ripped his heart out."

Valeria tipped her head back, and a tear trickled across the scar on her wet cheek.

Rhoda wrapped her arms around her sister and held her tight. "He's not lost yet. We know Jesus is calling him. Maybe this is just God's way of softening his heart enough for him to hear and come. Why would He have let us be Good Samaritans if He didn't mean to save Decimus in every way?"

♦

Valeria turned her gaze on her sister's face. It shone with such certainty of God's will. Maybe Rhoda was right. Jesus said we should have the faith of a child. God can do anything. She wasn't the only person He could use to lead Decimus to know and accept His love.

Valeria wiped the tears from her cheeks, took a deep breath, and stood up. "You're right. God's will cannot be defeated, no matter how it seems to me now. I mustn't give up hope."

Galen had been standing in the doorway, watching, silent for once. Now he walked over to Valeria, wrapped his arms around her, and held her close.

"I hate to admit it in front of Rhoda, but I think she's right, too."

Decimus slowed his horse to a walk and reached down to massage his leg. The muscles weren't back to full strength. He should have wrapped it, like Valeria would have. The jolting made it hurt to trot too long, but the horses shouldn't canter too far without walking to rest.

The problem with the horse walking was he didn't have to think about riding. He wanted to think about anything except what happened in the cottage.

He would have bet a million denarii that Valeria loved him, just as he did her. The horrible part of it was that she did. She'd just told him herself how deeply she loved him; the truth of her words shone in her eyes. Surely she knew he loved her at least as much.

But that wasn't enough. He had to love her god, too!

Galen told him during their first talk that she wasn't betrothed because no man had passed her test. He'd thought it was just some cryptic joke like Galen was always making. Galen had asked him if he was ready to pass it the day he kissed her. Finally, that odd comment about following Jesus made sense.

Many times, he'd heard her tell Baldric why she couldn't marry one of his sons, but he always thought that was just her way of graciously declining.

But it was a real test—and he'd failed it.

In the contest for her love, he'd come in second. Not to another man, but to her god!

What kind of god could own her heart so completely that she'd sacrifice anything to him, even their future together?

Why were so many who worshiped that god willing to give up everything for him? He'd watched them suffer agonizing deaths in the arena rather than deny their faith. They even died singing and praising him.

He was a true Roman, and this Christian god was an enemy of Rome. Or was he?

How could he be an enemy of anyone when he commanded his followers to love their enemies and they actually did it, even at the risk of their own lives?

Thoughts and questions kept swirling and twisting in his mind as he continued down the road.

Finally, he knew what he must do.

Her Jesus had said that any who seek would find. He needed to find someone he knew, someone he could trust, someone who knew enough about her Jesus and those who follow him to help him decide what was true. Once he knew what to believe, he could decide what he needed to do. But who could that possibly be, and how could he even begin to look for him?

He nudged his horse back to a trot.

Sometimes pain was good. It could help a man focus on something other than what he didn't want to think about. Right now, there were a lot of thoughts he wanted to avoid, and he welcomed the pain in his leg to distract him from the pain in his heart.

Chapter 44

No Longer Home

A few weeks ago, the ramparts of the legion fortress in the capital would have been a welcome sight to Decimus as he returned from the south. Good hot food and a comfortable bed had always been a welcome change from field rations and sleeping on the ground. But this time his return was not a homecoming. Home was a day and a half to the south in a small cottage with a loving child, a good-natured youth, and a kind, smart, beautiful woman...who had just ripped his heart out.

Commotion swirled behind him as he rode past the stone arches in the massive gate and deeper into the fortress. Many of the soldiers on duty recognized him, and a man presumed dead for several weeks tends to cause a stir. The troops peeled off, and only Cassius continued beside him. They reined in at the headquarters of the legion commander.

His first duty was to return the gold. The accursed gold whose presence in his box of scrolls had left him no choice except to return. Whoever was to lead the delayed inspection of the Augusta would need it. If there had been no gold...but there was, and duty denied him any other course of action.

Even without his full uniform, the guards at the commander's headquarters snapped to attention and saluted as he walked past.

The centurion in charge ordered a soldier to go at once to the governor and report the return of his son.

Governor Tiberius Cornelius Lentulus could not remember a time when he'd been more content. He'd mourned the death of his only surviving son when the legion commander declared him lost and presumed dead. His grief had been deep and full of regrets that he and Decimus had never been close because of his total fixation on political power to the neglect of family.

Now his son reclined beside him at this banquet celebrating his return. He'd thought he'd seen the end of his ancestral line, of generations of service to Rome. Tiberius's expectations for Decimus's rapid rise to the highest positions of power were reborn when he rode through the fortress gates that day.

It also gave him a second chance as a father.

He was just completing his tenure as provincial governor and would return for the present to civilian life at his villa near Rome. His time in Germania Superior had gone smoothly, and he was confident that he was secure in the Emperor's favor.

His return to Rome would allow him to fortify old alliances and make new ones. It would be the perfect time to have Decimus meet the people of power and influence that he would need to cultivate to achieve Tiberius's ambitions for his son. They could also grow closer as they planned Decimus's future together.

Tiberius offered his son the plate of fruit. "I'm glad you returned in time to command the troop that will escort me back to Rome. It will be good for us to spend the time together. We've done too little of that over the years. It should also provide opportunities for me to introduce you to important people who can help you in the future."

Decimus selected a cluster of grapes. "It will be good to visit old friends in Rome as well."

"Yes, that too." Tiberius's eyes narrowed as he lifted his goblet to summon the slave who would refill it.

He'd been surprised several times that evening by comments Decimus had made. There was something different about his son since he returned. Even though they hadn't been close, Tiberius could tell something was not right. He couldn't put his finger on what it was, but it was there.

Perhaps Decimus's close brush with death was still too much on his mind. The entertainments that awaited them in Rome should make him forget that.

Decimus masked his disinterest in his father's plan. The prospect of spending his entire time in Rome cultivating political alliances didn't appeal to him like it used to. There were people from his past without political power that he considered much more important than the men his father would choose to spend their time with. There was a German peasant woman he would have chosen over the daughter of the Emperor himself...if only she had chosen him.

The slave came to refill Decimus's goblet, but he waved him away. He had no interest in getting drunk. The evening meal should end with happy conversation and family prayers, not overstuffed stomachs and drunken stupor. His time with her had ruined him for enjoying many Roman customs.

At least he had persuaded his father to celebrate his return with a sumptuous banquet instead of gladiator contests. Deep sadness would have clouded her eyes if she thought he was celebrating his life with the death of other men. She was a day and a half away, but she was in his mind all the time. He was no longer purely Roman, and for the most part, that was good.

Valeria sat in Decimus's chair, her elbows resting on the table and her face in her hands. He'd been gone for two days. The chair had been hers at meals before he came. It was hers again. She couldn't bear to see it sitting empty while they ate, but it wasn't much better to sit where he used to pin her hand to the table as he teased her with warm brown eyes and a crooked smile.

She raised her head and stared out the door. Had the ride to Mogontiacum been too hard on his leg? Where was he now? Would he ever think about Jesus and how much he was loved? Must she live the rest of her life with a ragged hole in her heart that only he could fill, or would he return? And if he ever did, would he still be the Roman tribune who left or the changed man she dreamed he could be?

God, please let Rhoda be right. Bring someone else to lead him to You. She pulled at the corner of her eye, wiping away the start of a tear. *Then, if there's any way it can be Your will, please lead him back to me.*

She shook her head to clear it of the thoughts of him that lurked in every corner of her mind and kept leaping out unbidden. Every remembrance was shadowed by dreams of what might have been.

The distant call of Galen to Otto brought her back to the present. She placed both hands on the table and pushed herself up.

Baldric's deep voice spoke a greeting to Galen and drew her trembling smile.

God was the only true consolation for a broken heart, but right now she needed an arm with flesh on it to wrap around her and a human voice to tell her the pain would pass.

Baldric had walked this path with Elka. Having no hope of ever seeing the one you loved again—that pain he understood.

◆

Baldric glanced at the cottage. Valeria stood in the door, her hand raised in greeting. The droop in her shoulders told him what he already knew. He tied his horse to the railing and strode over to join her.

"Your Roman bought my horse at market day. I thought he should have left by now." The wetness of her eyes drew his arm around her shoulder. "Otto is always eager to see Galen, and I thought you might want company today."

She turned and tilted her head to look at his face. "I knew you'd understand. I'm so glad you came."

"The first week is the hardest. By a month...the pain is not so bad."

She tightened her lips and nodded. With one finger, she flipped away the tear that had escaped.

"At least your Roman left without trying to take you with him. I am glad he knew it could never work. Better you be alive here with grief that will pass than dead in Mogontiacum."

"But he did ask me to marry him." Again, she flicked away a tear. "I had to tell him no. Part of what hurts so much is how much that hurt him."

"His pain will pass, too. It is good you were wise enough to say no." He slid his hand up her arm, then down. "You need to find another to love, as I did after Elka died. Adolf would be pleased if it is him. You can follow your Jesus without risking your life if you marry my son."

"But I didn't refuse Decimus because it was too dangerous. I would have to deny my Lord to be with him. I can't do that, no matter the cost. Only a man who loves Jesus more than me would understand why I had to say no, and Decimus doesn't. I would let the governor kill me before I'd betray my Lord and worship the Roman gods."

"You will not have to worship any other gods with Adolf. I will even tell Adolf to add your god to those he worships."

"But following Jesus doesn't work that way. You can't just add him as one more god that you worship. It's all or nothing. No one who follows him can have any god but him. Nothing and no one can be as important." She wiped the corner of her eye before the tear could escape. "Not even the man I love with my whole heart."

Baldric frowned as he shook his head. "That is too high a price for any god to ask."

"But what Jesus did for me is far beyond any price I could ever pay. He died for my sins out of love. That gift—it's why I love him above all others, and if that means I remain alone, then so be it. If it's God's will for me to marry, He'll bring a man who follows the Way to be my husband. If not, loving Him will be enough."

"I do not understand why your god asks what he does." He squeezed her shoulder. "But I do not have to. If it is enough for you, then I guess it is enough."

Valeria tilted her head to offer him a smile. "It's always my prayer that you will understand someday."

She stepped away and rested her hand on his arm. "I'm so glad you came. It helps to know how soon the pain will fade from someone who knows." A quick pat before she withdrew her hand. "I was about to make lunch. Would you and Otto like to share it with us?"

"Yes."

Valeria entered the cottage as Baldric settled onto the bench. He cupped his chin and rubbed his bearded cheek. Valeria was a wise woman in many ways, but to love a god so much...

He shrugged before fixing his gaze on the Roman's stallion pacing in the corral. At least some good had come to her from saving the Roman, if only a good horse.

It had taken nearly a month to travel the distance from Mogontiacum to Rome.

Tiberius had followed the river road along the Rhenus to Augusta Raurica, then south to Aventicum and Octodurus before crossing the Alps into Italia. It had been an uneventful trip, but it had not been a pleasant one. Something troubled Decimus, and growing concern over what it might be gnawed at Tiberius.

Decimus had always been the life of the party, ready for an evening of good humor, good wine, and good women. He still laughed at many things, but the ribald, often cruel humor that he used to enjoy so much never elicited more than a weak smile and seldom even that.

Tiberius hadn't seen him drunk even once since he returned. When they stopped in a town, the other officers indulged themselves in the nighttime company of women. Decimus excused himself to stand alone in the darkness and watch the stars. Sometimes he just stared into the heavens with a wistful look, but other times he was clearly brooding about something.

Many times, Tiberius had gone out to draw him first into conversation and then back inside. The conversations were shallow and short, and Decimus chose solitude over the companionship of his own father.

Tiberius hadn't fully appreciated how much he loved his son until he thought he'd lost him. He'd always been proud of Decimus: his intelligence, his prowess as a swordsman, his intuitive grasp of military tactics that quickly made him the favorite of the legion commander. He'd reveled in the near certainty that his son would rise in the Roman power circles even faster than he had himself.

When he thought Decimus was dead, that no longer mattered. His grief had been intense. Memories of his failure as a father haunted him. Too many times he'd brushed aside young Decimus's requests to spend time with him so he could spend the time stroking the vanity of some powerful man who could help advance his own career.

The father of his son's best friend had been more of a father to Decimus than he had. At the time, he'd been happy to let Publius Drusus be his son's confidante and mentor because it freed his time for cultivating political allies. The sad result of his neglect? Decimus had grown into a man who always showed him respect but never the affection that a father and son should share.

This month traveling together should have nurtured a deeper friendship; it hadn't. Decimus remained polite but aloof, unwilling to talk about anything personal. Something haunted his son, something that made their intimate conversations impossible.

He could only assume it had something to do with the ambush, but Decimus wouldn't talk about that, either. Tiberius had no way of knowing what was wrong, so he couldn't even try to fix it.

In two days, they would reach Rome. Perhaps being home in the capital of the Empire would restore his son to what he used to be. Perhaps spending time together in the familiar places of Decimus's childhood would give them a chance to become real friends.

Tiberius stood at the door to his tent, once again watching his son stare at the night sky. What could he possibly be looking at or, more likely, looking for?

Valeria was working in the garden when Adolf rode out of the trees. She straightened and waved at him. Although Baldric had dropped by often in the month since Decimus left, Adolf hadn't been with him. Why the visit today?

She stepped out of the garden and closed the gate behind her as Adolf tied his horse to the rail.

"It's good to see you, Adolf. The mare your father gave me is with foal." She waved her hand toward the stable. "I'll get to use the stable you helped build soon."

Adolf grinned "I'm glad I was here to help. Your Roman was right about needing grown men to frame the roof."

"Yes, there are many things that are easier when there's a man around." Valeria couldn't quite keep the wistful note from her voice. There were too many places in the farmyard where images of Decimus slipped into her mind when she looked at them. The stable was the worst.

"Send Galen for me when you need one. I'll always be glad to help."

Valeria offered a smile. "Your whole family are such good friends to us. Thank you."

Adolf stared at his feet and kicked at the dirt. Then he turned his gaze on her.

"Actually, I came to ask you something." He looked past her toward the trees.

"What is it?

His gaze settled on her again. "Father told me the Roman asked you to marry him before he left. He said you refused because he didn't worship your God."

He ran his fingers through his hair. "I'm glad you refused, but I can't help wondering. Why was that so important? I wouldn't let a woman not worshiping my gods stand in the way of marrying her if I wanted her for my wife."

His head tilted as his eyebrows scrunched. "Your Roman didn't care that you were a Christian, even with the governor declaring it a crime. So why do you care so much?"

"Did Baldric send you to ask, or do you really want to know for yourself?"

"Father didn't send me. I want to know...for me."

Valeria gestured toward the cottage. "Come sit a while, and I'll tell you about Jesus and what he did for me."

As they walked side-by-side toward the porch, Valeria's smile slipped out and broadened with each step.

Chapter 45

SEARCHING

Decimus was eagerly anticipating his stay at the family villa near Rome. Not because of the beauty of the marble columns and perfectly manicured gardens or the luxury of a good library and sumptuous food, but because Graecus was there. As faithful steward for the house of Cornelius Lentulus for many years, Graecus had been there for Decimus through his teen years when his father never had time for him.

Graecus was waiting in the stable yard as the cavalcade arrived. Decimus dismissed the troops for them to proceed to the garrison. Then he rode to where the steward was standing before dismounting. Graecus's eyes lit with pleasure as Decimus swung his right leg over the horse's neck and slid off.

"It's good to see you again, Master Decimus."

Decimus placed his hand on the steward's shoulder and beamed at him.

"It's much better to see you, Graecus. It's one of the best parts of returning to Rome. I look forward to us talking later."

He slapped the steward's arm before leading his horse over to the stable slave for his rubdown.

◆

Graecus was skilled at concealing his thoughts, but the greeting from the young man he loved like his own son broke through the servant's mask. A broad smile lit his whole face. Decimus had been affectionate as a boy, but Graecus had expected his years in a position of power to make him more aloof, like his father was when other people were present. It was sheer delight to see that at least one of the best characteristics of his young master had remained unchanged.

The next morning, Decimus ordered his horse to be saddled. He had a problem to resolve, and for that, he needed a true friend he could rely on.

Titus Claudius Drusus had been his best friend since they were young boys. Of all the men he ever knew, Titus was the one man he could trust with his most intimate secrets. If there was anyone with whom he could discuss his dilemma over the Christian faith and the woman who followed it, it was Titus.

Titus had never been on the fast-track to political importance. He was serving his ten years as an officer in the military as expected of a man of the equestrian order, but he had no ambitions beyond completing the required service. His loyalty to Decimus was greater than his loyalty to Rome, so there was no risk in telling him about Valeria and her faith and her rejection of him because of it. If Titus was near Rome, he'd finally have the person he could trust to help him sort it all out.

When Decimus arrived at the Drusus house in the elite Fagutal section of Rome, it looked exactly as he remembered it. When he knocked, the door was opened by a house slave he didn't recognize. The slave only opened the door halfway and stood blocking entrance.

"I've come to see Titus. Tell him Decimus Lentulus is here."

"My master Titus is not at home."

"Where is he? I want to meet with him as soon as possible."

"That will be difficult, Master Lentulus. Master Titus is serving in Perinthus in Thracia. He hasn't been home for more than three years, and we don't expect him within the next year."

Decimus ran his fingers through his hair. Then a smile tugged at his lips. There might be an even better person for discussing at least part of his problem: Titus's father, Publius. In fact, if there was anyone in Rome who might be able to answer his intellectual questions about the Christian faith, it would be Publius. He was a historian and philosopher of some fame in scholarly circles.

More importantly, Publius was the man to whom he'd always brought his ethical quandaries. Publius was not a politician like his own father; he always judged based on moral rightness rather than political expediency.

Publius had always been ready for leisurely talks with Decimus and Titus about the meaning of life and how to make the right choices. His own father never had time for such discussions, so he'd learned to rely on Publius as his pole star when navigating the difficult decisions of young adulthood. If anyone could help him now, it was Publius.

"Is Publius Drusus at home today? I would speak with him instead if he is."

The door slave's eyes widened, and he swallowed hard. He peered into the atrium before answering.

"My former master doesn't live here anymore."

Decimus's shoulders drooped. The death of his own father couldn't have hurt more.

"When did he die?"

The door slave cleared his throat and glanced over his shoulder at the atrium again. Footsteps were followed by a grey-haired man passing the doorway of the *vestibulum.*

Decimus knew at once the slender form of the Drusus steward. "Malleolus."

"Decimus Lentulus!" Malleolus strode into the *vestibulum* and turned to the door slave. "Admit him. I'll attend to this business."

The door slave bowed to Decimus and swung the door wide open so he could pass. Malleolus motioned for Decimus to follow.

Upon entering the atrium, he turned into a small room to the right. Malleolus indicated with a flick of his fingers that Decimus should follow him to the far corner of the room, where he stood with his eyes fixed on the doorway. Then he spoke in a voice that was barely audible.

"I am so glad to see you, Decimus. Terrible things have happened this past week. My old master is no longer here, but he is not dead yet. I hope you can convince him to change his course so he will not be killed."

"What's happened?" Decimus whispered his question.

"Master Publius has become a Christian and is now in the cells at the Flavian Amphitheatre. He is waiting to be killed during the games this week. There is no one in Rome more loyal to Emperor Trajan than my new master Lucius. Because of that, he made the difficult choice of honoring Caesar instead of his father. May Rome have many more such patriotic citizens. He reported his father's treasonous rejection of the Roman gods. When my old master was charged with being a Christian, he would not perform the sacrifices to Caesar and was sentenced to die. In gratitude for his loyal service to Rome, the family estates were awarded to Master Lucius instead of being confiscated."

Decimus heard all Malleolus's words of praise for Lucius and his treachery, but they were only words spoken in case someone was listening. The pain in the old steward's eyes matched his own.

"What can I do?"

"Master Publius has always loved you like his own son. If he will listen to anyone, it is you. If you could go to him and convince him to deny the Christian god and return to the worship of the gods of Rome, he could be spared. That is all it would take."

Malleolus's eyes were pleading as his voice almost broke. "For more than thirty years I have served him. No man could be a better master and friend. I would do anything to save him, but I can do nothing myself. Even getting in to talk with him takes more influence and money than I have."

Decimus rested his hand on the old steward's shoulder. "I'll go speak with him this morning. Are you sure he's already in the cells at the amphitheater?"

Malleolus took Decimus's other hand in both of his as a look of intense gratitude overspread his face.

"Yes. I overheard Master Lucius tell one of his friends last night."

"I'll do all I can, but I may not be able to convince him. The loyalty of Christians to their god is beyond what I understand. They'll sacrifice what they love most to him, and nothing can turn them from that decision."

The memory of Valeria's tear-streaked face as she told him she loved Jesus even more than him tore at his heart again.

A trace of tears glistened in the old steward's eyes. "It is enough that you even try."

Decimus squeezed the old man's shoulder.

"I'll go right now. I will try, and we will see."

Malleolus escorted Decimus back to the door, and the door slave let him out.

As Decimus stood in the street outside, utter amazement flooded his mind. He'd come looking for his friend to have a listening ear as he tried to sort out his life. He was leaving knowing the perfect person to answer every question he had about the Christian faith and those who would follow it to their death. Publius, of all people, the one man he trusted most for guidance in this world.

Valeria would say it was her god's hand directing all this. She didn't believe in coincidences. Maybe she was right, maybe not. Would he know after he talked with Publius?

He headed home to don his uniform to ensure easy entrance to the cells and to get enough money to pay a bribe to get Publius out, if that was what it would take.

Chapter 46

THE LOGICAL CHOICE

Decimus had been to the amphitheater many times, but it had always been to sit in the premium seats close to the arena that were reserved for the senatorial order. He'd never walked through the passages beneath it, so it took him some time to locate the entrance.

He'd judged correctly that a tribune would be admitted without questions by the guards at the entrance. Finding his way to the cells where the condemned criminals were held was almost as easy. The first person he asked had volunteered to escort him, and he gave the man a sestertius, enough to be appreciated but not enough to be a topic of discussion.

The atmosphere in the cellblock repelled him. The passageways were dark and damp, and the cells reeked of human waste. The thought of Publius imprisoned in such a foul place was gut-wrenching, but an observer would never know it. He kept his face impassive, but he was reaching the limits of his skill.

He approached the guard station. "You have a Publius Claudius Drusus here. Take me to him."

The guard snapped a salute and lifted a torch off a wall rack. After lighting it, he led Decimus down a narrow passage to a tiny cell. The guard unlocked the cell door and swung it open. Decimus took the torch from his hand and stepped inside.

"Call when you wish to leave, tribune." The guard snapped another salute before he closed the door, leaving it unlocked.

Decimus's eyes swept the putrid darkness as he stepped deeper into the cell with the torch raised. His breath caught when something moved. Publius was sitting on the filthy floor with his back resting against the cold, damp wall. Decimus slid the torch into a ring on the wall and strode over to help his friend to his feet.

"Decimus!" A joyful smile overspread Publius's face. "I thought you were in Germania."

"I escorted Father back to Rome. He's finished his term as governor. I'll be returning to the province soon."

Publius pulled Decimus into a fierce hug before holding him at arms' length.

"I didn't expect to see you before I died. I thank God for this chance to say goodbye to my fourth son. How did you know I was here?"

"I went to your house to see Titus, and Malleolus told me. He sent me to persuade you to worship Caesar and be pardoned."

"He's a faithful servant and a good friend. I'm sorry my death is causing him such grief, but I won't change my course. I die gladly for my God. I can never deny Jesus to please Caesar."

Decimus looked first at the ground, then at Publius's eyes. "I knew you wouldn't. That's part of why I came. You've always guided me in everything that's truly important, and I'm facing the most important decision I've ever had to make."

Decimus paused, not quite certain how to continue. Publius placed his hand on his shoulder.

"What is it, son? Let me help you."

Decimus took a deep breath and blew it out.

"I'm in love with a Christian woman, and she loves me, too, but she rejected my proposal because I don't love her god. She loves your Jesus more than me, more than her own life, more than anything. I need to know why you're both willing to give up everything for him, and I need to decide if I can follow him, too." His voice broke. "Help me understand so I can decide."

The love and compassion in Publius's eyes mirrored Decimus's memories of Valeria. "Tell me all about it, and maybe I can tell you what God needs for you to hear."

Decimus told him about the ambush, how she risked her life to save him because of Jesus's command, about the miracles of him not dying from mortal injuries and of his sight returning. He told him about how they made him part of their family, how he read their scriptures and heard their prayers, and how much she wanted him to believe like they did. He told of how he fell in love and asked her to marry him, and how she loved him too but rejected him because she thought marrying him would mean denying Jesus.

"And now I'm back in Rome, and I find that the man I love and respect most in the world, the wisest man I've ever known, has made the same choice she did—to give up everything else for the love of Jesus. I must know why. How is it possible to love a dead man who claimed to be god enough to give up everything for him?"

Publius listened and nodded as Decimus poured his heart out. When he finished, Publius rubbed the back of his neck.

"Let me tell you how I came to my decision. Maybe then you will understand. It began as a problem with the philosophers I most admired. Aristotle. Plato."

Decimus crossed his arms. "I remember. You spent uncountable hours telling Titus and me about them."

A wry smile tugged at Publius's lips as he shook his head. "I bored you two sometimes, but I thought Aristotle and Plato so wise then. I was foolish to think that. They fail to explain how the world really is.

"I thought Aristotle the best of all philosophers. He taught that everything has an effective cause. When I looked deep enough or far enough back in time, I could see the causes of almost everything. He also taught that everything changes over time, that nothing lasts forever. I could see that, too."

Decimus's brow furrowed. "But that is how the world works. Why do you say he failed?"

"His failure lies in the contradictions. He taught that the universe was eternal and had no effective cause. But how could the universe as a whole be the opposite of all the parts within it? That wasn't logical. So I began my search for a philosophy that taught that the universe had a beginning and something that started it. I found it in the Jewish scriptures. They tell how God created everything from nothing, how He is the effective cause of the whole universe."

As Decimus's head tilted, his eyebrow rose. "I see your point."

"But there's much more. Consider the nature of man. Plato taught that we could be ruled by philosopher-kings: intelligent, self-controlled men who ruled based on wisdom and reason, for the good of the kingdom and not for their own desire for power and wealth. But such rulers don't exist now." Publius shrugged. "I doubt they ever have."

He pursed his lips. "Emperor Trajan is as good a man as has ever ruled an empire. By the standards of Rome, he's a shining example.

He's ordered that orphans be given food and education in Italia, but what about the rest of the empire? He sends his legions out to conquer, enslaving and killing, making new orphans who will starve. He lounges in the imperial box, happy to watch the lions rip apart small children who've done nothing worse than call Jesus their Lord."

Decimus covered his mouth and pulled his hand down across his chin. "I ordered children into the arena in Mogontiacum. I did it for Rome...I thought what I did was good then, but now..." He shifted his gaze to the filthy floor.

Publius rested his hand on Decimus's arm, and Decimus looked again at his mentor's eyes. Publius's voice softened. "You gave the order, but you only did what you'd been taught was right. So often good and evil get confused in our minds, but what else can we expect? Man is not good and wise; he naturally chooses evil. There are glimmers of beauty and kindness, but it's ugliness and cruelty that rule. Rome is brutal and rotten at her core, yet she rules vast lands."

Decimus nodded. "We use brutality to keep the provinces afraid. Fear makes them peaceful, but..." He shrugged.

Publius sighed. "War is the playground of violence, but we don't stop there. Man's love of violence led to the games. Tens of thousands of Romans watch as people are brutally murdered and consider it good entertainment. Man is naturally evil, selfish, and rebellious against God—a sinful being. Again, I found this understanding in the Jewish script—" He gasped.

Decimus jerked when Publius's hand clenched his arm in a vise-like grip. "You must return to my house and get my scripture scrolls. Lucius will only throw them away when he disposes of the things in my bedchamber."

Decimus rested his hand on Publius's. "I'll get them from Malleolus today."

Publius beamed as if Decimus had given him a magnificent gift. His grip relaxed, and he withdrew his hand. "I want you to have them. They contain the actual words of God, and I pray you will come to treasure them as much as I do. Promise me you won't let Lucius destroy them."

"I give you my word."

A serene smile lifted the corners of Publius's mouth as his eyes warmed. "At last, I had found a philosophy that explained everything I knew to be true about the world, but it was much more than a philosophy. In those Scriptures, I met the God who made the universe, and

I learned that He cares about men. He has always wanted us to know Him and love Him. So I became a God-fearer, worshiping the God of Abraham, Isaac, and Jacob. But the more I learned, the more I worried about a problem."

Decimus pushed back the lock of hair that had fallen onto his forehead. "What problem?"

As Publius looked past Decimus, he massaged his right shoulder "He's a holy God, and He can't tolerate sin in His presence. He gave His people a way to approach Him by covering their sins through blood sacrifice."

"How is that a problem?"

"Because it didn't remove the sin; it only covered it for a while. God said the sacrifice must be performed in His temple in Jerusalem every year on the Day of Atonement. For more than a thousand years, His people offered the sacrifices He commanded, but those ended when Titus destroyed the temple when he put down the rebellion in Judaea. But the payment for sins has always required blood sacrifice."

Decimus's eyes narrowed. "But with the temple gone, how was sin to be paid for?"

Publius slapped Decimus's shoulder. "Exactly! And how could the true God, the one so powerful that He could make the universe, let Rome destroy His temple and take away what allowed His people to approach Him?

A frown pulled Decimus's mouth down. "If the Jewish god is the true god, like you say, that makes no sense."

A smile crept across Publius's face, just as it had when Decimus suddenly grasped something years ago. "I know. I thought about it constantly, but I couldn't see my way to the answer." The gleam in Publius's eyes matched the growing smile. "Then I met a man who explained it all. He's from Thessalonica, and his grandfather heard the great apostle Paul teaching about Jesus. One of his grandfather's best friends had even been in Jerusalem on business when Jesus was crucified."

Decimus's eyebrows rose. "An eyewitness?"

Publius nodded. "Yes. He saw the dark sky, felt the earth shake, and heard of how the temple curtain had been torn from top to bottom. He saw the courage in the temple courts of Jesus's followers who had abandoned Him in fear the night of His arrest. His grandfather's friend heard the preaching of Peter in the temple and was among the first new followers after Jesus rose from the dead, proving His claim to be God. My friend's grandfather became a believer, and so have all his descendants.

"Don't you see? The temple could be destroyed because God made the perfect blood sacrifice Himself—Jesus on the cross more than eighty years ago."

As Decimus rubbed the back of his neck, his eyebrows lowered. "So you think the temple and its sacrifices were no longer needed?"

Publius beamed as he nodded. "God had Rome destroy it so people wouldn't cling to the old ways. The coming of the Messiah, of Jesus, was foretold in the Scriptures hundreds of years before He came, and God kept the promise He made to His people.

"No animal sacrifices were needed to cover my sin with their blood. I only had to believe in Jesus as the sacrifice for all sins, including mine." The grin relaxed into a satisfied smile. "My mind knew this was true, and I chose to follow Jesus as my savior, no matter what the cost."

Publius placed his hand on Decimus's shoulder, and a strange brightness lit his eyes. "And then I met God. He came to me and He lives in me. The day I decided to believe, to repent of my sins and commit myself to Jesus as my Lord, all the darkness and decay in my life was replaced by brightness and newness."

He stared past Decimus, as if he was looking at something only he could see. "It was as if I'd never seen beauty before, never tasted sweetness before, never known what it meant to be fully alive. Following Jesus is like the finest marriage; denying Him would be committing adultery against the most loving, beautiful, faithful wife a man could have. I could never betray my Lord that way."

The brightness faded, and Publius's eyebrows dipped as he lowered his arm.

"When Lucius reported me as a Christian, I knew what my sentence would be. The praetor who heard my case is Lucius's good friend. He's well known to hate Christians, especially those of the senatorial and equestrian orders."

His eyes brightened again, and his smile reappeared. "But I have no regrets. I'm content to die because it isn't death that matters. It's whether you have accepted Jesus as Savior. Death is a tragedy apart from Jesus. Without Jesus, I would be lost, in hell, forever separated from God. With Jesus as my savior, death has no power over me. I don't fear it. It will just usher me into life with Him in heaven."

Decimus sucked in a breath and held it. The echo of Valeria's distress when she thought Inge might have died before she chose Jesus rang in his head. She'd fought tears when he wanted to kill himself because she didn't want him to die while he was still lost. Her happiness every time he let her think he was interested in reading her Gospels, learning more about Jesus, trying to understand why she believed—it all made sense.

Publius's voice pulled him back to the cell. "I know Lucius betrayed me because he wants full control of his life and the family fortune. He wasn't content to wait until I died naturally. I've forgiven him, and I pray that somehow God will reach him so he'll choose to follow Jesus, too." His deep sigh revealed the pain born of that betrayal.

"I pray for Claudia and Titus, too." Wistfulness softened the tone of Publius's voice. "My only regret is leaving Claudia under Lucius's guardianship. I wish it was Titus. He would select the right husband. Marriage to the wrong man will crush her gentle heart. I know my arrest and coming death are devastating her, but I pray that God will care for her when I am gone.

"I've written Titus to tell him why I believe in Jesus, that I'm happy to die for Him so he is not to grieve, and that he must find a way to forgive his brother for turning me in. I've told him that I will be praying for all my children until I take my final breath and even after that in heaven."

Publius placed his hand once more on Decimus's shoulder and squeezed. That touch of compassion—Decimus was a man who never cried, but it almost breached the dam holding back his tears.

"I will pray for you as well. For many years, you've been my extra son. May Jesus claim your heart and mind as His own so you can know the joy and peace I've found."

Decimus's gaze was locked on his friend's face. The happy glow in his eyes, the gentle smile on his face—it was Valeria's face as he read from John.

He ran his fingers through his hair and shook his head. "All you say makes sense, but how can I know it's true? Just because something is logical, that doesn't mean it's true."

"But it is true. Jesus told us that He is the way, the truth, and the life. He promised if a man would believe in Him and follow, he would know the truth and the truth would set him free. If you let Him, Jesus will show you what is true. Open your mind to Him, Decimus. Open your heart. Know the truth and be free like I am, even in this prison as I wait to die."

Decimus shook his head again. "I can't do that. I have to know something is true before I can believe it, not the other way around."

"Let God help you. Know that Jesus loves you and wants you to come to Him."

"That's what she said." Decimus's voice caught. "But I don't know, and I need more help to decide."

He took a deep breath and squared his shoulders. "I'm not going to leave you here to die. You'll be in the arena with the lions before week's end. I have enough money with me to pay a bribe to free you. I can get you out of Rome and send you to her. She'll gladly take you in for as long as you need. You can safely follow Jesus there."

Publius rested both hands on Decimus's shoulders. "My son, I don't want to get out unless it's God's will to free me without bribery." The squeeze before he lowered his hands spoke more than words could. "To help a condemned prisoner escape...you know that's a capital crime. I won't let you destroy yourself trying to set me free. The lions kill quickly, and then I'll be with my Lord Jesus forever. Death comes to every man, but mine will open the door to eternal joy and peace and perfect life without end. My brothers and sisters in Christ who have already died await me across the threshold. I'm ready to begin my new life with my Lord Jesus forever."

Decimus stood motionless, staring at Publius. His friend's face was serene. His eyes glowed with a mixture of love and happiness and contentment that mirrored the eyes of Valeria after he'd listened to her singing that beautifully strange song the night after his sight returned.

"But—" Decimus began, but Publius placed his finger on his lips and stopped him.

"It's time for you to go. You shouldn't be here if the guards come again to take more of us up to the arena. They've already taken the people for the lions today, but they may take some for the gladiators this afternoon. I'll probably go up tomorrow. Don't grieve for me. Rejoice instead. I'm going to be with my Lord.

"I'll be praying for you, Decimus. For you to hear God's call to you and choose to follow Jesus with your whole heart, as I have. Then this parting will only be a farewell, and not a goodbye."

Publius wrapped his arm around Decimus and guided him toward the door. He called through the tiny window, "Guard, we're through."

The hinges creaked as the door swung open. As Decimus stepped through the doorway, he looked one last time into the eyes of his friend. Love shone from them—love like he'd seen in hers.

"Farewell, my son. I pray I'll see you again as my brother. May the grace and peace of my Lord Jesus be with you."

The guard closed the door and locked it. Through the small hole in the heavy door, Decimus heard singing. Suddenly the dank air of the cellblock was so oppressive he couldn't breathe. He spun and strode through the passageways to reach the sunshine and fresh air of the open street.

Decimus had promised he would return to the Drusus house to get Publius's treasured scriptures, but the thought of going there again tore at his heart. He recoiled from telling Malleolus about his failure to save Publius.

He rode to the house in silence. When he knocked, the same door slave answered.

"I'm here to see Malleolus." The slave bowed and escorted him to the small room where they'd talked before, then went to find the steward.

When Malleolus first entered the room, his eyes shone with hope, but that faded when he saw Decimus.

"My master refused to listen."

"He listened, and then he explained why he's made his decision to follow Jesus to his death. I couldn't even persuade him to let me bribe his way out to send him where he can safely be a Christian. He made me promise to collect a final gift from him. There are some scrolls in his bedchamber, a Greek version of the Jewish scriptures. He didn't want Lucius to destroy them."

Malleolus nodded. "I know the ones. He read from them every day. I am glad they will go to you. I will get them."

As the old steward left the room, the spring that had always been in his step was gone. Decimus understood exactly how he felt; knowing you've lost someone you love will do that every time.

Chapter 47

PROOF

As Decimus rode back to his father's villa, the turmoil of his part-ing with Valeria enveloped him again. She had chosen Jesus, first risking her life for her enemy, then sacrificing her love for him. Publius had chosen Jesus, embracing the death that choice must bring. The two people he loved most in this world loved Jesus more than anything. Both chose him above all, even if the price was their lives.

Should he make the same choice? Could he make the same choice? Did it make sense to give up everything for a crucified Jewish carpen-ter? A man who claimed he was the perfect sacrifice to reconcile man with the one true god? A man who claimed he could do that because he was God himself?

Publius had always been so well informed, so wise about every-thing. Everything Decimus heard in that stinking cell made perfect sense when he looked at it logically.

But was logic the same as truth? Was it something a man should hang his whole life on?

If he chose to believe and follow Jesus, his life as a tribune on the road to power must end. Was he willing to pay that price? Was it worth the cost? Publius and Valeria both thought so.

If he chose Jesus, he knew what he would lose, but what would he gain?

Surely the price was too high to pay without proof. He couldn't make that choice based on logical argument. He needed some undeniable proof.

Decimus rubbed the back of his neck before turning his face up to scan the sky.

He'd always thought it strange the way Valeria and her family spoke with their god as if he was a person in the room, but he was ready to try it. After taking a deep breath, he uttered his first prayer.

"God of Valeria and Publius, I don't know if you're really who they say, but if you are, send me the proof I need to believe and follow you."

He relaxed in the saddle and nudged his horse into a trot.

Her Jesus had said to seek and he would find, to ask and he would receive. Well, he was seeking and asking. Now he would wait to see if he would find what he was looking for.

Decimus was sitting by the window in his bedchamber. He'd begun reading Publius's scriptures and had reached the section where Moses was describing the Jewish god's laws for blood sacrifice when his father entered.

He set the scroll aside as his father approached.

Father was beaming. "I have excellent news. We've been invited to dine tonight with Quintus Flavius Sabinus. He's one of the men I especially wanted you to meet while in Rome, so this is most fortunate. He has great influence in the Senate and with the Emperor."

"I don't have any other plans for the evening."

His father's eyebrows rose, then dipped. "Quintus Flavius Sabinus is a man you would cancel any other plans for. This is a superb opportunity, and I hope you'll make the most of it."

"Of course, Father."

"Since you've already completed five years as tribune with great success, it's time for us to start positioning you to become a quaestor based in Rome in three years. Sabinus can be a great help to us in accomplishing that."

Decimus nodded his head but said nothing. Father obviously expected him to be delighted by the chance to attract the patronage of a man like Flavius Sabinus. Before the ambush, he would have been.

"Sabinus always serves superb food and has other entertainments as well. Dining with him is usually a memorable experience."

"I'm sure it will be an interesting evening."

His father's eyebrows dipped further. "It will. Also, I think tomorrow we should go to the games. They'll provide a good opportunity to run into some of the other people who can help with your rapid promotion."

Go to the games—the mere thought made Decimus's stomach knot. The roar of the crowd as lions tore Publius to pieces—he couldn't bear that. Before Valeria, he'd considered the games one of the best ways to spend an afternoon. How could he ever have thought watching men die brutal, bloody deaths was fun? She'd shown him a better way, and that had ruined the entertainments of Rome for him. He wanted no part of them now.

"I have something else to do tomorrow."

◆

Tiberius was shocked by that response. He made no effort to keep the irritation from his voice as he replied.

"There is nothing more important than meeting as many key people as you can while you're here. We'll be going mid-morning. Anything else you're planning can wait. I'm going out. I'll be back in time for us to go together in the chariot to Sabinus's."

Tiberius turned and strode out of Decimus's room. As he walked through the atrium, he shook his head as he replayed their conversation in his mind. What was wrong with his son, and how could he help him return to the way he used to be?

When Decimus and his father arrived at Sabinus's villa, a slave escorted them to the dining room.

Sabinus turned at their entry and stopped his conversation with a middle-aged man whose toga bore the wide purple stripe of a senator.

"Ah, Tiberius, I see your years in Germania have only made you seem younger and stronger." He held out his hand, and the two men grasped arms. "Trajan told me before he left for Armenia that you would leave your province in much better shape than you found it."

Sabinus swung his gaze onto Decimus as he released his grip.

"I've heard promising things about you, Decimus. Like father, like son. I expect someday that you, too, will be a provincial governor. That will be a good thing for Rome. She needs smart young men like yourself to rise in their service to her. I'm glad to get to know you now so I can enjoy watching you rise. And who knows, maybe I can be of some service to you as you do."

His smile reminded Decimus of a crocodile. The similarity probably didn't stop there. He detected masked ruthlessness in Sabinus's eyes. This was a man who would be better to have as a friend than an enemy. Maybe not better, but certainly safer.

Decimus smiled and nodded. His response seemed to satisfy Sabinus, who turned to converse with his father. A distinct relief...talking with a crocodile was touchy business, and he didn't feel up to playing that game tonight.

◆

Dinner was just as Decimus expected: too much rich food, too much wine, too much malicious gossip about the Roman elite. Only a few weeks ago, he would have drunk himself into a stupor with the rest of the dinner party. Tonight, he was the only one still sober.

As the wine began taking effect, Sabinus became less and less guarded in what he said.

"I've made it my goal to advance the careers of the sons of my friends who deserve my special attention. Many choose to express their appreciation for my contributions to their success. One is now a quaestor who organizes many of the games in Rome. He shows his gratitude by providing me with special entertainments sometimes."

He turned to the slave who was overseeing the banquet. "Bring the girl."

The slave bowed and left the room.

Sabinus wiped his mouth and smiled a suggestive smile at Decimus. "I like you, Decimus. I can see that you have a great future serving Rome. Tonight, I want to make you a gift of something my young friend sent me today. I have a Christian virgin who will be in the arena tomorrow. Normally I would have her myself, but I want to make a gift of her to you. She's a cripple, but her limp and the scars on her face won't make her any less enjoyable to take for the first time. Do what you want with her. She'll be returned to the arena cells early tomorrow for the morning's games."

As Sabinus finished speaking, the slave returned with the "gift."

Even before the ambush, Decimus had never enjoyed taking women who didn't want him to. For a wealthy, handsome man, there were always plenty of willing women. Even then, he would never have taken a willing virgin who was barely more than a child. The offer revolted him, but he masked his disgust. His father's beaming smile at Sabinus making such an offer disgusted him even more.

The girl stood beside the slave, her head bowed and her eyes focused on the ornate mosaic pattern of the floor. She couldn't be more than thirteen years old.

"This is a special honor. I will remember it. Would it be possible to go to a room where we won't be disturbed and we'll disturb no one?"

Sabinus's leering eyes matched his lecherous smile. "Of course." With a flick of his fingers, he instructed the slave to take Decimus to a secluded room.

The slave bowed and made a sweeping gesture with his hand. "Come, tribune."

Without raising her eyes to look at Decimus, the girl limped ahead of him as the slave led them down a hallway to a room far from the dining hall. The girl's lips moved, although she uttered no sound. Decimus forced his face to remain emotionless. She was praying for deliverance, as Valeria would have when Fabius grabbed her in the village.

As they entered the room, he turned to the slave. "I don't want to be disturbed by anyone tonight. No one is to come close enough to hear us until they come to take her to the arena in the morning."

"I understand, tribune. I will place someone at the end of the hallway to ensure your privacy tonight." The slave bowed and left them, closing the door behind him.

When the slave should have been out of earshot, Decimus opened the door. The hall was empty except for a slave standing guard at the far end. He closed the door and turned to the trembling girl. When he took a step toward her, she took a step back.

"Don't be afraid. I have no intention of taking you."

She stepped back again and almost stumbled. "But you told him you—"

"I only accepted the offer so you wouldn't be given to another."

Her eyes widened, and then her whole body relaxed as relief flooded her. "May God bless you for your mercy."

Decimus's jaw clenched as Rhoda's sweet smiles danced in his mind. She could be this girl in a few years.

"My mercy can extend beyond this night. We're alone. I can let you escape so you won't have to face the lions tomorrow."

A smile lifted the corners of her mouth until she was beaming, then it faded. "What will happen to you if I'm not here when they come?"

Decimus shrugged.

"Will they kill you?"

He couldn't tell her they wouldn't, so he said nothing.

Her face took on that same gentle glow he'd seen so often on Valeria. "I thank you for your mercy and kindness, but I'll stay here. I'm not even sure where I could go. My betrothed and my parents are at the arena now waiting to die for our Lord. I'll join them."

His jaw dropped. He'd just offered her life and freedom, and she was choosing to die for Valeria's god! First Publius and now her turning down his offer to free them so they wouldn't have to die?

"But why? How can you make that choice? I'm not asking you to deny your god and sacrifice to Caesar. I'm offering your life without asking anything of you."

"I can't buy my life with yours. Besides, I have nowhere to go where I can love and serve my Lord without ending up in the arena anyway. Life without Jesus is death, not life, and I don't want to live that way again. When the lions kill me, I'll still live on with Jesus forever."

He ran his fingers through his hair and stared down at her upturned face.

"I've heard those words before, but I don't understand them."

Something in her eyes pulled words out of him that he hadn't intended to speak. "I love a Christian woman who told me the same thing. I've read your scriptures, but I still don't understand. How can life be death and death be life? It makes no sense. Why are you choosing to die for this Jesus?"

Eyes of compassion softened her scarred face as a smile curved her lips. "Let me tell you why I love Jesus, and maybe that will help."

Those eyes—so like Valeria's as she sat beside him after his nightmare about killing her. So like Publius's eyes when he said Jesus loved him and wanted him to come.

He knew nothing about this girl, but what she had to say...did it hold the key? She was the age Valeria would have been when she became a Christian. Could this girl solve the mystery that haunted him?

"Tell me."

Her face lit up at his request. "When I was little, my father was not a good man. When he was sober, he treated us well enough. But he often drank too much. Then he got angry so easy."

Her eyes drifted toward the window as she paused. Then she focused once more on Decimus's eyes. "We never knew what would set him off. He beat me and my mother when he was drunk. Mother was afraid of him, so she wouldn't even try to stop him when he was hitting me. I couldn't understand why she let him hurt me, but I found out she had good reason to be so afraid."

Again, she looked past him. "One night when I was ten, he started beating her, and he kept on even after she wasn't moving anymore. I was so afraid he'd kill her that I tried to get him to stop. He did, but only because he turned on me. He hit me and kicked me again and again. I passed out when he stomped on me and shattered my leg. I think that's when he finally stopped. My scars and limp are from that night."

Decimus covered his mouth and rubbed his cheek. How could she be so calm as she described those many years of suffering with a brute who should have cared for her?

"The next day Father was so sorry for what he'd done, but that couldn't undo the night before. Then our neighbor told him about Jesus, how He died to pay for every wrong my father ever did, how Father could be forgiven and live at peace with God. When he heard, he gave his heart to Jesus. Everything changed that day. He never got drunk again, and his anger was gone. Father loves us so much now, and no one could ever be kinder.

"After seeing how Jesus changed Father, Mother and I decided to follow Him, too. I forgave Father for crippling me, and now I truly love him because Jesus helped me do it. My life has been all I could hope for ever since. I'll always follow Jesus, no matter what. I could never deny my Lord who saved me. He's given me peace and so much happiness."

Decimus massaged his neck as a frown dragged his mouth down. "So now you're willing to die for him? Do you understand what kind of death that will be?"

Her lips twitched. "I know I'll face the lions tomorrow. I can't say that doesn't scare me, but I pray my death will be quick." Her peaceful smile returned. "And then I'll see my Lord face to face, and I'll be with Him forever. I can never love Him as much as He loves me, but I love Him more than anything else."

Decimus ran both hands into his hair. As he held his head, he closed his eyes. How could she be so untroubled by what tomorrow held?

When he opened them, she was watching him, her lips in a gentle smile and her eyes soft.

"But can't you love him without giving up everything else?"

"Sometimes keeping something we treasure isn't possible. No matter how much I love life, I love Jesus more."

Those words pierced his heart. His jaw clenched as Valeria's tearful face and final words swirled in his memory. *No matter how much I love you, I love Jesus more.*

The girl's lips straightened, as if she thought her words had caused his pain. She reached out and touched his hand. "Please don't be sad! You should rejoice with me that I'll soon be with Jesus forever. If you knew Him, you'd understand." Her eyes warmed, and the smile returned. "I hope my story helped."

He stood in silence for a few moments, gazing at her face. The girl looked happy and at peace. Like Valeria when she watched him reading their scriptures. Like when she prayed to their god as they sat around the table. Like Publius when he talked about meeting God.

He finally nodded. He didn't want to tell her his real thoughts. What she'd told him astonished him, but he still didn't understand. Perhaps he never would, even though he wanted to more than anything. How could both she and Publius tell him to rejoice instead of grieve over their deaths? How could they be so content to die for their god?

He ran his fingers through his hair once more. No mystery solved, only more questions with no answers.

"Thank you for telling me. Rest now. The slave should keep anyone from coming to this room, but I'll stay for a while to make sure no one bothers you tonight. I'll leave when I'm certain you'll be left alone."

If she wouldn't let him save her, at least he could give her a final night without pain.

She stretched out on the bed, and he drew the sheet over her and tucked it in around her shoulders. She looked up at him with bright, hopeful eyes, like Valeria had when she asked him what he thought about the story in the writings of Luke.

Decimus laid his hand on her hair as he had so many times with Rhoda. "Rest in peace, child. I will think about what you've told me."

"Thank you for giving me this last night. God truly blessed me by having you here. I'll be giving thanks and asking Him to bless you for your kindness for the rest of my life." Her eyes grew serious. "I'll also be praying that you decide to love Jesus, too."

He forced a smile but said nothing. He turned away from her and walked to the window. There was an eight-foot drop to the ground. When it was time to leave, he could slip out through the window so the slave would continue to keep the room undisturbed until the guards came to get her.

His own heart remained in turmoil, but he could give her a final night of peace.

Chapter 48

CHOOSING THE WAY

It was well into the third watch of the night when Decimus climbed out the window and dropped to the ground below. The jolt was hard on his leg, and he sat down to massage it. It was about two miles to his father's villa. A long walk for a man with a bad leg, but it was worth it to have spared the girl what Sabinus had planned.

He entered the villa through the main entrance, waking the slave guarding the gate with his knocking. After telling him to stop the chariot being sent for him in the morning, Decimus retired to his bedchamber.

He lay down on his bed, but sleep wouldn't come. After tossing for what seemed like hours, he gave up trying to sleep and rose. He began pacing as his thoughts churned. Publius's logical arguments. The story of the crippled girl whose name he didn't even know. Everything he'd read in Valeria's codices.

He'd read the history of their Jesus and his claim to be the Son of God. His death on the cross was supposed to be the perfect sacrifice that paid for every sin and made peace between sinners and God.

Publius had always been a good man, and Decimus would bet any amount that Valeria had never done anything bad in her entire life. Following Jesus couldn't have made too big a change in what they did

But the girl's story of Jesus's love and forgiveness instantly transforming her father from a vicious brute to a loving husband and father—that shook him to his core.

He'd asked for proof from her Jesus, and here was the proof he'd been looking for.

People didn't change like that, not on their own and certainly not instantly. Something or someone must have changed him. The girl told him Jesus had transformed her father and given him and his family peace and love—like he'd seen every day with Valeria. But Jesus could only do that if he wasn't just a dead man; he must truly be the living son of God, as Valeria's codices and Publius said.

And if that was true, his sacrifice could pay the debts of sinful men like himself, just like he claimed. Jesus had paid the ransom, and he offered the chance for eternal life with him instead of death. All a person had to do was believe and accept it.

Only a fool would turn down such an offer.

Decimus was no fool.

His mouth pulled up into a crooked smile. *Ask and you'll receive. I asked you for proof, Jesus, and a brute changing into the best of fathers is enough.*

He wasn't a brute, but he had been a proud, selfish, violent man. In the eyes of the Christian god, he was a sinner. Her codex said to confess and believe. He was ready for both.

Decimus dropped to his knees and began his confession. It took a while to work through the many things that he'd done and many more that he'd failed to do.

When he could think of nothing more, he squared his shoulders, took a deep breath, and plunged ahead.

"Jesus, I ask you to forgive all my sins. I believe in you, and I want to follow you as my Lord and my God. I renounce my vows of loyalty to Rome and Caesar and offer all that I am to your service instead. Please accept me and save me and show me what I must do."

As he knelt in the dark on the cold marble floor, the room filled with brilliant, shimmering light. As the light enveloped him, an overpowering feeling of being loved washed over him, and a sense of total peace replaced the turmoil that had churned within him for so long. A bubbling joy that he'd never imagined possible filled him, and he found himself giving thanks in a language he didn't know.

He wasn't sure how long it lasted, but when the light faded, he felt...different. A smile tugged at his lips and grew until he was beaming. So this was what Jesus meant when he told Nicodemus he could be born again. God's presence burned within him. He would never be alone again. No wonder Valeria always prayed to her God like He was a person in the room with her. He was really there.

Valeria's song on the porch the night his vision returned—the hauntingly beautiful melody, the words he couldn't understand. The Holy Spirit was with her that night, just as Decimus had met Him tonight. The Spirit was there when she came to tell him good night and that God loved him. No wonder she'd been so certain her God was real and would heal him because God even loved a wounded Roman tribune.

He finally understood her: why she obeyed her God's command to save him, why she longed for him to know Jesus, why she refused to give herself to the man she loved when he didn't love her God.

That refusal—it had haunted him, but what a precious gift! This peace and joy would not be his if she hadn't loved Jesus over him. Only the anguish of losing her could drive him to seek Jesus as well.

Jesus was real, and he was alive. Decimus would follow Him as Lord, no matter what. Tomorrow he would tell his father he could no longer be tribune or follow the course of offices because he now followed Jesus. He would return to her in Germania...if Father didn't have him killed for his new faith. If his father declared him an enemy of Rome deserving death, he could face the sword or the lions without fear because life forever with Jesus awaited him on the other side.

He lay down on the bed and closed his eyes. The peace of God filled his heart and calmed his mind, and he drifted off into the sweetest sleep of his entire life.

Chapter 49

CROSSING THE LINE

Decimus had slept only a few hours, but he'd slept so well that he awoke at dawn feeling rested and relaxed. He rose and went to the dining hall, where he expected to share breakfast with his father. He would tell Father about his decision to follow Jesus and what that would mean for his future. It would be difficult, if not impossible, for Father to understand and accept his decision right away, but that didn't matter. His loyalty had shifted from Rome to Jesus, and he was ready for whatever that brought.

A slave was putting fresh sheets on the couches. He bowed deeply and bit his lip.

"I beg pardon for failing to have your breakfast ready, master. We didn't expect anyone to be up so early after the banquet last night. We should have known that a soldier like yourself would keep earlier hours than your father. I'll go tell chef you'll need it immediately."

"Don't bother. I can wait. I'm planning to eat with Father, and I doubt he's up yet after so much wine. I'll be in the library. Send someone for me when he's ready to eat."

The slave bowed again as Decimus turned and walked out of the room.

Decimus fought a smile as he strolled to the library. The shock on the slave's face at seeing a patient, undemanding Lentulus was the funniest thing he'd seen since reaching Rome.

His father was already reclining at the table when Decimus entered the dining hall. His eyes were bloodshot, and he probably had a beast of a headache even though Flavius Sabinus only served the best wines. His mouth was turned down in a frown that was replaced by a smile as Decimus entered the room.

"Ah, Decimus. You surprise me by rising so early when you don't have to. And reading in the library, no less."

"I don't like to waste the early hours of the day in bed, and a well-written history is always a worthwhile way to pass the time."

His father smiled as he shrugged.

"You always were more of a scholar than I ever was. Publius's influence, no doubt. After last night's banquet, I expected you to sleep even later than me."

The corners of his mouth turned suddenly upward in a satisfied and knowing smile. "Sabinus was very impressed with you. I didn't expect him to give you such a desirable gift upon first meeting you, but I'm delighted that he did. It bodes well for him working on your behalf to advance your career."

His father chuckled as he pulled a grape off its stem and popped it into his mouth. "He was most gratified with your response to his generosity. He said not many would have been so eager to leave the wine and food like that and spend the entire night with someone as ugly as that one. They're only virgins the first time. If you'd finished with her quickly, he'd planned to offer her to me as well. Sabinus is always a thoughtful host."

He popped another grape into his mouth.

"He was glad she pleased you enough that you wanted her for so many hours. I expected you to be through before it was time for me to leave. I would have sent the chariot back for you last night, but the slave said you asked not to be disturbed until they had to send her back to the arena. I didn't expect the pleasure of your company at breakfast, but I guess they needed to take her back early."

Decimus masked his disgust as his father talked about the girl as if it was admirable for Sabinus to treat her as some animal to be used for the amusement of his guests. He didn't remember seeing this side of Father before, but that was probably only his lack of attention. It was unlikely that Father had only now become so callous about how much a girl like her would suffer. Valeria's comments on how little human life was valued in Rome had certainly hit the mark.

His father tore some bread off the loaf that lay on the table.

"I think we should go to the games as soon as we finish breakfast. That gives us a greater chance of running into some of the other influential men I want you to get to know better while you're in Rome."

Decimus took a deep breath. "I can't go to the games with you, Father."

His father looked up, his eyebrows slightly lifted. "We discussed this yesterday. If you have other plans for the day, you can change them."

"Actually, I have other plans for my life."

His father swung his legs off the couch and sat up. A grimace declared that the sudden movement did not help his headache.

Decimus sat down on his couch and faced his father.

Father's eyes narrowed and a worried frown appeared. "What are you talking about?"

"I know we'd planned for me to follow in your footsteps, hoping I might also become a provincial governor. Something has happened that makes that impossible."

Decimus paused for a deep breath. What he was about to say would change his relationship with his father forever. *God, don't let Father be too badly hurt by what I'm about to tell him.* It was too much to ask that he understand right now.

"I can no longer follow the course of offices. I've decided to follow Jesus, and that means I can never fulfill the duties of each. I can never again offer worship and sacrifice to Caesar. I could never serve as quaestor and organize games where people are killed for entertainment. I don't even want to go to the games again. I must withdraw now while I'm only a tribune."

The look of shock on his father's face was beyond what Decimus had expected, but not by much.

"I know this is hard for you to hear. I know you've regarded Christians as enemies of Rome since my childhood, and that's why you've persecuted them for years. I can promise you that nothing is farther from the truth. We aren't enemies of anyone, and even if we were, by Jesus's own command we have to love our enemies as if they were our friends."

His father still hadn't moved or spoken. He just sat there, staring at Decimus.

The total lack of response was disturbing, but Decimus continued. "I know that by your own decree, I should be arrested and executed. I know that under Roman law, you can kill me yourself without penalty.

I hope you choose not to kill me or turn me in. But I must tell you that if I am arrested, I will choose death over denial of Jesus as my Lord and savior."

The silence coiled around Decimus as he waited for his father to respond.

His father rose to his feet, and Decimus stood also. Father began pacing, frequently looking over at Decimus with a steadily deepening scowl, shaking his head as he walked. Decimus remained standing by his couch, watching his father build toward the explosion he knew was coming.

Finally, his father approached Decimus and stopped just beyond reach. He ran his fingers through his graying hair and shook his head as he stared into his son's eyes. His eyes smoldered with anger.

"Have you gone mad? Only a madman would choose to walk away from family, fortune, power to follow...what? A dead man from a back-water province who claimed to be a god? What has happened to you? Why on earth would you make such an insane decision?"

"Because Jesus didn't just claim to be a god. He actually is God, and I've seen proof myself that everything He claimed is true. I haven't told you what happened in the ambush. I should not be here alive and seeing your face except for miracles of healing from God. I've been in battle; so have you. I can tell when a wound should kill. I had two of those."

He put his foot up on the couch and drew his finger along the scar on his leg.

"You see this scar? The cut was deep. I should have bled to death. I've never seen someone with a cut like this who didn't bleed out within a few minutes, and I was losing blood that fast. I lost a huge amount of blood, but somehow it didn't kill me."

He turned his head and pulled the hair aside to reveal the jagged scar on the back of his head.

"An ax split my helmet open but didn't cut into my skull. See the scar? Only my scalp was cut. The blow was so hard that I lay uncon-scious for two days. I should never have awakened. How did an ax do that without cutting my skull wide open?"

He turned to face his father.

"Even if the ax didn't kill me, that blow should have blinded me forever. I was blind for a week, and then my sight returned overnight. It shouldn't have. There was no reason why it would except for a mir-acle from God."

His father had been listening intently, but then he shook his head. "No. None of that had to be a miracle from the Christian god. You're a strong, healthy man. The healings must have been natural."

"I have more proof, Father." Decimus paused, not quite sure how to explain his encounter in the night. He wouldn't have believed it himself if someone told him, in spite of his conversations with Publius and his knowledge of Valeria and her codices. He would say nothing about her. In his anger, Father might go hunting for the woman who had begun leading him to Jesus.

"What proof can you possibly have? Proof of something that can't be explained in other ways?"

"I've met God myself. He surrounded me with light, and I felt like I was wrapped in a love that...it's nothing like anything I've ever experienced before, and it's impossible to explain to you. It was so warm, so deep, so passionate, so complete...I never imagined what that would be like. The peace in my heart, the joy...I can't explain it to you. God filled me with His presence, and I know He's here with me now."

"You're insane. Maybe the blow to your head has done this, but no intelligent Roman could ever believe what you're saying."

"Would you consider Publius Drusus an intelligent Roman? Isn't he the smartest man we both know?"

"Of course. He's admired as a historian and philosopher by all who know him. I'm proud to call him one of my closest friends."

"Do you know where he is right now?"

"At his town house, I would assume, or maybe in the country at one of his estates. If he is in town, I should take you there. You always hung on every word he said. Maybe he can talk you out of this foolishness."

"You're wrong, Father. He's at the arena, waiting to feed the lions because he won't deny his belief that Jesus is Lord and God. His oldest son betrayed him to get possession of the family fortune. If you go to the games today, you might see him die."

His father's jaw dropped as his eyes narrowed. "How do you know this?"

"I spent a long time with him yesterday trying to understand why he would choose to follow Jesus when it was going to get him killed. I even offered to bribe his way out of the prison to save him. He chose to die. I didn't understand why then, but I do now, after last night."

"Last night? You spent all last night taking that Christian girl."

"No. She slept. I only stood watch for a few hours to make sure no one touched her. It was after I got home that I met Jesus, right here in my room."

His father swung his arm sideways as if to sweep away Decimus's words.

"I've heard enough of this nonsense. You can't do this. You'll disgrace our family name. You're my only living son. You're destined to become a great Roman. I will not let you risk that."

"I no longer want to be a great Roman. I can't enjoy the murder of innocents as entertainment. I can't sacrifice to Caesar or the Roman gods anymore. There's a much better life following Jesus."

His father's jaw clenched as his eyes smoldered. "You're talking utter nonsense. There is no better life than being a Roman. The gods aren't real, so those sacrifices don't mean anything beyond loyalty to Rome. No one can meet what doesn't exist in his own bedchamber. To think you did is insane. If you won't give up this foolishness, you'll destroy yourself. No Lentulus can ever become a Christian. You'll destroy not only yourself, but me as well if you continue like this."

"It's not foolishness, and I can never return to what I was before, to what I wanted before. Let me explain to you more, and you'll see why I'm choosing a better way. There's nothing that would make me happier than for you to join me in this decision."

Decimus had watched the anger building in his father's eyes. His fury was now beyond anything Decimus had ever seen before.

"I've been a defender of Rome against her enemies all my life. The followers of this Jesus refuse to worship Caesar. They are dangerous to the Empire. If you insist on being one, you will have betrayed Rome. You will have disgraced our noble family. You will have disgraced me. It can never be known that you even wanted to make this choice. I won't have you arrested and tried. That would reveal the disgrace to all, and I cannot have that happen. You must stop this right now, before it goes any further."

His father ran his hand through his hair again and locked blazing eyes on Decimus.

"I've always honored you, Father, and I don't want to hurt you, but I can't turn back. There's only one way to life, and Jesus is it."

"So be it. If you are so determined to be what I've been trying to crush my whole life, that's the end. I have no son. I can't have this horrible truth about you revealed. This is the last chance I'll give you to abandon this insanity and come back to your senses. If you insist on being a Christian, you can leave this house without me reporting you, but you can never return."

The mixture of fury and coldness in his father's eyes signaled the end of the discussion. The red-hot lava had turned to black basalt. Father would listen no more.

Decimus drew a deep breath. "I understand, but I'm sorry you think we must part this way. I don't want us to end like this, but I'll leave if that's what you really want."

He paused, hoping his father would tell him he didn't mean what he'd just said, but Father stood in stony silence with anger still simmering in his eyes.

Decimus offered a half-smile, tinged with sadness. "I love you, Father, and I'll be praying for you. Goodbye."

He turned and walked out of the room.

It was so ironic. He'd been rejected by one of the people he cared about most because he didn't follow Jesus. He'd now been rejected by another because he did.

Chapter 50

A Father's Choice

Tiberius watched his only son walk away from him.

His grief had been so deep when he was told his son was lost and presumed dead. Then his son had been unexpectedly restored to him...but not really. Decimus had returned a different man. The son he lost had never returned at all.

He began pacing again. As his anger cooled, regret and sadness grew in its place. How could this have happened? Why had his son pushed him into disowning him? He never meant their argument to go that far. Decimus was the most important thing in the world to him—more important than Rome, more important than family honor, more important than his own life.

Decimus had made a fatal choice. As senatorial tribune, he was already an important man. It was impossible to keep his decision to be a Christian secret. As soon as it became known in Rome, he would be arrested and tried. He would dead within a week. If he returned to the legion as tribune and his new faith became known, Tiberius's own decree against the Christians could lead to his son's arrest and death if the new governor didn't rescind it. How could he bear being responsible for the execution of his own son?

Announcing Decimus's death before his return to the legion was the only way to ensure he wouldn't die. After the announcement, he would never be able to stay anywhere near Rome where someone might recognize him and reveal the lie.

To save his son's life, he must lose his son again.

The fewer people who knew, the better. No slaves were in the room while they argued. No one heard Decimus declare he was now a Christian. No one knew but him.

There was one man he could trust, one man who would never reveal the secret.

Tiberius was still pacing when a kitchen slave entered the room to clear away the remains of breakfast.

"Find Graecus and send him to my bedchamber immediately."

"Yes, master." The slave bowed and hurried out to find the steward who had been responsible for all Tiberius's property while he was serving in Germania Superior. He could trust Graecus with anything, even the future of his son. With Graecus, he would figure out how to save Decimus and help him start a new life.

Decimus stood by the window in his bedchamber, watching a slave pluck the faded flowers so new ones would grow.

He hadn't known exactly what to expect from the discussion with his father, but he hadn't expected what happened.

He had no regrets about his decision to follow Jesus. Everything that happened last night convinced him there was no other choice. Still, he was sorry Father had disowned him and ordered him to leave. He did regret that he would never see his father again.

He'd hoped to have some time to figure out what he was going to do next, but he wouldn't have that luxury now. He was still a tribune, and that posed a huge problem. He was only five years into his ten-year term of service. The new governor expected him to return to the legion in Mogontiacum. He could be a Christian and still fulfill many of his duties. Serving in Germania removed the problem of having to sacrifice at the temples in Rome. His absence there was sure to be noticed and an explanation demanded. But camp worship was mandatory for the enlisted men. How was it possible to avoid that?

The new governor might not be as determined to exterminate Christians as Father had been. But if he didn't rescind the decree, there was another huge problem. Decimus was the one who sent troops out to arrest Christians for their faith. He couldn't do that and not reveal that he was one, too.

He was still looking out the window when he heard footsteps behind him. He turned to find Graecus approaching.

"I'm glad to see you. I'd hoped to have a chance to tell you goodbye, but I was afraid you might have gone to check the estates before Father makes his tour."

Decimus's lips tightened as he fought a sigh. "I'll be leaving for Germania Superior in a few minutes. Father has disowned me and ordered me to leave."

He tried to smile at the man who'd done so much to raise him. Graecus and Publius had each been more of a father to him than his own father had. Today he would be losing all three.

Graecus rested his hand on Decimus's shoulder.

"Not really. Those were only words spoken in anger. You know your father's temper. He just told me about the choice you've made. He doesn't understand, and he certainly doesn't approve. But your father loves you, and he sent me to help plan your death so you can safely start your new life.

"To give you a future, Decimus Cornelius Lentulus must die. I think you should disappear between here and the northern estate, dragged off and killed by robbers, your body never to be found. Then you can go somewhere to live with a different name. Only we three will know the truth."

Decimus startled Graecus when he grabbed his arms, pulled him to his chest, and gave him a crushing hug. When he pushed Graecus back out to arms' length, he was beaming. If anyone could figure out what he should do and how to do it, it was Graecus. A report of his death was the perfect solution to all his problems. If the Roman tribune was no more, the Greek merchant could return...to her.

Chapter 51

THE BRIDE PRICE

Rhoda stood on the lower rail of the corral and whistled. The black stallion lifted his head from the trough, water dripping off his lower lip. With a swish of his luxuriant tail, Astro sauntered over to get his head scratched. She rubbed his star-shaped blaze as his head hung down where she could reach it. Suddenly, he jerked his head up and snorted. He stared over her shoulder. Then he started to dance in place, like he did when he first saw her in the morning.

She turned to see what had caught Astro's attention. A tall, bearded man on a proud Spanish mare emerged from the trees and rode toward her. He had two other equally beautiful mares on leads behind him. She held her hand over her eyes to shade them so she could see him better.

"Oh, Astro! It's him!"

She ran toward the rider. He slid off his horse and knelt to catch her as she threw her arms around him.

"Decimus! You've come back! I knew you would. I've been praying and praying for you to come since the day you left. Valeria will be so happy." She laid her head on his shoulder and hugged him like she'd never let him go.

◆

Decimus loosened her grip and held her at arms' length. "I'm glad to see you, too."

He braced himself before the question upon which the future he longed for hung. "Is your sister betrothed?"

Rhoda's smile was undimmed as she shook her head. Decimus swept her into his arms and twirled around before setting the giggling girl back on her own feet.

"Why do you have so many wonderful horses with you? They're almost as beautiful as Astro."

"I heard Valeria tell Baldric that three fine mares were an irresistible bride price."

"Oh, no!" Rhoda's hand flew to her mouth as her eyes saucered. "Decimus, she didn't tell him that. She told him no number of horses would be enough if a man didn't follow the Way. Please don't ask her to marry you. She'll have to tell you no, and that will break her heart again."

"Don't worry. I have something else to tell her that will convince her to accept my horses...and me."

Rhoda bit her lower lip and her eyes glistened as he stood up.

He took Rhoda's small hand in his large one and smiled down at her. "Don't cry. There's no need. I have a surprise for her that I want you to help me with."

Her head tipped back as she looked at him towering over her. "What do you want me to do?"

"When we get to the cottage, don't tell her I'm here. Just tell her a Greek merchant who's a follower of the Way needs her."

Rhoda's eyes widened as her breath caught. "You follow Jesus now?" His smiling eyes and nod gave her the answer he knew she wanted. She threw her arms around him again and held him tight as she pressed her cheek against him.

"I've prayed for this since the first night. I knew this had to be God's plan."

He stroked her hair as she looked up at him, grinning.

He tied his horses to the corral railing, and they walked hand-in-hand to the cottage porch. After a quick squeeze of his hand, Rhoda opened the door and entered.

He could hear her through the open window. "Valeria, there's a Greek merchant who's a follower of the Way on the porch. He needs you. He has three of the prettiest mares, too."

Valeria was wiping her hands on a towel, looking down as she came out the door.

"God's grace and peace to you, my brother. How can I help—" She froze as she looked up. Still holding the towel, her hands flew up to cover her mouth. "Oh!"

Decimus stepped close to her and cradled her face in his hands. "Is there still a place here for a Greek merchant who's become a follower of the Way?"

Valeria's eyes filled with joyful tears. She threw her arms around him and pressed her cheek against his chest. His arms wrapped around her as a satisfied sigh escaped. He rested his cheek against her hair as he held her close.

She pushed back so she could look at his face. "I see you brought my bride price. I'm still a wise woman, able to recognize a good horse..." She reached up and pushed a strand of hair off his forehead before laying her hand on his cheek. "And a good man."

He caressed her cheek, once more tracing the scar with his fingertip. Her smile brightened and became more beautiful than he'd ever seen before. Her eyes were glowing as he lowered his lips to hers and pulled her again into his embrace.

A deep peace descended on him. Now he had everything he would ever need—faith in Jesus...and Valeria. It was good to be the man who had finally passed her test.

COMING IN 2018

If you're not ready to say goodbye to the people in *Blind Ambition,* you'll have the chance to spend more time with them eight years later in the sequel. Turn to the next page for Chapter One of *Faithful.*

Faithful

Is the price of true friendship ever too high?

In AD 122, Adela is eagerly awaiting her marriage to a Germanic warrior when she's kidnapped and taken across the Roman frontier to sell as a slave. Otto wins her while carousing with her kidnappers and asks his trading partner, Galen, to take charge of her. When Otto is kidnapped by the same men, Galen must track them down before his best friend loses a fight to the death in a Roman arena.

Adela gladly joins Galen in the chase, hungry for vengeance. Will traveling from Germania to Rome with the kind man who would risk anything for his God or his friend open her eyes to choices she never dreamed she wanted?

A trip to the heart of the Empire poses mortal danger for a man who follows Jesus, especially when he must seek the help of an enemy of the faith if Otto is to survive. Will the risk Galen takes to rescue his friend prove too costly for all?

FAITHFUL

Chapter 1

Three days north of Germania Superior's frontier, AD 122

Adela felt the daggers as she hung her horse's bridle on the gatepost and swatted its rump to send it into the corral. When she turned to face the cottage, her stepmother spun and stomped inside.

She rolled her eyes. It was going to be another one of those days.

It had only been four months since Mother died. Why had Father been in such a hurry to remarry? He had a son, and she would marry soon to give him a son-in-law. She'd told him he should take his time. A chieftain of the Hermunduri could have his pick of the maidens whenever he decided to wed.

But had he listened? If her brother had spoken, he might have. All she got was a frown and a flick of a hand to shoo her away.

At the moment, they weren't at war. Marrying the sister of another chieftain just to seal an alliance was a bad idea when that woman was meaner than a weasel and had a nearly grown son and daughter herself.

She cringed at the thought of another day in the company of her mousy stepsister, Gunda, and Hildegard. She would not call that woman Mother, no matter what Father said.

Adela's gaze flipped over her shoulder when she felt the hand.

Gunda was holding two baskets. "The wild strawberries are ripe.

Olga had some this morning, and Mother wants us to go gather some, too."

"I didn't see any when I was riding."

Her stepsister hugged herself as her eyes flicked toward the cottage, then returned to Adela. "But Mother said they were ripe where the stream forks."

"That far? We won't be back in time for supper if we go there."

Gunda rubbed her nose and glanced at the cottage again. "I know, but when Mother says go, I'm not going to argue. Neither should you."

She held out a basket and gave it a small shake. "Your father already told you to do what Mother says. Do you want her to tell him you wouldn't go?"

Adela snatched the basket, jerking Gunda toward her when she didn't let go fast enough. "The sooner we go, the sooner we get back."

She set a fast pace as they entered the woods. Gunda had to scurry to keep up, but it wasn't Adela's fault that her stepsister was a scrawny little thing, even though she was thirteen. Hildegard spoiled her precious daughter, and spoiling made a person weak.

Adela squared her shoulders. No one would ever dare to call her weak. Father might not value her opinion about remarrying, but she'd heard him brag on her skill with weapons and horses. A daughter fit for a chieftain's son. That's what he'd said, and her heart warmed at the thought.

She was nineteen. Within the year, she would marry, and she knew exactly what kind of man she wanted. Tall, handsome, proud, afraid of nothing and no one—a warrior like Father.

Already Father was talking with the other chieftains with sons ready to take a wife. Adela's lips curved into a satisfied smile. Her marriage couldn't be soon enough to get her out from under Hildegard's aggravating control. After she was wed, she could finally tell that woman what she thought of her. That thought broadened her smile.

"Slow down, Adela."

Gunda's whining heightened the anticipation. One more thing she'd leave behind when she married her warrior.

When they reached the glade where the stream forked, Adela's brow furrowed. Lush, green...but no sign of red.

"I don't see any ripe strawberries." She spun on Gunda. "Did Olga pick everything already?" Her lips tightened. "Just like your mother to waste my time like this."

Gunda turned in a circle as she scanned the surrounding trees.

"But Mother said they were here." Her eyes caught Adela's, then flitted away. "Maybe we need to look among the deep grass and ferns." She pointed across the stream. "You look over there. I'll look on this side."

Adela jumped the stream and shuffled through the grass, pushing it aside with her foot before each step. No strawberries, not even green ones. Her back was to the stream when she heard hoofbeats behind her.

Then Gunda gasped. Adela spun. A man on a bay horse stood between her and Gunda, but she could see Gunda's legs under the horse's belly. She was backing up as the man leaned toward her. He nudged the horse closer and grabbed Gunda's arm.

Adela trotted to the steam bank and leaped across. "You! Leave her alone."

The man turned to face her, and his lips twisted into a sneer as Adela moved closer.

Gunda strained to pull free and started to cry. "No. Don't do it."

Adela sprinted toward the horseman as Gunda's tears turned to sobs. A feral laugh escaped his throat as he swung his gaze from Gunda to her.

Adela's eyes narrowed as she neared his horse's head. The man was brawny and she had no weapon, but she knew horses. She grasped the loose fabric panel that draped the front of her dress and flicked it into his horse's face.

With a panicky neigh, the horse reared, launching the man into the air. When the flailing hooves returned to earth, Adela was ready. She scooped up the reins, grabbed a handful of mane, and sprang onto its back.

Gunda stood like a statue, eyes enormous and hands over her mouth. Adela held out her hand. "Get up behind me."

Her stepsister started to move...backward.

The man moaned behind her.

"Gunda, now!"

Hoofbeats...two horses...coming up fast from behind. "Gunda!"

Gunda spun and ran into the trees and up the hill. Adela whirled the horse. Two men were coming straight for her.

"Keep running!" Adela bent low on the horse, drove her heels into its flanks, and hurtled forward...toward their attackers.

She shot between them before they could react. If only they would follow her. Gunda was running toward their home. Perhaps she'd get away.

The pounding of hooves behind her promised a chance for her

stepsister. Adela urged the horse forward. She reached the edge of the clearing and was forced to slow down as she wove between the trees.

The head of a horse moved up on her right side. Too close, but also close enough. Low branches lay straight ahead. As she pulled her reins to the right, she lay flush with her horse's neck. She barely cleared... but the tall man beside her didn't. His yell as the branches swept him from his horse was music to her ears. The trees thickened; the hill grew steeper. Her horse lurched as she pounded her heels into its sides to keep it lunging up the slope.

Hoofbeats behind her...closer...closer...

The front neckline of her dress cut into her throat as a hand grasped the back. The horse leaped forward as her thighs lost their grip. The canopy of leaves became a green blur as she was dragged across the horse's rump.

Then all went black.

A hill-country farm in Germania Superior

As Galen tied his bedroll to the saddle, Astrelo turned his head to watch.

"Ready for an adventure, boy?"

Astrelo's bridle jingled as he shook his elegant black head.

Galen slapped the stallion's neck twice. "I'll take that as a yes." A quick rub of the star-shaped blaze drew a contented nicker. "Let's go do some trading."

As he stepped away from his horse, two small boys dropped the sticks they were poking into the mudpuddle and ran to him. He scooped up four-year old Gaius and plunked him on his shoulders. Six-year-old Publius bounced at his side.

"I wish I could go with you, Uncle."

He tousled the boy's wavy brown hair. "When your mother and father say it's time."

Galen glanced at his sister, Val, as she walked toward him, a sack containing food and a change of clothes slung across her right shoulder and a giggling baby girl on her left hip. "Better if we ask Dec. He's more likely to say yes sooner."

He put his finger across his lips. "Don't tell your mother."

Val reached his side, a smile tugging at the left corner of her mouth. "Don't tell me what?"

Galen swung Gaius to the ground and slapped his bottom. "Run, before she gets an answer out of you."

The two boys sprinted away, giggling.

Galen took the sack from her. "Should be a good trip. We'll stop in Borbetomagus first. I already know someone who wants the mare there. Then we'll head south to Argentorate. Roman officers always have more money than they can spend out here, and the colts should bring top money at the legion fortress." He bounced his eyebrows. "I might even get a couple of the tribunes into a bidding war, like last time."

Val pushed a stray lock of hair back from his forehead. He fought a grin. She was always going to see him as her little brother who needed tending.

"My father would be impressed by how good you are at this."

Galen chuckled. "I learned from masters, watching you and Baldric."

"I know you'll only be gone for a week and a half, but be careful. I'll be praying for you."

"Don't worry, Val. I'll have Otto along to advise me."

Her eyeroll pulled another chuckle from him.

She planted her fist on the hip without a baby. "You know Baldric and I are relying on you to keep Otto out of trouble, not the other way around."

A grin split Galen's face. "You can tell Baldric I'll get a good price for his horses. I'll also make sure his young stallion comes home in one piece."

He whistled, and Astrelo trotted over. The sack joined the bedroll at the back of his saddle. As Galen jumped and swung his leg over his horse's rump, Val untied the lead rope of the first horse in the string from the corral railing. After he settled into the saddle, she handed it to him.

"May God bless and keep you on the journey."

Galen nodded once. "He always does. We'll head down to the river road as soon as Otto brings Baldric's horses to the village. See you in about ten days."

He nudged Astrelo into a trot and tossed his sister a backhanded wave as he entered the tree-lined wagon track that lead to the village. The sunlight made dancing patterns of light and shade as it filtered through the leafy branches. There could be no better way to start a journey of ten days with his best friend.

◆

Valeria shook her head as she smiled. Her brother was always joking, but he had a good head on his shoulders and a heart that wanted to please God. She'd be praying for his safe return, but he and Otto should be fine.

Historical Note

ROMAN PROVINCIAL GOVERNMENT IN AD 114: HOW TO DEAL WITH CHRISTIANS

Rome was a military power at its core, and virtually everyone who rose in the political ranks had extensive military experience. When only one legion was stationed in an imperial province, its commander was also the provincial governor. With multiple legions, one man, who had himself once commanded a legion, was appointed provincial governor by the emperor to oversee all legions and administrative affairs in the province.

A provincial governor of a major province might have already been a consul of Rome, but he had served, at the very least, as a praetor, whose duties included serving as a judge in Roman legal matters. This was excellent preparation for running a province, since the governor was the chief judicial officer for provincial residents. While Roman citizens living in a province could expect judicial treatment in accordance with written Roman law, that was not the case for the non-citizens.

The governor of a province had the authority to treat the non-citizens in whatever way he deemed best. Rome's general philosophy for provincial government was to tolerate local customs while insisting on strict standards of law and order. That meant provincials must acknowledge the state gods of Rome. While that was not a problem for the Empire's subjects who already worshiped several gods, it was something devout Jews and Christians could never do. Jews were allowed an exception because theirs was an ancient national religion, while Christianity was classed as a "new and illicit religion" that was denied that exception.

In AD 111, the Senate appointed Pliny the Younger as governor of the province of Bithynia and Pontus, which was located along the south shore of the Black Sea. Pliny died in his province in AD 113. During his brief term as governor, he was a prolific writer of letters, and copies of his official correspondence have survived to this day.

Of special interest is an exchange he had with the Emperor Trajan concerning his approach to the problem of Christians in his province.

"I have never dealt with investigations about Christians, and therefore I don't know what is usually either punished or investigated, or to what extent. I have hesitated no small amount about whether there should be some distinction in respect to age, or whether young people, however young, should be considered not at all different from more mature people; whether pardon should be given to those who repent, or whether it should be of no use to someone who was once a Christian that he has ceased to be one; whether the name itself, even if there are no criminal offenses, should be punished, or whether only the criminal offenses associated with the name should be punished. In the meantime, among those who were brought before me as Christians, I have used the following method. I asked them whether they were Christians. If they admitted it, I asked them a second and even a third time, threatening them with punishment. I ordered those who persisted to be led away for execution, for I had no doubt that, whatever the nature of their belief, their stubbornness and inflexible obstinacy surely should be punished. There were others who were afflicted by a similar madness, but I wrote in the record book that they should be sent to Rome because they were Roman citizens." — Pliny the Younger, *Letters* 10.96,97

Trajan's reply provided clarity. "You have followed the procedure which you ought to have, my dear Pliny, in investigating the cases of those who had been brought before you as Christians. It is not possible to establish a general law which will provide a fixed standard. However, these people are not to be searched out. If they should be brought before you and proved guilty, they must be punished, with this proviso, however, that anyone who denies that he is a Christian and proves this by his action, that is, by worshipping our gods, even if he has been suspected in the past, should obtain pardon because of his repentance."

The emperor's reply carried the force of law, but he made clear that it was not establishing an empire-wide policy. Individual governors kept the ability to deal with Christians in whatever way they saw fit.

One "criminal offense" ascribed to Christians was belonging to a secret society, which Trajan had forbidden as potentially threatening the security of the state. Since the days of the Republic, Rome had regulated the private meetings not overseen by a magistrate, requiring a license and restricting the frequency of such meetings. Membership in a secret society was considered treason and could receive the same punishment as participating in an armed riot—execution.

Another offense by Christians classified as treason was their refusal to show reverence to statues of the gods and the emperor. The superstitious feared the gods' favor could be withheld from Rome and her Empire if the rites weren't performed perfectly. Even a slight error meant the whole ritual had to be repeated. The Christian refusal might damage the perfection, putting the Empire at risk.

At the beginning of *Blind Ambition*, Decimus's father, Tiberius Cornelius Lentulus, is completing three years as governor of Germania Superior. He shares the common opinion that Christians are a treasonous group because of their refusal to participate in the state religion and has decreed a policy toward Christians modeled on the historical policy of Pliny the Younger.

Decimus Cornelius Lentulus is five years into his time as a senatorial tribune. Military service was required before beginning the "course of honors" that defined a Roman political career. He's the second-ranking officer of a Roman legion stationed in Germania Superior in AD 114. The provincial capital is Mogontiacum (present-day Mainz) on the Rhine River, and the fortress headquarters of his legion (XXII Primigenia) is there. The second legion in the province (VIII Augusta) is headquartered upriver (to the south) at Argentorate (present-day Strasbourg).

Law enforcement in the Empire was done by the military. As an officer of the legion, Decimus would have been involved in the arrest and execution of Christians in the portion of the province patrolled by his legion. He truly is a mortal enemy of Valeria and her family, but she chooses to obey Jesus and rescues her enemy despite the danger to herself and those she loves.

(Quoted letters are from Jo-Ann Shelton, *As the Romans Did: A Source Book in Roman Social History.* New York: Oxford University Press, 1988.)

For more about life in the Roman Empire at its peak, please go to carolashby.com.

Discussion Guide

1) How would you describe Decimus Cornelius Lentulus at the beginning of the story? Have you known people who remind you of him?

2) When Valeria found Decimus after the ambush, she was afraid to take him home. Why did she help him, despite the risk? What would you have done?

3) How does Decimus respond when he learns that the people he always thought were his enemies had rescued him? Have you ever discovered someone you thought was an enemy was actually a friend? How did you respond?

4) Baldric is a descendent of Germanic chieftains who once fought against the Roman occupiers. He has cultural bias against Rome and her military. He is also Valeria's friend and wants to protect her. What is his attitude toward Decimus at the beginning? How does his attitude toward Decimus change? Why?

5) Decimus pretends to be more interested in Valeria's god than he is because it makes her happy. She is excited because she thinks he's being drawn toward belief in Jesus. Have you ever known anyone in the same situation?

6) Valeria is faced with a choice between the man she loves and Jesus. Why did she choose Jesus over the man she loved? Do you know someone who's had to face the same choice? Did they choose as Valeria did? Were they content with their decision later?

7) How does Decimus respond to Valeria's choice? If you were him, how would you have responded?

8) When Decimus returns to Roman society, how does he react to things that he used to enjoy and take for granted? Have you ever

found yourself in the middle of a conflict between what society says is good and what God says?

9) When Tiberius learns that his son has rejected everything Tiberius values to follow Jesus, his response is extreme. Do you know anyone who's been rejected by family or friends for the same decision? How did they respond?

10) *Blind Ambition* is a story of the power of love to open the eyes of a man striving for worldly success to what's truly important. What touched you most? What made you think about what your own choices would be?

What does the future hold for Tiberius Lentulus?

Tiberius banished his son for choosing Jesus over Rome. Do you think Tiberius will ever regret that decision? If he does, what do you think he'll do about it? I'd love to hear your thoughts about what happens next. Please go to Contact Carol at carol-ashby.com (my blog) or carolashby.com (my Roman history site) and leave your thoughts in the comment box. I hope I hear from you!

Glossary

centurion	1st level officer over 80 men; rises through ranks based on merit
cuirass	metal body armor protecting torso
denarius	*denarii* (pl); 1 *denarius* = 4 *sesterces*; about one day's living wage
gladius	short thrusting sword used by Roman military
legate	commander of a legion
praetor	magistrate mainly serving as a judge; one level below consul
quaestor	magistrate in charge of finance and general administration; one level below praetor
tribune	high-ranking officer from equestrian or senatorial order
vestibulum	short hall between the entrance and the atrium of a Roman town house

Scripture References

Chapter 14: Luke 10:30-37 (ESV)
Chapter 17: John 11:25-27 (ESV)
Chapter 21: Matt 20:29-34 (ESV)
Chapter 26: Luke 15:3-7 (ESV)
Chapter 27: Luke 11:9-10 (ESV)
Chapter 31: Luke 1:1-5 (ESV)
Chapter 33: Luke 6:27-31 (ESV)
Chapter 36 Luke 6:46-49 (ESV)
Chapter 37 John 1:1-4 (ESV)
Chapter 40 Luke 10:30 (ESV)
Chapter 41 John 15:9-17 (NASB)

Acknowledgements

I'm most thankful to God for giving me this chance to write stories about the power of human love to crack open a closed heart so someone will consider and respond to the redeeming love of Christ. Nothing is more satisfying that watching that in real life. I'm so glad God is calling me to tell stories about people who love Jesus above all else and follow faithfully, no matter what the cost.

Special thanks to my critique partner, Katie Powner, who's an award-winning author herself, and my special trio of beta-readers: Regina Fujitani, Lisa Garcia, and Patti Stouter. Many thanks also to my wonderful friends who love to read and gave me many helpful comments. Some willingly read the earliest versions of *Blind Ambition* when I was first starting to write novels. My deepest thanks go out to each, and here they are alphabetically: Seaborn Ashby, Andrew Budek-Schmeisser, Tiffany Coble, Darcie Farrow, Eric Jones, Martha Kreklow, Christopher Miller, and Antoinette Smith. Your insights and suggestions made the characters more real and the situations more authentic. Many thanks!

My heartfelt thanks go to Wendy Chorot for her content editing. Her skill as an editor and her wisdom as a woman of God make working with her a true pleasure. If you're looking for an editor, look no farther than Wendy!

A cover should capture the essence of the story, and Roseanna White of Roseanna White Designs did it again! You may know her as the author of several top-selling historical novels. Well worth staying up way past my bedtime to read!

I especially want to thank my wonderful family. My grown kids, Paul and Lydia, are a true blessing. When I want to talk books, Paul is always willing; he's been writing himself since 8th grade. It's a joy to call Lydia one of my dearest friends as well as the best daughter in the world.

It would be so much harder to write without my husband, Jim. No one could be more supportive. He just pops another movie into the DVD player and keeps me company when I stay up past 2:00 because

I'm in the flow and can't leave a scene until it's finished. He'll even bring the dinner to me at my desk when I'd rather write than eat. Every writer should be married to a man who can be the model for the best parts of her novels' heroes!

About the Author

Carol Ashby has been a professional writer for most of her life, but her articles and books were about lasers and compound semiconductors (think the electronics that make cell phones, laser pointers, and LED displays work). Now she is having a wonderful time creating stories about human conflict and difficult friendships that grow into love as characters discover their own faith in Christ. Her fascination with the Roman Empire was born during her first middle-school Latin class. A research career in New Mexico inspires her to get every historical detail right so she can spin stories that make her readers feel like they're living under the Caesars themselves.

Read her articles about many facets of life in the Roman Empire at carolashby.com, or join her at her blog, The Beauty of Truth, at carol-ashby.com.

LIGHT *in the* EMPIRE SERIES

The Light in the Empire Series follows the interconnected lives of the members of three Roman families of the senatorial order during the reigns of Trajan and Hadrian. Join them as they travel the Empire, from Germania and Britannia to Thracia, Dacia, and Judaea and, of course, to Rome itself.

NOW AVAILABLE

Available in paperback and Kindle at Amazon.com

Forgiven

Are some wounds too deep to forgive?

With a ruthless father who murdered for the family inheritance, Marcus Drusus plans to do the same. In AD 122, Marcus follows his brother Lucius to Judaea and plots to frame a zealot for his older brother's death. But the plan goes awry, and Lucius is rescued by a Messianic Jewish woman. Her oldest brother is a zealot and a Roman soldier killed her twin, but Rachel still persuades her father Joseph to put his love for Jesus above his anger with Rome and hide Lucius until he heals.

Rachel cares for the enemy, and more than broken bones heal as duty turns to love. Lucius embraces Joseph's faith in Jesus, but sharing a faith doesn't heal all wounds. Even before revealed secrets slice open old scars, Joseph wants no Roman son-in-law. With Rachel's zealot brother suspecting he's a Roman officer and his own brother planning to kill him when he returns, can Lucius survive long enough to change Joseph's mind?

COMING IN 2017

The Legacy

What can you leave the ones you love
when Rome has taken all you own?

In AD 114, Claudia loathes her oldest brother Lucius, who arranged their father's execution for his new faith in Jesus to gain the family fortune. Suicide seems her only escape from a forced marriage to a cruel Roman power broker. Then the man who secretly led her father to Christ arranges for his son Philip to sneak her out of Rome and take her to her brother Titus a thousand miles away in Thracia.

A childhood accident scarred Philip's face. A woman's rejection scarred his heart. Claudia's gratitude grows into love, but what can a house-church leader do when the first woman who returns his love hates the God he loves even more? Can Claudia's love for the kind, brilliant man who rescued her survive her learning what he really is?

Claudia and Titus hunger for revenge on Lucius and the Christians they blame for their father's deadly conversion. His father's final letter commands the forgiveness Titus refuses to give. When Titus buys Miriam, a secret Christian, to serve his sister, he starts them all down a path of conflicting loyalties and dangerous decisions. What will it take to free Titus from the hatred that's poisoning his own heart?

You met Publius, father of Titus and Claudia, in *Blind Ambition*.

This is the story of why he made his choice and what happens to his grown children because of it.

Second Chances

Sometimes it takes more than love to conquer all.

In AD 122, Cornelia Scipia, proud daughter of one of the noblest Roman families, learns her adulterous husband plans to betroth their daughter to the vicious son of his best friend. Only over her dead body! Cornelia divorces him, reclaims her enormous dowry, and kidnaps her own daughter. She plans to start over with Drusilla a thousand miles away. No more husbands for her! But she hadn't counted on meeting Hector, the widowed Greek captain of the ship carrying them to their new life.

Devastated by the loss of his wife and daughter, Hector's heart begins to heal as he befriends Drusilla. Cornelia's sacrificial love for Drusilla and her courage and humor in the face of the unknown earn his admiration...as a friend. Is he ready for more?

Marriage to the kind, honest sea captain would finally give Drusilla the father she deserves...and Cornelia the faithful husband she's always longed for. But there are secrets in his past and unspoken misunderstandings born of the chasms between their social classes and different faiths. Will they keep two lonely hearts from the second chance at happiness that God so unexpectedly offers?

COMING IN 2018

Faithful

Is the price of true friendship ever too high?

In AD 122, Adela is eagerly awaiting her marriage to a Germanic warrior when she's kidnapped and taken across the Roman frontier to sell as a slave. Otto wins her while carousing with her kidnappers and asks his trading partner, Galen, to take charge of her. When Otto is kidnapped by the same men, Galen must track them down before his best friend loses a fight to the death in a Roman arena.

Adela gladly joins Galen in the chase, hungry for vengeance. Will traveling from Germania to Rome with the kind man who would risk anything for his God or his friend open her eyes to choices she never dreamed she wanted?

A trip to the heart of the Empire poses mortal danger for a man who follows Jesus, especially when he must seek the help of an enemy of the faith if Otto is to survive. Will the risk Galen takes to rescue his friend prove too costly for all?

Follow the continuing saga of the people you met in *Blind Ambition* from the frontier of Germany to the heart of the Empire.

I'd love to hear what you think!

If you enjoyed this book, I would really appreciate it if you would post a review at the retailer you purchased it from. A good review is like a jewel set in gold for an author. I'd love to hear from you.

What does the future hold for Tiberius Lentulus?

Tiberius banished his son for choosing Jesus over Rome. Do you think Tiberius will ever regret that decision? If he does, what do you think he'll do about it? I'd love to hear your thoughts about what happens next. Please go to Contact Carol at carol-ashby.com (my blog) or ca-rolashby.com (my Roman history site) and leave your thoughts in the comment box. I hope I hear from you!

Interested in the next stories in the
Light in the Empire series?

You can sign up for my newsletter at carol-ashby.com for advance notices of upcoming releases and other info about my latest writing adventures. I hope you will!

Carol Ashby

Manufactured by Amazon.ca
Acheson, AB